CRISANTA KNIGHT

The Severance Game

Book Two in The Crisanta Knight Series

GEANNA CULBERTSON

Virginia

Published in the United States by BQB Publishing
(Boutique of Quality Books Publishing Company)
www.bqbpublishing.com

978-1-939371-57-7 (p)
978-1-939371-58-4 (e)

Library of Congress Control Number: 2016953387

Book design by Robin Krauss, www.bookformatters.com
Cover concept by Geanna Culbertson

Cover design by Ellis Dixon, www.ellisdixon.com

Other books in The Crisanta Knight Series

Crisanta Knight: Protagonist Bound
(Book One in the series)

Crisanta Knight: Inherent Fate
(Book Three in the series)
Releasing in 2017

Dedicated To:

This book, like everything I shall ever accomplish, is dedicated to my mom and dad. You are my heroes, my coaches, my best friends, and I am thankful for you every day for more reasons than there are words in this book.

Special Thanks To:

Terri Leidich & BQB Publishing
You can go pretty far in life believing in yourself, but every once in a while another person's belief in you can make all the difference in the world. You are one such person to me. Thank you for believing in me, and Crisanta Knight. It has made my world more magical and exciting than I could have ever hoped. May our partnership never know severance, and may our success grow grander than a full-sized Therewolf.

Pearlie Tan
Yay! We did it, Pearlie! That's two down, six to go! I hope you know I am eternally grateful to you for all of the hard work you have put in to make Book Two the best that it can be. Whenever I describe my experience working with you, I always say, "You push me to be better," because I know it is the truth. And I will never forget or stop being appreciative of that.

Olivia Swenson
Glad to have you on Team Crisanta Knight. Like with Pearlie, I am grateful for your efforts, which cause me to evolve as a writer. From the moment I took a look at your work, I knew

this was going to be the beginning of a beautiful literary friendship.

I also want to thank the Fine Family, the Charettes, Gatito Suarez, Gallien Culbertson, Ian Culbertson, Andrea Lagatta, Girls on the Run Los Angeles, John Daly, the SMB team, Jaimee Beck for the battle in the conference room, & Ever Lee for the breakfast, making me smile, & paying it forward.

Bonus Dedication:

Since this is going to be an eight-book series, each book will issue a bonus dedication to individuals who have significantly impacted my life or this series in some way.

For this second book, I want to thank Alexa Carter a.k.a. Alexa Harzan. There aren't a lot of people in the world you can truly count on—people who you put your faith in, and who will always come through—and I count on you. Since we first met my freshman year in AXO, I have been grateful to have you in my life. I still remember that moment we met—I was a first-week pledge visiting the sorority house for the first time and we instantly connected over our shared love of Tokidoki purses and animated movies. Over the years you've taught me what it means to have a true sister and friend. So thanks, Big. Thanks for just being you.

PROLOGUE

The problem with being a protagonist isn't so much the external dangers that threaten you. When you put yourself out there, you anticipate them—the monsters, the enemies, the risk. What you don't see coming are the dangers that feed on your insides—the threats you create for yourself.

Those, I've learned, are far more treacherous. For while the former can be vanquished with swords and spears, quick thinking and cunning, and training and physical strength, internal threats are not so easily destroyed. Moreover, they are born when you least expect them and grow like weeds, taking you over from deep within. So much so that by the time you notice what's happening, it might be too late to resurrect yourself from their grip.

But I'm getting ahead of myself. Then again, isn't that how all great adventures start?

I still remember that day in the infirmary like it was yesterday, though it was actually several weeks ago when everything changed and this whole journey began.

The students from my school, Lady Agnue's School for Princesses & Other Female Protagonists, were on a field trip with the students from Lord Channing's School for Princes & Other Young Heroes. We were visiting Adelaide, one of two kingdoms by the sea in our enchanted, fairytale realm of Book, to learn about diplomacy. Though for me, the formal lectures given that week were buried beneath a far more important lesson, which was that your whole world can flip in an instant. And when it does you have two choices—take what the universe gives you lying down, or do something about it.

Despite the fact that I was literally lying down in a cot at the time of the incident, I'd chosen the latter. No easy task, considering where I come from.

I live in a world where people are selected to either be common characters (commons) or protagonists. If you are a common, you are not expected to be anything special; you are supposed to live an ordinary life and help make up the ensemble that highlights those of us chosen to be something extraordinary.

This might seem like the short end of the stick in terms of our realm's division, but being a protagonist has its own set of catches. As the rebellious daughter of Cinderella, I know the cost better than most.

Depending on what type of protagonist you happen to be (princess, hero, etc.), you are expected to live up to the very specific standard that goes along with it. That's why my kind attends the aforementioned private boarding schools. The institutions keep us in our place, streamlining us through curriculums designed to eliminate any personality traits that might deviate from what our realm's leaders consider appropriate "main character" behavior.

If I were to provide my humble opinion on the subject in as succinct a way as possible, I would offer but two words: It blows.

Some people, like my best friend SJ, were great at accepting their roles. She was the spitting image of her mother Snow White in nearly every way. And while I knew deep down she wasn't keen on the forced archetypes either, at least her princess-ness came naturally to her. For me, being everyone else's idea of a perfect princess came as naturally to me as vegetarianism came to the Big Bad Wolf.

Part of me was glad for this. I didn't want to be another glittering doll like the rest of my kind—shiny, fragile, useless. I was proud to be the bold, headstrong creature I'd grown into over the last sixteen years. I yearned to challenge the damsel in distress stereotype and become something more than a typical good princess, something better. And I figured my defiant personality was the best chance I had of getting there.

Alas, three main problems stood in my way.

First, I wasn't even a good princess to start with. Since the very beginning, I pretty much sucked in that department. While I excelled at things like combat and snarky comments, I lacked skills my archetype deemed important, like curtsying, singing, and keeping my mouth shut. I'd spent the last few years struggling through most of my classes at Lady Agnue's—from Damsels in Distress to Woodland Creature Fashions—and it had become evident to pretty much everyone that I was not up to par. As a result, I'd long been forced to wonder: if everyone just saw me as a screw up, then what chance did I have of defining who I was in a favorable light?

My second problem was that female protagonists weren't allowed to be heroes. Common (non-royal) female protagonists could be "heroic," but the best they could hope for career-wise was serving as feisty sidekicks to male heroes. If you were a princess, forget it. We were supposedly incapable of such strength.

Finally, the third obstacle I had to face was the Author and her prophecies.

Our realm's prophet has never been seen. She lives in an off-limits part of Book called the Indexlands where she chooses protagonists and writes their futures in actual books. These books tell the schools which children in our realm to take in, and they tell the children what fates to expect.

Traditionally all princes and princesses are protagonists, so they do not need to wait for their books to appear to know they're headed for main character school. Commons, however, have no way of knowing when or if the Author will select them as protagonists and change their lives unalterably. So they wait, but usually not for long. Common protagonist books appear in childhood or early adolescence. Except for a few unique cases, if you're not chosen by age thirteen or fourteen, it means you're stuck in the ensemble character class forever.

One thing all protagonists do share—whether royal or not—is the wait for their prologue prophecies. A prologue prophecy is the very first thing the Author writes in any protagonist book. These vague, typically rhyming lines are super important, for they prophesize the sum of that main character's destiny.

SJ hadn't received her prologue prophecy yet, but all my other friends had. For instance, Blue, the younger sister to the famed Little Red Riding Hood and another one of my best friends, received hers a few weeks ago.

While I didn't know exactly what it said, she'd told us the gist. The main takeaway being that it sucked. Her prologue dictated she was going to have to marry our friend and fellow protagonist Jason—younger brother to Jack from *Jack & the Beanstalk*. This was as awkward as it was infuriating.

Jason was a cool guy and everything, and we were all really good friends, but no one should be forced to marry someone they didn't pick out for themselves. And the fact that Blue—my cloak-wearing, knife-wielding, independent, fearless, heroic dear friend—didn't have a say in such an important part of her future was maddening.

But that's life. Protagonist life, anyways. You're dealt a hand and you play it. No one ever thinks about folding or requesting a change in the cards. No one until me, that is.

Which brings us back to that afternoon in Adelaide's infirmary.

When my prologue prophecy appeared that day, it revealed that I would live a boring, subservient life and marry the intolerable Prince Chance Darling. In response I didn't just reject the hand the Author assigned me, I swept the cards off the table completely, refusing to participate in the game any longer.

In a mad, brilliant, beautiful moment of inspiration, I decided that I would find the Author and get her to rewrite my fate. And in an equally delirious, wonderful moment, I convinced my friends to come with me.

As a result, SJ, Blue, Jason, Daniel (ugh, Daniel), and I had run away from school on a quest to do just that.

The Indexlands were protected by an extremely powerful In and Out Spell, one of four in Book that kept people from entering in or out of specific locations. These spells had been cast by the Fairy Godmothers, so we'd gone to visit my mother's former Fairy Godmother (and my own regular godmother), Emma, to see if she knew how to break it. Lo and behold, she did. And now we did too.

Emma told us that in order to break the In and Out Spell around the Indexlands we needed "Something Strong, Something Pure, and Something One of a Kind." More specifically, we needed three elusive items that fit that bill:

- A Quill with the Might of Twenty-Six Swords,
- The Heart of the Lost Princess,
- And a Mysterious Flower Beneath the Valley of Strife.

Which brings us to the here and now. The here being the sky—me and Blue riding on Pegasi; the others inside a carriage pulled by three more amazing flying horses—and the now being sunset—the day after we'd left our respective schools, and only an hour after fleeing our realm's capital, Century City.

The good news at this point was that we had acquired the first item on our enchanted shopping list. The quill in question now resided safely within Blue's boot. Plus, we'd eluded a giant dragon that had attacked the city during our visit and had come very close to roasting us like lamb on a spit.

The bad news was a much longer catalogue. Given that collecting the first item to break the In and Out Spell had almost gotten us killed in a myriad of colorful ways, I had a bad feeling about finding the next two. Because while the five of us were all capable and formidable in our own ways, a lot of equally formidable factors had just been introduced.

I inadvertently shivered at the thought. As our group of five flew toward the fading cherry-colored horizon, I could still feel cold steel against my throat. Twilight may have been falling, but the memory of Arian and his sword was sharp as the midday sun.

Arian had presented himself as the head of a team of antagonists charged with hunting down protagonists whose prologue prophecies posed a threat to them.

This was a disturbing notion, especially since I'd learned that I was one of their targets. It was also extremely confusing.

Although Arian claimed he was hunting me because my prologue prophecy posed a threat to the antagonists, as far as I knew there was no indication in my prophecy as to why. The destiny I'd read in my book was beyond doldrums.

For me, becoming Prince Chance Darling's obedient, elegant wife was a fate worse than death. But I could see no reason why the antagonists would take issue with it. It just didn't make any sense. And while we were on the subject, neither did Arian himself.

Despite the boy's new role in my life—hunter, enemy, theoretical executioner—what I found most puzzling about his existence was the fact that he was the boy of my dreams.

No, I don't mean like that.

Yes, the twenty-year-old antagonist had fiercely dark, wavy hair that offset his black eyes, and the physical form and sword prowess of your above-average Lord Channing's hero. But that was so not where I was going with this.

I meant to say that he was the boy of my *nightmares.*

I'd suffered from viciously real dreams for years. However, it wasn't until recently that their content had begun bleeding into my reality. Arian was one such example. His voice, his presence, had permeated my sleeping consciousness for some time; I just hadn't known it. The moment I'd come face to face with him in Century City, though, I'd recognized him. Without ever having met him, Arian had been in my head for months now.

I still didn't know how or why this was possible, but I did know that I was not prepared to talk about the matter openly. As such, I hadn't told my friends about my second encounter with Arian when our group had gotten separated in the capital and I'd run into him, nor what he'd said to me during that confrontation.

Granted, my crew hadn't had much time for discussion since fleeing the city. But regardless, I knew I wanted to withhold the information from them. And in acknowledging this compulsion, I felt a subtle shift in the way I regarded my friends.

I mentioned earlier that there were three main problems that stood in my way to breaking the expectations of my princess archetype and becoming something better. However, I didn't realize at this point in my journey that a fourth, much more toxic obstacle was about to reveal itself. And unlike the other problems (which were all external threats), this fourth one would come at me from a source I never thought I'd have to guard myself against, and one that was much more powerful:

Me.

CHAPTER 1

Beginnings

hey say the calm comes before the storm. What they don't say is why.

Maybe it's the world's way of drawing you in to a false sense of security. Or maybe the world never knew devastation was imminent, and was just as surprised as you were when chaos streaked the sky.

Up 'til now my life had by no means been a picnic, but I had experienced the good fortune of having wonderful friends who I never fought with and never doubted.

I'd met SJ and Jason on my first night at Lady Agnue's School for Princesses & Other Female Protagonists. Blue had joined our gang two years later when her protagonist book appeared, courtesy of the Author, and she'd enrolled at Lady Agnue's as well. If I disregarded the newest addition to our group, Daniel (which I so often preferred to do), the four of us had been pretty tight knit for a while.

Little did I know our easygoing friendship was but another calm before a storm. And little did I know that the "why" behind this particular storm would be my own actions.

At the moment the clouds were beginning to brew (figuratively and literally). Gray manifestations of coldness were coming across the late twilight sky as steadily as they were encircling our group. As they stirred, I found my mind wandering to brighter days—memories, beginnings, milestones. In particular, my thoughts drifted to the eventful evening when I'd first met SJ and Jason.

I couldn't say why I let the recollection consume me so vividly. Maybe the hesitation I felt toward my friends in the aftermath of today's events had me feeling guilty, and my subconscious was trying to remind me that, given our history, trusting my friends should have been the easiest thing in the world.

Or maybe I was just bored. After all, it's not like you get complimentary snacks or inflight entertainment while riding a Pegasus.

I very clearly remembered my first interactions with Jason and SJ six years ago. In all my life I had never felt so crowded, yet so alone.

The giant hallway intersection of Lady Agnue's was bustling with activity. Most of the other ten-year-old, first-year students were huddled around the Treasure Archives, admiring their magnificence. I did not join the herd. I was sure there would be time to regard our ancestors' fairytale relics later. I would be attending this school until I was eighteen, after all.

Besides, despite being Cinderella's daughter, the treasures displayed in those cases weren't so much exciting to me as they were annoying. From Aladdin's genie lamp to my own mother's glass slipper, they were shiny reminders of every tradition I was walking in the shadow of.

I hung around the back of the room, leaning against one of the cold, grand windows that allowed moonlight to spill through. Its ghostly glow caught on the shimmering material of my light purple gown, particularly the smooth, pearly beads that decorated its bodice.

I looked on at the myriad of first-year girls flocking the space. The school seamstresses had made each of us a custom gown in preparation for our first ball at Lady Agnue's tonight. How they'd divined our sizes ahead of time, I did not know. Maybe our parents had sent them in. Or maybe it was just a "one size fits all" deal and if you happened to be a plus-sized protagonist you were out of luck.

I clawed at the uncomfortable corset of my dress. None of the girls here had even hit puberty; why in Book was it necessary to wear dresses that defined our waists when most of us didn't even have waists?

It was frustrating, but at least I wouldn't have to wear the dress for very long. While my mother's famous ball had expired at the stroke of midnight, the first-year students only had to be at tonight's ball for an hour in the middle. It would be kind of silly for us to be present for more than that. None of us knew how to dance yet; our formal ballroom training didn't start until our second year. And it wasn't like any of us were keen on the boy-girl socializing aspect of such functions. We were all still in our respective "boys are gross, girls are strange" stage of life.

The lot of us younglings from Lady Agnue's and Lord Channing's were instructed to meet in front of the Treasure Archives at eight o'clock, at which time the Damsels in Distress (D.I.D.) teacher, Madame Lisbon, would escort us inside and teach us about ball decorum, fanciness, and other things I didn't care about.

I sighed as I stared on at the masses.

I would have been lying if I'd said I wasn't worried about the journey ahead. I'd been looking over my course schedule for this semester and was as far from thrilled as physically possible. I mean, Grace for Beginners, Singing with Nature, A Young Lady's Guide to Diction—forget graduating at the top of my class, I'd be lucky if I didn't get bored to death before my adult molars came in.

It didn't help that the only courses that did intrigue my interest were off limits. Stuff like Boomerangs for Beginners, Tracking in Nature, and A Young Tomboy's Guide to Tomahawks were classes exclusively for the common protagonists at my school. I was told that in later years I might be able to take more stimulating electives. However, in the meantime I was doomed to an academic curriculum that had the equivalent excitement of dry toast.

In spite of all this, as I stood there and fiddled with the fabric of my dress, what filled me with the most anxiety was the realization that I might have to go through this alone.

It was true a lot of kids here didn't know each other, especially the common protagonists. While the children of royals tended to meet one another at some point as a result of our parents' friendships, common protagonists did not have that advantage. Common protagonists were either Half-Legacies (the relatives of non-royal fairytale characters) or new protagonists entirely—chosen by the Author for a greatness yet to be determined.

Yet, despite their lack of familiarity with one another, I could already see friendships starting to form, particularly between roommates.

This made sense. When you were dropped off at a brand new boarding school—ripped away from everything and everyone you were accustomed to—your immediate reaction was to attach yourself to somebody going through the same.

Sort of a safety in numbers, we're-in-this-together kind of thing.

Alas, I had not been afforded such a luxury. After arriving at Lady Agnue's with my mother, I'd learned that I'd been assigned two roommates. Both were Legacies (protagonists whose parents had been protagonists *and* royals), and one of them I already knew.

The girl in question was Princess Mauvrey Weatherall. She was the daughter of Sleeping Beauty, and because of our kingdoms' close proximity and parents' congenial relationship, we'd already known each other for a long time.

From what I could remember she hadn't been so bad at first. But apparently evil and narcissism were characteristics that needed to lie dormant for a while before fully manifesting. Because in recent times this golden-blonde princess had fine-tuned a unique kind of malice that would've made a mutilated magic hunter look sweet.

She hadn't spoken to me since we'd arrived at school (unless you count getting shoved out of the way to our shared bathroom as talking). If so, after she pushed me aside in her haste to get ready for the ball, I'd definitely done my share of "talking back."

Needless to say the girl and I were not bonding.

In her case our lack of roommate connection didn't matter. She appeared to be doing just fine in the friend department. Although she was about as kind as an eel, her inherent princess charm gave off a conductive spark that drew others toward her. I didn't know if the electricity cackling in her personality and dangerously sharp blue eyes were inspiring the other princesses to listen to her out of faith or fear, but they were drawn to her circle either way. And as a result, I knew with every passing minute my chances at befriending them were slipping. Mauvrey would not hesitate to get a jump on spreading word about my weirdness. She was just vicious enough to view poisoning the other girls' opinions of me as a sport. And thus far it wasn't hard to tell she was winning.

With this unfortunate turn of events, I held onto the hope that my other roommate was not going to be so blind or catty. Though I didn't allow that hope to get very high. For my second roommate was to be Snow White Jr. (And yes, I do mean the daughter of *that* Snow White.)

I'd never met the princess before. But given her lineage, her appearance, and the shocking number of glittery dresses in her suitcase, I had a feeling we weren't meant to mesh well.

Looking at her now, I was all but sure of it. She'd gotten here extra early and was following Madame Lisbon around asking questions, offering to help, and carrying the professor's pre-ball checklist. Her dress was silver silk and incomparably graceful. Her face looked pale and cold like an antique doll. And her long black mane was braided neatly behind her, unlike my own brown hair, which fell thickly and thunderously around my face.

It may have been rash to judge her off the bat like that, but after growing up around princesses like Mauvrey I didn't have any evidence to support the possibility that she might be different. Whether she was or not, though, I still hadn't had the chance to verify.

By the time I found our room this afternoon she had already left for the two o'clock tour of the school. I had been forced to miss that tour and take a much later one because our headmistress, Lady Agnue, held me back to scold me after orientation. I'd helped myself to the snacks before the program started, which apparently was some kind of major transgression.

She said she would think of a punishment appropriate for the crime and get back to me. As such, I was doing my best to avoid her. Mom would flip if she found out I'd gotten into mischief on my first day, let alone my first hour at school. She'd asked me at least a dozen times on our way over here to do my best to keep out of trouble. Granted, I think she suspected that with my bold nature and disinclination toward obedience I might not be able to avoid it and would inevitably provoke difficulty. But she also hoped for the best.

Me? I wasn't sure what I hoped for when it came to my development at this school.

The brochure in our welcome packet stated my path pretty clearly. I was meant to follow convention and become everybody's idea of a proper princess. But despite being only ten years old, I already had a strong enough sense of myself to know this probably wasn't going to work out.

I did want to be a good princess someday, but not in the way this school or my realm deemed fit. Moreover, I didn't want to be limited by the role. My brothers had attended Lord Channing's School for Princes & Other Young Heroes and were trained to be valiant protagonists. So, much as I did truly want to make my princess-ness my own, my greatest hope was that I might someday combine that with something more, that I might somehow branch out and be part of a new breed, a stronger kind of archetype—a hero-princess, if you will.

Sadly, I seemed to be alone in thinking I could achieve such a thing. As it stood, most of the other princesses in my year were already starting to avoid me due to Mauvrey's warnings of my weird personality. The common female protagonists in our class, meanwhile, didn't seem to want me near them either. I may have been a different kind of princess, but to them I was still a princess, and therefore my presence in their circles weirded them out just as much. Evidently I was too much combat boot for the prissy girls and too much glitter for the tough ones.

I absentmindedly tugged on one of the silver pumpkin earrings hanging from my ears and turned my back on the noise and clutter to look out at the grounds.

The campus on the other side of the window was bathed in shades of dark blue, but occasional fireflies that resembled mischievous, moving stars added a warm twinkle to the landscape. It was unusually windy for a September night. I watched the trees sway in the forest that separated us from Lord Channing's. They moved with purpose, I thought. And at the thought, I found myself feeling jealous. For I wished I could do the same.

My pensive ten-year-old wonderings were interrupted by a sudden impact against my right arm. I rotated around to find a boy in a khaki pantsuit that was slightly too big for him. He'd tripped on an untied shoelace and rammed into me.

"Oh, sorry," he said, his cheeks turning red from embarrassment as he bent down to retie the misbehaving shoelace. He stood when he was done then glanced around and gave me a bashful grin as he rubbed the back of his neck. "I feel so stupid," he said. "Balls are weird and I feel like I don't know what I'm doing."

"I don't either," I replied. "But then, I'm used to it."

The boy smiled brighter. His blond hair was kind of messy, making me wonder if he'd just been playing outside, or if an older classmate had given him a noogie. He had a naturally pleasant, happy-go-lucky look on his face, but the color of his bright blue eyes was intense for anyone, let alone a kid.

"I'm Jason Sharp," he said, extending his hand.

"Crisa," I said, shaking it.

"What are you doing over here by yourself?" he asked.

"Just observing," I said, nodding my head toward the little groups of girls and boys scattered around the corridor, each huddled together tightly like the protons and neutrons of a chemical element.

"Mind if I join you?" Jason asked. "I don't feel like picking a flock yet."

I gestured to the spot beside me, extending an invitation. Jason put his hands behind his head and stared out at the crowd. "Girls at balls are like bears in forests—only look them in the eye if you mean business," he said.

I turned my head and raised my eyebrows in confusion. "What?"

"It's the only piece of advice my brother gave me for tonight," Jason explained. "He went to Lord Channing's a while back."

"Who's your brother?" I asked.

"You'd know him as Jack from *Jack & the Beanstalk*."

"You're a Half-Legacy."

He nodded. "What are you?"

I hesitated at the question. Maybe that was stupid. But pronouncing myself as a princess did not feel right as I was not sure what the title even really meant. Introducing myself as Cinderella's daughter didn't sit well with me either. It would've been a form of false advertising; I was nothing like my mother and anyone who spent more than three minutes with me knew it.

Furthermore, going with "Legacy" as my official brand seemed just as wrong. It implied that the greatest part of my identity was being an extension of someone else's. And while I may not have been the kind of kid parents bragged about, I really believed my life had to amount to more than that.

"Crisa?"

I blinked. I guess I'd been staring off into space. Jason had his head tilted at me like a perplexed puppy, waiting for my response. "I said, what are you?" he repeated.

"Um, let's go with undecided," I replied. "Anyway, if you believe your brother then why are you talking to me, eye contact and all?"

"I haven't met a lot of the other guys yet," he admitted. "And, well, I guess you're not as scary as the other girls."

"Should I take that as a compliment?"

"I would."

"Children, children!" Madame Lisbon called out, waiving a handkerchief at us with both excitement and aggression.

The lot of us cut off our conversations and instinctively took steps closer to the teacher out of good manners, not necessity of hearing. This woman could project.

Despite her booming voice, Madame Lisbon was not an intimidating person. At barely five feet in height, she was a lot closer to our eye level than, say, Lady Agnue who towered in at six foot two. She was also kind of thick and squishy-looking, reminding me of the many stuffed bears I had in my room back home. Frankly—from her rosy complexion to her soft and sparkly eyes—everything about her seemed non-threatening.

I supposed I was grateful for that. These ballroom lectures were the extent of our D.I.D. training this year. But once we began taking the subject in a classroom next year, I garnered it would be a lot easier to not pay attention if the teacher didn't intimidate me.

"Welcome, my little protagonists," Madame Lisbon gushed, "to your first ball at this fine institution. I am sure these monthly gatherings will become a favorite pastime of yours in the wonderful years to come. Now then," she waved theatrically to a corridor on the right, "it is time to go in. Please proceed behind me in single-file order. The first forty minutes of the itinerary will be a lecture. Following that you may wander about the ballroom on your own. But please stay to the sides, do not inconvenience your older classmates, and do stay out of trouble."

We moved into a line like Madame Lisbon had requested. Jason filed in behind me and leaned in for a whisper. "I think I can make two of those work."

I smiled in the shadows of the pillar we crossed under. I liked this kid already.

Once we'd entered the ballroom Madame Lisbon began her lecture. The topic was the importance of formal introductions when meeting someone new. I guess Jason and I had already failed at that, what with the ramming into each other and all.

I would have liked to have made a sassy comment about this to him, but upon entering the ballroom Madame Lisbon had separated us into two groups—boys on the left and girls on the right. As a result, I was on my own again (psychologically, anyway).

Squished in between the fine fabrics of other gowned princesses, I tried my best to focus on what the teacher was saying. I found this difficult, though. Past my tendency to mentally wander whenever boring subjects were being shoved down my throat, it was kind of hard to hear. The

orchestra never stopped playing, and the conversations
of the older protagonists in the room didn't help either.
There were so many of them, and they all looked so . . .
romanticized.

That's a word right?

Yeah, let's go with that. Romanticized.

Watching them was just plain mesmerizing, making
me feel like a June bug drawn to the light of a lantern. I
wondered if I would be as graceful and glamorous when
I got to be their age. Then I laughed to myself at the idea.
Like even.

When our lecture had concluded I thought I might
reunite with Jason only to discover that he and a few of the
other boys were hitting it off now. I decided to leave him
alone.

Mauvrey and most of the other girls had taken to the
sidelines to observe the flowing wonder that was the formal
dance circle in the center of the room. Boys in tailored suits
and girls in glittering dresses that fitted them way better than
ours did us moved with such elegance it was as if the music
pulsed through their veins, a body-enveloping extension of
their heartbeats.

I decided I would try to join my future classmates and
stood next to the princess farthest away from Mauvrey. She
had white-ish blonde hair and a navy dress with a matching
choker.

"Hi," I said. "I'm Crisa."

"My name is Princess Marie Sinclaire," the girl responded
formally, curtsying and then extending her hand. "How do
you do?"

"Wow, you really took that lecture to heart, didn't you?"
I replied, shaking her hand.

A tantalizing smell wafted under my nose and I turned my head to where it was coming from. Across the ballroom I saw members of the school's kitchen staff setting out a fresh round of fancy appetizers, among which I could definitely detect something wrapped in bacon.

While the dancing may have been an enjoyable spectacle to observe, and Marie seemed nice, the aroma won out. I bid goodbye to the princess and headed toward the food. On my journey to the snack table, however, I encountered two obstacles.

The first occurred about halfway there when I had to quickly sidestep to evade a couple in mid tango. In my haste I bumped into another one of my new peers. Alas, unlike Jason, I instantly disliked this boy.

"You should watch where you're going," the boy said condescendingly. "A small princess like you could get trampled if not careful."

I glared at him. "Dude—"

"Chance."

"Chance," I continued. "We're basically the same height."

"Yes, but princesses are so much more fragile. You're damsels. Besides, I am in the middle of a growth spurt."

"I hope for your sake it's a big one. You might look disproportionate if that big head of yours doesn't get a matching set of shoulders."

Chance eyed me like a boxer sizing up an opponent, but also like a dog meeting a raccoon for the first time—with careful consideration. I eyed him too. But my version of it was like a mongoose observing a proud snake—amused and insulted, for the snake had no idea what I was capable of.

I noted that for a ten-year-old, Chance had a lot of confidence. It practically radiated from him. And he was cute, I guess. (Again, for a ten-year-old.) But the boy had a smugness in his eyes that made me certain that if I'd ever run into him on a playground growing up, I would have surely shoved him in the mud.

"Pay no mind to her, Prince Chance."

A surprisingly stealthy Mauvrey slipped next to us. Her arms crossed, she bumped Chance's shoulder playfully. "She is hardly worth the attention of our kind."

"You're so right, Mauvrey," I replied, unfazed. "Allow me to direct you to something of interest that's more on your level." I tore a few sparkly beads from the bodice of my dress and tossed them across the floor like marbles. "Go get the shiny, Mauvrey. Go on, go get it girl."

Mauvrey narrowed her eyes at me but didn't retort. She simply grabbed Chance by the arm and led him in the other direction. I was sure I would pay for my snarky comment in some way later. Maybe Mauvrey would plant peanut butter in my shoes or use her perfect vocal chords to persuade the mockingbirds outside our room to mock me. For now, though, she'd been foiled. And that was good enough for me. After all, I had bigger fish to fry, and by that I meant eating the fancy, bacon-wrapped fish sticks arranged in towers at the snack table.

Unfortunately, that was where I encountered the second obstacle between me and my quest for treats: my height. The fish stick towers, modeled to look like the skyscrapers of Century City, were on top of a two-foot-tall display stand at the back of the table close to the wall. Even on my tippy toes I couldn't quite reach it.

There were plenty of other snacks within reach. In fact, pretty much all others were. But I was hardly the type to let things go. Once I got an idea in my head, I would follow that path no matter how dangerous or potentially problematic it could be. It was not the wisest way, but it was my way. And most of the time that kind of cement-headed persistence tended to yield fruitful results. Right now, though, it was just making me feel stupid.

I gripped the edge of the table with my hands and boosted myself up. Then I balanced my weight on one hand while I outstretched the other.

Almost . . . Almost . . .

"Here, let me help you with that."

Startled, I looked up to see an older girl, about fourteen and fairly tall, reach past me and grab a fish stick. I released my grip on the table and landed on the ground just as she handed it to me.

"Thanks," I said.

"No problem." The girl shrugged, her impressively curly, chestnut brown hair bouncing off her shoulders. "When I was younger I had the same kind of face-off with a fondue fountain. Needless to say it did not end well."

I opened my mouth to respond but was cut off.

"Ashlyn!"

An elegant girl with tan skin that glowed like bronze and dark hair pulled into a regal bun, scurried over. Her pale yellow dress matched the canary diamond earrings hanging from her ears. When she reached us she excitedly grabbed onto the arm of the girl who'd just been helping me.

"Come on," she said. "Prince Daryl is looking for you. And you know if you do not swoop in now, one of the other princesses will snatch him up."

"Right." The girl (Ashlyn, I guess) nodded. "Go time then."

She pushed some loose curls out of her face, adjusted

the lift of her strapless bra with a subtle pulling motion, and then gave me a nod. "Good luck, little duck. Try to keep out of trouble."

As she and her friend rushed off, I ate my fish stick and wondered why people were always telling me that. I guess while Chance radiated confidence and Jason emitted amicability, I must've given off an aura of mischief.

I'm not sure if that's something to lament or embrace, but I guess I'll roll with it.

After a few minutes of dawdling by the snack table I got bored and decided to try and find some place where I might have more fun. I was on the other side of the ballroom now, pretty far from most of the other kids in my year and surrounded on all sides by our bigger, more majestic counterparts.

I knew my older brother Alex was somewhere in that mess, but I didn't look for him. My mom and I had traveled to school separately as he'd planned to meet up with some friends along the way. Besides that, I'd long promised myself that I wouldn't bother him when we got here. He and I were close, but he had a good thing going at school. At Lord Channing's he was popular—royal, handsome, heroic—and he didn't need a ten-year-old kid sister cramping his style. He would've never actually said this to me, of course, but I was realistic enough to know it was true.

With no one to talk to and nothing to do, I found my way to the stage at the front of the room. The forty-piece orchestra was playing animatedly, framed by heavy, light pink curtains.

There was a door ajar that led to the backstage area. I subtly slipped through it. Sixteen steps later, I found myself surrounded by a myriad of pulleys and levers that controlled the curtains and lighting equipment.

I peered onto the stage. I was just behind the orchestra, which was elevated on platforms facing outward. Spotlights in assorted pastel colors rotated around the musical ensemble, reflecting off the instruments and mimicking the rhythm of the songs. They were so bright and spellbinding that the tiny particles of lint dancing in the air looked like magic dust.

Only Lady Agnue's could manage such a trick of the light, I thought, and make something so bland and inconsequential resemble something so inexhaustibly sparkly.

I was surprised that there was no one back here monitoring the equipment. But on further inspection I realized that all the lights were on timers. And the curtain ropes did not need supervision. They were secured in place—tightly wound and held by a sturdy padlock to keep their knots fortified.

The orchestra had its back to me. The side area I stood in led to some curtained-off corridors, which likely ran to a greenroom. I knew there would be no performers or professors back there now as the ball was midway through. Other than the random cricket I saw perched on one of the control boards, I was completely alone.

As such, in the cover of the secluded alcove I finally felt comfortable letting myself feel like myself. And what that meant was drawing out my wand.

A few years ago, my godmother (my mother's Fairy Godmother, Emma) had gifted it to me on my birthday. Since then I had become attached to it in the way most girls grew fond of their dolls.

It was about a foot long and off-white. In dark spaces it gave off a silvery glow, but the luminescence of the stage area was so bright that the effect was counteracted for the time being.

I'd never really had a proper place to store the wand. (Emma hadn't exactly included a carrying case in the gift bag.) And since I'd always been dead set on preventing anybody—my parents, my brothers, my teachers—from finding out about it, I had a tendency to keep it shoved in my boot.

I lifted the hem of my gown, exposing the inappropriate footwear I had on beneath it.

Despite my mother's famous origin story and the laws of society that dictated I would eventually have to master walking in high-heeled shoes, I loved nothing more than wearing one of my many pairs of boots.

It went without saying that my mother was not a fan of this proclivity, even after I pointed out that if she had been wearing boots the night of her famous ball she could've gotten away a lot faster and not twisted her ankle in the process (an unfortunate truth so often left out of her fairytale's retellings).

However, regardless of her disapproval, she had allowed me to pack a few pairs for school. And as I was already going to be on my toes figuratively tonight, I'd opted to secretly wear a pair beneath my dress.

So far it had proven to be an inspired choice. Nobody was the wiser *and* I had a place to keep my wand for the evening.

I knew I couldn't very well store the precious thing in my boot forever. If I kept it there for more than an hour it seriously started to press into my calf, causing me to walk with a limp. But it had been worth the irritation tonight. I wasn't relaxed enough at school yet to feel comfortable leaving it in my room, even if it was hidden. Moreover, messing around with it had a calming effect on me. After the stressful day I'd had that was definitely something I needed.

I twirled my wand between my fingers with ease. Then I smiled and let out a whisper.

"Knife."

The moment the word escaped my lips, or rather the moment the thought escaped my brain, the wand changed in my hand. The bottom part of it thickened and formed a leather grip. The top widened and sharpened—morphing into a glistening, unbreakable blade (the likes of which no kid my age should've been allowed to handle). When it had fully transformed I twirled the knife with just as much effortlessness.

My Fairy-Godmother-issue magic wand was enchanted to turn into whatever weapon I willed it into. It made for a very intriguing, adaptable toy to say the least. Though I wished I had more use for it.

I'd always wanted to be good at combat like the heroes at Lord Channing's, or even some of the grittier common female protagonists at Lady Agnue's. However, that was a hard undertaking when you were a princess.

My mother and father would've sooner invited the Wicked Witch of the West to stay in one of our guestrooms than let their little girl train for combat. They loved me and wanted me to be happy and everything, but fighting was just not a princess thing, despite some of the scuffles I'd gotten into during play dates as a toddler that suggested otherwise.

My brother Alex had secretly been giving me lessons in combat and fighting when he was home from school for the summer. As a result, I had picked up a bit of skill and know-how over the last few years. But I knew this small amount of practice was not going to turn me into any kind of hero. It definitely wasn't going to be enough to feed the desire I had to grow beyond my damsel princess archetype.

I had hoped that at school I might occasionally get some more intensive combat training, but without a partner I didn't know how I would ever improve on a practical level.

Then again, it wasn't as if I could use my wand even if I did find somebody to spar with.

Only Fairy Godmothers were supposed to have wands (powerful magic like theirs required sturdy conductors), and really, the magical items were supposed to be useless without a Godmother's magic. My having one was definitely not above board. I didn't know how Emma had managed to acquire the wand or, more importantly, how it functioned for me, but I did know that if anyone ever caught me with it, it would be as good as confiscated.

With two new roommates, a school full of protagonists, and an army of teachers who would be watching me with the intensity of a hundred female hawks, I didn't know when I'd get to use my wand. This might well have been my last moments with the thing for a very long while. Hence my decision to take it out of my boot.

The knife glided through my fingers. I tossed it into the air with flourish like I'd been practicing. It spun three times before I reached out and caught it perfectly by the grip.

On guard! I thought as I pointed the weapon at the cricket on the control board.

The cricket chirped but did not seem impressed. Luckily for me, I did not care. For the next several minutes as the orchestra played on, I continued my game. The music became the soundtrack to which I fought imaginary enemies—transforming my wand between a knife, a sword, an axe, and a shield.

My mind whirred with scenarios. I had a knack for quick thinking and creativity, so there was no shortage of fight scenes that ran through my head. I was in the middle of fantasizing about wielding an axe against a lizard monster when suddenly the game altered in a way I never anticipated.

"What are you doing?"

I was so surprised by the voice that I leapt out of my skin and—in the process—let go of my axe. Time seemed to move in slow motion in the moments that followed.

My axe flew from my hand with such force that its unforgivably sharp blade chopped through several of the curtain ropes on the control board. I turned and found my new roommate, Snow White Jr., standing behind me—Madame Lisbon's checklist in her left hand and a small, sparkly purse in her right. She and I blinked at one another for a second before our attention shot upwards.

The ropes were unraveling and there wasn't time to stop them. Seconds later, pounds of pink curtains were cascading on top of the orchestra, followed by screams and crashing symbols. The cellists' chairs toppled off the stage. Flutists took each other down like dominos.

One of the swinging curtain ropes flung a cluster of hooks at a sector of stage lights, knocking them out of their intended vectors. And as if the universe's premier planners had orchestrated this embarrassment for an exhibition of their finest work, one of the spotlights was redirected to the backstage area—directly at me.

With many overhead curtains having knocked down orchestra members, and several side curtains that had been previously shielding me on the ground too, a perfect window of visibility was created. It was narrow. But it was enough.

I held up my hand to shield myself from the blinding

glare. In doing so I caught a glimpse of the last person I wanted to see.

Lady Agnue.

She was across the ballroom, dark brown hair in a tight bun and wearing a blood-red dress with long sleeves and elegant ruching. The crowds separating us were thick and disorderly. Nevertheless, even if it was just for a second, it was unmistakable that she saw me too.

"Crisanta Knight!"

I dashed back into the shadows where Snow White Jr. was still concealed. Without thinking I grabbed my axe from the ground, transformed it back into a wand in mid-run, slid down the banister of the stairs, stuffed the wand in my boot, and slipped out the door.

My boots and natural quickness allowed me to merge back into the ballroom crowds without drawing much attention to myself. Some people may have heard Lady Agnue call out my name, but I had moved with such swiftness that I doubted that more than a few had seen me slide out the door.

In that continued gait of stealth I inconspicuously but hurriedly darted in and out of the gown-clogged sections of the dance floor. The poofy dresses, combined with the confusion and sheer number of students in the room, were my allies as I maneuvered across the area. But I knew their concealment wouldn't last forever, because that's when I heard Lady Agnue's voice.

She was talking to a teacher about fifteen feet away. I could just barely hear her over the other students, and I could just barely evade her line of sight as I hid in the shadow of a tall prince with red hair and big coattails.

"When you find her, bring her to me," the headmistress

snapped. "I do not care who her mother is, she will be made an example of."

I felt myself gulp as I slowly backed up.

"Crisa," someone whispered from behind.

I spun around, panicked. Thankfully it was just Jason standing next to the snack tables. He'd picked up the edge of one of the floor-length, deep purple tablecloths and was gesturing underneath it. "Hide," he said.

I zipped over to him. The two of us ducked beneath the tablecloth. I scooted toward the wall on the other side of the table, but Jason stayed on his hands and knees.

"I'm gonna go draw some attention on the other side of the ballroom," he said. "Buy you time to think of a plan."

"I already have a plan," I responded. "Dig a hole through the floor, escape on wild Pegasi, and live a long and healthy life as a traveling acrobat."

"I meant more along the lines of a story you can tell Lady Agnue to lessen whatever punishment she's plotting."

"Yeah, I know. My plan just sounds so much more feasible." I knocked my head against the wall with a groan. Eventually I sighed. "All right. I'll think of something. I always do."

"Good. So like I said, I'll go buy you time."

"Maybe you shouldn't," I protested. "You're not in any trouble and you haven't done anything."

Jason smiled at me. It was a goofy, sympathetic, boyish smile. "I know," he said. "And neither is how I want to end my first day."

He scooched toward the tablecloth's draping barricade.

"Jason . . ."

He paused and looked back at me.

"Are you sure?"

"Yeah, Crisa. I am. You've been dealt a bad hand. What kind of person would I be if I just let you crash and burn?"

"An unscathed one," I replied.

He shook his head of unruly blond hair. "A selfish one," he corrected. "I may not know anything about being a hero or a protagonist yet, but I'm smart enough to know that neither would turn their back on a friend."

Jason ducked beneath the tablecloth and disappeared before I could fully appreciate the statement.

For the next minute I sat lost in thought. Had I just made a friend? Could it honestly be that easy? This kid hadn't known me for more than an hour and was offering me his trust like we'd been pals for ages. It was confusing, but if he actually was for real then maybe that's just what we would end up becoming—pals for ages.

However, the part of me that was always on guard made me think that the odds of this were very, very slim.

I looked up quickly when I saw the tablecloth rustle as a small hand began to lift it anew.

"Jason?" I whispered.

The hand pulled up the tablecloth. It wasn't Jason.

Snow White Jr.'s head peeked beneath the tablecloth. My mouth hung open with surprise and dread. She stared at me curiously. Her giant gray eyes blinked; her expression showed no signs of emotion. I truly expected her to call out for Lady Agnue or Madame Lisbon or an equivalently responsible adult. But much to my surprise, she didn't.

She looked over her shoulder—checking to make sure no one was watching her—then without invitation or explanation ducked below the tablecloth and joined me.

Snow White Jr. sat across from me and put down her

checklist and the small, sparkly purse she'd been carrying. I watched her elegantly straighten the wrinkles out of her pure silver gown so that its shimmering fabric lay gracefully enough to be painted for a portrait.

"What are you doing?" I asked.

"Straightening my gown," she replied. "You never want silk to wrinkle. It would require a steamer to return it to normal."

"No," I said more pointedly as I pointed to the spot of ground between us. "What are you doing *here*?"

"I gathered you could use some company," she responded.

I crossed my arms. "Even if that were true, why would you want to provide it? I just caused a major catastrophe, took out the orchestra, and ruined the first ball of the semester."

The increasingly hard-to-read princess shrugged without worry or judgment, as if I'd just told her I collected stamps or something. "That was an accident," she stated simply. "You are my roommate; I am hardly going to avoid you because of one mistake."

"Well there are plenty of other reasons to avoid me. Haven't Mauvrey and the other princesses spoken to you yet? You must've heard the rumors about me being a trouble-making, weapons-loving princess who can't sing, can't curtsy, and basically doesn't belong here."

"I have," Snow White Jr. nodded.

"Well, don't you think I'm weird?" I asked.

"Maybe a little," she admitted. "But who says that is a bad thing?"

Um, pretty much everyone I've ever interacted with.

We stared at each other without saying a word. It was like a cat meeting a dog for the first time—two creatures entirely different in nature and perception sizing each other up, deciding whether or not they could accept the other's dissimilarity.

I crossed my legs and sat up a bit straighter, as uncomfortable in my dress as I was in this situation. The commotion outside continued, so I still couldn't get out of here. But I wondered if braving a run for the ballroom exit would be less awkward than continuing to sit under this table. I focused on the barricade of tablecloth intensely, like I was trying to see through it.

"Your name is Crisanta Knight, is it not?" Snow White Jr. asked, startling me.

"Um, yeah," I responded hesitantly. "But I go by Crisa. And you're Snow White Jr."

"Yes." She nodded. "But I go by SJ."

I raised my eyebrows. "SJ? Really?"

"Is there something wrong with that?"

"No," I replied. "It's just not what I expected. Kind of . . . unconventional."

"Says the princess hiding beneath the snack table."

I allowed myself a slight smirk. "Touché. Although technically you're hiding under here with me."

SJ glanced around at the enclosure then let out a slight huff. She got onto her knees and grabbed my wrist with one of her hands. "Not for much longer," she said. "Come on, no more hiding. We must face Lady Agnue sooner or later, so it might as well be now."

"I don't know, later sounds like a pretty compelling option," I countered, pulling my wrist away. "Besides, what's all this 'we' stuff? I'm the one in trouble. Whatever consequences are out there, I have to face them alone."

SJ sat back, meeting my gaze. Studying her now, I no

longer saw coldness. She may have been polished and proper—an inherently flawless Legacy like Mauvrey—but there was something unique about her. I saw a deep kindness in her eyes, which had been evident the moment she'd popped her head under the table and hadn't judged me.

For whatever reason, SJ was willing to accept my flaws right out of the gate, no questions asked. Moreover, despite barely having met me five minutes ago, it seemed she was willing to stick her neck out for me too.

"You will not have to face the consequences alone," she said decidedly. "I shall tell Lady Agnue that the accident was my fault as well. That we are both to blame for what happened."

Part of me thought I'd heard her incorrectly. Confused words stuck in my throat like cotton wool. I pushed my hair behind my ears and leaned my head on the heels of my hands.

A strange wave of apprehension set in.

Growing up, I had never had any good friends. Not fitting into your designated slot in a world defined by archetypes and stations made your life a study in isolation and spurn—the combination of which taught you to never truly rely on anyone.

This made me tougher in a lot of ways. It also made me unafraid to be bold and take chances. But whether you think this was a character-building way to grow up or a lonely one, it was what I had gotten used to. Which was precisely why SJ's kind gesture felt as foreign to me as it did unbelievable. Things never worked this way. People never worked this way.

"SJ, I—"

"You can thank me later," SJ interceded, a little

unexpected sass in her tone. "And do not worry. I will not tell anyone about your wand either."

My heart stopped for a second. I'd forgotten that she'd seen my wand—seen that I had it and seen it transform. Instinctively I tried to scooch away, but my back was already against the wall. I had nowhere to go.

SJ saw my reluctance and sighed. She picked her handbag off the floor and opened it. Within its silver-lined interior I saw a crumpled quill, several wrinkled pieces of parchment covered with scribbled thoughts, and a few small glass vials with cork stoppers. Each of these vials was filled with some kind of colorful liquid. The instruments struck a chord of familiarity, and I realized I'd seen similar (albeit empty) vials on my tour of the school.

"Did you get those from the school's potions lab?" I asked.

"I did," SJ responded. "I have a weakness for potions study and sought special permission from the potions professor to work on some experiments in between orientation activities."

"SJ, schoolwork before school even starts—"

"She said no," SJ interrupted.

"What?"

"I suppose I understand," she continued. "Giving a ten-year-old permission to mix chemicals in a laboratory is hardly something a responsible teacher would do. It is not as if I could provide her with proof that I have been studying and practicing potion formulation in the basement of my castle for two years."

"I don't understand."

SJ closed her purse. "I love making potions, Crisa. And I am very good at it. But I have never had the opportunity nor the means to develop my skill without being judged. And while I know students here are not permitted to take potions classes until our second year, being in that potions lab today, I was just so excited that I am afraid I could not help myself. In between tour groups I mixed these anyways. They are harmless—just some height and hair-coloring potions I read about in a book last month. But the chance to use such wonderful equipment and refined ingredients . . . I am ashamed to say it was too great a temptation to pass up."

"SJ," I finally said. "That's some could-totally-get-you-into-trouble stuff and . . . you don't even know me. Why are you telling me this?"

SJ got back on her hands and knees, scooped up her purse and checklist, and made for the edge of the tablecloth. "Well," she said, "I suppose I trust you, Crisa. Now the question is, will you trust me too?"

That night I had done something quite opposite my nature. I'd trusted someone. I'd trusted SJ. And as a result, we'd forged the beginnings of a vibrant friendship—one that continued to grow in the years that followed.

It seemed that SJ and Jason had been meant to be my good friends from the beginning. And when Blue eventually enrolled at Lady Agnue's, she too earned an immediate spot in my heart when on the very night of her arrival the two of us got mixed up in an adventure involving underground troll poker and unicorn vomit.

Over the years the three of them had consistently been true in all aspects of their word and friendship. Even as recently as this afternoon in Century City, they'd demonstrated what an unstoppable team we could be when we worked together.

This made the growing compulsion I felt toward keeping secrets from them pretty conflicting. On the one hand, doing so made no sense. They were my best friends. On the other hand, I didn't like the idea of increasing the vulnerability I was already feeling by sharing it with other people.

I guess I needed time. I needed to think. I needed . . .

Well, firstly I needed to get off this Pegasus. I was starting to get a serious butt cramp.

CHAPTER 2

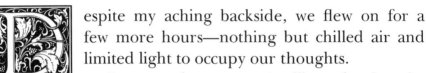

Friction

Despite my aching backside, we flew on for a few more hours—nothing but chilled air and limited light to occupy our thoughts.

Just as the moon (smiling despite the circumstance) reached the center of the sky, we landed in the kingdom of Harzana. The field we selected was not far from the Forbidden Forest, which most people stayed away from after dark. So it seemed like a decent place to lay low for a while.

I scratched the ear of my Pegasus, Sadie, when we landed—both to thank her for the ride and to apologize for the near-death experience I'd put her through when we'd faced off with the dragon in the skies over our realm's capital.

Blue swung her leg over her own Pegasus while SJ, Jason, and Daniel jumped out of our levitating carriage. They began to survey the area while I continued to pet Sadie. At least I thought they were surveying the area. When I turned to look at them I realized they'd been surveying me.

"I think we should make camp for the night," I said, ignoring their stares as I went to unload our sleeping bags from the trunk of the carriage.

Daniel blocked my way. "Is that all you have to say?" he asked.

"It's all I'm going to say," I responded, pushing past him with little regard.

While SJ, Blue, and Jason had been my friends for years, I'd only just met Daniel a couple of months ago. And frankly, most of the time it was all I could do not to kick him in the shin.

The moment we'd laid eyes on each other, I'd felt apprehension about the boy's presence. For while my school nemeses like Mauvrey and Lady Agnue regularly showered me with malice and insults, Daniel made me feel something much worse: doubt.

Despite being the person in our group who knew me the least, he spoke to me with the familiarity of someone who'd known me for ages. And the words that came out of his mouth were nothing short of unsettling.

Since our first meeting Daniel had managed to hone in on my insecurities. He possessed the uncanny ability to read me like a book. And for someone like me, who preferred to keep people at a distance, this was very disconcerting.

Like the rest of us, Daniel was on this mission because he wanted to find the Author and have his fate altered. But even though we shared the same goal, this didn't make up for the fact that I did not trust him. His prophecy, like pretty much everything else about him, was shrouded in mystery.

The perplexing boy had a naturally aloof demeanor and tended to dodge more questions than I did. Which was really saying something.

In addition, since he was a common before being selected as a protagonist, he had no fairytale lineage to provide context or backstory. He was something completely new and someone completely unreadable. The combination of which made me very uneasy.

"So, we're not going to talk about what just happened?" Daniel asked, following me to the rear of the carriage.

"What's there to talk about?" I countered. "It's called slaying a dragon. I hope you were taking notes."

"I wasn't actually, because (a) You didn't slay a dragon, you froze one with SJ's portable potions. And (b) You know that's not what I meant."

Mental sigh.

I knew it wasn't what he meant. Between the dragon and fleeing Arian's antagonists in Century City, we'd been running for most of the day, which had prevented the others from asking me a lot of tough questions. We hadn't really spoken since leaving the capital. Now that there was nowhere left to run, I had to face them—the questions, my friends, and Daniel too.

In truth, I understood why they thought I might have answers. I was the one who had led them to a bunker beneath Century City's Capitol Building where we'd discovered files on countless protagonists in our realm—me, Jason, Blue, and Daniel included. And of all the protagonists in those files, I was the only one the antagonists were presently trying to kill.

But the cruel fact remained that I could not explain any of this. Discovering the bunker had been an accident. I'd somehow dreamed about the passage leading up to it, and when I'd seen the markers in the Capitol Building, I'd followed them out of curiosity.

And given that my prophecy was so lackluster, I could see no reason why the antagonists were hunting me, let alone what they wanted with all the other protagonists they weren't trying to kill but were still interested in.

I released a deep breath and rotated around to speak

sincerely. "Look, I don't know what you expect me to say. I don't know anything about that bunker below the Capitol Building with those protagonist records. I have zero idea why all of us except for SJ were mentioned in those files. And I certainly don't know why those guys we ran into down there were trying to . . . why they wanted to . . ."

"Kill you," Daniel said bluntly.

"Yeah. That," I muttered.

Jason cleared his throat. "All right," he said. "Maybe we don't know why those antagonists were after you, Crisa. But since there were other kids from Lady Agnue's and Lord Channing's in those files, we should probably go back to school and find them. Find them and warn them that—"

"That what?" I interrupted. "That on our way to steal a quill that'll help us break the spell around the Indexlands, we stuck a sword into a dragon statue, discovered a secret bunker beneath the realm's oldest building, and then broke into a filing cabinet that contained suspicious paperwork for a bunch of protagonists with absolutely no relation to one another?"

Jason rubbed his arm sheepishly. "Well, it sounds crazy when you put it like that."

"It is crazy. We don't know why those antagonists are interested in those kids at school, let alone why that girl wants me dead."

Blue tilted her head. "What girl?"

I stopped short. "What?"

"You said a *girl* wants you dead," Blue clarified. "The only girl in that group chasing us was the member of the kitchen staff who I guess ratted us out to those creepy antagonists in the first place. Who are you talking about?"

"I, uh . . ."

Oh, crud.

Earlier today we'd all shared in the fun of being pursued through the Capitol Building by Arian and the armed antagonists set on (to quote that stupid file) "eliminating" me. But when the dragon had appeared and chaos had ensued throughout the city, there had been a short period when my friends and I had been separated. During which time I had suffered the misfortune of being cornered by Arian.

I shuddered just thinking about everything dreadful the boy had come to mean to me since our short period of introduction.

I was never one to feel fear. I just didn't allow it. I couldn't if I had any hope of ever being taken seriously as a hero, or at the very least being seen as a non-damsel princess. But when I'd come face to face with Arian I'd felt . . . *something*. It was a bit of fury, a touch of indignation, and a dose of anxiety. What that amounted to was what I could best describe as troubling intrigue. For while I wanted to keep Arian as far away from me as possible, I also felt the compulsion to dig deeper into the can of worms he'd opened, starting with that girl I'd just mentioned to Blue and the others.

When we were alone Arian had explained the whole "antagonists hunting me because of my prophecy" bit. But he'd also told me that he and his team were acting under the orders of a girl called Nadia.

I had zero idea who this chick was. But anyone who could order the doom of so many protagonists without our realm's leaders noticing was not a threat to be taken lightly. Given that, I deemed the best thing I could do was bide my time until I learned more.

In the meantime, her existence, like my run-in with Arian, was a topic I didn't feel comfortable talking about. Not with my friends, and certainly not with Daniel. So in response to Blue's inquiry I thought fast and evaded the truth like an explosive dodge ball.

"That's who I was talking about," I replied quickly. "That kitchen girl clearly had a death wish for me if she ratted us out to those bad guys."

The others' expressions were hard to read, the moon casting a ghostly luminescence on their features.

"All right," Blue finally declared, ending the horrible pause. "Since that's settled, can we move on to discussing our next move?"

"Yes," SJ said. Then she turned to face me, crossing her arms with an expectant look on her face. "Unless there is something else you would like to tell us, Crisa."

I looked my best friend in the eye. It was obvious that she wanted me to tell the others about Natalie Poole. She wanted me to reveal to them that the girl who'd been another recurring character in my nightmares for the past several years was not only a real person who lived in our neighboring realm of Earth, but also the subject of her own elimination file in Arian's bunker, just like me and Paige Tomkins (a former Fairy Godmother who was a good friend of my godmother, Emma).

Regardless of SJ's wishes for full disclosure, this was something I simply could not bring myself to share either.

I mean, I'd only just found out about it myself. And despite the fact that SJ had seen the file by accident, and that she'd learned about my dreams of the bunker, I was resolute that these were still my secrets to wield until I had a better grasp on what was happening to me.

None of it made any sense. Why were my dreams seeping into reality? Why was Natalie so important? She didn't just have a file in the antagonists' bunker; I'd also found a similar file in Fairy Godmother Headquarters a few weeks prior. And most importantly, why were all these weird things converging on me?

The sad truth was I didn't know the answers to any of these questions. But I did know that they were bizarre, unsettling, and confusing enough to make me want to keep them private. At least if I actively chose to handle their burden alone it gave me a sense of control. The thought of unveiling all my issues to the others prematurely felt too violating to bear.

Which was why—standing there in the shrouds of nightfall and my own self-preservation—I locked my gaze with SJ's and I lied.

"No," I responded flatly. "There isn't."

She glared at me. I glared at her. Then Jason abruptly cleared his throat a second time. It broke the staring match between SJ and me, which was good. Alas, his subject change added a newer, deeper layer of tension to the conversation.

"Um, guys, what about Mark?"

Mark.

I felt guilty that I hadn't thought about him until now. Though in all fairness there had been a lot going on.

Mark was a friend of ours from Lord Channing's. He was a prince and he'd been Jason's roommate for a couple of years. However, at the beginning of the semester their school's headmaster had made the announcement that Mark was taking a leave of absence for health and personal reasons. Incidentally, it was his absence that had brought Daniel to us; he had been assigned as Jason's new roommate at the start of the semester.

Until this afternoon we hadn't thought twice about

Mark's specific reasons for being absent. We just assumed he was sick or something and would return next semester. But after finding a file in Arian's bunker with Mark's name on it, along with the words "threat neutralized," a horrible thought had been born. What if our friend's leave of absence was way more suspicious and permanent than the school had let on?

The words "threat neutralized" could mean a lot of things. But—combined with the understanding we now had of what those antagonists were capable of—one interpretation was something far too dark to comprehend. It very well could've meant that Mark was, you know . . . that he'd been . . .

No. I can't even say it.

It had to be something else. It had to be.

"I think as far as this Mark kid is concerned, if we want to find out more, our best bet is still the Author," Daniel asserted.

Blue cocked an eyebrow. "How do you figure that?"

"Well, Mark was a protagonist, right? That means he has a book, a book the Author wrote. If we find the Author, maybe we can look at it, see what really happened to him, and if it was something messed up then it'd serve as the proof we need to show the schools."

A beat of reflection passed.

"He's not wrong," Blue said eventually. "Plus, if we find the Author we can also use her original books as proof that the realm's ambassadors have been forging protagonist books."

Ah yes, I'd almost forgotten about that little chestnut.

The trusted ambassadors of our realm's twenty-six kingdoms (not including the antagonist kingdom of Alderon) were evidently in cahoots with the Scribes and the

Fairy Godmother Supreme, Lena Lenore, to manipulate protagonist selection by both creating books for royals who weren't chosen as main characters and destroying those for people who were but didn't fall within their "realm quota."

I had no idea how long they'd been doing it, but their reasons had become clear to us when we'd eavesdropped on their meeting in the Capitol Building.

Evidently they considered putting a cap on the number of main characters allowed in our realm—and sticking with the tradition of all royals being protagonists—to be a vital part of keeping order in Book. The five of us, however, saw it as a twisted betrayal by the very leaders charged with keeping this kind of malevolence at bay. It was a problem that we somehow, someway needed to bring to an end.

We all thought on both Blue's and Daniel's proposals. It made sense to continue heading for the Author. In the meantime, we just needed to push past our worried feelings and trudge onwards. It sucked. But realistically, it seemed to be our best option.

"Fine then," I agreed, looking around at the acquiescing nods of the rest of our group. "I guess it's decided. We keep searching for the Author. Which means that now that we have the first item on Emma's list to break the In and Out Spell, we should probably figure out how we're going to find the second."

"I actually have a few thoughts on that," Blue piped in. "I think we have to go to Adelaide. Well, to the Forbidden Forest first, and then to Adelaide."

Blue began to recount the gears that had been turning in her head about how to find the next ingredient for deconstructing the In and Out Spell around the Indexlands (i.e., "The Heart of the Lost Princess").

While she wasn't quite sure what the whole "heart" thing was referring to, Blue (like the rest of us) was sure that Book had only one "Lost Princess." Princess Ashlyn of Adelaide— daughter of our land's most famous hydrodynamic main character, the Little Mermaid.

A small spark tickled my brain at the thought of her. Being several years older than me, I'd only seen Ashlyn in passing at school. But suddenly I remembered that I had actually met her once. It had been during my first ball at Lady Agnue's. The introduction had just been so many years ago, and for such a brief moment, that I'd forgotten.

When Ashlyn vanished a year and a half ago, all signs pointed to her being lost at sea, off the coast of her home kingdom in Adelaide. If we were going to find her, that was where we should start our search.

Of course, to search for anyone in the ocean, you have to hold your breath for more than a couple of minutes. That's where the Forbidden Forest came into play.

Many mythical and magical entities were rumored to exist deep within our realm's infamous forested area. The most whispered-about was called the Valley of Edible Enchantments. This place was said to house an assortment of different magical foods that people could consume to achieve a myriad of goals.

Blue's obsession with fairytale history (and the fact that she was from Harzana, which bordered the Forbidden Forest) made her pretty familiar with its legends. She informed us with relative certainty that one part of the Valley had something we could use to breathe underwater for a prolonged period of time.

My friend's logic was sound, and it made sense that the

Valley should be our next stop. Our only hesitation was that it was a gamble to enter the Forbidden Forest at all. You had to be wary of monsters and magical creatures when you set foot in most forests in Book, but the Forbidden Forest was different. Few people had ever made it out alive, and even fewer had managed to find the legendary Valley we were seeking.

Then again, I supposed it was also a gamble that we would even be able to locate Princess Ashlyn, given that tons of people had already failed to find her.

Since risk, faith, and presumption were all we had to work with at the moment, we all agreed to the course of action anyways. Next stop—the Forbidden Forest and an accompanying order of highly probable doom for five.

Yeah, I know that's not a real optimistic outlook. But I've had a long day.

As we proceeded to make camp for the night, I could tell SJ was still a bit uncertain about the idea, while Blue and Daniel seemed unfazed.

He hardly ever showed emotion, so I couldn't tell if his indifference was due to lack of worry, or lack of ability to show it. Blue's calm, on the other hand, was genuine. Things rarely got under her skin. And in this particular case, she was the most prepared of all of us.

The combined knowledge she'd acquired researching the Forbidden Forest in her books, and from the accounts of people in her village who'd survived its trap was impressive. For goodness' sake, even her own older sister (Little Red Riding Hood) had firsthand experience of the Forbidden Forest.

Red's journey had allowed my inquisitive friend to glean

a very rare inside understanding of some of the Forbidden Forest's internal workings. Knowing that, I understood how Blue could be so even-tempered about the mission ahead.

Not worried about her, my eyes drifted to the area of the campsite where Jason was chopping wood for the fire. He hacked away with his trusty axe at a steady pace—silent, focused, and keeping to himself as he tried not to burden us with the emotions that must've been whirring around his head in regards to Mark.

I felt bad for him. Our friend's unknown state was gnawing at the back of my mind just as it was no doubt gnawing at the back of Blue's and SJ's. But the three of us didn't know Mark anywhere near as well as Jason did. Up until this year, we typically only saw the boys once a month for our school balls. Jason, on the other hand, had been Mark's full-time friend and roommate for two years. He must've been really worried.

Despite how he was probably feeling, Jason remained stoic. Not because he was too proud or closed off to admit such feelings, but because he didn't want to weigh down our mission. It was his way—putting aside his needs for the needs of the many and the greater good.

I admired him for that, just as I admired Blue for her bravery, SJ for her compassion, and even Daniel for how secure he was with himself. They were all pillars that stood for something. What with everything going on, I wasn't sure I felt that kind of power in any part of myself anymore. How could I when my life was becoming an epicenter for change and conflict?

Jason, Daniel, Blue, and SJ continued to move about the campsite. We'd packed more than enough supplies in the trunk of our carriage. While SJ rolled out the sleeping bags,

Jason prepared the fire and Daniel removed the harnesses from the Pegasi and set up an area for them to sleep. I, meanwhile, went to aid Blue with unpacking the food.

As I helped her, my focus was not so much on the various cans of beans she'd brought with her, but on the journey that lay ahead—the fate that awaited us in a place that so few had ever dared explore.

It would be a tricky, risky endeavor, and I was anxious just thinking about it. But despite my initial skepticism over the likelihood of our success, I wasn't afraid of the Forbidden Forest. The term "forbidden," in my opinion, had always been more of a suggestion. And honestly, the stories I'd heard about the place sounded far too far-fetched to be taken seriously . . .

CHAPTER 3

Secrets & Lies

eace.

Peace and quiet.

In my experience there was nothing comparable to the calmness of a crisp ocean breeze paired with the smell of saltwater. I smiled contentedly with my eyes closed—basking in the pleasant atmosphere. Everything was perfect. Then I opened my eyes and saw myself standing about five feet in front of me.

And I wasn't talking about a reflection. There was quite literally another Crisanta Knight standing before my eyes.

Other me was at the edge of a dock. She was wrapped in a blue blanket and clenching her fists nervously, a slender, gray boat with a scarlet sail passing across the water in front of her.

In a trance, I walked over to her and reached out. My hand went straight through her like she was a ghost. Or rather, since it was my hand that seemed to dematerialize as it passed through her, *I* was the ghost.

I figured I had to be dreaming. But no matter how realistic my dreams were, I always knew they were just that—dreams. For one, they were usually fairly blurry. Two, I'd never been a character in them; I was just an observer.

Yet there I was, standing right in front of me. So what other explanation could there be other than insanity?

"Hey, you sleepwalking or just taking in the sights?"

Me and other me spun around to find Blue trotting toward us. She approached the other me though, not *me*, me. And her not being able to see *me*, me reaffirmed that I was actually dreaming.

"Just getting an early start to the day," dream me told her.

"You sure you're okay?" Blue asked. "You look pretty beat. And SJ's been looking out the kitchen window to check on you all morning with this worried expression on her face. But when I asked her what was up, she wouldn't tell me."

Dream me nodded absentmindedly. "Yeah, I'm fine."

Then she raised her eyebrows—seeming confused by whatever realization had just occurred to her.

"I'm surprised though," she said. "Between your Bruce obsession and what happened back in Book, I wouldn't have expected you to notice . . . or even care for that matter."

"Well, I'm not over either," Blue said slowly, "but I think Bruce would want us to move forward. Don't you?"

"I do," dream me agreed.

A beat passed and she bit her lip—processing some unknown thought. Then she glanced in my direction.

I could've sworn she was looking at me. But she couldn't have seen me because I wasn't really there. This was but a dream. A vivid one, mind you, but a dream nonetheless.

Turning her attention back to Blue, dream me exhaled and continued her conversation. "Which is why . . ." she began slowly. "Which is why I need to tell you something, Blue. Something important."

Whatever dream me was about to tell Blue must've been

big because I'd never seen so much conflict wrought across one person's face. It made me cringe to witness. Imaginary or not, that was still *my* face. And seeing that much pain so deeply etched into my own features was as strange as it was unsettling.

Dream me's eyes drifted toward the floor as she got ready to reveal whatever grand secret was weighing down on her. Unfortunately, I never got the chance to know what she intended to say. As quickly as I'd been deposited into the scene, I was ejected from it.

Ripped away from the dock, my consciousness was flung to the sandy shores of Adelaide. I hadn't been on those beaches since our schools' field trip weeks ago. Nevertheless, I instantly recognized the cave-dotted cliffside.

SJ, Blue, Jason, Daniel, and dream me were running down the beach with great haste. Something was wrong. They dashed inside one of the cliff's cave openings and merged into a great tunnel system. When they rounded the corner, though, dream me vanished.

I wasn't sure where she'd gone, but the others were now running on without her. They proceeded through the cliffside labyrinth, passing countless caves, many of which were half-submerged in water. All around them the ceilings and floors sprouted large, luminescent crystals—clear like sea foam and sharp like daggers.

Eventually they turned into a low-roofed cavern. Jason and Daniel continued ahead to make sure the coast was clear, leaving SJ and Blue behind.

An unfamiliar, heart-shaped silver locket outlined in lime green crystals swung from SJ's neck. Blue drew her hunting knife and paced as she waited for the others to return. SJ started to bring her fingers to her temples as she always did when she was stressed, but stopped short and stared off in the direction they'd just come.

"We should not have let her go off alone," she stated abruptly. "It was a mistake."

"I may still be upset with Crisa, but her plan makes sense," Blue reassured her.

"It does if we assume she was being honest about all the factors in play."

"She told us the truth," Blue said firmly.

"Yes, but are we certain she told us *all* of the truth?" SJ responded. "Lately Crisa has been a need-to-know-basis type of girl."

"That's only because she was trying to deal with everything on her own instead of bugging us with it," Blue replied.

SJ gave Blue an incredulous look. "And who is to say she is not doing the same thing now?"

Just then I was yanked away from Blue and SJ's conversation. My consciousness zoomed through the elaborate tunnel system until it came to a stop in front of dream me. I didn't know where we were. The surroundings had faded to indiscernible black and we were squared off in a void, me watching her and her concentrating on a threat I could not see.

It was weird to be staring at myself like this. What was substantially weirder though, was when my consciousness was suddenly absorbed into that body.

The feeling was like having your soul suctioned out by a giant, electric toilet plunger. I merged with dream me and looked through her eyes just in time to see a massive purple blast shoot out of the void in my direction.

The horizontal tornado pulled me off my feet and dragged me forward, consuming me inside its swirling abyss.

No matter how I struggled, the strange force would not let me go.

At the last second I felt someone grab my arm—trying to pull me out of the vortex. But it was too late. The help was not enough to hold me, or keep me out of the vortex's grasp. I was gone—trapped within its power as I was sucked deeper into some kind of black hole heart.

I was about to make full impact with this dark endpoint when I was curtly dumped into another room entirely.

The forceful tornado, the cave, and whoever had been holding onto my arm had all disappeared. I was in some kind of theater now—surrounded by the vague outline of a vast audience and the dim light of torches lining rock walls.

There was a performance taking place on an enormous stage across from me. Blue was there (on the stage, I mean), only instead of her typical blue cloak she was wearing a blood red one like her sister used to.

I blinked, and a moment later found myself on the stage too. Trace remains of green smoke were dissipating from the area, and the curtains to the left had collapsed—blocking the audience from view.

My eyes widened when I realized that standing right in front of Blue was a twenty-foot-long black wolf baring its teeth. Even more surprising still was the expression on Blue's face. It was filled with . . . *fear*. Total, unrestrained fear that I never would've thought she was capable of showing.

"Blue!" I yelled.

She didn't hear me.

"Blue!" I yelled again.

I ran for her as fast as I could, but as I did I began to evaporate into the air. Blue didn't notice. She was busy using what looked like a rubber band around her wrist to fire something at the wolf lunging at her.

I didn't get the chance to see what it was or what became of my friend. In the next instant I was pulled out of this strange vision too—my last view of the scene being the giant monster barreling down on my best friend.

"We should approach it from the side," Daniel said.

I turned my head to find myself facing him, a completely new setting around us. Daniel looked a little older, more tired. But his expression was hard and determined as always. He nodded directly ahead of us. I followed his gesture and discovered an enormous white compound indented into the side of a desert mountain.

"Or we could just take the driveway," said another familiar voice.

I felt a chill go up my spine and turned to my left to see Natalie Poole standing beside me. She, too, seemed older. Usually my dreams featured Natalie as a teenager. Here she looked about twenty.

Her curly, maple-colored hair cascaded around her. Her brown eyes were stained red like she'd been crying, though they reflected just as much strength as Daniel's.

"After what they've already done, you don't think they've accounted for a driveway? No way. There's zero chance Arian hasn't thought of that. It'd be too easy," Daniel replied.

"Nothing about this is easy," a third voice said.

I turned to look at the fourth member of our group. Mauvrey. Her golden-blonde hair was scooped up in an uncharacteristic ponytail. There was a pair of weird metallic contraptions around her wrists that looked like futuristic fingerless gloves. And the eyeliner around her blue eyes was black, like the strange vein pattern on the right side of her neck . . .

The scene blurred around her image until she was the last thing left. In an instant, she was gone too.

Everything that followed was pretty unclear and without connection. Images streamed through my head in a flood of bright flashes—a glowing red watering can, rocks crumbling around me in a cave-in, a set of plastic patio furniture with a tray of sandwiches, bronze animals running in every direction, a huge wave of lava crashing into a sea of fire, and then . . .

Stars in the sky, the smell of burning wood, grass beneath my fingertips.

I was awake again.

Sitting up, I wiped some of the cold sweat from my forehead and glanced around the still campsite. The fire was almost extinguished except for a few dying embers that glowed orange against the black night. Just knowing they were real was enough to calm me a bit, and I exhaled deeply as I tried to expel the feelings of anxiety my nightmares had stirred.

"Bad dream?"

I whipped my head around to find SJ wide awake in her sleeping bag.

"You scared me," I said as I pushed loose strands of hair behind my ears. "What are you doing up?"

"You are not the only one who has trouble sleeping, Crisa," she replied. "So tell me, which beach was it, Adelaide or Whoozalee?"

"Sorry?"

She sat up and lowered her voice to a whisper so as not

to wake the others. "As I told you before, Crisa, you talk in your sleep. Blue has never noticed because she sleeps so deeply." SJ gestured to a nearby Blue whose face was buried inside her puffy sleeping bag. "I, however, have been woken quite frequently by the things you say while you dream. Just minutes ago you were going on about running down a beach and hiding from something. So I ask again, which beach was it?"

"Adelaide," I said absentmindedly. "I dreamt that we were all on the beach there. And that . . ."

"That what?"

I hesitated, but then sighed and conceded to giving her a recap of my dreams. I told her about the gray boat with the scarlet sail, all of us being on the beaches of Adelaide, the heart-shaped locket she'd been wearing, and that at some point I was alone and saw some kind of purple tornado coming toward me. I explained the vision of Blue with the wolf in the theater and the short vision I had of Natalie, Mauvrey, and Daniel. Finally, I described the image flashes I'd seen—the glowing watering can, the patio furniture, and so on.

SJ listened the whole time without interrupting. When I finished she shook her head in what I gathered was disbelief, disapproval, or a combination of the two.

"You should have told the others about your dream, Crisa," she said.

"SJ, I just had it."

"No, not this one," she clarified, "the dream you had last week about that bunker we found beneath the Capitol Building. You knew all those things were down there without ever having seen them. How is that even possible? And then there is the whole Natalie Poole revelation. Crisa, before today were you aware that she was *real?*"

I rubbed my neck awkwardly. "Well . . ."

SJ's eyes widened. "You knew. You knew and you . . . chose not to tell me?"

"It's not like that," I replied rapidly. "I've only known since our trip to Fairy Godmother Headquarters. There was information about her in a folder I took from the Grand File Room before we met Lenore. But I didn't know that bunker and all that other stuff we saw today was real. I swear."

SJ blinked, still in shock. "You should have told me."

"I just . . . didn't know how."

Her blank expression suddenly sharpened. "And did you also not know how to tell me what really happened to you when we were separated in Century City?" she asked.

"I got lost. I found my way back. That's all there is to it," I responded flatly.

I gritted my teeth but held my ground. I hated lying to her. At the same time, I felt like I had no other choice. While closing myself off to SJ may have stung, I didn't feel comfortable letting her in on all the things that were eating away at me, especially when I couldn't even bring myself to fully come to terms with them.

After a moment of silence SJ shrugged. "Okay. Be that way," she said. "You do not have to tell me what happened back there, Crisa. But as I said before, you certainly should have told the others about your dream concerning that room beneath the Capitol Building. And all these other dreams you are having for that matter. They mean something, Crisa, and our friends deserve to know all the facts. You need to let them, *and me,* in on what is happening with you."

"SJ, the truth would only freak them out."

And freak me out.

"They are already 'freaked out' as it is. A bit of trust on your part would not overwhelm them, I assure you."

"Oh, *you* assure me. That changes everything," I said sharply, my instincts going on the defensive before I could stop them. "Look, SJ, I'm just not ready to tell them. So I don't need you passing your high-and-mighty princess judgment on me and the morality of my choices in the meantime. It's my secret and I'll tell them when the time is right."

SJ eyed me in a way that made the guilt brewing inside me start to simmer.

"Fine," she replied after a pause. "But think about this, Crisa. From the moment we took off after that carriage in Adelaide and followed you to Fairy Godmother Headquarters, we have all put our faith in you. Maybe you should consider returning the favor."

SJ lay back down and rolled to her right so we would no longer be facing each other. As if on cue, the last ember in the fire burned away. Sitting there, I watched it go out and witnessed darkness once again consume the silent world.

CHAPTER 4

A Pig Called Chauncey

he five of us woke at the crack of dawn and readied ourselves for the journey ahead. It wasn't the most pleasant of mornings. Remnants of yesterday's revelations hung in the air like personal shadows. Add to that, SJ wouldn't even make eye contact with me the whole time we were cleaning up the campsite. It bothered me, but for now I chose to give her space. I would try talking to her later.

Before heading into the Forbidden Forest our group stopped at the town closest to it. After breakfast we figured it would be a smart idea to leave the carriage and Pegasi at a stable during our indeterminable absence while finding the Valley of Edible Enchantments. It didn't cost much, but we did have to sign a waiver stating that if we didn't return from the Forbidden Forest in thirty days, we were presumed dead and thereby relinquished ownership of our property.

Part of me wanted to ask the bearded stable owner just how many times this policy had been enforced over the years, but I realized the answer probably wouldn't be very comforting.

I elected to keep my mouth shut—a decision that took all of my restraint, especially when one of the workers stumbled and the owner called him "weaker than a princess on a promenade." Every fiber in my being wanted to berate the bearded man for this comment. Though for the good of our transaction I knew I had to let the matter slide.

A few hours later when we were at the threshold of the Forbidden Forest, I was somewhat surprised to find no guards, no toll bridges, and no obstacles to prevent us from gaining access. All that stood in our way was an aged sign that read, "Forbidden Forest: Proceed at Own Risk," and another sign immediately beneath it that stated, "Seriously, Turn Around if You Know What's Good for You."

Evidently we didn't, because we trudged past the warnings with hardly a second thought.

A thick wall of trees didn't announce the start of the Forbidden Forest as I'd originally anticipated. We were eased into it by means of a smaller forest comprised of rolling hills with trees thinly interspersed at the base of the climb, thickening in density as we ascended. I had to watch my footing as we made our way through—roots stretched everywhere like twisted, wrinkled fingers clawing into the earth.

When the ground at last leveled off, we were enveloped by trees from every angle—signaling our full-on penetration into the actual "forbidden" part of the Forbidden Forest.

As we delved into the denser woods, Jason brought up the idea that maybe while we were there we could try searching for the Scribes.

The Scribes were a powerful band of Fairy Godmothers charged with guarding all of our realm's protagonist books and monitoring the portal through which the Author regularly sent them. Since said portal was supposed to reside in the Forbidden Forest, Jason reckoned that if we found the Scribes we could check their collection for Mark's book and find out what had happened to him much sooner than if we waited to find the Author.

This was a nice idea, but SJ pointed out that while there were a few documented accounts of people finding the Valley of Edible Enchantments, no one had ever actually seen the Scribes. The Forbidden Forest was, like, a hundred miles thick. And although Blue had a pretty rough idea about how to get to the Valley, there was no way of telling which direction to go if we were looking for the Scribes. Finding them was a lost cause.

The subject squashed, we spent the next couple of hours hiking without much to discuss, but also without much to complain about either. By midday we'd yet to come across a single vicious monster, talking tree, or any of the other weird stuff I'd been expecting to encounter. So far this place just seemed like an ordinary forest.

It was a creepy forest, sure. The trees reached so high they nearly blocked out all sunlight. Cobwebs draped over everything like foreboding, intricately crocheted curtains. Ambiguous sounds echoed back and forth periodically, as if warning us to keep on our toes. But apart from the stereotypical creepiness, everything seemed fairly normal.

Blue had assumed the role of guiding our group. Her fairytale research, exposure to the place growing up, and tracking abilities gave her the greatest working knowledge of how to navigate through the labyrinth of trees.

Of course, she'd also told us that the Valley was supposed to be located toward the center of the Forbidden Forest. So as long as we made our way in that general direction we should've been fine too.

I'd been keeping to the back of the group for most of the morning. It wasn't until the afternoon that I finally garnered up the courage to try talking to SJ. I trotted up to her just after we'd finished climbing down a mossy hill that let out by a stream.

"Hey," I said awkwardly.

"Hello," she responded in her usual pleasant tone.

"So, I wanted to talk to you," I continued as I rubbed my arm anxiously. "Um, about what I said last night."

"What about it?"

I wanted to apologize for snapping at her and not telling her about Natalie and keeping my dreams a secret and lying to her and so much more. But the only thing I managed to get out was, "Promise me you won't tell the others about my dreams?"

She raised her eyebrows in surprise. "*That* is all you have to say?"

I sighed, aggravated. "SJ, I don't get what is happening with me. The whole thing is weird and very unnerving. Keeping it to myself is the only way I know how to protect you guys from dealing with the same disconcertedness. And besides that . . . I'm just not ready to tell the others. I'm not ready to . . . to trust them with this stuff."

"And what about me?" SJ asked slowly. "Would you even have trusted me with the truth if I had not found out on my own?"

The rest of our group had passed through a tunnel ahead, so SJ and I were alone in the small clearing. I stopped and looked at the ground. Then I said something I'd only then been forced to realize.

"I don't know," I replied.

I'd never seen SJ look so hurt. Her gray eyes were wide from shock. Her ordinarily pale skin lost even more of its color as my admission struck her like a cruel gust of wind.

"Why?" she asked once she'd overcome the speechlessness.

Pain and remorse tinged in my throat, but my expression remained resolute.

"Do I really need to explain, SJ?" I asked in return. "In the last twenty-four hours I've found out that I have a secret magical power. The places I dream about actually exist. And there's a shady group of antagonists out there who want me dead. It's a lot to deal with and I don't want to make things even worse or more confusing for myself by letting others in on the details. Can't you try and understand that?"

"I am trying to understand, Crisa; believe me. And I sympathize with you. There is a lot going on right now and you must be overwhelmed and stressed and afraid—"

"SJ, I'm not afraid," I suddenly snapped. "I just need a little space."

SJ crossed her arms and glared at me. A bird in the distance chirped and some far-off frog croaked. Despite the friendly chatter of wildlife around us, all I could hear was the sound of the steel wall that'd just been lowered between my best friend and me. It was loud—like the death of a loved one, or the loss of a dream you could never return to no matter how hard you closed your eyes. And I knew it was entirely on me.

"Then space you shall have," SJ responded evenly. "I hope it helps you in the ways that you will not allow us to."

"SJ," I started to groan, full of regret at having lost my temper and barked at her like that.

But she wouldn't hear anymore. She walked right past me and followed the route the rest of the group had taken, entering the tunnel.

Ugh. What was the matter with me? SJ was my best friend. After everything we'd been through together I had no reason not to trust her. Why did I not feel comfortable doing so?

I took out my wand and absentmindedly twirled it in my hand for a moment. Fiddling with it always made me feel a bit better.

The wand's sheen caught on the rays of light that peeked through the trees. I thought about how Emma had secretly given me the wand so I might have a means to protect myself. When we'd visited her to learn the secret of breaking the In and Out Spell, I'd also discovered that she'd transferred a sole spark of her Fairy Godmother magic to me so I alone could operate it.

Alas, while the weapon was extremely versatile, I knew it was as useless to me in this situation as that spark of magic, which was supposed to develop into a single ability. No weapon or amount of Fairy Godmother power could protect me from the rift I'd created with SJ and the distrust crippling my perspective. I would have to find other means to resolve those threats and other means to protect myself from their harm.

When or how I would locate such means, however, I did not know.

I realized too much time had passed, so I stored my wand back in my satchel and jogged into the tunnel to catch up with the others.

The passage dove a long way underground. The atmosphere felt damp and the walls were constructed mainly of undergrowth. As I made my way through I began to hear loud crackling noises in the distance. The further I went, the louder these crackles became.

After a time, I finally saw light at the end of the tunnel. I swiftly cantered up to it. Alas, the second I emerged into the light, my foot unexpectedly caught on a tree root at the edge of the tunnel, which launched me to the ground headfirst.

I hit the forest floor with a thud, but (wind getting knocked out of me aside) I was more taken aback by the bed of yellow flowers I'd landed in. I was surrounded by beautiful, canary-colored daffodils. They carpeted the earth, protruding from every nook and cranny within this pocket of the forest.

SJ was off to my left, some forty-five feet ahead, but wasn't moving. A quick look in the distance revealed that Blue and Jason were in front of her, but also standing perfectly still. Each of them was silent and facing away from me—majorly creeping me out.

Slowly I rose to my feet. "Guys . . ."

"Don't move!" Blue called back.

"Why?"

The sound of lightning nearby startled me and I jumped. That was the noise I'd been hearing within the tunnel. But it didn't make any sense. It wasn't storming. Where could lightning possibly be coming from? I heard it strike again, but this time much closer. And then . . .

"Look out!" Daniel shouted as he tackled me.

A daffodil some three or four yards over released a giant bolt of lightning—striking the spot where I'd previously been standing. The grass there was now charred and dead, much like I would be if Daniel hadn't pushed me out of the way.

"We have ten seconds. Move!" Jason ordered.

Daniel grabbed me by the arm and pulled me up. I followed him and the others as we dashed across the blanket of violent flowers.

"What did I say about saving me?" I said as I ran next to Daniel.

"You're right. Sorry. Next time I'll just let you get fried," he replied.

Another snap of lightning echoed through the trees.

"Everybody stop!" Blue yelled.

We all froze and listened.

"You know, instead of going ballistic every time I help you," Daniel continued as we waited, "you could try saying thank you once in a while."

The second bolt in the series crackled somewhere nearby.

"Thank you?" I scoffed. "I'd sooner say . . . *Hit the deck!*" I spotted the puckering daffodil just in time and tackled Daniel out of the way just as lightning shot itself in his direction.

"All right, that's three strikes; let's go!" Jason shouted.

"*Thank you*, Knight," Daniel said sarcastically as we made a run for it.

"Save it," I said as we plowed through the flowers. "We're even. That's what matters."

Our group continued like this for a few minutes—pausing for each series of three lightning bolts, and then covering as much ground as possible in the intervals between them. While there were some definite close calls along the way, we made it out of the floral death trap without being barbequed.

With no more yellow flowers in sight, we stopped for a moment to catch our breaths. This part of the Forbidden Forest didn't look too exceptional. The trees seemed ordinary enough, though they did have a light blue tinge to their bark. And the ground was covered almost entirely in moss.

Much to our displeasure, this calm setting was a deception. Moments after we set foot in the area the moss at our feet started to climb up our legs. It tried to consume us like giant green leeches. No matter how we stabbed at them, the living plants continued to work their way up our limbs.

Luckily, SJ was able to destroy them. Using her trusty slingshot, she fired a couple of her marble-sized, homemade red portable potions, which set off medium-sized explosions that temporarily dried up the moss and gave us a chance to make a break for it.

Next we arrived at a spacious clearing where dozens of logs surrounded a skinny stream. It appeared peaceful at first. However, when we approached the waterway to take a well-earned drink, all the logs in the vicinity suddenly began to tremble and then link up.

They were suctioned together by some invisible force—connecting like links in a chain to one particularly contorted log in the center. The different log extensions formed legs, arms, and a body the height of a redwood tree, which proceeded to angrily lunge at us.

Jason jumped into action, removing his axe from its sheath and chopping away at the creature's arms as they swung in our direction. The rest of us swiftly joined the defensive. Blue's knife and Daniel's sword didn't seem to make much of a difference, but I was able to morph my wand into an axe and aid Jason with his efforts. SJ, meanwhile, managed to fire off the occasional portable potion, which caused the creature to stumble back and lose portions of its limbs altogether.

After a minute of battle, it was clear that the chopping and potion attacks were not giving us the advantage. The creature may have lacked dexterity and higher-thinking functions, but it was still super-fast and aggressive. Plus, it kept calling more logs over to replace its arms and legs faster than we could remove them.

Wait, that's it; they're being called *to it.*

I remembered the first log that had set off the chain reaction was the janked-up one at the center of the body. Of all the pieces we'd severed, this was the only one that had been untouched because the creature kept maneuvering itself to protect it. That must've been its heart.

I rolled out of the way as a massive wooden foot attempted to stomp me.

"We need to destroy the log in the middle," I called to the others. "It's what's attracting the other pieces."

"It's thirty feet up and this thing isn't holding still," Jason responded. "Suggestions?"

I glanced around and did a few trajectory calculations. Then I sprouted an idea that fit the bill. "Blue, climb!" I yelled, gesturing to the tree behind me. "We're gonna need one heck of a tackle, so get as high as you can!"

"SJ," I continued, "I need a fire over there; make it big!" I pointed to an area forty feet behind the river. "The rest of you, we're on distraction duty." I chopped at the creature's arm when it tried to crush me again. "Jason, when the time is right I'll give the signal and we'll set you up while you take out its left foot. Okay, everybody. Move!"

I had to say, I was surprised at how rapidly they followed my instructions. They didn't question my guidance in the slightest. Then again, I'd led them into way crazier scenarios than this and they'd never questioned my plans on any of those occasions either.

SJ snuck around the wooden monster as Jason, Daniel, and I distracted it. She used one of her portable potions to start a fire in the area directly behind it while Blue scaled the tree I'd pointed out. When all the conditions were right, I gave the order.

"Jason, now!" I shouted.

Daniel and I continued to use our respective weapons to occupy the creature's attention on its lower right side while Jason made a break for its left. With one grand motion he swung and chopped off a sizeable chunk of its foot.

The monster now off-balance, Blue took the opening to draw her knife and jump off the tree she was clinging to. She shot straight down on the wooden menace—the force and trajectory of her tackle mixing with the creature's lack of a left foot to knock it over. It toppled to the ground. Blue used her knife to dig into its body and hang on as they fell.

When the monster hit the floor its center landed within SJ's pool of flames. As it caught fire, Blue quickly removed her knife. She hopped off just before the entire middle log was fully engulfed.

The rest of us chopped off the monster's limbs, separating them from the rest of the body before they got caught in the flames too. Those logs rolled away toward the stream— safe from spreading any forest fires—while the creature's enchanted heart burnt to a crisp.

That obstacle out of the way, we moved forward again without another word.

A couple more hours went by and soon it started to get dark. The sun must have gone down somewhere beyond the Forbidden Forest's walls, and our limited sky was now ushering in the beginning of nightfall.

As twilight draped over the trees, the eerie atmosphere began to escalate. The eyes of owls began to spontaneously appear in the branches overhead. I was relatively sure that some of the vines drooping from the trees were moving. And the gossamer spider webs hanging between them seemed to be growing when we weren't looking.

All of a sudden I heard a noise coming from a nearby bush. Instinctively I drew my wand from my satchel. "Did you guys hear that?" I asked.

"Relax, Crisa," Blue said, coming to stand next to me. "It's probably just a rabbit or something."

Then I heard a similar rustling coming from the bush next to my friend's foot. "Blue . . ."

A chipmunk with a goofy face popped out of the bush.

"See," Blue said calmly. "The Forbidden Forest feels creepier at night, but you can't let it get to you. It's all in your—"

Shield.

While Blue had been lecturing me, I'd seen the chipmunk's eyes flash bright red and his body puff up. I'd managed to morph my wand into a shield just in time to protect us from the sizeable spurt of fire that burst from his mouth like a flame-thrower.

"Go! Go! Go!" Blue and I yelled to the others once the flames subsided.

Alas, the warning came too late. Every bush in the area had begun to rustle. And in a matter of seconds, dozens of the adorable yet terrifying pyromaniacs had emerged. They charged toward us, ejecting fire from their tiny guts and herding us together.

SJ tried to go for a potions attack, but in the darkness and chaos she rammed into Jason and dropped her slingshot. The left flank of chipmunks cut her off before she could retrieve it. Meanwhile, the rest of us quickly discovered that although we had weapons, none of them would keep us from getting flame-broiled by these little monsters. We were now surrounded, and my shield wasn't going to protect us all.

Oh, dang. Their eyes are starting to glow. Maybe if I—

BAM!

One of the chipmunks was curtly nailed in the back of the head with an acorn—knocking him unconscious on the spot.

What in the world?

Out of the trees suddenly came a full-on assault of acorns. They barreled forward in a constant and powerful stream, pelting the demon chipmunks with merciless precision. The woodland creatures began to scurry in panic—many getting hit over and over again by the unexpected attack. It wasn't long before they'd all either scampered away or been knocked out by the ambush.

When the crazy had passed and everything had returned to silence, I squinted through the night to try and pinpoint the source of the offensive. A figure emerged from the shadows—measuring at about four feet with blue overalls, brown eyes, and a curly pink tail.

"Name's Chauncey," said the talking pig, holstering the massive acorn-firing mechanism to his back like a crossbow. "And we'd better get out of here before the sonic frogs find you."

Being led through a forest by a talking pig was nothing to write home about; as far as tour guides went, he was pretty lackluster.

He barely said two words to us the whole way. The fully loaded acorn-shooting machine that he had holstered to his back made more noise than he did.

Still, the five of us followed him without objection. We were just relieved to have been found by someone who knew his way around the Forbidden Forest *and* who didn't want to kill us like half the other things living here did.

Eventually Chauncey took us through a tunnel made of stone, stucco, and thick tree roots. When we emerged we were in a clearing with a brick house at the center.

"A brick house . . ." Blue thought out loud, startling us.

Realization hit her and she smiled at her own brilliance, pointing at Chauncey incredulously. "You're one of the Three Little Pigs, aren't you?"

We recognized, of course, she had to be right. Talking pigs weren't exactly common, and the ones from the aforementioned fairytale were said to live in this very forest.

Chauncey didn't respond to the accusation. He simply grunted as if annoyed by his minor celebrity status and then shouldered on toward the house.

It was a small dwelling. Understandably so given that the owner stood only four feet tall on his hind legs. We managed to fit inside just fine, but Jason and Daniel did have to stoop to fit through the door.

We entered into a rustic living room, the sole source of light emanating from an old, brick and mortar fireplace. It filled the space with warmth that was a nice break from the cold outside.

Chauncey unhooked the strap of his acorn-launcher and set it on the floor before leaving the room. In awkward silence we sat down on the corduroy couch and the three wooden chairs surrounding the fireplace as we waited for him to return.

Blue and I originally chose two of the chairs as our seats. However, when we sat down we discovered that they were covered in dust and other filth, so we opted to join the boys on the couch instead.

It was not comfortable. And it smelled like turnips and

mothballs. I managed to distract myself from the smell by looking around the room.

The coffee table held a bowl of mushrooms, some haphazardly drawn blueprints, several dirty mugs, and copies of assorted magazines—everything from *Enchanted Architect Monthly* to *Tournaments Illustrated*. Three caps and checkered scarves hung on coat hooks next to the door beside a calendar featuring various towers from Century City. A floor mat made of straw was lying in the entryway. And there was a budding tomato plant hanging in the windowsill.

As my eyes continued to wander the room, I came to notice the painting residing above the fireplace. It was of Chauncey and his two brothers. They were standing in front of the brick house we presently sat in and were holding shovels like proud construction workers. I would have considered it a nice pig family portrait had it not been for the large rip marks I saw going across it—as if someone had torn the image apart and then put it back together in remorse.

Chauncey reappeared in the doorway holding a steaming cup of coffee. Immediately upon entering he glared at SJ, who was sitting in the third wooden chair, which apparently hadn't been dusty like the others.

"You're in my seat," he said flatly.

SJ hastily got up and apologized. She came to join us on the couch. When she realized the only available space was beside me, we exchanged an unsettling look. I moved out of the way so she could sit, choosing to stand rather than endure the tension of her gaze and close proximity.

"So," Chauncey said as he eyed our interaction and settled into his chair, "what kind of crazy mission are the five of you on?"

"Who said we were on a crazy mission?" Blue asked defensively.

Chauncey shook his head. "Spare me. Only a person with a death wish or a crazy mission sets foot in this forest. Less than a hoof full of people have ever made it out alive, you know. So tell me, what's your business here?"

There was a pause, but after a beat SJ let out a small exhale and looked Chauncey in the eye. "We seek the Valley of Edible Enchantments," she responded.

"Obviously," Chauncey scoffed. He took another swig from his cup then set it down on the table beside its dirty counterparts. "Like I said, people that come into this forest come because they have crazy missions, and they always need some sort of magical doodah from the Valley to accomplish them. So I'll ask one more time, what are you kids here for— invisibility bread, truth jerky, magic beans maybe?"

The five of us glanced at one another, unsure of how much information to divulge.

"We're searching for something lost beneath the sea . . ." I finally replied on behalf of our group. "In order to go after it, we need a way to breathe underwater and we figured the Valley is the best place to find something that will let us."

SJ gave me a sad look. "Really? Him you trust?"

The others seemed confused by her comment, but Chauncey changed the subject before any of them could inquire what she'd meant.

"Well then," he huffed, "I'll tell you what I've told all the others that I've found wandering through the Forbidden Forest. Turn back now if you know what's good for you. Don't, and the wolves alone will pick you off like sitting ducks."

"We can handle wolves. I assure you," Blue said as she

lifted the hem of her cloak and proudly patted the holster her knife was stored in.

"These are no ordinary wolves," Chauncey warned. "One of them blew both my brothers' homes down with a single huff and puff combo."

Blue let out a slight, patronizing snort. "I'm sorry, but didn't your brothers build their houses out of hay and sticks?"

"Do you have the lung capacity to blow down an *entire house* made of sticks with one exhale?" Chauncey asked.

"No," she admitted.

"Then don't knock what you don't know. These wolves are like nothing you've ever seen. If they find you, they will kill you. That is, if the witch in the Valley doesn't rip you apart first."

This caught Blue's attention. She, like the rest of us, had been under the impression that the witch who once guarded the Valley of Edible Enchantments was already dead. There was a whole book about it.

After being lost in the Forbidden Forest for several days, protagonists Hansel and Gretel had ventured into one of the Valley's cottages and been trapped inside by the witch that resided there. Luckily, when the witch had tried to cook them alive for trespassing, they'd pushed her into her own oven and—bing, bam, boom—the wicked old witch was baked to a crisp and the Valley was freed from her terror forever.

Or, according to Chauncey, apparently not.

In hindsight, I supposed we could have put together some of what Chauncey went on to tell us for ourselves. My godmother Emma had already explained that magic could not be killed or destroyed; it could only change forms or change hands. So when Hansel and Gretel's witch had perished, her powers passed into something or (in this case) *someone* else. And that person had become the Valley's new witch as a result.

Chauncey confirmed this moments later, telling us of the horrible witch that now lived in the Valley and served as its caretaker.

"I've never seen her," he continued. "But she's supposed to be a real piece of work. At least the witch before her used to let a *few* people go with their lives and what they came for. This one, well, let's just say she's not too fond of trespassers unless they can offer her something in return."

"Offer her something? Like what?" I asked.

"I don't know. Your guess is as good as mine," Chauncey replied.

"Oh, come on," Blue pressed. "You've lived here for years and you have no idea what she's after?"

"Sorry, kid, but I don't exactly invite the witch over for Sunday brunch. I've never met her, and I don't intend to. But I'll tell you what I will do," Chauncey continued. "I'm gonna help you kids out another way. Tomorrow I'll make you a map that'll allow you to find your way to and from the Valley without wandering through any more hot zones for dangerous Forbidden Forest activity."

"Really? That's awesome. Thanks," Jason said.

"Seriously," I seconded. "We really appreciate your help."

Chauncey shrugged. "Yeah, well, the more deaths that happen in this forest the lower the property value around here gets, and I'm thinking of selling next year."

CHAPTER 5

Self-Acceptance

awoke to the smell of bacon.

At first this delighted me. But then my eyes widened when I remembered that our host was a *pig*.

With great haste I jumped up from the floor and raced into the kitchen. Chauncey was rinsing his arm in the sink. When he saw the panic on my face he gestured to a pan on the stove. "Settle down. I just burnt myself while I was cooking."

"Oh," I said sheepishly.

Feeling a bit embarrassed, I walked over to the side window. As I yawned, I noticed my reflection; the bags under my eyes were enormous and my hair was bird's-nest-shaped at best. I rubbed my eyes and looked past the unflattering image to the paling sky above the trees.

I'd been up late last night. We all had. None of us could really sleep considering everything we'd just been through.

SJ and the others stayed up making light conversation. Blue talked about the first time she ever wrestled a bear. Jason spoke of his apprenticeship last summer mastering an underground form of kickboxing called Fing Wa. And SJ described the array of portable potions she was still carrying around with her, explaining how their color signified the type of enchantment contained inside.

The silver potions temporarily froze things. We'd used a few yesterday to freeze that dragon over Century City. But SJ made it clear that that much power was not to be consistently relied upon. The only reason yesterday's potions had managed an effect that large was because we'd gotten them inside the dragon's mouth, which set off a chain reaction by combining with the creature's blood, blah blah blah.

SJ explained that part in much more detail, but I was too tired to listen. Bottom line, the dragon was a very specific case and ordinarily the silver potions could only freeze an area between two and twelve feet in radius (depending on exposure and power of impact).

The other potions SJ was presently packing were jade, red, and yellow. The jade ones emitted a potent slime that glued people where they were standing. Red—as previously demonstrated—emitted fiery explosions. And yellow was a weird body-switching potion. Shoot it at someone and that person would temporarily switch bodies with the next living being he or she touched.

SJ had made four copies of that potion just in case. I didn't see how they would be terribly useful. But she was the master potionist, so she could brew whatever kind of portable concoction suited her.

While my three friends kept each other's minds occupied with casual chatter, I too had stayed up, but on my own and off to the side. I felt awkward talking to SJ. As they shared stories, reminisced, and exchanged memories, I lay on Chauncey's wooden floor beneath a flannel blanket and counted the tiles on the ceiling, the questions in my head, and the insecurities burning inside of me like splintered wood.

Daniel remained silent all evening too—keeping to himself like he always did.

Unlike me, I gathered this wasn't due to any form of residual internal conflict. Rather, it was probably just another symptom of his strong conviction to remain aloof.

Late into the night, when the others had finally fallen asleep, I noticed him taking out his golden pocket watch. He'd had that thing for as long I'd known him, but he never took it out when he thought anyone was around to see. I supposed he thought the coast was clear, but I hadn't fallen asleep yet.

Chauncey's fire shone off the pocket watch's shell. Daniel stared into the contents concealed within. I wondered what they were. He always had that watch with him and kept its meaning a secret from everyone. So I gathered whatever was inside was both immeasurably important and immensely personal.

The late night taking its toll on the lot of them, my friends and Daniel were still sleeping as Chauncey worked over his stove. I was tired but had no trouble coming to the conclusion that being half-awake in this kitchen was way better than going back into the living room where I'd risk waking up the others or having more nightmares.

My night's sleep had been jam-packed with awful dreams. They were growing so clear now that it was becoming harder to write them off. And this development was just the tip of the iceberg. As of two nights ago, I was beginning to contend with a factor that made the dreams all but impossible to forget. I was becoming a regular character *in* them.

In my latest nightmares the dream version of myself had

faced two enemies. Based on my past interactions with them, I wasn't sure which posed more of a threat to my actual well-being. Just as I wasn't sure which caused greater disturbance to my subconscious one.

After falling asleep I found myself opening my metaphysical eyes to the sight of Lena Lenore. The leader of our realm's Fairy Godmother Agency—Book's Godmother Supreme—was a fuzzy image at first.

I was lying on the silver carpet of her Fairy Godmother HQ office. There were hundreds of glittering ice shards on the floor. My body felt drained like a thousand leeches had just gone to town on me.

I hesitantly lifted myself onto my forearms, swallowing the pain and blinking hard to bring the scene, and the woman, into focus.

The office was just how I remembered it—pink walls, black chandelier, glass desk with a leather chair behind it. Lenore, too, was exactly how I recalled her. The forty-something woman possessed a beautiful face, a regal stature, and a cold sharpness in her eyes that put any of these shards of ice to shame.

I tried to speak, but the words were dry in my throat. And my head was too dizzy to think straight.

Lenore said something to a massive Fairy Godfather standing in the corner. He had a crewcut and a tan face. His muscles bulged with apprehension when the Godmother Supreme snapped at him.

Looking down, I discovered my arms were clothed in the sleeves of a cobalt dress. The fabric was soft and strange. Spreading from the wrists to the underside of my elbows, a tiny star pattern ran down the sleeves in the pattern of the veins I surely had beneath my skin. The design was elegant and slightly off-putting, much like the woman who suddenly grabbed me.

Lena Lenore was beside me now. She'd bent over and grasped my chin in her smooth, manicured hand. Her long pink fingernails grazed my cheeks like small knives, and she forced me to look at her.

Despite the aching in my body, the hatred I felt for her burned even more intensely. Lenore had kept me apart from Emma for ten years. She and her higher-up Godmothers had been conspiring with our realm's ambassadors to manipulate protagonist selection. And in the brief introduction we'd had last month, she'd basically threatened my friends and me to learn our places and stop messing with things we couldn't control.

"*Answer me*, Crisanta," Lenore hissed.

I locked my gaze with hers and detected frustration and anger in her expression. Those ardent hazel eyes were the last image I held from this scene. I blinked again and I was in a different place but with the same enemy.

This time, however, I was watching from a distance.

Dream me and Lenore were in the infirmary at Lady Agnue's. It was night and the windows were open, allowing a biting winter air to breathe through. The white lace curtains fluttered, the moonlight outside making them take on an even more ghostly palette.

The Godmother Supreme had her back to one of the windows. The icy air should've made her cold, but she seemed unfazed by its touch. Not a goose bump could be seen on her arms, both of which were exposed due to the sleeveless nature of her sleek, silvery pink dress.

Lenore strode away from the window. Dream me got up from her cot and crossed her arms. She was wearing a floor-length, black silk robe. I'd only ever seen such a robe once when Princess Marie Sinclaire had come down with a life-threatening case of toadstool fever and been bedridden for weeks. That was the kind of robe the infirmary kept on hand for long-term patients; its silk was made from enchanted silkworms found in the kingdom of Coventry.

"You don't scare me, Lenore," dream me said as the woman sauntered over.

"Well you scare me, Crisanta Knight," Lenore replied coolly. "And you know what I do with the things I fear? I make sure they never see the light of day."

Lenore drew closer. The sound of her heels against the stone floor caused an echo in the otherwise deserted room. Dream me stood her ground, but I could tell it was difficult. She seemed tired and weak. The flames of the candles in the room quivered like they were nervous.

The Godmother reached for her right hand. Dream me reacted quickly and went for something in the folds of her robe. As Lenore removed the silver ring from her finger, dream me produced a sparkling hairpin. Both accessories instantly transformed into wands, only mine kept extending until it was in the shape of my spear. The two women regarded one another, their individual weapons glowing ominously.

The scene changed again with a flash and I was left observing a new pair of mortal enemies: dream me and Arian. They were squared off somewhere dark. I figured it was outdoors based on the way the wind was rushing around them.

One minute I was watching them fight—a brutal, vehement combat that made my pulse quicken to the speed of a hummingbird's heart. Then before I knew it my consciousness was absorbed inside my dream form again.

I didn't have time to digest the convergence. Arian swung at me, and I ducked. I jabbed at him and he came at me with increasing force. The contorted sounds of fast winds and grinding metal whirred around us. The void we fought in was intermixed with disorienting flashes of silver and starlight.

Suddenly Arian grabbed me. He had me by the throat and—sweeping my leg out from under me—slammed my body to the floor.

My head hit metal. When I opened my eyes I expected to see him bearing down over me, but instead a blaze of light consumed my vision. All of a sudden I was dangling from something precarious. Everything around me was a blur, but I gathered from the way I was holding on for dear life that I was somewhere high above the ground.

I looked up and saw Arian once more. He was crouched on the platform above me. I stared into his cold black eyes and saw a scar where I'd struck him back in Century City.

He raised his sword. My heart stopped.

I didn't remember letting go, but without warning I abruptly found myself plunging through darkness in free fall. Eternity was quiet at first as I dropped through the endless abyss, but then I heard one word: "Knight!"

Daniel was calling out to me. I didn't know where he was; everything was lost in the void. Nevertheless, I was certain it was him. His voice was etched into my memory so deeply it might as well have been a part of my conscience.

I continued to hear him call out to me, a resonating echo that made me simultaneously resentful and relieved. As this went on, more images spun around me. Short, sharp visions of that red watering can, light pink high heels walking across a glowing floor, snow falling in the woods, wolves and torches and a theater, and then . . . Well, and then I woke up.

Given all this, you could understand why I preferred to force my tired eyes to remain open in Chauncey's kitchen. It sure beat going back to the traumatizing world I'd just risen from.

After a minute in the warm silence I decided to help our host finish preparations for his breakfast. He had been kind enough to take us into his home. The least I could do was help him with some of the housework.

Together, he and I sliced and diced and chopped and charred various ingredients. When the food was ready Chauncey offered me a seat across from him at his quaint, handcrafted table. He offered me some of his breakfast too, but much as I loved a good home-cooked meal, I had to decline. A kale omelet with a side of sautéed truffles was not exactly how I wanted to start my morning, as I was neither a vegetarian, nor insane.

I suddenly heard a noise behind me and glanced in the direction of the living room. For a second I worried that my friends had woken up. I sighed with relief when I saw that it was just a bird at the window.

"In a fight with one of your friends?" Chauncey asked through a mouthful of his breakfast.

My head spun back around, surprised that he'd guessed correctly.

"Uh, kind of," I said.

"It's Little Miss Perfect out there, isn't it?" he went on, referring to SJ. "Why am I even asking, of course it is. I could tell. It was the same with me and my brothers at first, you know—avoiding eye contact, questioning what the other said but pretending to everyone else like there wasn't anything wrong. So what happened with you two?"

"Nothing," I replied. "I mean, I'm just sort of going through some stuff right now and she got mad that I didn't trust her or the others enough to be honest about it."

"Why didn't you?" he asked.

I shrugged. "It's all pretty strange and I didn't want to freak them out."

He looked up from his truffles. "And?"

"*And* nothing."

Chauncey raised his piggy eyebrows in suspicion. I pretended like I didn't know what he was implying but soon realized I wasn't fooling him.

Dang, this is one perceptive pig.

After a moment Chauncey shrugged too. "Okay, kid," he said. "You don't have to tell me. But the way I see it, you should probably take the opportunity to."

"How do you figure that?"

"To start with, you're probably never gonna see me again, right?"

"Well, yeah," I agreed. "I mean I don't see us coming back here for our winter vacation or anything."

"That, and there's a pretty good chance you're gonna get killed before you make it out of the Forbidden Forest."

"Gee, thanks for the encouragement," I huffed. "So what's your point exactly?"

"My point," Chauncey continued, "is that whatever's eating you, you're obviously nowhere near ready to admit it to your friends. So you might as well tell me. Get it off your chest to a complete stranger while you have the chance."

It wasn't a terrible suggestion. Strangers did make the

best listeners at times. The problem was, I didn't even know if I was certain about what was "eating me."

For a long time, I'd been operating under the notion that my secrecy over things like my dreams and Natalie Poole was a path I'd taken *for* my friends, not *because* of them. However, I knew now that the matter was not so simple.

Not wanting to tell my friends the truth because it would put unnecessary stress on them was one thing. But realizing that I didn't trust them with it felt like something entirely different.

"All right, Chauncey. Here it is," I began slowly. "I don't know why I didn't trust them enough to tell them. I thought I did it because it would be better for them not to know— that I was protecting them from this giant burden I've been dealing with on my own, but now . . ." I shook my head. "Now I don't know."

The sound of Chauncey's pensive chewing filled the room as he sat there analyzing me. When he finished his last truffle he wiped his snout with a cloth napkin and took a long sip from his coffee mug. After he'd allowed my words to hang in the air sufficiently, he smacked his lips together and pointed at me with his hoof.

"You know what I think, kid? I think you really are trying to protect your friends, but that's only part of what's going on here. I think the bigger part is that you're trying to protect yourself from facing a much bigger, personal issue."

"That's ridiculous," I said, crossing my arms defensively.

"Actually, it's not," Chauncey countered. "As a matter of fact, I read about this in *Maidens' Home Journal* last month. According to their self-help section, you're not going to trust anyone until you trust yourself and everything that comes with that. Matter of fact, now that I'm thinkin' about it, I can boil down your problem to one thing. You wanna know what that is?"

"Fine," I reluctantly sighed. "Hit me with your best shot."

"Okay," he said. "You don't accept yourself. Plain and simple. That explains why you won't admit any of that stuff to your friends, or to your own conscience either."

"Yeah," I scoffed. "I think you missed the mark there, Chauncey."

"Really?" he said. "All right, prove me wrong then. Tell me what makes you, *you*."

I sat up straighter—accepting his challenge. "Okay, I will. Just give me a second."

A list of adjectives immediately popped into my head. But they were all just a bunch of miscellaneous traits like opinionated, headstrong, and snarky—not exactly character defining. Chauncey was asking for more than that.

I thought harder.

Nothing that proceeded to come to mind, though, seemed important enough to be an all-defining personal quality—not like SJ with her kindness or Blue with her fearlessness. Consequently, the more I concentrated on the issue the more I discovered that Chauncey's claim may have been more accurate than I'd initially asserted.

I guess I really didn't have an internal consensus about what made me, *me*.

My prologue prophecy would have me believe that what made me, *me* was the fact that I was a normal princess destined to be the ordinary and subservient wife of Prince Chance Darling. Our headmistress Lady Agnue and my archenemy Mauvrey had been trying to convince me for years that I was a terrible princess, a sorry excuse for a hero, and a damsel on both counts. My teachers thought I was spunky but naive. My classmates considered me a girl without direction or purpose—just someone who identified with being unexceptional in any role she tried to embody, be it a hero, princess, or otherwise. And as for my friends . . . Well, I genuinely wasn't sure how they saw me. And that fact alone, I realized, made me the most uneasy.

"Just as I thought," Chauncey said, interrupting my self-reflection. "You've got nothing."

"Hang on," I protested. "It's not that I don't have *any* idea; it just kind of depends on who you ask."

"I'm asking *you*," he replied fervently. "So, can you tell me or not?"

I opened my mouth to speak but found my lips without words at the ready. Embarrassed by this more than I cared to admit, I looked away.

Chauncey sighed. "Don't beat yourself up, kid. Truly accepting yourself is one of the toughest things a person can do because there's so much that goes into it—strengths, weaknesses, wants, fears—basically everything that you are and everything that you're not. It's a tall order, and one that most people struggle through life trying to fulfill. But if you really want to overcome what you're going through, you're gonna have to try. Because I have a feeling that in your case it's either what's gonna make you or break you."

I huffed, blowing a strand of hair out of my face.

Maybe he was right.

On our way to Emma's, Daniel had called me on my inability to be open with myself about who I was. And while I'd acknowledged this was true, I still hadn't been able to solve the riddle of *why* it was true. My reaction to Chauncey's challenge just now caused me to wonder if his assertion contained the answer. Then after a minute of reflection I was sure that it did.

He wasn't wrong. I didn't accept myself, at least not entirely anyways. If I did, I wouldn't have been at such a loss for words a moment ago. I wouldn't have been filled with so much insecurity whenever Daniel or anyone else made judgments about me. And I probably wouldn't have been burdened with all this relentless doubt.

Hmm. I guess I need to work on that . . .

I really hadn't expected to be fed such deep, fairly accurate advice so early in the morning, and as a result I now found myself feeling mentally exhausted. I needed a cup of coffee, or a scone. Actually, forget the coffee. I just wanted a scone.

There were no baked goods in sight, though. So I exhaled deeply and leaned back in my chair as the weight of this unsolicited self-revelation set in. "You know what, Chauncey," I said. "Pig or no, you're a pretty insightful guy."

Chauncey snorted in amused response.

"Yeah? Tell that to my ex-wife."

CHAPTER 6

The Magic Watering Can Branding

t seemed that neither my friends nor Daniel liked kale.

Once they'd woken up, Chauncey offered each of them a sample of his breakfast specialty and they respectfully declined his offer just as I had. We all, however, gladly feasted on the bread and cheese he brought out. That, paired with the cup of coffee I'd been craving, really hit the spot.

When we were all fed, Chauncey proceeded to keep his promise and construct us a map of the Forbidden Forest. Before we left he gave us several more warnings about how "tree-stump stupid" it was for us to continue this journey. But these warnings, as he suspected, went unheeded. We trudged on.

Chauncey's map proved to be extremely helpful as we ventured deeper into the Forbidden Forest. It marked all the paths we should take and, more importantly, the ones we should stay away from. This was a lucky break considering some of these paths hosted butterflies that fed on human hair, spontaneously appearing tar pits, and a clan of ten-foot-tall praying mantises wearing hats (i.e., a lot of things you generally wanted to avoid).

We hiked all day. Thanks to Chauncey's map it was actually pretty pleasant, despite the lingering tension between SJ and me.

When this day, too, grew tired and the sun began to set somewhere in the distance, we came upon a wall of giant weeping willow trees. The branches were so thick and numerous that they shielded the area beyond like organic curtains.

We'd arrived.

"Now remember what Chauncey told us," Blue cautioned before we continued. "There's a new witch in town and apparently she's not the most congenial. So we've gotta move quickly and quietly—get in and get out before she finds us. Got it?"

We nodded and began to move into the dense natural barrier.

After pushing through it for several minutes I began to wonder if we were lost. The willows went on for what felt like ages, and the further we delved in the harder it became to perceive anything but green around us. That is, until I saw a streak of orange sunlight flickering through some leaves ahead. I eagerly pulled the branch aside and there it was— the Valley of Edible Enchantments.

Before us lay a clearing designed by the gods; or rather, the gods' personal chefs. There was an orchard at least a couple acres in length consisting of every possible fruit tree you could imagine. Pears, oranges, apples, lemons, and so on—each such a pure and shining shade of its individual color that from a distance the fruit looked like jewels.

Beside the orchard there was a garden producing

vegetables just as bright and boldly-colored, which were planted in the straightest of parallel rows.

A series of cottages lined the edge of the Valley. They were simultaneously beautiful and weird and made my mouth water. One cottage appeared to be made entirely of cheeses. A second was constructed out of deli meats and was conveniently located next to a third cottage built from various types of bread.

Needless to say the prospect of making a sandwich out of the houses' window frames was enticing. Especially given the pit in my stomach that had long digested Chauncey's breakfast spread.

Regardless of these impulses, I stayed focused. Our target was not any one of these three cottages; the house we wanted was the fourth in the lineup. It was on the far right side of the Valley, and it was built entirely of sweets.

After reading *Hansel & Gretel* so many times growing up, I'd always thought I had a pretty good idea of what the witch's enchanted gingerbread house looked like. But in truth, my previous mental picture was nothing compared to seeing the structure for real. This thing was seriously no joke.

The gingerbread roof was tiled by a rainbow array of gumdrops, which were cemented in place by white frosting. The bricks of the house were a mosaic of different colors of rock candy. Chocolate bar shutters shielded each window and were rimmed by large licorice window frames. Intricate gumdrop designs that matched the roof edged the cottage alongside bunches of marshmallow bushes. And the pathway leading up to the solid caramel door was lined with lollipops the size of my head, which sprouted from the ground like jumbo sunflowers.

It. Was. Awesome!

Our group made its way over to the house as swiftly as it could, treading lightly through the orchard and then across the garden.

I couldn't help but notice SJ pause when we passed an apple tree in the orchard. The branches contained dozens upon dozens of the same type of enchanted ruby red apple that had been used to poison her mother, Snow White.

We'd always known that the cursed fruit from her mother's story had come from the Valley of Edible Enchantments. But seeing it in real life had to be quite jarring for SJ. Right here was where they grew. This was where her evil step-grandmother had stood and selected the apple that would cause Snow White's doom. And this was where one of our land's most famous fairytales had been sealed and her mother's legacy born.

It must've been a strange thing to behold, and I could only attempt to fathom what was running through her mind as she stared up at the ripening fruit.

Blue leaned over to me and whispered. "If those apples cause a sleeping curse, then what do you think the grapefruits in this orchard do?"

I shrugged and tilted my head toward Jason, who was ahead of us. "Can't be any worse than what the beans do," I whispered back.

We emerged from the orchard and began to walk through the garden, specifically past a plot where magic beans were flourishing.

I imagined the experience of running into the magical objects that defined Jason's family heritage had a greater effect on him than the apples did on SJ. Not to underplay her psychological trauma or anything, but Jason had been alive to witness his brother Jack's magic bean-induced adventure and its consequences, whereas SJ had not yet been born when her mother bit into the poisoned fruit.

Despite whatever degree my two friends were affected by their encounters with the magical edibles, they pushed past the shadows of fairytales gone by and continued to the doorstep of the candy cottage with the rest of us.

I nudged Blue. "You're on."

She nodded and twisted the chocolate chip cookie doorknob.

Immediately the smell of sugar hit us like a gust of wind. Everything inside the cottage was as sweet as that which made up its exterior. However, while the outside of the house had filled us with mouthwatering awe, the inside of the house was as creepy as an abandoned lighthouse. The sweetness in the air seemed more ironic than inviting.

"So what does it look like?" Jason asked as we started scoping out the candy-coated place.

"It should look like normal taffy," Blue explained while she checked the contents of a few jars. "But, you know, more magical."

Daniel started opening cabinets above the stove. "That's not very much to go on," he said. "There are different kinds of taffy in all of these. How will we know when we find it?"

"Oh, believe me, you'll know."

My blood froze. The voice that'd just spoken had been a girl's voice, but Blue and SJ were both standing in front of me and neither of them had opened their mouths.

With trepidation we all looked around the room trying to find the source of the comment. It sounded like it had come from the bed against the back wall, so I drew my wand and tiptoed over.

There was definitely something big and clumpy concealed beneath the blanket. I promptly ripped the sheet from the bed, but merely revealed a giant sack of caramel corn lying on the mattress.

"Oh, come on, girlie. Did you really think it'd be that easy?"

I whirled around. There it was again—that high, almost childlike female voice. But where was it coming from?

Suddenly the chocolate bar blinders on the windows snapped closed. The door, too, shut on its own with a slam. On the right side of the room, the oven burst open and released a blast of flames so strong it caused half the frosting countertop to melt.

The gingerbread ceiling started to shake—cracks formed and threatened to cave in the entire roof. Fissures formed in the crumbling rock candy walls and spread quickly in every direction.

I thought we were about to be buried or eaten alive by the monstrous house when, as abruptly as it'd begun, the shaking stopped and everything became still. That is, until a moment later when the front door was kicked in and flew across the room.

Light streamed into the darkened house. On top of the crumbs of the fallen door walked a small girl in a white dress. She couldn't have been more than twelve, and she had blonde curls and freckles gracing her rosy cheeks. She looked like an adorable, delicate child. Yet the way she strode confidently into the room with her eyes smiling wickedly told me she was anything but.

"Well, what do we have here? It's been a while since anyone's made it to the Valley for a magical food item," she said as she marched toward us. "I'd be impressed that you made it through the Forbidden Forest if I wasn't so averse to people trespassing on my property."

Blue started to go for her knife, but the small girl reacted first. She waved her dainty hand and all of Blue's weapons, along with Daniel's sword, Jason's axe, SJ's slingshot and potions sack, and my wand shot against the back wall.

"Sillies. Only I decide when it's play time around here." She waved her hand again and Blue's hunting knife bolted back across the room and levitated in front of our group. "Now then, who wants to go first?" she asked.

"I'm sorry," Blue said bluntly, "but *you're* the witch that lives here?"

"Yes, well, Mummy's Pure Magic had to go somewhere when she was killed, now didn't it?" the witch replied.

"The witch that used to guard this place was your *mother*?" I heard myself asking in utter disbelief.

"That's right," the witch hissed as she gestured toward the kitchen area. "I was only a toddler when those sorry excuses for protagonists, Hansel and Gretel, shoved my mother into that oven. I had an aunt who lived in the bread house next door at the time, but she died about a year ago. Now I have both their powers and I look after the Valley in their place. So on that note, I'll ask again—who wants to be first?"

The levitating knife pointed at each of us as its mistress posed her question. But no one had an answer for her. Instead, we just looked at one another in shared, silent agreement that none of us wanted to be the person to ask, "First for what?"

Soon the itty-bitty witch grew tired of waiting and summoned the knife to her hand. She began twirling the blade like a seasoned sous chef as she readdressed us.

"Let me spell it out for you," she said. "Option one: I

could kill *all* of you, which would be fun and everything, but even with magic I really hate cleaning up afterwards. Or we could go with option two and you could each give me something in exchange for your miserable lives."

Blue stepped forward, completely unshaken. "What do you want, Tiny?"

Our blonde, bite-sized captor grinned maliciously and snapped her fingers. In response, a cabinet below the kitchen sink opened. From it emerged a red watering can, which floated over to our confrontation and levitated in midair— glowing so brightly it nearly blinded us.

"This Valley feeds on different kinds of strength," explained the small enchantress. "And while a lot of that comes from the enchanted earth that naturally grows in this forest, the orchard and garden still crave an extra, outside boost of strength from time to time. That, kids, is where you come in. Every person has one vital quality, a piece of their personality that is the strongest part of who they are. It is what empowers them and gives them their root strength. Place your hand on the handle of this watering can and that part of you will be absorbed into it—providing me with fresh food for the plants outside. You five do that, and I'll call us even. Don't, and I'll call for a mop to clean up the bloodshed."

Although I was processing what the witch had said, I was more taken aback by the watering can floating in front of us. I'd seen that can before. At least, I was pretty sure that I had. It looked . . . it looked just like the one I'd envisioned in my—

"What happens to us?" Daniel asked the witch, pulling me back to the present.

"It's not that complicated." She shrugged. "That piece

of your personality is sucked out, and for a couple of weeks you'll simply act as if that element was not inside you at all."

"A couple of weeks?" SJ repeated.

"Well, fourteen days to be precise," the witch replied. "On day fifteen you'll be back to normal, if the altered versions of yourselves haven't killed each other by then. You'd be surprised how quickly people turn on one another when they're not themselves. Although, if you're not feeling this option I could just obliterate you where you stand . . ."

"But if we do this, you let us go?" I clarified. "*And* you'll let us take what we came for?"

"Yeah, yeah. It's the same agreement I make with most people that come through here poking their noses through my stuff looking for magical help," she answered. "Of course, very few people can actually give me the kind of strength I'm after, so I usually end up having to smite them anyways."

'Smite'? Really? This chick is twelve. I know she's evil and apparently insane, but no kid that age should talk like a middle-aged dictator.

SJ raised her eyebrows, surprised by the witch's comment. "I thought you said every person has one of these vital qualities, these root strengths."

The witch rolled her eyes. "Ugh, I get so tired of explaining this every single time. Look, yes every person has a specific piece of their personality that gives them their internal strength. But if they haven't realized what theirs is yet, or they're suppressing it for some reason, then the watering can can't absorb it and it's as useless to me as it is to them."

The dimming light pouring in from the doorway suddenly seemed to call the witch's attention. The sun, wherever it was, had almost set. Sensing this, our captor responded by exhaling in a manner that indicated she was getting impatient and possibly in need of a nap before dinner.

"Well then," she said as she cracked her neck. "You're all starting to bore me and I want to get some unicorn hunting in before it gets too dark out. So let's get on with this. You first, Pretty Pretty Princess." She gestured to SJ. "What'll it be: the watering can or a quick killing?"

SJ was clearly frightened, but what could she do? What could any of us do? It was either the can, or let this malevolent child execute us in the middle of her candied home.

My friend swallowed her nerves, reached out, and grasped the handle of the watering can. The instant she did, the thing glowed even brighter and SJ winced painfully as crimson light enveloped her hand and arm. It spread all the way up to her shoulder. As it did her hand started to wobble—not in a natural, jittery kind of way, but slowly and voluptuously like oil flowing through water.

When the effect receded and her arm was no longer bathed in crimson light, we were astonished to see that SJ's hand looked like liquid metal. Shining and silvery, it stayed that way for a few moments as she gritted her teeth in pain. Then with a flash her skin returned to normal.

SJ released her grip from the watering can and took an unsteady step backward. I could hear her hand searing. It was like the sound of a fish in a pan of hot oil.

We all leaned over to get a better look at SJ's hand and saw that the word "kindness" had been burned into the center of her palm. The word shimmered blood red for a moment before darkening like a tattoo—branded into her skin as a memory of the experience.

"Did it work?" I asked.

"Could you be any more stupid, Crisa?" SJ snapped.

"Of course it worked. Are you really that dense, or are your trust issues messing with your head and keeping you from noticing the smell of my *literally* burning flesh?"

Okay, it definitely worked. While my best friend's comment had been aimed at me, our entire group was shocked by the harshness of SJ's words. They were completely incompatible with the sweet-natured temperament we'd always known her for.

Up 'til that point I couldn't remember SJ saying an outright cruel thing in her life. Like, ever. But I gathered that was what the witch meant when she said once the source of our inner strength was absorbed into the watering can we would behave as if that part of our personality didn't exist.

In other words, SJ's greatest strength had been her kindness, and now that she was stripped of that, she was no longer kind in the slightest.

"The mark on her hand," Jason said, gesturing to the word imprinted in SJ's palm. "Is it permanent?"

"No," the witch responded. "It'll disappear after the fourteen days too. Now stop stalling. Who's next?"

We hesitated.

"Need I remind you of the alternative?" she asked.

The witch waved her hand and our weapons flew forward and encircled our group with their respective blades aimed directly at us.

"I'll go," Blue said confidently.

The process with the watering can repeated itself. When it was complete I was horrified to see the word "fearless" burned into my friend's hand.

It was obvious that this was the internal strength that gave Blue her power. Unfortunately, I was immediately put off when I realized this meant she was now *full* of fear.

Jason went next and was branded "selfless."

I'd never really paid much attention to this defining quality of his. But it did make sense when I thought about it. He was always putting others before himself. He'd even set aside his own feelings over Mark's disappearance so our group could continue with its mission. However, now that his selflessness had been thoroughly absorbed by the can, I gathered his personality was about to take a very abrupt selfish turn.

Next in the line-up came Daniel. I'd have been lying if I said I wasn't super interested to see what word the watering can branded him with. This would finally reveal something about him—something big and important that might solve the endless riddle of who he was.

Regrettably, the king of cryptic-ness was one step ahead of me. Not only did he use his less-dominant, left hand to grasp the can, but the second he removed it from the handle he balled it into a fist before any of us could see what had been imprinted there.

The others were still too drained from their ordeals to care, so I was the only one frustrated by his resolute secrecy.

It was finally my turn to face the watering can. So I stepped forward and grabbed hold of its handle—ready for whatever would come. What I got, though, was seriously anticlimactic.

The can's glow spread over my arm. But I didn't feel the same level of pain my friends had felt. Frankly, I'd experienced more potent high-fives than this. For all the watering can's supposed dark magic, the weird burning episodes I sometimes experienced in my hands were twenty times more severe.

These burning episodes happened at random times,

like on our bedroom balcony the first day back at school or by the fountain the night of the ball in Adelaide. They were absolutely awful, and felt like I was holding fire. This watering can, meanwhile, felt more like touching ice. When the magic glow left my arm, its touch merely emulated the aftereffects of rubbing menthol on your skin.

At that point my hand turned to liquid metal, but it snapped back to normal almost instantly. I removed my grip from the watering can to learn what quality I'd been stripped of, but there was no word imprinted on my palm. Instead there was a glittering, blurry, scarlet blob, which flickered and faded into an unattractive splotch on my skin that looked like smudged ink. Stranger still, I didn't feel any different. For better or worse, all of my personality felt intact.

"What happened?" I asked as I looked my hand over.

The witch snapped her fingers and the watering can flew to her. She shook it for a second then shrugged. "It couldn't take anything from you. You're not finished yet."

"What do you mean I'm not finished?" I asked, kind of insulted.

"It's like I said before," the witch responded. "You, like all people, have a source of internal strength. But *you* haven't yet fully realized the specific trait that gives you your strength, so the watering can can't take it from you."

"And the blob on my hand?"

"Just a side-effect," the witch explained. "If you ever figure out what your strength is and quit suppressing it, the right word will appear on your hand like it did for your friends minus the whole 'watering can strips you of the quality for two weeks' thing. Sadly, I doubt you'll ever reach that day."

"Why's that?"

"Because unless you can give me something else of value,

I still have to kill you. Rules are rules, and what kind of person would I be if I broke my own?"

"She has magical powers," Jason abruptly piped in.

"Jason!" I snapped.

"What? I am not getting killed because of you, Crisa. Just give the girl your magic so I can get out of here in one piece."

Great. Unkind SJ has me on her hate list, and now selfish Jason is ready to throw me to the wolves at the drop of a hat if it means bettering his own odds.

"Relax," our tiny captor said. "I don't want your magic. For starters, magic I've got. And second, magic isn't strength; it's power. There's a huge difference. Any fool can have power. Strength, however, is something special. So as I was saying, unless you have something else of value to offer . . ."

She motioned with her hand and an invisible force grabbed me by the throat and threw me against the back wall. I struggled against it, but was unable to break free. My attempts to do so only made the little witch snicker.

"You princess types are too easy," she said. "Such damsels; it's almost not even worth my time to kill you."

The force from the witch's push had caused my satchel to slip off my shoulder. It fell to the floor with a thud and the magic mirror I'd been carrying around tumbled out.

The little witch's eyes widened when she saw it—the beautiful relic from *Beauty & the Beast* that my friends and I had taken from the Treasure Archives earlier in the month. We'd borrowed it from the Treasure Archives to find Emma; its powers allowed you to see and hear anybody whose name you spoke into its looking glass.

Originally we'd intended to put it back after getting the information we needed. Unfortunately, that same night someone else broke into the Archives after us and stole the replacement mirror we'd left as a decoy, along with three other items: Aladdin's empty genie lamp, the corset used to poison Snow White before the apple, and the enchanted pea from *The Princess & the Pea*. As a result, we'd decided to keep the mirror with us to prevent it from being stolen by whoever wanted it. We figured that until the culprit of the other items was caught, it was safer in our possession. Alas, this no longer seemed to be the case.

Holding one hand in the air to keep me pinned to the wall, the witch motioned to the mirror with the other. It levitated across the room. When it reached her, she examined it with great care.

"You have a Mark One!" she exclaimed.

"A what?" Daniel asked.

"A Mark One magic mirror, you dolt," she scorned, gesturing at the engraving on the back of the mirror. "I thought they'd all been destroyed ages ago . . . Do you have any idea what one of these is worth?"

"It's not ours to give," Blue blathered nervously. "See, we only borrowed it from our school. We were going to put it back. Now we're just sort of holding onto it to protect it from whoever was really trying to steal it. But we have to take it back eventually otherwise we'll get in serious trouble and—"

"Blue, shut up!" SJ barked. She whipped her head around. "You can have it," she told the witch.

"SJ, we can't—" I started to say. But then the witch tightened her fist, magically squeezing my windpipe shut.

She levitated me forward then released me from the chokehold when I was three feet in front of her. My body dropped to the ground. I coughed violently as air returned to my lungs.

The witch smiled and patted me on the head. "Thank

you very much, Crisanta Knight. I accept your offering and will gladly take this mirror off your hands as payment for my hospitality."

I looked up at her in surprise. "How?" I choked. "How do you know my name?"

"I got a message from some friends in Alderon to be on the lookout. Let's just say you're lucky I'm more interested in feeding my garden than I am in the going rate for the head of some stupid teenager."

"Alderon?" I repeated.

That must've been where Arian and his lackeys were getting their orders from. Which meant that's where this Nadia chick was too.

It made sense, I supposed. The desolate kingdom of Alderon was where our realm's officials and Fairy Godmothers imprisoned any antagonists they caught—depositing them indefinitely within its one-way In and Out Spell border.

But if Arian was originally from Alderon, how had he and his followers managed to escape its boundaries to come after me and the other protagonists? And of all the potentially powerful main characters out there, why did they seem so adamant about wanting *me* dead?

It had to be more than my lame prologue prophecy. Unless they knew something about it that I didn't.

I thought back to what Arian had said in Century City: *"Oh, you poor, dumb princess. You really have no idea, do you?"*

What if he was right? What if there was something about my prologue prophecy that I was missing? What if there was more to it than I knew?

If this was the case, I had no way to verify it. The only thing I could garner in that moment was that my prophecy must've been really important to the antagonists. Otherwise why else would word of their mission have made it all the way from their blocked-off kingdom on the outskirts of the realm to the middle of the Forbidden Forest?

"Here," the witch said curtly, interrupting my train of thought with another wave of her hand. "You said you wanted taffy, right?"

The top cabinet on the left flew open. Inside there were several jars of the blue, sticky candy. "I assume you mean saltwater taffy," the witch said. "It's the only kind I have that's of any use. One bite and you'll be able to breathe underwater for up to four hours without resurfacing."

"Yeah," I said, standing and dusting myself off. "That's the stuff."

"Good," the witch responded. "Then take what you came for before I change my mind. And *get out*."

Like the others, I tore my attention away from the witch and moved for the kitchen cabinet. I opened a jar and each of us shoved a piece of the candy into our pockets.

This enchanted saltwater taffy was just what we needed to breathe underwater, find Ashlyn, and hopefully retrieve whatever "Heart of the Lost Princess" Emma's list had been referring to.

By the time we turned back to where the small devil had been standing, she'd vanished without a trace.

Everything seemed colder in her absence. Even the wind had picked up. It blew open the chocolate window shutters with a great deal of ominous force.

After we'd gathered our weapons from the back of the room and made our way outside, that same wind caused the branches of the weeping willows on the edge of the Valley to sway. The motion created an unsettling effect, which was enhanced by the gloom of nightfall and the clouds that had rolled in. They were thick and stormy, concealing every star behind fifteen shades of gray.

SJ rammed into my shoulder, knocking me out of my thoughts. "Stop admiring the scenery, Crisa. We have to go. There will be more time for you to be enigmatic and self-indulgent later, I am sure."

Wow, okay. Unkind SJ is so not going to be fun.

Still, my feelings for her new state aside, something told me she was right about us needing to go. Whatever other surprises the Forbidden Forest held likely didn't get any better after dark.

We followed Chauncey's map as best as we could when we left the Valley, but it became next to impossible to read in the dismal light.

As we continued to fumble along the darkening paths of the Forbidden Forest, it was probably for the best that we didn't say much to each another. None of us were ourselves.

Well, except for me. But apparently I'm "not finished," so what the heck do I know?

The only sounds we heard came from Blue and SJ. Blue released periodic squeaks of terror whenever a twig snapped beneath her feet or a wandering animal scampered out of a bush and startled her. SJ would then mercilessly shush Blue in response. Of the two, it was hard to say which sound was more difficult to take.

Daniel, meanwhile, appeared reluctant to open his mouth at all—probably afraid that he might say something that would give away the secret he was concealing within his hand.

Maybe I should go over there and try and trick him into revealing what he's hiding? Or maybe I could just run up to him and unclench his fist by force to see for myself.

Both seemed like plausible plans, but my further formulation of their execution was cut short. A deafening howl pierced the woods, tearing through the silence.

Blue quivered nervously. "Wh-what was that?" she asked.

"It was nothing," I said, trying to reassure her.

"No, no," Blue insisted. "There's something out there! You're lying!"

"It would not be the first time," SJ huffed.

Blue's eyes darted around. "What does that mean? What's out there? Oh, we're all doomed, aren't we?"

"Shut up, Blue!" SJ ordered.

"Whoa," I interjected. "Cool it, SJ. That watering can is messing with her head *and* with yours. So just calm down, okay?"

"Guys," Daniel said, trying to get our attention.

"Do not tell me to cool it, Crisa," SJ snapped. "Do not tell me to do *anything*. We are here because of *you* and *your* big ideas. Neither of which I care for at the moment since you cannot even be honest about—"

"Guys," Daniel repeated.

"What?" SJ and I shouted in unison.

Then we saw it. A gigantic wolf was leering at us from atop a nearby hill. He slowly descended through the tree-entwined slope, making his way toward our group. The creature's eyes were glowing green and his twenty-foot long body was a carpet of thick, black fur that was almost flawlessly camouflaged with the darkness.

Blue screamed. Jason took out his axe. I stood frozen.

"We can take him," Daniel said a bit unsteadily.

The raised hairs on the back of my neck made me think

otherwise. As did the three other, equally large wolves that suddenly emerged from the trees and began to encircle us.

"You want to rethink that statement?" I muttered.

I began to feel nostalgic for the fire-breathing chipmunks.

The wolf closest to me snarled malevolently. He was a mere five feet away. He was so close, in fact, that I was able to see my reflection in his eyes like a shimmering bullseye. As he bared his fangs—sharp like daggers and white like moonlight—all I could think was:

My, what big teeth you have . . .

CHAPTER 7

Therewolves

ther than the crunch of twigs beneath our feet and the occasional pensive hoot of an owl in the distance, all remained quiet.

Of course, this had less to do with the tension between the members of my group and more to do with the enormous wolves forcibly escorting us through the Forbidden Forest. They hadn't exactly said anything to us. But for the past half hour they'd made what they wanted pretty clear. They simply herded us along, pushing us deeper into the trees with their growls and massive bodies.

As we traveled, it crossed my mind to break out my wand. But, tempting as it was, four giant monsters against a girl with a spear didn't seem to offer the best odds. I was gutsy, not stupid. These things could probably swallow me whole in one bite.

In accord with this, the other thought that consumed my mind as we walked was why they hadn't just eaten us already? Were they taking us back to their lair to share the wealth with their wolf friends? Or did we just need to be seasoned properly before being swallowed?

I caught glimpses of my friends' faces during the seemingly endless journey. Blue looked terrified, making me feel sorry for her. She really had gotten the shortest end of the stick with the watering can, especially given our current situation.

The others seemed solemn—no doubt wondering how this wolf situation could play out. However, as I observed them I realized that there was something more to their expressions than that. Or rather, something less. Now that I had the chance to really notice, I saw just how empty they all appeared, even Daniel.

It was strange to think that a person's personality could be so dependent on one defining characteristic, and that without it they became ghosts of their former selves. It made me feel guilty. I mean, here they were, my friends, their natures changed like unicorns with their horns ripped off—while I remained unscathed.

The thing was, not only did I feel guilty, I also felt kind of insulted.

How dare that awful little witch call me "not finished" like I was some haphazard arts-and-crafts project?

I glared at my palm. The blur persisted, mocking me with its lack of clarity.

My self-pity was put into perspective a minute later when we came upon a massive cave guarded by several other epically-sized wolves. Out of instinct I stopped in my tracks. But I was pushed forward in the next moment by the growling wolf behind me.

Hesitantly, I continued with the rest of the pack through the cavern's opening.

Freaking out, freaking out, freaking out.

On our way down, the cave merged with several other tunnels like an underground maze. As we descended farther into the labyrinth's heart, I noticed the usual accouterments—bats hanging from the ceiling, undergrowth here and there, bones scattered periodically, and torches lining the walkway. Although I didn't quite get how wolves would go about lighting torches in the first place.

The atmosphere went from terrifying and eerie to terrifying and confusing as we began to pass shelves built into the cave's walls. It wasn't so much the shelves themselves that raised our eyebrows (the craftsmanship wasn't *that* bad). But the contents that sat upon them were weird. There were ballet shoes, wigs, musical instruments, and a bunch of other strange junk.

What, did they just eat a theatre troupe for breakfast and an orchestra for lunch?

It wasn't long before we entered an immense round room, no doubt the center of the tunnel system. It was lit from every angle by torches and had a high roof that converged into a point like a pyramid. Tree roots from the outside world poked through—some gripping the ceiling tightly, others dangling out as if reaching for us.

Built into the front of the room was an impressive stage. It was elevated at least fifteen feet above the floor and was adorned with meaty red velvet curtains.

What really caught my attention, though, were the people in the room. They were hammering, painting, dancing. Many seemed perfectly content. But maybe fifty or sixty of them were working with balls and chains shackled to their ankles.

I felt like I wanted to ask a question, but I couldn't think of the right one to pose. It was all so random. Before I could form the words, the wolves herded us into the center of the room and circled us like prey.

Seriously, is this how it ends—eaten by wolves in an underground community theater?

I was truly expecting them to lunge at us, and I slipped my hand into my satchel in preparation, ready to go down fighting. But instead of attacking, each wolf was abruptly consumed by an emerald tornado.

The vortexes appeared out of nowhere and expanded rapidly—shrouding the theater in a thick cloud. After a few seconds the smoke faded away. In place of the colossal wolves were ordinary-looking people, all of whom were dressed up and possessed glowing green eyes.

A man emerged on the stage behind them. He had orangey hair, a suspicious mole, and wore a petticoat with matching teal tights.

Yes, you read that correctly. *Teal tights.*

He descended the stage and bowed to us formally. "Welcome, children," he said. "I am Gustaf Pepperjack."

As he bowed, a chain around his neck dangled forward and I caught a glimpse of the big ring that was hanging from it. It was gold and tacky, like a cross between a prize from a cereal box and a promise ring a teenaged boy might give to a steady girlfriend. The stone set into the ring was as bright and deeply green as the eyes of Mr. Pepperjack's colleagues.

Daniel raised his eyebrows. "Werewolves? Really? That's kind of predictable isn't it?"

A girl at my twelve o'clock with big curls and bigger eyebrows crossed her arms. "We are not *Were*wolves," she said. "We are *There*wolves."

Now it was my turn to raise an eyebrow. "I'm sorry. What now?"

"*There*wolves," Pepperjack repeated. "The 'th' is an abbreviation of Thespian."

"Is that kind of like a windsurfer?" Jason asked.

"Thespians are actors," I whispered to him.

Pepperjack shrugged. "We prefer Performance Artists or Stage Masters or—"

"Scripted Chameleons," another Therewolf added.

"Sydney, we vetoed that name at our last table read. Let it go, man," Pepperjack growled.

The two continued arguing, and I took advantage of the distraction as best I could.

Looking around, I knew there was still no way we could fight them all and win. But after seeing the imprisoned workers, I got the feeling that whatever they had in store for us didn't involve a quick execution. Which meant there would be time to think of an escape plan later. In the meantime, since these creatures were humans as much as they were wolves, I didn't want them to discover my wand and find out about my magic. I had to camouflage it, fast.

I subtly dipped my hand into my satchel, grasping the wand tightly.

Okay, don't transform it into anything too fancy. Just pick something commonplace.

Pepperjack suddenly removed his glove and slapped Sydney across the face with it before throwing it to the ground.

Snap! I have never seen anyone literally and figuratively throw down the gauntlet. I guess I can check witnessing the fulfillment of an age-old idiom off my bucket list.

Sadly, Sydney did not accept the challenge. He looked like he wanted to at first, but Pepperjack's daggering stare stole whatever courage he'd been mustering. He simply rubbed his bruised cheek, sucked in his equally injured pride, and stepped back subserviently to join the other Therewolves.

I hurriedly concentrated on the first weapon that came to mind and morphed my wand into a kitchen knife.

"As I was saying," Pepperjack continued as he readdressed us. "To use the peasant and overly colloquial term—we are *actors*. To be precise, we are a race of hyper-talented actors that transform into giant, hyper-intelligent wolves."

Jason scratched his head, trying to understand the strange revelation. "So . . . what do you weirdos want with us exactly?" he asked.

"Jason, do not be a moron," SJ said. "They obviously want to eat us."

"They come anywhere near me and I'm stabbing them in the sternum and making a break for it," he replied bluntly. "The way I see it, I don't have to outrun them; I just have to outrun a few of you."

"Will you shut it?" SJ huffed. "Just because you can only think of yourself now does not mean you have to say every awful thing that comes into your simpleton head."

"Says the princess donning a new heart of darkness," Jason responded. "You can't speak without it being an insult. Right now you have more in common with your witchy step-grandma than you do with your own mother."

"Take that back," SJ barked.

"Make me," he responded.

I saw SJ reach for her slingshot, but I rushed between her and Jason before she could shoot any potions at him. If she opened fire now these Therewolves would kill us first and ask questions later. We needed time.

Surprisingly, Daniel also stepped in. He pried Jason farther away from SJ and told him to cool it. Even more surprisingly, Jason listened.

As the Therewolves snickered at us, I delicately put my hand over SJ's, which was holding her slingshot. "Not now," I muttered under my breath. She tensed at first but thankfully released her grip on the weapon.

Geez, that was close. That tiny witch in the Valley had been right; it was easy for people to turn on each other when they weren't themselves. I almost just witnessed two of my best friends—and two of the nicest people I've ever met— get into an all-out brawl.

Pepperjack cleared his throat, calling everyone's attention back to him. "Well now, that was . . . spirited," he said. "I guess we will have to assign you children to different groups."

"Groups?" Daniel repeated.

"Yes," Pepperjack replied. "You will all be assigned to different work groups to help out our troupe."

"So you're not going to eat us then?" Blue stammered.

Pepperjack chuckled. "Oh no, we're definitely going to eat you, but not until after the show. You see, we Therewolves roam the Forbidden Forest hunting travelers for three reasons. First and foremost, we like to have audiences for our theatrical productions, even if they are being held against their will. Second, good stagehands are hard to find and the free labor our prisoners provide helps us mount the most lavish of shows."

"And the third reason?" I asked, although I had a pretty good idea of the answer.

"Naturally," Pepperjack mused, "so we can have food at the after-party. Now come, opening night is in two weeks and we're dreadfully behind with costume design."

CHAPTER 8

The Light Bulb Moment

ays one and two of Therewolf captivity consisted of sewing sequins onto gender-neutral leotards within the confinement of my solitary cell.

Since we were new recruits, the Therewolves didn't trust us with any important stage crew work, or to be in close contact with one another yet. Separated from my friends and Daniel for a couple of days, I found myself constantly wondering how they were doing. Had they also been driven within an inch of their sanity from so much sewing? Or had they been forced to perform other, equally monotonous tasks like highlighting lines in scripts or shining shoes with smelly polish?

Throughout the ordeal I'd been racking my brain trying to think of a way to escape. But my prison, like that of the others I was sure, lacked much to work with.

Since we were underground, there were no windows. And when they'd shoved me in here, I'd noticed the absolute heftiest of padlocks clinging to the outside of my cell's solid steel door. The walls were also without weak spot. Plus, I had to contend with an enormous ball and chain clasped around my right ankle, which weighed close to thirty pounds.

At least if I'd had my wand there would have been some possibility of finding a way out—its unbreakable nature would've easily allowed me to hack through the chains and maybe even the door too. But the Therewolves had confiscated it and our other weapons. Now the only thing I had in my corner were my lock-picking skills.

After fiddling with it in between guard patrols, I'd managed to pick the lock on my ball and chain with my sewing needle.

This was definitely a win. However, since the lock to my cell was on the other side of the door and I had no way of reaching it, for the time being the small victory served no purpose. As a result, I'd decided to keep the ball and chain around my ankle and the lock-picking option in my back pocket until I had a follow-up move for escape.

On the third morning of captivity I was sewing my ten thousandth sequin when a very plump Therewolf wearing a tight corset appeared in my doorway.

"You, combat boots," she said as she unlocked my cell, her arm fat waggling as she jiggled the rusty bronze key. "Come on, you've been reassigned to wardrobe and set design."

She and another Therewolf led me through a series of torch-lined tunnels to a huge area that housed every kind of design material you could fathom. It was so big and winding I had no way of ascertaining just how far back it extended. Craning my neck, I saw that the space twisted into a myriad of extensions like a maze.

The ceiling here was high like in the main theater; it had to be to accommodate the storage of so many massive set fronts. Tables bearing everything from spray paint to chicken wire covered the floor, causing me to up my agility in order to avoid bumping into them. Costume racks provided rows and rows of color.

It was pretty packed, but I immediately smiled with relief

when I spotted Blue and SJ. They were busy cutting fabric at a table in the corner—balls and chains clasped around their ankles as well. I was instructed to go over to them and gladly did so.

The second she saw me, Blue smiled too—unlike SJ. The cold shoulder she gave me sent shivers up my spine as I approached them.

"Crisa, I'm so happy to see you," Blue whispered as I sat down beside her.

"Back 'atcha." I nodded. "How long have you guys been here?"

"Since yesterday," she responded. "I'm scared. They've been giving us weird looks."

"Sure they have. We're their groceries," I said as jokingly as I could in order to try and ease her nerves.

Blue shook her head worriedly. "No, I mean besides that. They keep coming by to sniff my cloak and ask questions about where we're from. It's really freaking me out."

I made sure no one was within hearing distance and then leaned in close to her. "Do you know what happened to our stuff?" I asked.

"I . . ." Blue stiffened as a Therewolf on the other side of the room glared suspiciously in our direction. He went back to his business a moment later, and I put my hand on Blue's arm to calm her.

"It's okay. We're fine. What were you gonna say?"

"I . . . I heard one of them say they keep all confiscated supplies in the props closet over there in case they want to use any of it in their play," she said, gesturing to a door. "But, Crisa, I still can't get over what's happening here. I mean, actors that morph into wolves? This doesn't make any sense."

"Yeah, well I pretty much gave up on sense when I almost got barbequed by a daffodil the other day."

Suddenly SJ threw down her fabric. "Are you really making jokes right now?"

I raised my eyebrows. "You have a problem with that?"

"Yes, I have a problem with that," she growled. "I do not know if it has escaped your notice, Crisa, but we are in serious trouble here. And it is all your—"

A Therewolf wearing a black leotard, suede kilt, and purple boa flounced around his neck came over to our station and interrupted SJ before she could finish. "The director has some questions for the two of you," he said, nodding to Blue and SJ.

Blue's face paled and panic filled her eyes. I squeezed her hand for reassurance. It was strange; usually she was the last person that needed any such comfort. But now fear was running wild inside of her and I realized that she had no experience with how to handle it.

"You'll be okay," I tried to convince her as she got up to leave with SJ.

After they'd left, I repeated the statement aloud once more—this time to convince myself.

Over the next few days it was all I could do not to punch Jason in the face.

I'd eventually been reassigned from the wardrobe and set design department to work with him and a half dozen other prisoners backstage on the physical set construction. The work was hard, but it was the least of my worries considering what Jason put me through.

My friend, whom I now realized really *had* always put

others before himself, had transformed into the ultimate selfish twit.

Whenever a Therewolf came round with a new task to be done, he volunteered my services instead of his own. And he did so even more speedily if the assignment happened to involve any hard labor or potential danger. Then if he screwed up, he pinned it on me and I had to deal with whatever punishment our captors dished out in return. Usually this involved treating blisters on the feet of the troupe's director, Mr. Pepperjack.

Ugh, you would've thought the man was a triathlete by the number of disgusting sores around his toes. They were almost as green and bulbous as that ridiculous piece of costume jewelry he constantly had hanging from his neck.

All this was nothing in comparison to some of Jason's other antics though. For example, on day five of our captivity one of the sets we'd made—a wooden front for a cottage—came crashing down. Only I hadn't seen it coming because I was busy building a trapdoor in the stage floor. Jason, however, had seen it coming. Except instead of warning me, he just took off. By the time I saw what was happening it was too late and I got totally squashed.

Many similar scenarios continued throughout the week, including mishaps with buckets of paint, falling curtains, and a nail gun that almost took me out arrow-through-an-apple style.

Overall, let's just say it was a good thing that the Therewolves had first aid kits and fire safety equipment backstage. Otherwise they would've had to revise the sign in their lounge that read: "This troupe has gone 273 days without injury."

To put it mildly, my patience with Jason was wearing

thin. But I restrained myself from losing it with him since his current state (like SJ's, Blue's, and Daniel's) was on me. Yes, the watering can had made them like this. But it was my ideas about finding the Author that had led us to the Forbidden Forest in the first place. SJ may not have been able to finish her comment the other day, but she didn't need to. I knew this was my fault.

By day seven of captivity, Jason and I had different shifts. He was working on lighting backstage while I'd been relocated to work in the audience section of the theater. This safe distance was a small comfort, though, as I was becoming fairly preoccupied with concern for the others. I hadn't seen SJ and Blue since my brief time with them in wardrobe and set design. And other than having spotted Daniel once in passing a few days ago, I hadn't run into him either.

Needless to say that as the days went by I was growing increasingly worried about them. It was almost to the point where, if I didn't know any better, I would've said I felt myself becoming a little . . . *afraid.*

My whole body cringed with defiance at the thought. I hated even sort of admitting that.

I hastily swallowed down the feeling like a spoonful of the vilest vinegar. The clock was ticking. Opening night was one week away, and I needed to think of a plan to get us out of here.

This proved to be a difficult task when the four other members of my group were nowhere to be found. Not having SJ and Blue around meant that I was missing the sounding board of my usual co-conspirators.

Yes, normally I took charge of developing our elaborate plots. But it was Blue and SJ who I'd always considered the geniuses behind their success. The combination of Blue's daring with SJ's sound judgment gave our plans balance and made them work.

Then again, even if I'd had my friends with me it probably wouldn't have helped. Blue was a terrified mess and SJ's head was clouded with meanness. Right now I was the only one who was able to think clearly, the only person whose inherent qualities could be relied upon. Which meant I had to ask myself, what did I actually bring to the table on our various adventures?

I found myself dwelling on this as I scrubbed blood spots from the Therewolves' shirts and tried to avoid wondering where the stains had come from. Hopefully it was just fake blood from the make-up department, not the vestiges of a human snack. I assumed the odds of this were good given that only about ten of the Therewolves could physically transform into their wolf halves at any particular moment.

Evidently they were all on different cycles with the moon and could only morph into monsters if it was their time of the month.

I shook my head and tried to concentrate on something else. On stage, the troupe's members were undertaking their first full dress rehearsal. It was an adaptation of *Little Red Riding Hood* of all things.

The production the Therewolves were putting on was a showcase of "re-worked" fairytales. That's what they called them at least. In reality they'd just changed the endings of every story so that the tales' protagonists were eaten by wolves. Oh, and they added a few musical numbers too.

I gazed at the set meant to portray the grandmother's cottage in the show. The Therewolf playing the part of the grandmother was busy at her fake stove pretending to cook.

That's when I saw it.

On set in the form of the kitchen knife I'd transformed it into, my wand was sitting on the countertop next to several other basic cutlery props.

If that wasn't good enough fortune, I was even more elated when I noticed a glass bowl filled with SJ's portable potions sitting on the set's coffee table. The Therewolves definitely hadn't known what they were and had decided to use them as decorative tchotchkes.

Just having the potions and my wand in close proximity gave me hope that escape was possible. In fact, the second I saw them, the gears in my brain began to turn like runaway carriage wheels. My eyes darted about the place calculating strategies and configuring scenarios. As I stared at the stage—its layout, its elevation, the giant curtains that framed it—ideas sparked inside my head and my heart sped with excitement.

I had the incunabula of plan.

Alas, my temporarily heightened spirit was extinguished at the sight of SJ and Blue being led into the theater. Seeing them for the first time in days should have made me ecstatic, but when they sat down next to me, I saw that Blue was practically in tears.

Their Therewolf guard instructed them to assist me with the shirt scrubbing. When he left I dropped my steel wool and turned to Blue. "What's wrong?"

She shook her head in response—unable to get out a single syllable. SJ sighed and rolled her eyes before she brought herself to explain what had happened on Blue's behalf.

The reason the Therewolves had taken such a strong interest in SJ and Blue was because they'd suspected my friends were protagonists. The higher-up's in the troupe had interrogated both of them over the last few days trying to verify this theory. But in the end it didn't matter how many times Blue and SJ denied the allegations, because one Therewolf knew the truth.

This Therewolf was the brother of the same Therewolf that had tried to eat Blue's sister Red when she'd wandered into the Forbidden Forest many years ago. One look at my friend and a sniff of her cloak for confirmation, and the vengeful actor-hunter hybrid confirmed Blue's protagonist identity on the spot.

You would've thought this meant that our captors intended to eat Blue right away. But as it turned out, they actually had bigger, more sadistic plans in mind.

Evidently the whole "wolf eats main character" thing was an ongoing theme in all of their productions, not just the fairytale adaptations. And this recurring ending was made possible by the fact that the Therewolves only cast prisoners in those roles. Meaning that the eating of the characters at the end of each show was not acting but *real* devouring.

Getting one of Book's actual protagonists to play such a sacrificial part was, like, the ultimate prize. So when they found out who Blue really was they immediately cast her in the role of her sister for their production of *Little Red Riding Hood*. Within the next few days she would be forced to memorize lines, get fitted for a costume, and learn a brief tap number in preparation for being eaten alive during the play's premiere performance.

SJ had barely finished her story when the Therewolf who'd escorted them in came to collect Blue. He was carrying something in his left hand. When he reached us, he threw the brightly colored garment at her with great disdain.

"Let's go, protagonist," he said. "They need you in wardrobe."

Blue held the red cloak with such terror you might've assumed she thought actual blood had given it its color. I also regarded the thing with dread, but for a very different reason.

Blue stood up and followed the Therewolf without question. I stood too, but not to go after her. I backed up a few feet and *really* looked around me for the first time since I'd been in this room.

The red cloak, the theater, the torches, the giant wolves . . .

Oh no. This is . . . This was . . .

My mouth dropped open as the images that my consciousness had tried to forget came flooding back.

I'd dreamed about this, about *all* of this. But how? How could I have possibly known about this place? How could I have known about that bunker back at the Capitol Building? Or the glowing red watering can? Or any of it?

I felt dizzy. Then I noticed SJ standing next to me. I had told her about this particular dream, and as she gazed around the room she was no doubt connecting the same dots I was.

Sure enough, when the spark of recognition flickered in her eyes she tersely punched me in the arm.

"Ow! Geez, SJ. What was that for?" I asked.

"This is all *your* fault," she said bitterly. "You and your big ideas. You fill our heads with nonsense about taking our lives into our own hands and being who we want to be, drag us back and forth across the realm, and for what? Only to have you lie to us along the way and then get us eaten by predatory actors."

"SJ, I—"

"You what, Crisa? Care about someone beside yourself? Want to be honest with the others?"

I grabbed SJ by the elbow and yanked her down. I pretended to get back to work and gestured for her to do the same so the Therewolves wouldn't notice our argument.

"Not that again, SJ," I whispered. "In case you haven't noticed, Blue is about to be eaten during a poorly directed theatrical performance. Can we please put aside our personal issues for the moment and concentrate on the big picture?"

"This *is* the big picture, Crisa," SJ hissed. "How can you not see that? This whole time you have been making the excuse that your dishonesty about what is going on with you was to protect us from dealing with your burden. But look around. We are not protected. We are all in this mess together. And maybe if you had trusted us with the truth, we might not be."

"That's not fair," I protested. "How was I supposed to know what to do with a dream about Blue being attacked on stage by a giant wolf?"

"You tell me; you are the one who can apparently see the future," SJ snapped.

I blinked. "Say that again?"

"I said you can see the future," she reiterated. "That is the only explanation, is it not?"

It felt like someone had turned on a light bulb in my brain. That was totally it! I could see the future! That was why my nocturnal visions always felt so real. That was why the places and people I had been dreaming about actually existed.

I felt like such a dunce. How could I not have put two and two together sooner?

To be fair I'd had a lot on my mind recently. And having

"psychic abilities" was not a natural assumption for any person to come to. But I still felt stupid regardless.

I stared into space, processing the revelation. It was weird and unsettling and incredibly cool all at the same time. Part of me was super freaked out because I didn't know how or why I was able to do this. But another part of me felt somewhat relieved and more confident now that I had some understanding of what was going on inside me.

Suddenly I felt a strange, icy tingle emanating from my fingers. I glanced down and realized that my entire right hand was liquid metal. The watering can's magic was fluctuating.

Really? I rolled my eyes. *You're telling me that the strongest part of my personality is being able to see the future? It's a pretty cool development and everything, but that's not even a trait so much as it is a skill. I feel like I'm being gypped here.*

After a moment the silvery effect evaporated into my skin. I flipped over my palm, expecting to find a word branded there. However, much to my surprise the smudgy tattoo merely flashed scarlet before returning to its normal, blurry state. There was no word, just the same blob.

Hmm. Okay, I guess that's not it.

I wondered why the mark had started acting up even though I hadn't solved the watering can's riddle but decided it was probably just another side effect of the enchantment.

"All right," I said at last, looking at SJ. "I can see the future. Apparently. That's, um, different."

"Different is one word for it," SJ replied. "Another would be ill-timed. It would have been a lot more helpful if you had figured out this was your Fairy Godmother-induced power sooner, Crisa."

"Wait, what do you mean? This isn't my power, at least

not the secret one that's supposed to develop from the magic Emma gave me to make my wand work."

"That is ridiculous," SJ scoffed. "Be logical, Crisa. Of course this is your power. Why in the realm would it not be? Psychic abilities do not fall from the sky. This skill of yours is clearly something magical."

I paused but then shook my head decidedly. No offense to SJ, but logic didn't matter in this case—instinct did. And mine told me that despite what the facts were suggesting, seeing the future in my dreams was not my magic power. It just wasn't. I could feel it.

"Look, SJ," I finally responded. "Emma said that when I discovered my power I would know it, like I would sense it in my gut or something. And if that's true then I can tell you with utmost certainty that whatever *this* is, it's not my power. I'm not saying it's not something magical, I'm just saying that it's something . . . *else*."

SJ rolled her eyes. "Fine then, Miss Know-It-All, maybe it is not your power. In any case it is what we have to work with at the moment, so hurry up and use this 'something else' of yours to get us out of here."

"How am I supposed to do that?"

"Well, what have you dreamed about lately?" SJ asked, the annoyance in her tone rising.

"Nothing," I admitted.

"Crisa, you lie to me again and I *will* punch you."

"SJ, you already did that; pretty hard, by the way. And I'm telling you the truth. It's the strangest thing. I haven't had a single dream since we've been here. Frankly, I haven't slept this peacefully since I was home for the summer."

"Wonderful." SJ scowled. "In that case, what else do you have?"

"What do you mean?"

"Crisa, *you* are the one who always directs our mad plans. You must have something up your sleeve."

I sighed. "SJ, we both know that you and Blue are the ones that make our plans work. Past the inherent crazy that helps me come up with them, I'm not even sure what I contribute."

"Wow, you can be dense. That is an easy one," she scoffed.

"Is it now?" I replied, genuinely curious. "Well then enlighten me, Oh Mean One."

"And inflate your ego?" SJ crossed her arms. "I do not think so. Tell me what you have in terms of a plan for escaping and then let us see if you can figure it out for yourself."

I glanced around to make sure there were absolutely no Therewolves within earshot and then scooched closer to her. "All right, fine. I do have something," I admitted. "Look up on the stage. You see what's on that coffee table?"

SJ turned her head and her eyes widened. "Are those—"

"Yes," I interrupted. "My wand's up there too. It's disguised as one of the kitchen knives. I've been doing some recon over the last week during shifts and between that, your potions, and my wand—I think I've finally got a few ideas in the works. But in order for them to pan out we're going need a list of our job assignments for opening night, a script with stage directions, three rubber bands, a jacket, and, most importantly, I'm going to need you to do something that I haven't been able to do myself and that I definitely don't deserve."

SJ looked at me skeptically. "And what, dare I ask, is that?"

"*Trust me*," I said.

CHAPTER 9

Stage Frights

"And now I shall surrender, for you are clearly better than I. So what can I do, but lay down and die . . ."

"You really sold it that time," I said sarcastically as Blue threw down the sorry excuse for a script she was being forced to memorize.

Out of nowhere a rock suddenly hurtled by our heads—barely missing Blue and bouncing off the metal pipes behind us.

"Ten minutes, kid," the Therewolf who'd thrown the stone barked as he passed by.

Blue began to hyperventilate. I grabbed a paper bag and handed it to her.

"Calm, calm," I repeated. "Everything is going to be okay."

I was anxious, as every human within the tunnel system probably was. But Blue's worries were on an entirely different level. The circles under her eyes were immense from lack of sleep. Her nails were bitten down. And her knees shook more than mine did after an extreme day of training drills in the practice fields back at school.

School . . .

It felt like ages since I'd even thought the word. We still

wore the same clothes as the day we left—crisp and clean as ever thanks to SJ's nifty invention, the SRB, which we wore around our wrists. These Soap on a Rope-like Bracelets were laced with a potion of her own design that kept wearers clean and fresh no matter what the circumstance. Even if we fell in the mud or a pool of egg cream, as soon as we removed ourselves from the dirtying environment, the bracelets released a series of silver sparks that returned us, and our clothes, to dry and clean states. Needless to say, this was an extremely handy accessory to have on a quest and in an underground theater prison.

Other than our unchanging outfits, however, it seemed like everything in the world was different now.

I wondered if this was a fact to mourn or rejoice. I'd always wished to escape the confinement of my school's walls, rules, and routines. But then again, I definitely hadn't fantasized about coaching one of my best friends on her acting prior to performing in a play put on by bloodthirsty actor-wolves.

I really hoped my plan was going to work.

I'd managed to get my hands on everything I needed and, based on the list of work duties that SJ had procured for me, I'd assigned jobs to carry out our plan accordingly.

Considering what I had to work with, I thought I'd done a decent job, especially considering that opening night fell on day fourteen of the watering can's curse and my friends would not be themselves again until tomorrow.

I supportively patted Blue on the shoulder then went to retrieve her picnic basket filled with goodies from the props closet. *Fake* goodies, that is. Had they been real I would've eaten them on the spot. We hadn't had a good meal since being here. This was a prison after all, not a five-star resort.

The props closet was at the front of the wardrobe and set design department. I dragged my ball and chain through the maze of costume racks, fake scenery, and tables loaded with set design materials. I accidentally rammed into one of the tables and knocked over a tube of super glue and one of the many cans of spray paint, causing me to get a glare from a Therewolf nearby.

There was a huge line in front of the props closet when I arrived as other human helpers were also retrieving objects for the production. The chafing of my shackle against my shin irritated me more than usual as I inched farther up the line. I began to yearn for when I would finally be able to remove it.

The metal that cuffed it to my ankle was not locked anymore. I'd picked it loose this afternoon in my cell. Now all I had to do was unlatch the hook and step into freedom, something I fully intended to do in the very near future.

I'd confirmed that Blue, Jason, and Daniel had also figured out how to pick their locks during our stay. Accordingly, the boys had their shackles unlocked and ready to be discarded at a moment's notice. Blue, meanwhile, didn't need to worry about such an impairment. As an actress in the show, she didn't have to wear her shackle tonight due to the Therewolves' concern with the show's "realism."

SJ, on the other hand, remained bound by the lock on her ball and chain. She was not familiar with lock-pickery like the rest of us. And since we were never left unwatched for very long when let out of our cells, none of us had found the opportunity to show her how to do it.

I wasn't worried though. I'd taken that factor into account and had adjusted our plan so that it would not be an issue.

My turn in the props closet line arrived. The Therewolf monitoring the door took my name and the name of the object I was after. He nodded, checked something off his clipboard, and went to retrieve the basket I'd come to collect. As he turned his back I scanned the storage area one last time to make sure everything was where it should be.

After Blue told me that all the prisoners' personal items were kept in this room, I'd volunteered to take props from the closet to the stage and vice versa throughout dress rehearsals. This allowed me to familiarize myself with the items' whereabouts inside.

That evening it was vital that everything was in its proper place. As such, I mentally checked off my own list of important "props" before the Therewolf returned with Blue's basket. Since I was the last person in line, once he'd handed it over, he closed the door and fastened it shut with a ginormous padlock.

I heaved my shackle back through the department's twisting and turning labyrinth. When I reached Blue I found her sitting in a fetal position with her back against the wall. Most of her body was hidden within the red cloak she was being forced to wear, but a corner of her blue cloak peeked out from beneath it.

I stood in front of her. She looked up at me for a moment to acknowledge my presence then gazed back at the ground.

"Crisa . . ." she mumbled. "I don't know if I can do this."

I placed the basket on the floor and sat down beside her. "Blue, of course you can. You're *you*."

"No. I'm not," she said as she shook her head. "Haven't you been paying attention? I've been absolutely useless lately—terrified, jumpy, rattled right to my very core. I'm so scared I can barely breathe half the time. You should have thought of a different plan, one that didn't involve me needing to be someone that . . . I'm just not anymore."

"Blue," I began. Then I noticed she was still staring at the floor so I elbowed her in the arm. "Hey. Listen to me. That one part of you that's fearless is just that—*one* part. Your skills, your strength, your faith in yourself, they're not gone. They're still in there. *You're* still in there." I yanked at the corner of her blue cloak that was showing, pulling it so she could see it. "And you *can* do this."

She met my eyes wearily. "Are you sure?" she asked.

I hopped to my feet and extended my hand to her. "I wouldn't send you out there if I wasn't. Now come on, we have a show to put on and we can't do it without you."

"All right," she said after a pause. "I trust you, Crisa."

Guilty conscious—party of one?

I helped Blue up. She handed me the jacket I'd nabbed earlier in the week from one of the costume racks, I put it on, and together we began to make our way backstage.

It bothered me immensely that Blue and the others put their trust in me so completely when I apparently could not do the same. At least not entirely anyways.

After all, I seemed to have no trouble trusting them to handle different aspects of this escape and upcoming fight. But even after being imprisoned together for two weeks, I still couldn't bring myself to entrust them with the secrets that had been weighing down on my shoulders like dumbbells. And that was definitely not fair. For I felt certain that if they knew just how many things I wasn't telling them, they would put no such faith in me.

I was glad I at least knew why I was acting this way. Chauncey had been right. The root of both my doubts and my inability to trust my friends was that I needed to fully accept myself. But understanding this problem was not enough to solve it. And without any guidance, right now that challenge seemed as enigmatic as it did impossible.

Blue and I passed the props closet and proceeded through the left tunnel exit. The center tunnel would've taken us to the amphitheater where the audience was seated, and the one on the right led back to our cells. Our current path, meanwhile, took us directly below backstage.

The area we came into was dark except for a few lanterns and scant traces of light escaping through the stage's special effects trapdoors thirty feet overhead. If it weren't for the constant stream of people getting into their places, it would have been creepy. Like this, it just felt off-balance.

Unfortunately, it now came time for me and Blue to part ways. She had to go up via the lift on the right, while I had to take the one on the opposite end.

I double-checked that she was still wearing the rubber band I'd given her around her wrist (matching the ones SJ and I wore tonight). Then I hugged her hard and watched her ride up to the main stage with the other actors. When their lift had risen out of view I loaded myself into my own transport and made my way up.

No backing down now, I suppose.

Literally.

My job during the show was to work the levers that lowered the different set fronts onto the stage. I'd been assigned to work this task alongside SJ and Daniel.

Current bumpy relationships aside, it was actually super convenient that the three of us had been given crew duty in the same area and only Jason was cast off as an audience member for the night. Together, this would be a lot easier.

After I ascended the thirty feet to the main level, I hauled myself along the crowded backstage hallways toward my post. As I was passing through a corridor of thick, velvety curtains though, I stopped at the sound of familiar voices.

"That friend of yours can construct one heck of a plan," Daniel said on the other side of the divider. "I'll give her that much."

"You think it'll work?" Jason asked.

"I didn't say that," he responded.

"Well, I'll tell you one thing," Jason continued. "If something does go wrong and we can't save the other prisoners like she says we're supposed to, I'm makin' a break for the exit. You can stay behind and get killed for your nobleness for all I care. The way I see it, when it comes down to the wire, it's every man for himself."

There was a slight pause in the conversation, but soon enough Daniel found the right words to reply to Jason's awful comment.

"You know, you're kind of a jerk when you're like this. You get that, right?"

"Shut up," Jason snapped. "I'm thinking of myself for a change instead of everybody else, the greater good, and all that other crud; it's liberating. You of all people should know."

"I think about others," Daniel asserted.

"Could've fooled me. You keep to yourself as if socializing was bad for your health."

"If you're talking about Knight, you know she bugs me. And when she's around I can't help but mess with her, so it's better for the both of us if I keep my distance."

"*I* wasn't thinking only about Crisa," Jason said in response. "Why are you?"

"I'm not," Daniel replied a little too defensively. "She

just sticks in your brain like crazy glue. It's driving me nuts, especially now thanks to that stupid watering can. I can't get her out of my head no matter how hard I try."

There was another pause.

"You don't—" Jason began.

"Oh, heck no. Are you crazy?" Daniel interrupted. "It's the opposite really. I wish she was as far away from me as possible."

"Then I think you picked the wrong quest, man," Jason scoffed.

"No kidding," Daniel scoffed in return.

A few beats passed then and I began to wonder if their conversation was over. But in the next moment Jason broke the silence by posing the very question I'd been longing to know the full answer to for quite some time.

"What exactly do you have against her anyways?" Jason asked.

"Honestly?" Daniel said. "She *ruined* my life."

"Dude, that's kind of an exaggeration," Jason replied. "She comes on strong, but you did just meet her a couple months ago."

"Yeah," he said reluctantly, "but the only reason I'm here, the only reason I'm on this stupid mission to see the Author, is because of *her*. See, the thing is she—"

"Hey, show starts in five minutes; get into places!" an angry Therewolf said on the other side of my eavesdropping curtain.

The boys parted ways to head to their designated stations. When they'd gone, I scowled in frustration.

Of course I get this close to hearing Daniel be open about what's been going on inside that thick skull of his and he's interrupted.

I wanted to chase him down and force him to finish that sentence.

I mean, you can't just say a person "ruined your life" and then not explain why! And what was all that nonsense about him only being on this mission because of me? He was the last person I wanted on this journey with us, and was more than welcome to leave at any time. In fact, nothing would thrill me more.

"Problem?"

I spun around to meet SJ's suspicious gaze—a look I was becoming quite familiar with.

"Uh, no," I answered casually. "Just . . . hearing things."

"I am assuming one of those things is not the voice of reason," SJ replied. "Because honestly, Crisa, I must say this is by far your most dangerous, irresponsible, *insane* plan yet."

"I didn't hear the word 'bad' in that description," I countered.

"Well, that remains to be seen."

All of a sudden, three Therewolves in minstrel costumes rushed by us with zero regard for common courtesy. I jumped out of the way to avoid getting plowed over, but the buxom girl in the group still managed to step on my foot. I rubbed it for a second before readdressing SJ.

"Have a little faith in me, will you."

SJ huffed in amusement. "Funny, I could tell *you* the same thing."

"All right, fair enough," I replied. "But look, SJ, this *is* going to work. I know it will."

"For all our sakes I hope you are right," she responded, pushing past me to continue walking down the corridor.

I followed. It was time to get into our places too, and that meant being by the control levers.

"So I take it by all of this that you finally figured out what you contribute to our team's metaphorical table?" SJ said as we hustled along.

I shrugged. "Based on the perspective you were so unkind to provide a minute ago, I would say either insanity or irresponsibility."

"You really do not see it, do you?"

I expected another patronizing insult to follow, but when I saw the expression on her face I realized she was more confused than upset by my cluelessness. As if the part of me she was talking about was obvious and I was just too stubborn to admit it.

"Come on, SJ," I sighed. "I rely on what you guys can do more than anything else in these situations. I'm just the one that figures out how we can come together to use those skills to the best advantage of our group. And then, you know, convinces people that it'll all work out no matter how crazy or unlikely it sounds."

"Which makes you . . ." SJ egged on.

I stared at her blankly.

"Oh for goodness' sake!"

SJ threw her arms up in frustration as we rounded the corner. The lights started to flicker as we joined Daniel at the levers station—directly next to the main curtain ropes.

"Jason went to take his seat in the audience," Daniel told us as we approached. "Third row, left of center."

"Noted," I said, holding his gaze.

One of the Therewolves came over to SJ with some final instructions about the levers. I started to turn away, but Daniel's hand touched my shoulder. It was a light tap that only lasted a second, but it was so surprising it might as well have been an electric shock.

"Knight, a favor?"

"Um, okay," I said.

He leaned in close and whispered in my ear so that no one else would hear. "When you get down to the props closet, make sure to grab my sheath."

"Don't worry, I'll get your sword."

"No," he said. "It's not about the sword. You have to get my sheath."

There was an earnestness to his voice that I found startling. As a result, I reacted seriously. "Yeah, okay. I'll make sure I get it."

"People, people," one of the Therewolves announced to the cast and crew. "I've locked down the shafts to the lifts. The performance will be starting in a minute and there will be no access to the lower levels until intermission. So I hope you have everything you need. Actors, crew, human-slave work force—places, everyone, places!"

I cracked my neck and took a deep breath.

All right. Showtime.

CHAPTER 10

Stage Fights

 rolled up the sleeves of my baggy jacket and helped SJ and Daniel work the pulleys that lowered the sets onto the stage.

Once we'd finished, the backstage manager Therewolf raised the stage's massive curtains by pulling on their corresponding ropes. Dude must've had a serious amount of upper body strength. Those curtains were so thick and ginormous they would've buried a dragon like a kid beneath a king-sized comforter.

As the curtains went up, the whole dome filled with applause from the audience. The backstage manager Therewolf secured the ropes in place—putting a massive lock around the rigging to prevent them from being lowered for the remainder of the show.

When he'd gone, another Therewolf (the one called Sydney) took up residence beside our group. "I can't believe Pepperjack cast me as an understudy," he muttered as the performance began with a vivacious jazz number. "I can sashay way better than Terry Johnson."

"Tough break," I whispered.

Daniel smirked.

Sydney proceeded to lean against the curtain ropes and watch the show unfolding twenty feet away. I fixed my attention on the fire safety equipment against the wall between us. When Jason's selfish attitude had caused me to get set on fire during a special effects rehearsal, I had become quite familiar with the fire safety equipment in the back of the theater.

Currently I had my eyes on three cases. One contained first aid supplies, the second a fifty-foot-long hose, the third an axe. All these contents were on display in their individual cabinets behind moderately thick panels of glass. And each case had its own sturdy lock, thereby requiring Therewolf supervision to open it.

About thirty minutes into the production Blue's character found her way onto the set that resembled the grandmother's cottage. I held my breath for a moment then removed my jacket, bundling it up in my arms as I did one last perimeter check.

Daniel was standing a few feet away from Sydney. SJ had a rubber band around her wrist just like I did. My wand in its knife form and SJ's portable potions were both on set. And I could see Jason in the third row of the audience. He was seated near the aisle in a sea of other shackled prisoners, none of whom seemed to be enjoying the production any more than we were.

"My, Grandmother . . . what big *ears* you have," Blue said meekly.

I turned my attention to the stage.

"My, Grandmother . . . what big *eyes* you have," she continued.

Daniel started to shift closer to Sydney.

"And, my, Grandmother . . . what big *teeth* you have!"

I wrapped the jacket around my fist as the Therewolf

playing the grandmother rose from her cot. Squared off with Blue, her green eyes flashed as she finally declared: "All the better to eat you with, my dear!"

The grandmother Therewolf was engulfed in a rush of scripted emerald smoke as she transformed into her ulterior form. The cloud grew faster than she did and rapidly expanded over the entire stage, consuming everything from view of the audience.

Daniel abruptly turned and punched Sydney in the face. The blow was so hard it sent the Therewolf toppling over. I bent down and unlatched the shackle from my ankle. Free from my impairment and Sydney temporarily down, I used my jacket-wrapped fist to punch through the glass of the fire safety case containing the axe.

I pulled out the weapon and tossed it to Daniel. With one mighty swing he chopped through the ropes holding up the stage's curtains. So much like my first ball at Lady Agnue's, the curtains came plummeting down—concealing the action on stage from the audience.

As the curtains fell, Daniel used the axe to shatter the glass case containing the fire hose. I pulled out its head just as the smoke cleared and a full-sized Therewolf revealed itself before Blue. Amidst the general confusion and angry yelling on the other side of the curtain, I ran center stage, unraveling the hose as I went.

The Therewolf lunged at Blue. My friend dove underneath the monster and rolled out the other side. Then she used the rubber band around her wrist to fire a yellow portable potion she'd snagged during the Therewolf's transformation.

I rushed to the set's coffee table and snatched one of

SJ's silver portable potions from the bowl, stashing it in my pocket. Newly unshackled Daniel raced past me and grabbed my wand from the fake stovetop.

A yellow cloud of smoke erupted around the grandmother Therewolf when Blue fired her potion. Now my friend dashed beneath the Therewolf, placing her hand directly onto the creature's massive, furry chest.

I threw back the set's decorative carpet—revealing the trapdoor I'd been working on last week.

Daniel hurled my wand/knife backstage. It stabbed into the wall directly behind SJ. She yanked it free and used its unbreakable blade to slice through the chains of her shackle in a way no other weapon could.

Two more eruptions of yellow smoke consumed Blue and the grandmother Therewolf as SJ ran on stage. Sydney rose to his feet and transformed into his beastly other half. And I—clutching the hose—dove through the trapdoor.

As I plunged downwards I looked up just in time to see Sydney the Therewolf leap over the exit I'd taken.

A second later my hose reached the end of its length—leaving me dangling just five feet above the floor beneath the stage. I released my grip and landed more gracefully than expected.

The thud of my impact was drowned out by the panicked shouts, wolf snarls, and general sounds of chaos escalating overhead. The Therewolves in the audience were no doubt already transforming (at least those who could) and about to tear down the stage curtains to address the massive conflict beginning to ensue.

Uncharacteristic hesitation streaked through me like a pulse of lightning. I glanced up at the trapdoor. The opening was too far above me to see anything though, so I tore my gaze away from it and began to race through the tunnel.

As concerned as I was for my friends, and even Daniel, I couldn't allow myself time to worry about them. They had their roles and I had mine. And the first part of that required that I reach the props closet.

It took me no time at all to make it back to the wardrobe and set design department. The whole area had been vacated when the lifts were locked down.

When I arrived at the props closet I stepped back and put a moderate amount of distance between the door and me. Then I used my rubber band to fire the silver portable potion at the door's hefty padlock. The moment the glass ball plowed into the lock, a blast of silver fog burst outwards.

SJ had explained earlier in the week that the science behind firing her potions basically translated to the closer the range of the target, the smaller the resulting blast on impact and vice versa.

Ergo, from about eight feet away the snap of my rubber band released this potion with enough *umph* to cause the blast to be contained within a few square feet. If I'd fired it from, say, thirty feet away the resulting explosion would have been large enough to entirely encase one of the Therewolves' heads in ice.

The prop closet's padlock and some of the door successfully frozen over, I turned on my heel. I marched up to one of the nearby water pipes and kicked a section of it loose with a powerful thrust of my foot. Water began to pour out, but I didn't care. I grabbed the dislodged metal pipe and headed toward the closet.

With one massive swing I shattered the frozen padlock with my blunt instrument.

I turned the handle of the door then, but discovered that ice had formed around the doorframe and it was stuck. In response I threw my pipe aside, took a step back, and released the strongest kick I'd ever summoned to knock the door off its iced hinges.

The entire thing sailed inwards and fell flat on the floor. I dashed inside and climbed the shelves until I reached the plastic jar perched on the highest one. Inside was our enchanted saltwater taffy from the Valley of Edible Enchantments—confiscated from each of us and stored together in this jar by the Therewolves.

I jumped down and snagged my satchel off a nearby hook and shoved the jar inside it. Then I proceeded to grab SJ's slingshot, Daniel's sword and sheath, Blue's knives, Jason's axe, and as many other weapon-wielding scabbards as I could carry.

Moments later I was barreling through the tunnel that led to the front of the theater—the combined noise of screams, howls, and explosions echoing louder as I drew closer. When I surged back into the enormous room I was met with a scene that greatly surpassed the chaos of the preceding sounds.

Fights were unfolding everywhere. The theater was erupting with bursts of fire, ice, and goo. Prisoners free from their shackles were either defending themselves or running toward me.

During the final week of rehearsals, the Therewolves had required prisoners to work in much closer capacity with one another. Additionally, they'd had us go from department to department as needed. These factors had created the perfect opportunity for my friends, Daniel, and me to get to know our fellow inmates and spread the word of our escape plan.

I'd learned that the other prisoners had all been stuck here for varying amounts of time. I think the girl who'd been here the longest was a teenage chick named Blaire who'd been abducted three months ago. Others—like my man Robbie whose snark rivaled even my own—had only been here for a few weeks.

Over the course of those few days I'd gotten to know many of them. And based on that information I'd adapted our plan even further. This one kid named Devon, for instance, was great with weaponry. Despite being only twenty-three years old, his combat talent had allowed him to own and operate a private sword-fighting studio in Harzana. And this one muscular woman named Sylvia was a meat cutter at her local butcher shop, which made her very familiar with hacking away at things with heavy blades like cleavers and axes. And this other dude named Savron . . . well, you get the gist. The point is that many of the prisoners we talked to had the potential to bring something unique to the table tonight.

In truth, there were only two things they all shared in common. They'd each been abducted by a Therewolf when they'd wandered into the Forbidden Forest for one reason or another. And none of them needed much convincing to follow my lead.

My plan having been passed along quite quickly, all my fellow prisoners were aware of what was happening tonight. That's why they'd known to expect me coming out of the tunnel just then. And it was also why they were ready to accept the weapons I passed out.

I handed out swords, knives, axes, and whatever else I

had, sending my new friends back into the fight once I'd done so.

The idea was for the lot of them to just defend themselves while they tried to get out of the theater, not actually win the battle. After all, this was still a gang of twenty-foot-long wolves we were talking about. We wouldn't have lasted fifteen minutes in a raw, head-to-head challenge. However, with these reclaimed weapons and SJ's potions, we at least had a shot of escaping in one piece, especially since we had our own band of Therewolves helping the cause.

Three of SJ's four body-switching portable potions had been put to good use to achieve this outcome. Blue had switched bodies with the grandmother Therewolf that had intended to eat her. Daniel and Jason had shot two more Therewolves and taken their forms.

Now the three of them were in the theater—protecting the escaping prisoners from the seven very confused but angry regular Therewolves. The only thing differentiating Blue, Jason, and Daniel from these actual Therewolves were slight traces of yellow smoke that escaped their nostrils when their breathing got particularly heavy.

In the heated battle, bursts from SJ's other portable potions aided their efforts. Once freed from her own ball and chain, my friend had poured the remaining potions into her pocket and taken to the audience to assist with the fight.

Now she was running back and forth across the theater firing whatever potions she pulled out of her skirt at our furry, malicious opponents. She was really booking it too— bobbing, weaving, rolling underneath Therewolf after Therewolf as she added to the bedlam. Using the rubber band around her wrist, her red portable potions were blasting back attacking Therewolves. Her silver ones froze their limbs, and her green ones released grand splashes of a mucus-looking substance that stuck to the Therewolves' feet and kept them temporarily glued to wherever they'd been standing.

As I ran by her, SJ ducked beneath a super-sized hairy tail that would've otherwise swept her off her feet.

"SJ, heads up!" I shouted and threw over her slingshot.

She turned just in time to snatch it out of midair.

"On your left!" I called as I slid under a pouncing Therewolf.

SJ spun around and fired a silver potion at the monster. Since she was a relatively good distance away, this blast fully encased both of the creature's front legs in ice.

I scaled the struggling Therewolf's back to survey the area from an eagle eye position.

"SJ, we need more cover over by the main exit tunnel!" I shouted. "Those Therewolves are tightening their funnel around it!"

My friend nodded and headed in that direction.

"Robbie," I called to the unarmed boy on my right. "There are more weapons in the props closet! Devon," I directed my new friend, who did have a sword, "cover him!"

They both took off for the wardrobe and set design department while I slid down the tail of the thawing Therewolf and headed toward the next problem area that needed addressing.

After SJ had used my wand in its knife form to free herself from the ball and chain, she'd passed it on. Prior to body switching with the Therewolves, Daniel and Jason were meant to have gotten it to the other prisoners so they could slice through their shackles too. But past that I didn't know where my wand/knife had ended up.

It could've been anywhere in this mess, and until I found it I had to do my best to contribute to the fight with what I had. I'd shoved Blue's hunting knife into my bag with her throwing knives as a backup option, but for the time being I used Daniel's sword.

Reaching my desired target just in time, I used the blade to deflect the claws of a Therewolf closing in on an unarmed female prisoner. Following through, I jabbed the blade into his paw.

The pain the strike inflicted gave my co-captive and me the time we needed to escape. I escorted her to the exit tunnel on the other side of the room.

"Go!" I ordered. "Tell the others who have already made it out to get to the rendezvous point as fast as they can."

She nodded and dashed away. A humongous Therewolf paw suddenly came crashing down and I barely avoided being crushed.

I rolled out of the way then jumped to my feet and slashed Daniel's sword at the Therewolf's lower leg. It cut him pretty deeply. As he stumbled, I made a break for it—maneuvering my way around the edge of the theater.

I saw one of the younger female prisoners, Blaire, trapped on her back. A Therewolf was currently leaning over her. His mouth was open wide, and my eyes popped with panic.

There was an extinguished torch lying on the floor nearby and I kicked it over to her.

"Tent-pole him!" I shouted.

The girl grabbed the torch. Just as the Therewolf was about to swallow her whole she jabbed it vertically into his mouth—propping it ajar and keeping him from biting down. She tried to scramble away, but the Therewolf's thrashing movements made it difficult for her to get up without being punctured by his claws.

"Allan!" I called out to an unarmed boy on my left.

I swung my satchel off my shoulder and tossed him the bag, gesturing to the girl. "Go help, Blaire! Use the knives inside! Don't try to finish him, just get her to the exit before that torch snaps!"

Allan (whom I'd learned had spent three summers with Book's traveling circus as a performing knife thrower) followed my instructions without question.

When he took off I dove to the side to keep from being rammed into the wall by a Therewolf who'd just been thrown against it.

The creature got up and blinked at me, monstrous fangs not two feet from my face. I would've totally gone on offense had it not been for bright blue eyes and the slight poof of yellow smoke that escaped the beast's nose.

"You doing okay, Blue?" I asked.

"You know it," she said as she straightened out to her full, impressive size. "You were right. I am terrified beyond reason, but I am totally doing this! And I'm loving it! Is that weird?"

"No, it's just you!" I turned my head and saw that the pair of Therewolves who'd evidently tossed her this way were coming back.

"When you're done here head to the west side of the theater. Some of the others are getting herded there and they could use the backup," I said.

"You got it, chief," Therewolf Blue growled elatedly as she cantered off.

I watched proudly as she tackled the enemy Therewolves—

plowing them into dozens of chairs that snapped like twigs beneath their combined weight.

My temporary gladness faded when I saw that another prisoner was in serious trouble. The heel of a boy's back foot had gotten slightly affected by the one of SJ's silver potions, and now the ice was preventing him from getting free. Out of the corner of my eye I saw a distant Therewolf take notice of the same thing and begin to bound in his direction.

There'd have been no time to cut my inmate loose with Daniel's sword by the time I got over to him. So instead I stored the blade in its sheath and ran with all the force I had. A mere moment before the Therewolf reached him, I threw all my body weight at the prisoner and tackled him out of the way—breaking the hold the ice had on his foot and narrowly allowing us to escape the Therewolf's pounce.

The boy and I tumbled to the side. Then I popped back up and went after the monster. His back was to me now, and rather than wait for him to turn around I went straight for him. When I was close enough, I jumped onto a still upright chair without breaking stride and leapt onto the Therewolf's thigh.

I climbed quicker than he could react and soon found myself clutching onto the hairs on his back. He bucked furiously to toss me off, but I held on. When I reached the spot directly behind his neck, I drew Daniel's sword and made to take my shot. But, just as I was about to, a large rock struck the side of my head.

The blow made me lose my grip and I was thrown off the Therewolf. In the next instant, right before I was meant to hit the ground, another beast happened to whirl his rear end in my direction. His tail slammed into me like a massive battering ram.

The assault sent me flying backwards several dozen yards into one of the surrounding tunnels. I crashed onto the stone floor—wind completely knocked out of me, body reverberating with pain.

Ow.

My vision danced furiously as I tried to refocus. But this proved to be a difficult task. I'd been hit hard.

Somehow I'd managed to hang on to Daniel's sword through the ordeal, so I used it as a boost to help me up. I was not sure if it was the shock of being tossed across the room like a rag doll, or the general calamity of the atmosphere, but my head was reeling. Everything felt off-balance and very hot too.

Wait. Off-balance was to be expected after that much head trauma, but *hot*?

Oh no.

Not now.

It was happening again. Like earlier in the semester with those flowers on my balcony and that fountain in Adelaide, my hands were heating up for no foreseen reason.

Darn it, this is so not the time!

I tried to shake off the feelings, but it was no use. Worse still, this burning episode was stronger than the ones I'd experienced before. The heat and pain may have been most potent in my hands like usual, however this time the feelings were not isolated to them. The searing pumped powerfully through my arms, consuming my face and diaphragm too.

I dropped Daniel's sword and hunched over, clutching the rock on the cavern wall to steady myself—my head bent down as if I was going to throw up.

Just breathe, Crisa. It'll pass. Just breathe.

The heat and pain only continued to escalate, though. And while I was squinting to deal with the pain, I realized that my hands had randomly begun to glow. Like *really* glow. They were emanating a bright golden light that pulsed in tune with the way the awful, fiery sensation surged through my body.

Bracing myself, I grasped the rock wall harder.

Come on, focus. Just pull yourself together and go crush some Therewolves. Come on!

"Hey, you!"

I nearly jumped out of my skin and whirled around to see Blue standing in front of me. Not Therewolf Blue, whom I'd just seen out in the theater kicking butt and not taking names. No, this was Blue's normal, human body with the soul of a Therewolf temporarily inside it thanks to SJ's portable potion.

I reacted immediately. I punched her in the gut with one hand while the other circled around and jabbed forward—throttling her by the neck as my leg swept hers out from under her.

Not Blue slammed into the ground.

I kicked Daniel's sword back into my hands. "You'd better stay down," I said as I pointed the blade at her. "Just because you're in my friend's body and I can't damage you permanently doesn't mean there aren't still plenty of ways for me to hurt you without doing so."

Not Blue coughed and sat up slowly—raising her hands in surrender. "I'm not trying to attack you; I'm on your side."

"Yeah, okay," I scoffed as I edged away from her toward the tunnel's exit.

"No, really!" Not Blue insisted. "Whatever that stuff was that you used to switch our bodies, it cancelled out the spell!"

I stopped short. "What spell?"

"We Therewolves are not evil. That son of a stickmole, Gustaf Pepperjack, got tired of always being an understudy in our troupe, so he made a deal with some antagonists and cast an enchantment on us nearly two decades ago. We've been trapped by his will ever since."

"I don't buy it," I responded. "You all were going to eat us after the fourth act of your stupid show!"

"We had no control over that!" Not Blue exclaimed. "Gustaf's power keeps us from going against his wishes. Please, you have to believe me."

I bit my lip, unsure of whether or not I should. She seemed genuine, but then again she was looking at me through the eyes of one of my closest friends. I clenched my fist and thought quickly. However, my first thought had nothing to do with the current situation at all. It was:

Hey, my hands stopped burning!

I unclenched my fingers and gazed at my palms. The glowing was gone, as were the accompanying pains that had been imploding my body.

Just for a beat, I was relieved. That had been a bad episode, and a weird one too. I fully intended to look into the whole "glowing" thing further when there wasn't a giant wolf battle going on. But for the meantime a scream from the theater shocked me back to the present. I had to make a choice in regards to Not Blue's proposed dilemma.

"Look, I have to get back in there. So, for the sake of argument . . . let's say I believe you. What exactly do you want from me?" I asked.

"You have to help us," Not Blue replied earnestly. "Some of the prisoners are competent fighters. One of my brethren could get hurt or killed out there. You're the perfect example.

If I hadn't thrown that rock at you, you'd have seriously hurt my friend Bernerd, or worse!"

"Wait, that was you?" I instinctively touched the injured spot on my head. "You could have killed me!"

"Yes, and I'm sorry. But like I said, *you* could have killed *him*! And anyways it got your attention, which me and my colleagues trapped in your other friends' bodies have been trying to do since this whole fight began so that we could *tell you* all of this."

"Well, couldn't you have found a way to do that, which didn't involve knocking a few dozen IQ points out of my head?" I snapped.

The sound of chaos coming from the theater beckoned for my return. I glanced down the tunnel, then back at Not Blue. I had the feeling that if any of my friends were here, they would tell me not to believe her. But as foolish as it may have seemed, I trusted my instincts. And I willed the courage to make a different call.

"Pepperjack," I said, "where is he and how do we stop him?"

"He's the Therewolf with the golden collar," Not Blue told me as we ran toward the tunnel's opening. She pointed to the center of the theater. "Right there; look!"

I followed the direction of her gesture. Sure enough, I saw a Therewolf with a golden collar. He was a bit bigger than the others, and the collar he wore had a bright green gemstone on the top that flashed angrily like his eyes.

"I've learned a lot of things living in the Forbidden Forest," Not Blue continued. "And one of those things is that powerful magic needs a conductor. Like Fairy Godmothers and their wands, Gustaf's ring is his conductor. Now that I'm free of his control I can see that. It explains why he's always wearing it, and why it morphs into that collar with the giant power crystal whenever he transforms. The way I figure—destroy it, you destroy the spell."

I huffed, a bit exasperated. "If that's true then why didn't you just do that when you were free of his control?"

Not Blue rolled her eyes. "Hello, I'm an actor not a fighter. Therewolves are trained in the arts, not combat. None of us would last two minutes against Gustaf like this, and we certainly couldn't rely on anyone else to get the job done, like that dainty friend of yours for instance. As if we could entrust our protection to a princess. They're glorified damsels in distress."

I felt my fists tighten as I swallowed the bitterness of the insult, and the reminder of my archetype's unsavory stereotype.

"First off, that 'dainty friend' of mine is a lot more than people give her credit for," I stated firmly. "In case you haven't noticed, if it wasn't for her the others would have no chance out there right now. And second, if you want my help, watch what you say about princesses. Because they can be a lot more than you think, and technically I'm one too."

Not Blue raised an eyebrow. "Really? You, a princess? That's . . . surprising."

"Yeah," I said as I re-drew Daniel's sword. "I get that a lot."

I bolted back into the theater—no plan fully formed, but my brain racing like a horse on a caffeine high.

Okay, to destroy the collar I have to find a way onto Pepperjack's back. To do that I need a distraction and a boost.

A Therewolf with yellow smoke purging from his nose passed by just then and I called after him. "Hey!"

He halted in his tracks. "What?"

The Therewolf turned around and I could tell by the color of his eyes and the sound of his voice that it was Jason.

"Jason, I need a ride. Now, please!"

Therewolf Jason snorted indignantly. "Crisa, I've got my own fights to worry about. Whatever you need doing, do it yourself."

Jason bounded off and my brow furrowed in annoyance. Ugh, he'd been intolerable these last couple of weeks.

That plan shut down, I tried to come up with a second option.

Come on, universe; give me something.

In that beat, I spotted it. My wand (still in knife form) was about forty yards away lying amidst a ton of strewn chairs and an unfolding Therewolf fight.

Brilliant!

Ludicrous ideas started popping in my head left and right and I rapidly began to set them, and my feet, into motion. Instead of going after my wand, I headed to where the latest explosions were coming from. SJ was by the stage area driving back her own Therewolf problem. As I approached I hoped she was in a good enough mood to humor me.

She wasn't.

"I need to borrow a red portable potion," I told her when she'd finished gooping the Therewolf at hand with a jade orb.

"No way," she replied.

"SJ, just give me one, please!"

Another Therewolf came into view and charged us.

"Crisa, absolutely not," SJ hissed as she pulled a red orb from her pocket and readied her slingshot. "I cannot afford to spare any so long as we are in this situation. How else am I supposed to stop these things from swallowing us?"

"Oh, for crying out loud." I stored Daniel's sword in its sheath.

The impending Therewolf was ten feet away. I hastily grabbed one of the chairs, leapt in front of SJ before she could fire her potion, and swung the chair forcefully just as the enormous creature came within arm's length.

It smacked him powerfully across the face, causing him to stumble off to the side. Before he could regain his senses I slammed the chair down onto his lowered forehead. Then I thrust it back across his face with just as much power and again directly between his eyes—fully knocking him unconscious.

He'd be all right, maybe a headache when he woke up. But at least this way he wouldn't try to eat anybody else before I could shut down Pepperjack's collar.

"There," I said, throwing down the chair and pivoting to readdress SJ. "I saved you one. Now gimme."

SJ's eyes were big with surprise, but she relinquished the potion I sought nonetheless.

"Much obliged," I said as I stuffed it into my pocket. "Keep up the good work."

With that, I raced toward my wand. The two Therewolves who'd been battling one another were still there—their cumulative eight gigantic paws dancing violently around the area. I threw myself inside their trample zone with little to no regard for personal safety.

"Knight, what are you doing?" one of the Therewolves growled. "Get out of the way!"

I ducked and swerved to keep from getting crushed by Therewolf Daniel and his opponent.

"In a second!" I yelled as I dove under the regular Therewolf's front paw.

With a handspring of my bodyweight I cartwheeled over an additional furry foot and landed right next to my wand with the accuracy of a gymnast. Blue would've been proud. Therewolf Daniel, on the other hand, was not impressed. Perhaps it had been my landing . . . or perhaps it was the fact that I was now directly in front of the regular Therewolf's fangs.

The creature opened his colossal jaws, readying himself to chomp down. Sadly for him, I dove out of the way before he had the chance. After I summersaulted underneath his snout I was given a perfectly clear view of Therewolf Daniel head-butting him so hard that he skidded off to the side. The Therewolf did not get up again, evidently having been bashed into unconsciousness.

I returned to my previous spot and picked up my weapon, transforming it back from a knife to its original state and giving it a twirl between my fingers. Therewolf Daniel's shadow blanketed over me. Just for fun I turned around, reached up, and gave him a good, patronizing pat on the nose. "Aw, there's a good Daniel," I cooed.

He growled warningly. "You want to lose that hand?"

"Relax, scruffy. I was just kidding."

"Yeah, well, while you're kidding, I'm working. Now get out of here. I'm gonna make sure that Therewolf doesn't wake up again."

Therewolf Daniel moved to attack the downed Therewolf, but I jumped in front of him. "No, don't!"

"Knight, move," he snarled.

"Wait, listen!" I persisted. "I know it sounds crazy, but they're not evil. They're under a spell. We can't kill them; it wouldn't be right."

"You've completely lost it! Knight, if I leave that thing alone, what happens if it gets back up and tries to eat you and I'm not around to help?"

"What'll happen is I'll be just fine because your help is not needed," I replied. "I had everything under control even without you and your giant head intervening."

"Really? Well, next time an oversized monster is going to snack you down I guess I'll just let you fend for yourself and let him have at it!"

"Maybe you should!" I snapped.

"Maybe I will!" he snapped back. Therewolf Daniel snorted a puff of yellow smoke at me furiously then bounded away toward a new, less me-based opponent.

I stomped the ground in frustration before swiftly moving on with my search for Pepperjack. I easily spotted him and his gaudy, golden collar chasing a group of prisoners about fifty feet away.

The area between us was abundant with the theater's tipped over chairs, but a few were still upright. I calculated the trajectory of one in regards to its distance between the beastly director and me.

Yup, that should work. Assuming SJ's potion blast sizes stay consistent with what I've seen so far, and my timing and thrust are correct, it should totally work.

I clutched my wand tightly.

Boomerang.

My wand morphed into the desired metallic weapon. With the utmost precision I hurled it across the theater. My aim was perfect. The boomerang smacked Pepperjack right on his snout before ricocheting back to my hand to be returned to its original state.

Pepperjack jolted his head in my direction. His focus narrowed decisively and he began sprinting toward me. I took a deep breath and sprinted toward him as well.

Pepperjack and I were on a collision course for one another, but I had no intension of ever reaching such a suicidal point of impact. My destination was an upright chair that stood between us. I had gauged that we'd simultaneously reach it just before plowing into each other. As I ran I grabbed SJ's red portable potion from my pocket.

Five seconds.

I brought the potion up to my wrist and pulled back on the rubber band around it.

Three seconds.

Without breaking stride, I fired the orb at spot directly below the chair.

One second.

I leapt onto the seat just as the potion exploded beneath it. Pepperjack's fangs were barely three yards from my face, and he rapidly closed the distance just as the eruption unfolded the way I'd projected.

The blast launched the chair into the air with me still on board. I soared with the burst of force instead of fighting it. My body hurled upwards and forwards—flawlessly throwing me into a flip over Pepperjack's head.

Spear.

My wand transformed as I was in mid-flip. I twisted my body around so that I landed on the back of Pepperjack's neck. Then I grabbed hold of his collar with my free hand and with one strong strike plunged the point of my spear into the gemstone of his accessory.

The blade of my staff pierced the crystal. Cracks spread across the stone; chunks imploding within themselves like a shattered ice rink. I barely had time to jump off Pepperjack before a torrent of powerful magic exploded from the jewel's center and shot through the theater.

Everyone in the room—humans and Therewolves alike—shielded their eyes as the force made the entire space pulsate. I, however, had no time for such a luxury. I transformed my wand back to normal while I dove to the ground and rolled away to avoid being crushed by Pepperjack's flailing paws.

He howled as the potent magic exuded from his collar. It blasted in all directions and seeped into the rocky walls, the strewn chairs, the curtains, everything and anything. The whole theater shook violently from the power of the eruption. Between that and the blinding light, I could barely keep my balance. Then Pepperjack's giant tail abruptly swatted me with great force.

In a very unpleasant instance of déjà vu, I was flung across the room before coming to rest on a patch of cave floor.

In all honesty I might have blacked out for a second. By the time I opened my eyes, the shaking and magical lightshow had subsided. When I looked up I found another Therewolf bearing down on me.

I felt like a dead sparrow that'd just hit a window, so I did not react as quickly as I should have. Luckily, I didn't need to. The green shade of the Therewolf's eyes suddenly changed to a deep brown. He remained in his beastly form, but all vicious intent vanished from his expression. He withdrew his fangs and began blinking like he'd just been staring into the sun.

Everything in the theater was silent apart from the hoarse voice of the Therewolf standing over me, which echoed across the chamber for everyone to hear.

"We're free," the Therewolf cried in disbelief.

Not Blue ran up to the Therewolf and touched him on his face. "Sydney, it's me, Merilyn. This girl broke the spell! Shattering Gustaf's collar released us from his hold!"

The Therewolf standing above me (who apparently was Sydney) looked around at his reoriented comrades before meeting my gaze again. "You saved us," he said. "We tried to kill you and your friends, and you saved us."

I shrugged despite the ache in my shoulders. "No harm, no foul. Besides, it wasn't your fault. It was his." I pointed at a very flustered Pepperjack Therewolf who was stumbling about in the center of the theater, not quite over the traumatizing expulsion of magic.

Sydney glared at his former director and magical overlord. "You," he growled. "You made us your slaves for eighteen years!"

Pepperjack's expression filled with alarm. All the other Therewolves started to encircle him slowly and threateningly. That is, until the ceiling began to collapse.

The magical explosion had severely shaken the tunnel system. The whole thing had been structurally weakened and was now on the verge of crumbling around us. The first chunk of rock came crashing down, barely missing one of the Therewolves. A dozen more pieces fell a half second later and panic surged through the room.

"Everybody out!" Sydney hollered.

The Therewolves and two dozen or so remaining prisoners began to make a break for the exit. Unfortunately—because the day hadn't already been challenging enough—our escape was suddenly hindered by magical obstacles.

The objects touched by the explosion from Pepperjack's collar had absorbed some of its malevolent power. This was living proof that Emma had been right in her assertion that magic couldn't be destroyed; it could only change forms or change hands. Now that I'd destroyed the cursed gem, the vicious, bloodthirsty magic of the broken enchantment had gone wild and infected a slew of inanimate objects in the vicinity.

The chairs in the theater began to levitate and chase people. The torn down stage curtains came to life like enormous, velvet snakes, wrapping themselves around the Therewolves. Even the scattered programs from the production swatted at anything that moved.

Remarkably, the curse-free Therewolves and the remaining exhausted prisoners did not abandon each other. Understanding that they were now on the same side, they fought the magical hindrances to the exit together. And when they made it, the Therewolves scooped the humans onto their backs and carried them through the tunnels that led outside.

Everything seemed like it was going to be okay until a Therewolf suddenly jumped in my path. "Your friend's in trouble!" she said.

"What are you talking about?" I asked as I morphed my wand into a shield to block an oncoming chair.

The Therewolf transformed into Blue, then back into a Therewolf, then into Blue again.

"It's me, Merilyn; the Therewolf that's been in your friend's body," she responded. "I saw her charge through one of the tunnels a minute ago and when I was on my way up to the surface *this* started happening! My friends are still fully trapped in those boys' bodies, so it's not the potion that's malfunctioning. Something's happened to her."

"Which tunnel?" I asked as I thrust back the assailing chair once more.

"The one that leads to the cells in the eastern tunnel system. Come on, I'll go with you."

Merilyn started to take off, but she abruptly halted when she morphed into her full Therewolf size again. This transformation only lasted for a second. She immediately shrank back into Blue's body.

Once she did, she moved toward the designated tunnel, but I put my hand up to block her. "No. Like this you could get hurt. Get out with the others. I'll find her."

Merilyn seemed a bit reluctant, but she agreed and took off for the exit tunnel—continuing to morph between her two forms as she went.

I ducked to elude another flying chair and then jumped aside to dodge a chunk of falling ceiling. The whole place was coming down, we were running out of time, and one of my best friends was missing. Blue was lost somewhere in the tunnels, possibly hurt . . .

I transformed my shield back into a wand as worrying thoughts began to fill my head. What if there had been a cave in or something? What if she was trapped in there?

I needed a fully functioning Therewolf, but they were all either engrossed in their own efforts to escape, or had already made it out.

Just then I spotted a Therewolf I recognized. The giant version of Jason charged by me—yellow smoke billowing from his breath like a chimney.

He either didn't see me or wasn't planning to stop if he did. Before he was out of my reach completely I shoved my wand into my boot, grabbed the back of his tail, and—holding on—began to skid along the floor in his wake.

"Jason!" I shouted as I was dragged across the theater. "Jason, stop!"

Only then did he notice me clinging to him and tersely put the brakes on. I tumbled forward from the suddenness of the stop.

"Trying not to die here, Crisa," he snarled as I crashed against the stone floor beside him. "What do you want?"

I jumped up and dashed around to face him. "It's Blue. She got caught in one of tunnels. I think she's in trouble."

"I missed the part where that was my problem."

Oh, that is it!

He started to move, but I leapt in his way and stared at him dead on. "Jason, it's Blue!"

He rolled his eyes and tried to move again, but I refused to back down. "Look, I get it. That watering can won't let you be selfless. But, Jason, that's only one part of you; so suck it up cuz right now I need the rest!"

"This is all I can be, Crisa," he growled. "The rest of me is gone."

"Seriously? If that were true then you would've just booked it out of here the second you transformed into a Therewolf. But you didn't; you stayed and stuck with our plan to help the other prisoners escape through all of it. You may not be selfless anymore, but you're still loyal and determined and a good friend. Darn it, Jason, you're still you! So for crying out loud get a hold of yourself, and let's go get Blue!"

Jason's shield-sized eyes locked with mine. The hold of his glare was so intense that for a moment it seemed like the scrambled, jumbled, pandemonium around us had slowed down. Until he bent his head down to my level, that is.

"Get on," he said.

Now that's what I'm talking about!

I hopped onto the back of his neck and the two of us made a break for the tunnel where Blue had disappeared.

Our way there was treacherous in itself. Therewolf Jason had to evade squashing members of the stampeding crowd. I transformed my wand into a shield to keep from being bludgeoned by the possessed objects flying about. And we both had to avoid being taken down by rocks falling from the disintegrating rooftop.

Eventually we dove into the desired tunnel and Jason was able to pick up speed.

The noisy panic from the theater was drowned out by his panting and pounding heartbeat as we raced deeper beneath the earth. The tunnels were much more dimly lit here, as the torches were spaced farther and farther apart from one another. Even so, I did not need the extra light to see we didn't have long. Every rock and pebble that made up the walls was shaking, threatening to completely collapse within a matter of minutes.

After a few more seconds Jason came to an abrupt stop when we reached a dead end. Only this was not a natural stopping point; it was a collapsed area of the tunnel. And there, amidst the fallen debris, was Blue. I couldn't see much of her, but she was trapped beneath the pile of rocks. Her body kept shape-shifting, trying to break free by means of returning to Therewolf form. But the stones crushing her consistently got in the way. She was only able to hold the Therewolf transformation for a few seconds before the rocks' weight inevitably overpowered her will and caused her to return to human form. On the last occurrence of the phenomenon she stayed human—too drained to change any further.

I hopped off Jason and he began to dig at the rocks.

I wanted to help, but knew I would've just gotten in the way. The massive claws on his massive paws tore through the rock pile in no time—allowing our crumpled friend to tumble out.

"Blue!" I raced to her side and tried to help her up, but she was slipping into unconsciousness fast.

"There were people, other prisoners, in their cells," she muttered under her fading breath. "SJ and I . . . we got them out before the cave in."

"Get her on," Jason said as he lowered his head.

I quickly draped Blue over the back of his neck. However, just before she was fully out cold she raised her head ever so slightly.

"Crisa . . . I . . . I don't know if SJ made it out. She might not be . . ."

Blue blacked out, but her unfinished comment sent another wave of panic up my spine.

"Crisa, come on. We gotta go," Jason ordered, waiting for me to hop on his back.

"No way," I said. "You heard her. SJ might still be down there."

"Well, I gotta get Blue out of here."

"I know. So go, both of you. I know my way from here. It's the same route we've been taking for the past two weeks from our cells to wardrobe and set design. I'll check to make sure SJ's not there then I'll make a break for the exit."

Jason nodded. "You sure?"

"I'm sure. She's my best friend, and there's no way I'm leaving without her."

I made my way through the tunnel Jason had just cleared while he turned on his heels and headed back to the theater with Blue.

Relying on my own two feet proved a lot less convenient than it had been counting on his. I was running as fast as I could, but the ground I was covering was not nearly enough. I barely made it to the cells without being buried.

By the time I arrived they were deserted anyways, so that was good. But I only had a moment to verify this because the whole area caved in a second after I checked.

Bolting in the other direction, I headed for the wardrobe and set design department. When I arrived I maneuvered through the maze of unused set fronts and costume racks searching for SJ. Suddenly a hand grabbed me and pulled me behind a rack beneath a fake storefront.

"SJ!"

"Not so loud, you idiot," she whispered.

"Why?"

A giant, furry paw swatted away our hiding place—revealing a very angry Therewolf wearing the remains of a shattered golden collar.

Pepperjack was not pleased. Being at the receiving end of his grudge and intimidating teeth, I couldn't say I was that thrilled either. He snarled and pounced. SJ and I dove underneath him.

He plowed into a whole mess of dress racks as we ran in the other direction. After a few yards, SJ spun around and fired a silver portable potion that encased his entire face in ice. I paused for a second to behold the precision of her strike, but SJ grabbed me by the arm and yanked me the other way. "Now is our chance!"

"What about your potions?" I asked her as we ran. "That

one's not gonna hold him alone. You need to fire a few more!"

"I only have one left," she said as she held up a single scarlet orb. "Not enough to hinder him for long."

SJ and I pushed past scattered costumes and tables with abandoned set design materials. The tunnel that rerouted to the theater had already collapsed, so we were headed for the tunnel that led below backstage. But then I realized something.

With the lifts shut down, the only way out of the below-stage area was via that hose I'd left dangling through the trapdoor. There would be no time for one, let alone both of us to fully climb it before Pepperjack caught up with us. He was already starting to get up and shake free of his icy head case.

"SJ, give me that potion!" I said.

She tossed it over to me without breaking stride. "Crisa, do not do anything stupid!"

"No promises!" I called back.

I slowed down—allowing SJ to pass ahead of me into the tunnel. Right as she did, I rapidly spun back around and ran in the other direction. By the time she discovered what I was doing and skidded to a halt, it was too late for her to stop me.

"Go for the exit!" I yelled. "I'll buy you time!"

"Crisa, do not even think about—"

I fired the potion at the top of the tunnel's entrance with my rubber band. The blast (amplified by the quaking) caused that portion of the ceiling to collapse. The avalanche of rock created a large barrier, which completely blocked off access to the tunnel SJ was now safely inside of. Meanwhile I was left exposed, but by choice.

From observing Jason, I'd realized that a Therewolf could easily sweep away a sizeable barrier in less than fifteen seconds. That was barely enough time for one person to scale half that hose. So I'd elected to let that be SJ's route to freedom. I would stay out here, drawing Pepperjack away from the tunnel to pursue what seemed like a simpler target. Me.

Pepperjack was still stuck in the ice. I grabbed a can of familiar-looking spray paint from a table of set design equipment then brought my fingers to my lips and whistled. Despite the ice, Pepperjack heard me and looked in my direction.

"Hey, fluffy!" I called. "Catch me if you can!"

Pepperjack banged his head against the wall violently, causing cracks to spread across his frozen face prison. He would soon be free to chase after me, which meant I had to book it, fast. Without further delay I zipped inside the tunnel I'd just come out of a minute ago.

Thirty seconds later I heard a loud howl echo in the remnants of chamber behind me.

Okay, I guess that's my cue.

I grabbed two blazing torches off the wall and set them on the floor. From there I held up the can of spray paint I'd nabbed. It was the same brand of paint that Jason had accidentally sprayed on me, which caused me to get briefly set on fire during that special effects rehearsal.

"Caution: Highly Flammable" read its bright orange label.

Yeah, I'm aware, I thought as I sprayed the paint onto the blaze.

Just as I'd been hoping, the fumes instantly responded to the torches' flames by exploding them in size. After a few moments they grew into a great wall of fire that burned like a flamboyant barricade.

Pepperjack rounded the corner and sped toward me. However, he came to an abrupt halt when he reached the immense fiery obstruction. He glared at me bitterly through the screen of orange and red—unable to pass through without being barbequed.

My plan had worked; he was stuck. Having confirmed this, I turned and continued my dash down the corridor.

I made it a solid hundred yards before I felt a disturbance. This had nothing to do with the rumblings of the cavern. No, these jolts felt quite different. They seemed to be emanating solely from behind me.

Reluctantly I spun around. Through the flames I could see Pepperjack ramming his body into the ceiling just before the fire wall. Two more impacts later and that part of the roof gave way completely. Earth and stone poured from the spot—blocking Pepperjack from view.

I wasn't sure why he'd caved in the area at first. But then the pile of rubble started to be scraped away from the other side.

Oh no . . .

The fallen rock had extinguished the flames and now Pepperjack only needed to dig through the mound to have an unblocked access to the tunnel and to me.

Move girl, move!

I drew my wand and sprinted with everything I had. Pepperjack howled and I glanced back to discover he'd broken through and was now in full pursuit.

Chunks of the cavern fell all around me. Alas, while weaving around them slowed my speed, they did nothing to hinder Pepperjack's. He plowed through everything in his relentless chase—closing the distance between us more rapidly than I'd hoped.

At that point I was not far from rounding the corner that led back into the theater. But Pepperjack reached me before I reached it.

Spear.

My wand transformed, but not fast enough for me to make any kind of strike. Pepperjack stretched out his paw and swatted. I was thrown against the cavern wall and fell to the ground, forcing myself to roll to avoid the paw that I instinctually knew was coming.

Pepperjack's paw crushed the spot where I'd landed. Then he swung it back around and I spun to thrust my staff upwards, keeping his giant claws from skewering my face.

"You little twit," he growled, pressing down harder and bringing his teeth closer to my face. "You ruined everything!"

I continued to push up with all the force I had, desperately trying to keep his sharp nails from digging into my head. I couldn't keep this up for much longer. My strength was about to give way.

That, however, was when the crazy escalated to a whole new level.

Out of nowhere a large blast of horizontally moving rock shot toward Pepperjack and threw him off me. At least I thought it had been a blast of rock. I sat up to learn it was actually a monster comprised entirely of stone.

It began grappling with Pepperjack. The peculiarity threw me for a loop, but I decided to just take the lucky break and get out while I had the chance. With my track record, the two of them probably weren't far from teaming up.

I could see it now—the rock monster would pound me

to a pulp then Pepperjack would finish the job by eating me up like ground beef.

Blech. Not a nice image.

Gasping for breath, I made it back to the theater. It was completely empty now, aside from the magically altered objects, which were still zipping about every which way.

Oh, duh. That had to be where the rock monster came from. The magic from Pepperjack's collar had seeped into so many things in the theater. It must've affected the very rocks of the cave, forming that monster as a result.

I bobbed and weaved my way across the abandoned room. But it was a tough endeavor. Now that I was the only living thing left in the area, I was attracting way more rogue flying chairs and pamphlets than before. Worse still, I'd barely made it a quarter of the way when one of the possessed stage curtains projected toward me and wrapped itself around my right leg like a squid.

It pulled me off my feet and dragged me across the theater. The sensation was as abrupt as it was terrifying— akin to what children must've imagined it felt like to have monsters reach out from under their mattresses and drag them to a netherworld beneath the bed frame.

As I was pulled along the floor I noticed that the stage had also been affected by Pepperjack's dark magic. The entire thing had morphed into some kind of giant living mouth, pieces of plywood forming splintered teeth. They were chomping down like an eager garbage disposal as the curtain yanked me closer to their death sentence.

I thought things couldn't get any more difficult. But then the rock monster came back. He stomped out of the tunnel with purpose. When he saw me he began marching in my direction.

Knife.

I tried to cut through the serpentine curtain with my blade, but with the way it was yanking me I couldn't get the right angle on it. By the time I did, it was too late. The stone monster had arrived.

He bore down on me with his massive frame and I was mortified to realize there was nothing I could do to fight him. No shape of my wand, no amount of gumption or strength was going to be enough to stop him.

The monster grabbed me—ripping me out of the curtain's clutches and into his own. He raised me up to his boulder-sized face and his enormous golden, glowing eyes.

I desperately tried to squirm free. But, well . . .

Have you ever tried to find a weak spot in a monster made entirely of rock? Let me tell you, weak spots are definitely not a thing.

Gravel shed from him like sweat as he stared at me. I cringed and braced myself for what was about to happen. Eaten, crushed, beaten to the ground like a spider—whatever my imminent fate, I was sure it was not going to be favorable.

But then, in a reversal of the scene moments ago, a Therewolf suddenly plowed into the stone monster, causing it to drop me to the floor.

Why would Pepperjack be helping me? I wondered as I clambered to my feet.

The rock creature temporarily downed, the Therewolf spun around to face me. It wasn't wearing Pepperjack's collar and had familiar gray eyes.

"SJ?"

"Come on!" SJ growled as she bounded over.

I hopped onto the back of her neck and the two of us

charged across the room—crashing through anything that tried to get in our way.

We ducked into the exit tunnel just in time. The cavern ceiling collapsed—burying everything behind us and starting a domino effect that was dead set on taking this last standing tunnel with it.

An avalanche of stone chased us like wildfire. Wand in hand, I clutched tightly onto the back of SJ's neck. She increased her speed as much as she could.

Several heart-racing beats later, we shot out of the tunnel. SJ crashed into the forest floor, narrowly making it out before everything that was once the Therewolves' elaborate, underground domain imploded.

I tumbled off her as the dust settled. My heart felt so high up in my throat that it might as well have been roommates with my uvula.

When both SJ and I had caught our breaths, we returned to our feet. I looked back at the wreckage. All that remained was a large crater. At its center was a single tree—the one whose roots had clung down from the middle of the theater roof.

"I thought you were all out of potions," I said as I surveyed the area. "You said that red one you gave me was your last one."

SJ cracked her neck and shook the dirt from her fur. "After I escaped through the trapdoor I discovered there were still a few left behind on the stage floor. They must have fallen out when I poured the contents of that bowl into my pocket. I almost did not reach them because of those magical theater obstacles, but in the end I was successful in scooping them up. And when I reached the surface with the other prisoners and Therewolves, I discovered one of the potions was the fourth yellow one I had made—hence the four legs and giant teeth."

"Right. Lucky for me, I guess . . ." I responded.

A few wordless beats passed then, which I was actually grateful for. Everything was still for the first time in a long time. And despite the dreary darkness that blanketed the Forbidden Forest's nocturnal state, as SJ and I breathed in the fresh air and accompanying freedom I felt more at ease than I had in weeks, inspiring me to try and clear the air between us.

After what we'd just been through, I had obtained nothing if not some serious perspective on what really mattered. One such example was my friendship with SJ. While I knew it was far from being mended, I didn't want it to continue rotting away. I may not have been able to take back what I'd said, or change the way I felt about certain things, but I could try and make her understand my deep remorse.

With a sigh I kicked at the dirt and turned to her.

"I can't believe you came back for me," I said. "I thought between you already hating my guts and that watering can's effects, you'd have left me there to fend for myself. That's what I deserved anyways . . . after not trusting you."

SJ didn't look at me. She kept her giant eyes focused straight ahead, again allowing a long pause to hang in the space that separated us. Eventually she took a deep breath and exhaled a steady stream of yellow smoke through her nostrils.

"I would be lying if I said there was not a moment when I considered it," she said slowly. "But however mad I am at you, Crisa, or however unkind that spell has made me, when you sacrificed yourself so I could get away I realized none of that mattered. I was still me, and therefore I could not leave you behind. In spite of everything—your stupidity, your selfishness, your lack of rationale—you remain my best friend, and I care about you. So whether I like it or not, or whether you deserve it or not, I will always come back to help you. Even if you do not want me to *or* trust me enough to do so."

I tried to muster something to say that would convey even a portion of what I wanted to tell her. "SJ," I began. "It's not that . . . I mean, I just . . ."

"Save it, Crisa," she interrupted. "Do not say anything that you think you have to in order to make me feel better. I do not want to hear it."

SJ turned on her huge heels and began to walk away. I watched her go, leaving epic paw prints in the earth as she moved through the clearing.

"Aren't you going to at least tell me to thank you later?" I called after her. This was something she always said to me after doing me a favor or helping me get out of some mischief. The good-natured, slightly sassy comment had been a part of our escapades, and our relationship, since the very beginning.

SJ stopped but didn't glance back. I clenched my fists as silence roared. The distance that had drifted between us felt colder than the sharp wind blowing through the trees.

"Is there a point?" she finally asked, still facing away from me. "You never do. And while much has changed since we began this journey, can you honestly say that *you* have?"

I bit my lip as I seriously thought on the question. In doing so I inadvertently thought about the Author and my reasons for remaining so ardently, adamantly committed to finding her.

Avoiding marrying Chance Darling was a big reason. But more than that, my desire to take control of my life, augment the possibilities for my archetype, and define my fate for myself pulsed through me with such heat and fire it was a wonder my blood didn't boil.

So much of my world (both internally and externally) had become shrouded in mystery and ambiguity. The only thing that still felt right anymore was my deep belief that I had to keep moving forward in defense of these motives.

It may have been dangerous. The caved-in Therewolf camp was a pretty strong indicator of how close I'd come to digging my own grave today. But I was as certain now as I had been the night we'd left Lady Agnue's, and the afternoon we'd escaped Century City, that we were on the right track.

We still had a long way to go if we wanted to meaningfully change our futures. And I still had a long way to go if I wanted to meaningfully change myself. However, as far as this journey was from being over, I couldn't deny that things felt different, that *I* felt different. And that, I supposed, was because of this sense that I was onto something.

It was like the majority of me still felt lost but somehow, even amidst this torrid fog of confusion, I had found a direction. And the more steps I took toward it, the more pieces of myself and my future were coming into focus.

With all this in mind—swirling across the plains of my head and heart like a storm of the soul—I held my ground and told SJ the honest truth for all I knew it to be.

"Maybe I haven't changed," I replied. "But I think I'm starting to."

CHAPTER 11

Shadows & Foreshadows

t figures that some of the best sleep of my life happened *while I was incarcerated.*

I had gone to bed feeling calm. Unfortunately, after two weeks of being absent, my nightmares chose that night to return.

I was subconsciously transported to a bathroom: the public kind. White tiles yellowed by time—at least I hoped it was time—lined the walls and floors. Stalls creaked with age. Three rectangular mirrors with residue dirt and backwash splatter were mounted behind the sinks.

A malicious-looking blonde with black eyes suddenly pushed the main door open. I recognized her instantly. She was the same blonde I'd seen tormenting Natalie Poole in one of my previous nightmares, one I'd had while I was in Adelaide.

When she first entered I froze. But then when she went about her business without paying me any mind, I realized she couldn't see me. I may have had a physical form in this dream, but unlike the ones where I'd been fighting Arian or absorbed into that purple vortex, in this scene I was just an observer, witnessing something from a perspective I was never meant to have.

Once the blonde had completed a perimeter check of the

bathroom, she approached the center mirror and removed something from her pocket. It was a compact mirror with the words "Mark Two" engraved on the outside.

Inside the compact was a sponge, assumedly for dabbing on the powder makeup caked beneath it. However, instead of touching up her perfect yet stone-cold face, the girl used the sponge to apply the powder to her own reflection in the looking glass.

Whatever was inside that compact was evidently not concealer. The powder sparkled when it was wiped across the mirror and the entire glass began to flicker. When the effect dissipated, someone else's face appeared.

Arian.

With the long stint I'd spent in Therewolf captivity, it'd been a while since his presence had daunted me. Seeing his face again made my body shudder.

Can you blame me?

The last time I'd seen him in real life he'd cornered me and nearly slit my throat. And the last time I'd seen the guy in *non*-real life hadn't exactly been a picnic either.

That nightmare of facing off with him had given me the shakes back when I thought it was merely a manifestation of my sleeping consciousness. Now, though, I knew better. My dreams were real. Which meant that what I'd seen unfolding between us was actually going to happen. He and I would be seeing each other again. It was inevitable.

I forced myself to take in his image rather than cower away from it.

His face in the bathroom's looking glass replaced the space where the blonde girl's reflection should've been. It was crystal clear, as if the only thing that separated him from the room was a window.

In that clarity I couldn't help but notice that something was different about him. The area around his eye where I'd hit him back in Century City . . . it wasn't right. There was a mark where I'd knocked him, but it was nowhere near fresh. In fact, it had faded sufficiently to form a fully healed scar on his face as if months, not weeks, had passed since I'd imprinted it there.

"This better be good news, Tara. I'm in the middle of something," Arian's image said.

"I made a lot of headway this week," the girl called Tara responded. "Natalie Poole is strong and resilient, but hopefully with a bit more pressure she will be broken soon."

"Hopefully isn't good enough," Arian barked so starkly I felt a chill. "I sent you there because after all your years of service, I convinced Nadia that there was no one better to manipulate the girl than you. So if you cannot assure me beyond a shadow of a doubt that you will be able to destroy her by the deadline, tell me now. This is far too important to leave to chance."

"I can handle this," Tara insisted. "I've given you and Nadia nearly ten years of my life. I've proven that I can get the job done, haven't I?"

"You proved you could get *that* job done," Arian replied. "Our confidence in your ability to do this one is wavering. I sent some allies to check on you last week, Tara. I didn't tell you because I wanted an unbiased assessment. Do you know what I found out when they returned? They reported that Natalie is nowhere near breaking point. They say that while she is often upset or aloof, her spirit remains intact."

"Arian, I—"

"Have been exaggerating your progress," Arian snapped. "You're lucky your last assignment earned you so much credit. With what's at stake here, if you were anyone else I would have you hanged for the transgression. I mean honestly, Tara, what have you been doing over there, taking in the sights?"

"Arian, I'm doing everything the other antagonists assigned to targets on Earth have," Tara responded ardently. "I've more or less eliminated what family Natalie has, I've made her lose her job, publicly humiliated her over and over again, and I've kept her away from that O.T.L. of hers. She's just . . . I don't know; she's difficult."

"Natalie Poole is not like the others we've destroyed, Tara. If her downfall has the power to open the Eternity Gate, then of course she is going to be difficult. Which means if she is going to be broken, it has to be in a big way."

Arian sighed and shook his head. Then he looked back at Tara with a bit more consideration. "You said you *more or less* eliminated her family?" he clarified.

"Her father's been taken care of, but her mother's still alive. The poison you gave me for her wasn't strong enough. You want me to finish the job myself?"

"No. If eliminating her father didn't break her, losing her mother would probably only temporarily make her more vulnerable. If her spirit really is as strong as they say, then she'll recover eventually. Which means we need something more than that."

Arian thought for a moment. Then an idea flashed across his cruel face. "You said you've been keeping her away from that guy of hers, right?"

"Uh-huh. Ryan Jackson. It's getting harder, though. No matter what I try, I know he still has eyes for her. I suppose that kind of attraction is inevitable with O.T.L.s. But I've never seen any pair of One True Love designees so drawn to each other. I can feel their pull like a magnet. Frankly, I'm not sure how much longer I can distract him away from his true feelings. Maybe I should just kill him now. You did say a key part of this would be taking her true love away from her, right? Perhaps the whole 'me stealing him' thing has just been too subtle a tactic."

"Maybe it has been the wrong tactic entirely," Arian responded pensively.

"So do I have your approval then?" Tara replied. "Can I end Natalie's little soul mate right out?"

"No," Arian said. "Actually, I want you to do the opposite. Instead of keeping them apart, I want you to let them be together."

Tara's eyes practically popped out of her head. "What? Are you crazy?"

"Far from it," Arian replied. "I think we've been going about this the wrong way. Our mission is to destroy the girl and take away the true love between her and this guy before she reaches her twenty-first birthday. But in retrospect, you can't take away that which never existed."

"Meaning?"

Arian rolled his eyes. "*Meaning*, now that I think about the kind of girl we're dealing with, taking Jackson away from Natalie before they've developed a connection is a waste of time because their love hasn't had the chance to fully form."

Tara nodded slowly, beginning to understand. "So you want me to back off?"

"In regards to him, yes. Keep provoking Natalie; keep causing her misery in every other way that you can. But do not interfere anymore with her and Jackson. Given the nature of her destiny, I believe that our best shot is to try and make her vulnerable in every aspect of her life except one—him. That way when we do eventually take him from her, she'll snap because she has nothing else to lean on."

"All right," Tara said. "And how long do you want me to do this for exactly?"

"This is delicate work, Tara. It can't be rushed."

"I get that. But I've been trapped doing Nadia's bidding at this stupid Earth high school for what feels like an eternity. My vernacular has been reduced to acronyms and urban slang. I think I've developed black lung from this city's dense smog. And without magic or murder, I've had to take up Pilates to work out my aggression."

"Pilates?"

"Forget it. Just tell me what you want me to do to Natalie and Ryan and for how long."

"Allow me to spell it out for you," Arian said. "In regards to Natalie specifically, let her mother rot, torment her at school, and make every part of her life a living nightmare so that she is primed to break. As for Natalie and Ryan Jackson, let them find each other and fall in love. Then rip them apart, kill him, and crush her soul on the exact day of her twenty-first birthday."

Tara was so shocked and angry she nearly ripped the bathroom sink off the wall. "Are you kidding me? Arian, you know perfectly well about the time difference between these realms. That may be like two or three months to you, but what exactly do you expect me to do here for another *four years*?"

"Oh come on, Tara, a little age isn't going to kill you," Arian said patronizingly. "We need to give Natalie as much time as possible so that her feelings for the boy can get as strong as possible. Targets are at their most vulnerable when they reach their Key Destiny Intervals. It is a risk to wait, but it is also a risk not to. Continuing to rely on our current tactics to break her like we have with other targets is inefficient and foolish. If Natalie Poole is supposed to open the Eternity Gate then she must be utterly destroyed in one fell, powerful swoop. And that will require time and effort. Understand?"

"Yes," Tara sighed. Then she angled her face away from the mirror. "There goes another chunk of my life pretending to be someone else," she muttered under her breath.

"What was that?" Arian asked.

"Nothing," she replied.

Arian smirked condescendingly. "Look on the bright side, Tara. You pull this off and Nadia will reward you beyond measure when her new order is established. So, buck up. Go and be a good little team player and see what you can do to help our friend Natalie get a date with her One True Love. Need I remind you, clock's ticking."

Tara crossed her arms and began to pout, but a second later her eyes flashed with mischief. "I guess in retrospect I really shouldn't complain about *my* assignment," she said as she cocked her head toward Arian. "I heard it through the grapevine that my old friend Crisanta Knight has been giving you quite a bit of trouble over there."

"Through the what?"

"The grapevine," Tara repeated. "It's an expression in this realm. Now seriously, boss. Is it really as bad as they say?"

Arian furrowed his eyebrows, causing a crinkle to form in the very scar I'd produced. "She's nothing I can't handle," he responded flatly.

"And you accuse me of exaggerating," Tara scoffed. "Don't forget, I've known the girl a long time, Arian. So I'm perfectly aware of how difficult she can be to destroy."

"Maybe for you. But putting aside what happened with our ally in her inner circle, I've taken extra measures to assure her destruction and have everything under control."

"I don't know," Tara chastised. "You've been saying that for months now, Arian. And after what transpired in Big Bear, our fearless leader has to be wondering if she put her faith in the wrong right-hand man. Need I remind you that while I have all the time in the world on my end, it is truly *your* clock that is rapidly tick-tocking away."

A crack abruptly streaked across the face of the mirror they'd been talking through, but neither Arian nor Tara acknowledged it.

"Contact me again in three weeks Book time," Arian scowled, abruptly ending the conversation without addressing Tara's last comment. "We'll need to be in contact more frequently as our appointment with the Eternity Gate approaches. Got it?"

"Yes, sir," Tara said, throwing in a mock salute.

My dream consciousness jumped back as the entire mirror shattered then, but Tara hardly blinked. Arian's image gone, she simply side-stepped to the adjacent mirror to fix her hair, and then calmly exited the restroom.

I drifted forward to get a closer look at the broken mirror. But a soft, distant voice captured my attention.

"Crisa . . ."

I stopped cold. The female voice sounded like it had come from within the mirror. I touched its broken shards but halted when the same voice called out to me from somewhere else.

"Crisa," it called. "Crisa, can you hear me?"

This time it sounded like it came from behind me. I whirled around but there was no one else in the restroom.

The voice spoke again a moment later, but volume-wise I could barely hear it and comprehension-wise I only caught a few words. It sounded like garbled nonsense.

"Crisa, when *sdaikrflorglklfldsk* but she *fgsgljlfsowjansffsg* I don't know *dfsahkfsglsasldfhjb* but you *fdsjlsdjlgfwwppskdf* dragon."

The jumbled words spun around me, seeming to come from everywhere and nowhere all at once.

I gripped the sink in front of the broken mirror and tried to steady myself—concentrating on my own fragmented image until a very different sound pierced the restroom and drowned out the whispers.

A noise like a large snap echoed through the lavatory. It bounced off the tiles and caused the room to tremor. The voice went silent altogether. In the next instant I was pulled out of the dream by a flash of light that sucked me up like apple cider through a straw.

My eyes opened to a giant moon surrounded by the tops of pine trees in the Forbidden Forest.

My racing heart immediately jolted me to a seated position. The darn thing was pounding in my chest like a drum—making me feel like we were under attack again.

I glanced around the area to see if there was any just cause for the unease.

Our camp appeared tranquil. Therewolves and humans alike slept peacefully, and the campfire we'd lit was burning in the center of our group. Nothing was out of the ordinary.

Then I heard it again—the snap from my dream, followed by rustling sounds. They came from the trees to my right.

Grabbing my satchel, I instinctively went in the direction of the noise.

I relied solely on the glow of the moon and my wand to see. They got the job done, but with everything drenched in shadows, the branches of the trees looked like crooked arms, the moss on boulders imitated sleeping monsters, and every root could've easily been mistaken for a kraken's tentacle.

Everything remained quiet, still, and inanimate, though. And after a while I began to wonder if I'd just imagined the rustlings. No sooner did I think this than I heard the sound anew. This time it was accompanied by various crunchings and what sounded like someone sliding down a hill.

I went after the source, making my way quickly but carefully down root-laced slopes between rows and rows of pine trees.

When the ground leveled out, I found myself in a relatively open area. There was no one around to explain the sounds I'd heard, but something else here earned my attention. On the other side of the clearing was a very, very large tree. And at the base of that tree was a very, very large hole.

Overcome with intrigue, I made my way over. When I reached the tree, I stored my wand in my boot and slowly got down on my knees. The round hole was some three feet in diameter. The depth of the hole, however, was a total mystery, as its interior was a silver, sparkling void. Curiously, I inched my hand toward it.

When I dipped my fingers inside the hole I was startled to see them vanish before my eyes. As I continued to extend my hand farther inside, I witnessed every inch disappear within the void as well.

"What in the . . ."

"Hey, get back!"

I ripped my arm out of the hole and backed away from the spot like a kid caught with her fingers in the candy drawer. "Sorry," I said out of reflex. "I just . . ."

But then I realized I couldn't see who I was talking to.

"Look down."

I looked down and saw a White Rabbit perched on his hind legs, arms crossed. He wore a white T-shirt (which seemed redundant) beneath an open black vest. A poofy cottontail poked out above his rear end through a pair of tiny black corduroy pants. On his wrist was a fancy watch with a brown leather band, a rose-gold face, and buttons all around the rim.

I glanced back at the hole then at the rabbit before me. My face brightened as I put two and two together in a total fairytale history nerd moment à la Blue. "No way. Are you—"

"*The* White Rabbit?" interrupted the rabbit. "No. That's my Dad. I am *a* White Rabbit, though. But you can just call me Harry."

"Harry?" I repeated, raising my eyebrows. "*Really?*"

"Hey, I've got it pretty good in comparison to my brother Whitey."

"Fair point," I said as I stuck out my hand. "I'm Crisa. Crisanta Knight, that is."

Harry made a motion to extend his paw, but a pained expression crossed his face as he did so, causing him to wince and withdraw his arm.

"You okay?" I asked.

"What? Oh, it's nothing. I was protecting this hole, keeping watch around the area—you know, checking things out—when I came across, like, ten giant wolves sleeping in a clearing. I got a little freaked out and fell down a hill in the process."

"Oh, sorry about that," I said as I realized *he* had been the noises I'd heard in the trees. "They're with me. And they're Therewolves by the way—completely friendly. I wouldn't worry about them."

"Friendly or not, I don't trust anything with teeth that are bigger than my entire body."

"Not a bad rule to live by."

Harry tried to smile, but winced again. I noticed that he'd been subtly rubbing his arm the whole time we'd been talking.

"Are you sure you're okay?" I asked him.

"I'm fine," he insisted.

But then a drop of blood fell onto the fur of his foot.

"No, you're not. You're hurt." I tore a piece of fabric from the hem of my dress and got down on my knees. "Come here. Let me help you."

Harry rubbed his arm self-consciously. "I really don't think—"

"I said come here, Harry."

He sighed. "Okay, okay. Just please tell me you're certified in this kind of first aid."

"Are you kidding?" I smiled. "I'm a princess. Taking care of injured talking animals is practically in my job description."

Moreover, it was one of the few courses I'd taken at Lady Agnue's that I didn't totally suck at. My Animal First Aid elective had hardly been my favorite subject at school, but I was grateful now that I'd paid attention.

Harry seemed a bit reluctant, but he hopped to my side nonetheless. He sat down next to me and I began to clean the wound on the back of his arm. After a few moments I worked up the nerve to ask him the question that had been buzzing in my head since he'd told me who, or rather *what* he was.

I cleared my throat as I kept tending to his arm. "So, um, Harry. About that hole you're guarding . . . Does it really lead to—"

"The Wonderlands?" Harry interrupted. "Yeah. It does."

I paused. "Hold on. Did you just say Wonder*lands*? As in, plural?"

"Yup. The holes in this realm's outer In and Out Spell create portals to *all* of the Wonderlands—my hometown, which is actually called Wonderland is one example. But there's also Oz, Neverland, Camelot, Cloud Nine, Limbo, and a bunch of others. It just depends what route you take once you get down there."

"Seriously?" I asked. Then something else clicked. "Wait . . . did you say *holes* in the In and Out Spell?"

I thought back to ages ago. On the night of the ball in Adelaide when I'd ditched the dance and found a secret route to the beach I'd met a mermaid named Lonna Langard. She was a sassy, outspoken girl and (as it turned out) one of the princesses of the underwater kingdom of Mer. What was most interesting about her, though, was the information she'd let slip.

"Someone said something to me about that once," I continued slowly. "Can you tell me what it means, *holes* in the In and Out Spell?"

Harry scrunched up his nose. "You don't know?"

"Would I be asking if I did?"

"Fair point to you," he countered.

Harry thumped the ground anxiously with his foot as

he thought on the matter. "Um, okay, look," he eventually said. "You're pretty nice, and you're helping me out, so I guess it's only right that I level with you. But I should warn you—some of this information can be a bit overwhelming. You don't have a weak constitution, do you?"

I huffed in amusement. "No. I don't."

"Alrighty then." Harry twitched his nose a bit, but his ears relaxed. "First off, you do know that Book isn't the only realm with an In and Out Spell protecting its borders, right?"

"Um, no actually," I said, super stunned. "I didn't."

"Well, it isn't. There's a protective barrier around every realm—Wonderland or not. They're what keep our worlds separate. I don't know when exactly they were cast. In the beginning, I guess."

"By the Fairy Godmothers?"

"That's what they'd like us to believe, I suppose. But who knows really. Anyway, whoever's responsible, they did a heck of a job with those spells for them to last this long. But all things, even magic that powerful, wear away over time. And in terms of an In and Out Spell, the more it disintegrates, the more holes—or wormholes if you will—start appearing in its walls. These are essentially tears in time and space, cracks that allow things to slip from one realm to the next."

"How many are there?" I asked. "Holes, I mean."

"There used to be just a handful," Harry explained, "but more have been showing up in the last couple of years. There's enough now to keep me and the other White Rabbits on duty practically twenty-four seven. That's what my kind does, see—we monitor the holes."

"All of them?"

He gave his head a quick shake. "No, just the ones to the Wonderlands. I'm one of the rabbits assigned to Book, so I try to show up wherever holes appear here. It's usually not that hard—a majority of them are concentrated in this forest. Although they do pop up kind of regularly in Century City, Midveil, Clevaunt, and a few other kingdoms too."

"You said you guys only keep track of the holes leading to the Wonderlands," I thought aloud, connecting the dots. "Are there holes that create portals to other lands too?"

Harry shrugged. "A few, like Earth, Ickblat Five, Dreamland. But we're not responsible for those. Mainly because we can't usually get to them. They're really sporadic and only turn up in really inconvenient places like the deep ocean, Alderon, or random caves in the northern mountains. Out of our reach, but out of anyone else's too, so I guess it's fine."

I completed the final knot on Harry's makeshift bandage. "All done," I said.

"Thanks," he said as he admired my handiwork. Then panic streaked his face. "Oh no, what time is it?"

Without warning, a second White Rabbit popped out of the silver hole beside us. This rabbit (I suspected) was the *actual* White Rabbit from the *Alice in Wonderland* stories.

That wasn't me being racist—not all talking White Rabbits look the same to me. But based on the monocle, red suit jacket, collared shirt, and the bronze pocket watch in this White Rabbit's paw, I felt like I had a pretty good foundation for the assumption.

"Junior, you were supposed to come back down two minutes ago," lectured the White Rabbit. "We're going to be late for the next hole."

"Dad, relax. I was just talking to this girl here." Harry gestured to me.

I raised my hand awkwardly. "Hi there."

The White Rabbit's ears flared up in the rabbit form of rage. He whipped his head toward Harry. "Cotton head! Your mother and I have told you not to talk to humans when you're on Rabbit Hole Patrol. Now come on, we only have a few minutes before the next shift starts."

"Yeah, yeah, Dad. I'm coming. Just give me a minute, okay?"

"Fine. But that's it, son. Sixty seconds. I mean it this time."

The White Rabbit tapped his pocket watch as he glared at Harry. Then he shot me a small glare, along with a cordial nod, before diving back into the sparkling hole and disappearing into its depths.

Harry rolled his eyes. "Sorry about that. Punctuality is kind of his thing."

"So I've heard," I replied. "I take it that it's not yours, though?"

"Eh, let's just say the old guy and I don't have a lot in common. I'm not exactly what he or any of the other White Rabbits expect me to be."

I smiled slightly. "Believe me, I know the feeling. But that's a conversation for another day. I've already kept you long enough. You'd better get down there before your dad's whiskers fly off."

"Yeah, I guess." Harry shrugged sadly. Then his eyes and ears perked up at the thought of a new idea. "Hey, you wanna come with?" he asked. "I could show you around the Wonderlands when my shift is over."

I was intrigued to say the least. Frankly, it sounded awesome. It took all my willpower to stop myself from accepting his offer.

"Tempting," I said, "but I actually have a previous engagement at the moment. Rain check?"

"Definitely." He nodded.

Something seemed to cross his mind. His ears twitched then he swiftly removed the timepiece from his wrist. "Here, take this," he said. "It's a Hole Tracker. We use them to monitor hole locations in whatever realm we're currently in."

I blinked, shocked at the gift. "Don't you need it?"

"Nah, White Rabbits are taught how to make these when we're barely old enough to hop. I'll just whip up another one later. Now come on, I insist. My way of saying thanks for the patch-up. Plus, when you finally decide to cash in that rain check, you'll have a way of finding me."

Harry fastened the watch around my wrist right next to my SRB. I held the timepiece up to the moonlight. It was terribly intricate and there were multiple hands on the face pointing to twenty continuously moving, tiny circles with numbers next to them. Most of the circles were gold, but a few pulsed with different colors. Currently three pulsed silver, two pulsed orange, one pulsed red, and another pulsed black.

"Wow, thanks," was all I could think to say.

"Junior!" The White Rabbit's voice bellowed from down below.

"You're welcome," Harry replied. "Now I gotta go. This thing's about to close and my dad's gonna flip if I don't meet him."

Harry got up, straightened his pants, and shook some twigs from his vest. I stood up to dust away a bit of the dirt clinging to my leggings too.

"See you down the Rabbit Hole some time," I said.

He turned and winked. "Count on it, Crisanta Knight."

With that, Harry dove back through the hole. Just seconds after his hind legs vanished, the entire thing disappeared. The ground sealed itself shut like the fascinating, inter-dimensional wormhole had never existed.

Well, that's just . . . phenomenal, I thought as I started to head back to where the others slept. Of course, then something *else* caught my eye, altering my plan.

No, not another wormhole in the ground. A flash of golden light.

Although it had only been visible for an instant, it had appeared just beyond the trees no more than forty feet away.

Curious, I pushed my way through a handful of branches and cobwebs, ignoring the eerie sounds of forest nightlife and the darkness that consumed the terrain as the moon was gagged by clouds.

A few moments later I came upon another clearing. It was about half the size of the Valley of Edible Enchantments and had its own very distinct brand of weirdness.

Quills, wooden baskets, artwork, candles, and other miscellaneous objects were strewn about as if someone had just dropped them from the air. The clutter was especially dense in the center of the field.

I saw a spot where the grass looked like it had been flattened out from people walking on it. Lying there amongst the bric-a-brac was a large book with gold sparks trickling off it. The book was brown with the name "Russell Caulfield" imprinted on the front cover like a title.

I picked it up and flipped through it. The pages were all empty except for the last page. There, inked delicately in the parchment, I discovered a simple signature: *The Author.*

Holy Cow; this is a book! This is a protagonist book!

I whirled around and looked at the place with fresh eyes. This was where the Scribes lived! This was where the Author's fate-prophesizing, life-ruling, realm-order-keeping protagonist books appeared!

On the other side of the field I suddenly took notice of a cave. I put Russell's book back on the ground and ran to the cave as fast as my legs could carry me. As I entered, my mouth hung open in wonder. The passage seemed to stretch underground for an eternity. There was a single shelf running along each side wall for as far back as I could see, and every inch was lined with protagonist books. The books varied in color and size, but each copy emanated a sense of importance that made it sit erectly on its shelf with pride.

Levitating candles illuminated my way and called me inward. I began to wander through the cave and gaze at the names on the spines. The books didn't appear to be in any kind of order, but I imagined the Scribes had to have some kind of system for keeping track of them.

Most of the volumes I passed were unfamiliar, but there were a few titles I did recognize. Some old like *Rapunzel* and *Jack & Jill*, some new like *Mauvrey Weatherall* and *"Blue" Dieda*.

Part of me wanted to give Mauvrey's and Blue's books a little looksee. But I quickly thought better of it. Blue had more or less told me about hers, and I respected my best friend's privacy too much to go rifling through the specifics of something so personal. Meanwhile I really couldn't have cared less about what the future held for Mauvrey. It was likely just built around extravagant jewelry, gowns, and snootiness. Or (if we were lucky) a long episode of unconsciousness like her mother, Sleeping Beauty.

The candles began to grow scarce when I was some hundred feet deep into the cavern. The thought occurred to me at that point to go back and fetch the others without wasting more time. But before I could commit to such a decision, I came to a fork in the road. The route on my right led to a door marked "Placeholders." The path on the left was aimed for a door with the words "Other Realms" printed on it.

I chose the one on the left.

The door was heavy, and I had to give it a good shove to get it open. When I managed to squeeze inside I found myself in a huge, stone room. It was tall and round, much like the library back at the Capitol Building in Century City where I'd almost gotten killed.

And where you saw that book on Shadow Guardians, my subconscious whispered.

The fleeting memory surprised me. I barely recalled seeing that book in the Capitol Building library when I'd been running from Arian's forces. Add to that, the term "Shadow Guardians" meant nothing to me—making it a mystery why it had even stuck to my subconscious at all.

Hmm. Weird.

I shrugged off the strange memory.

Continuing with its similarities to the Capitol Building, the Scribes' library also had a rooftop window carved into a spiral design. The intricate shape mirrored the temporary burn marks we received when our prologue prophecies appeared.

I guess in hindsight the architectural similarities made sense. If the ambassadors and the Scribes, along with Lena Lenore, were taking protagonist selection into their own hands, it was only fitting that their bases of operation were marked with a common symbol—the symbol we received on our foreheads the moment our fates were taken from us.

I shuddered in disgust.

That spiral design had always reminded me of being branded like a cow—marked like an animal that had been selected by the Author to serve a certain purpose. However, now I knew that the herders charged with wielding the hot iron had their own agendas too.

I shook my head bitterly. While I wasn't sure how yet, I swore to myself that I would find a way to put this right one day. Now that I knew the truth, I had a responsibility to.

I stood beneath the center of the spiral window. The floor and shelves of the library were flooded with foreboding moonlight. The tiles on the ground appeared to be constructed of moonstone, which absorbed the luminescence and reflected it fervently.

This would have been a beautiful effect had it not been for the way the floor felt. As I moved across the space, it was as if a steady heartbeat was pulsing beneath the stone— causing my boots to vibrate ever so slightly with each step.

Trying to keep from wondering about the cause of the reverberation, I focused on the books that encircled me. At first I didn't recognize any of the names on the spines. But then on the fifth shelf of a mahogany bookcase a title caught my eye: *Alice in Wonderland*. Soon after I noticed a few more familiar names. *Peter Pan* sat on a shelf several cases over. Directly next to it, *King Arthur*.

I wasn't sure which of these volumes to pursue first, but then another book won the battle for my favor. This book was electric red and had the name *Natalie Poole* inscribed on its spine.

Heart and mind racing, I bolted for the bookshelf and

stopped in front of my great discovery. I'd first experienced this type of anxious curiosity when I'd snagged that file with Natalie Poole's name on it back at Fairy Godmother Headquarters. Then I'd undergone the same blood-surging intrigue beneath the Capitol Building when I'd found the Natalie folder that belonged to the antagonists.

Alas, neither source had provided me with answers. If anything they'd only filled me with more questions about the mysterious girl who consistently haunted my dreams.

But this book, this *protagonist* book, was different. It could tell me everything. Like for starters, why did Natalie even have a protagonist book? She wasn't from this realm. She lived on Earth and shouldn't have any connection to Book or to me. And yet, as the evidence piled up, it was becoming increasingly clear that somehow Natalie was tied to us both.

I suppressed my nerves and began to reach for her book, regarding the precious object with trepidation and excitement.

Finally, I would have some answers. Finally, I'd—

BAM!

Something akin to a bolt of lightning struck the back of my head. The blast surged powerfully through every cell in my body and shot me against the shelf. I dropped to the ground, some of the books on the shelf falling to the floor with me.

I heard the mumbling of voices. Fading scarlet sparks of leftover magic fell around me as the voices drew closer.

Several pairs of footsteps echoed off the moonstone. They accompanied the floor's steady pulse and my own wavering one like a half-dozen hushed metronomes. Most of them stopped a slight distance away. However, one set came closer.

A pair of light pink pumps with glittering silver straps

stopped in front of me. I'd seen a flash of these high-heeled shoes in one of my visions many nights ago, the night we'd spent at Chauncey's.

I tried to look up, squinting to see who they belonged to. But it was too late. The magic bolt had zapped me too fiercely. My vision blurred and I fell into unconsciousness.

CHAPTER 12

Reacquainted

omething exploded.

Well, something exploded in my dream. But it was still pretty intense.

I had to say, while I was aware that I was asleep, this newfound clarity to my nightmares was making them a lot more action-packed.

In this particular episode of subconscious exploration, I once again saw a dream version of myself. However, this time she was not on the beaches of Adelaide or some random dock. This time she was in a forest.

No, wait.

That wasn't just any forest. I recognized the slope of the hills and the way the trees thinned in density as we descended. This was the smaller forest that led up to the entrance of the actual Forbidden Forest—the one we'd passed through a couple weeks ago.

Dream me, SJ, Blue, Jason, and Daniel were making their way through it, walking back toward town. No sound accompanied this image. Not because dream me and the rest of the group weren't talking—it seemed like they were. It was more like someone had muted the audio of my subconscious and only I couldn't hear them.

Even without sound, one thing was clear. Dream me was worried. She appeared anxious, like she was trying to convince the others of something with little success.

Like a candle being blown out, in the next instant everything and everyone in sight was extinguished from view. All that was left was blackness, leaving me unable to see anything past my own hand.

Wait, my own hand . . .

My spirit was no longer adrift witnessing this dreamscape. I was whole again. I could feel the ground beneath my boots and the cold air on my skin. I was here. Wherever here was anyways. For all I knew, I could've—

CRUNCH!

The sound came from behind me, and while logic indicated that it was just the noise of a branch being trampled beneath someone's foot, my gut told me otherwise. It was too horrible a sound, this crunch. It was a noise comparable to that of a spine being crushed by the clenched fist of a giant.

"Get down!" a voice that sounded like my own suddenly shouted through the void.

I turned my head in the direction of both the crunch and the voice. The moment I did, I was forced to leap out of the way. A giant fireball plowed into the ground where I'd been standing. I may have avoided being hit, but I was still blasted back by its force.

Ugh, can dream versions of yourself suffer from head injuries? If so, I think I'd like to report one.

I was lying on my back on what felt like grass. My ears were ringing, and I clutched my head as I slowly sat up. I smelled smoke. I heard the distant sound of cannon fire. But I had no visuals to account for either. I couldn't even see the flames from the explosion that'd just occurred. The ball of fire had disappeared as suddenly as it had appeared. All that remained was the void.

I stood and dusted off my dress. That's when I took notice of a distant glimmer.

I started toward the shining object. When I got closer I discovered it was another compact mirror similar to the one I'd seen in my last dream. Like Tara's, it was contained within a sleek shell and had the words "Mark Two" engraved onto it.

As I approached the object, a silhouette began to come into view. I realized that the Mark Two was not simply free-floating in space, but being held up by a girl. Her figure was hunched over. Her sparkly black pumps had four-inch, silver-sequined heels. And she was shrouded in both shadow and a familiar, hooded purple cloak.

Between the shoes and the cloak, I recognized her as the same partially concealed figure I'd seen in my dream of the Capitol Building long ago, the one who'd led me to the antagonists' bunker and who also seemed to be working for Arian.

I was getting quite close to her when I abruptly came to a barrier that wouldn't allow me to go any farther. It was like an invisible wall that prevented me from getting a better angle on the girl and seeing her face.

Despite the hindrance, I still managed to see the face reflected in the mirror she was holding. It was Arian's.

Unlike in my dream of Tara, the mark I'd left around Arian's eye appeared relatively fresh here. It looked like I'd just done it. Which meant that this slice of the future was not far from coming to pass in my timeline . . .

Cloaked girl was having a conversation with Arian through the compact. Alas, it was at a volume of muddled whispers. I had to concentrate very hard to discern what they were saying.

"She's better than you said she was," Arian told the girl.

"Please," cloaked girl responded. "She is just lucky."

"I'd say very lucky given that she's managed to elude us three times now."

"She can only outrun you for so long. With that new toy of yours, you should be able to snuff her out no matter where she is hiding."

"No thanks to you," Arian said. "It's a good thing our small, wicked friend was able to get us what *you* failed to."

"Hey!" cloaked girl replied defensively. "How was I to know that the first one was a fake?"

Arian waved his hand dismissively. "Forget it. That doesn't matter now. The point is that we need to change tactics. We started using the stupid thing back in the forest like you suggested, but it has only helped us find her, not capture her."

"What do you mean *capture* her?" cloaked girl asked. "I thought our orders were to *get rid* of her."

"Well, sorry to disappoint, but there's been a change of plans. Nadia wants this one alive."

Although I couldn't see the cloaked girl's face, I could tell by her sudden change in tone that she was definitely not happy. Her hand tightened around the mirror's shell. "Please tell me you are joking."

"Afraid not, sweetheart. Now that the girl has proven to be more of an adversary than you initially described, Nadia is actually looking forward to a little confrontation. You know our leader, big fan of the big dramatic moments."

Cloaked girl was obviously pouting because Arian

smirked and responded, "Don't make that face, beautiful. It might freeze that way."

The cloaked girl scowled.

Arian suppressed a chuckle. "Look, we're still going to kill her eventually," he reassured his hooded accomplice. "But this way it'll be rubbed in her face a bit before it happens. You of all people should appreciate that."

"Hmm." Cloaked girl mulled over the thought. "I do like that idea."

"I thought you might," Arian said. "Now then, the other item you have is just what we'll need to take the girl when we cut her off at the beaches of Adelaide tomorrow. I'll be coming by tonight to pick it up, so meet me in the usual spot at half past two."

"All right." Cloaked girl nodded. "But why exactly? I understand its purpose in regards to Paige Tomkins, but how can it possibly be useful in this situation?"

"Four words," Arian responded. "Crisanta. Knight. Has. Magic."

"Crisa? Crisa!"

I bolted upright and glanced around.

Friends? Check.

Forest? Check.

Therewolves? Also check.

Okay, I was definitely awake.

The campfire was extinguished and both Therewolves and former prisoners were lazily greeting the morning. I squinted up into the sunshine to see Blue, SJ, Jason, and Daniel standing around me—returned to their normal human forms now that SJ's potions had worn off.

"What time is it?" I yawned as I rubbed the crust from my eyes.

"You tell us," Blue said. "You're the one with the fancy new watch. Where'd you get that anyways?"

I looked at my wrist and saw the strange timepiece strapped to it.

The Hole Tracker . . .

Realization hit me like a battering ram and my memory came flooding back. I put my hand to my head and felt a bump where I'd been magically struck last night.

"I found the Scribes!" I gasped.

Jason blinked twice in surprise. "Wait, what?"

"I found the Scribes and the protagonist books! All the protagonist books!" I repeated as I hopped to my feet.

"Sydney," I called to our Therewolf friend who was stretched out like a cat. "Hold down the fort!"

I bolted like a madwoman through the trees, skidded down the steep hills, and pushed branch after branch out my way. The others pursued me without question. After a minute I passed through the clearing with the tree where I'd met Harry last night.

I didn't stop to explain, though. There'd be time for that later. The clearing with the Scribes' cave was not far now, and whatever had knocked me out last night couldn't keep me from finding it again. At least, that's what I thought.

When I broke through the part of the Forbidden Forest that should have opened up into the desired field, I discovered a massive crater. Everything that had been there the night before—the cave, the books, the miscellaneous junk that littered the grass, even the grass for that matter—was gone. It was as if some vindictive colossus had uprooted the whole lot with an impossibly large shovel.

"It was here, I swear," I said earnestly. "There was a field with all this weird stuff and a whole cavern filled with protagonist books. Blue's was there, and Mauvrey's, and everyone else's I'm sure too. But I went into one of the back rooms at the end of the cave and when I wasn't looking, someone—*something*—hit me from behind and the next thing I knew I was waking up at the campsite this morning."

I stood there, sure that none of them would believe my mad rantings. Thankfully, Blue put her hand on my shoulder. "Calm down, Crisa. We believe you. The Scribes must've just moved everything when they realized you'd found them. They're all-powerful Fairy Godmothers, remember? Uprooting everything and zapping it somewhere else was probably a snap."

"Great," I grunted. "I guess that means they could be anywhere."

"Hey, guys," Daniel interrupted. "What's that?"

He pointed up. About ten feet above us and thirty feet from the ledge where we stood was a single, folded-up piece of parchment levitating in midair.

"Blue . . ." SJ started to say.

"I got it." Blue drew one of her throwing knives and stepped forward.

She took aim then hurled the blade across the depression. The knife soared overhead and pierced through the parchment. Like an anchor, its weight yanked it out of the sky and to the ground. The five of us eased our way down the slope in its pursuit.

Blue was the first to reach the mysterious note. She picked it up and unfolded the parchment.

"So, what does it say?" Jason asked.

Blue raised her eyebrows as she read it out loud. "Nice Try, Miss Knight."

"It does not," I said, thinking she was joking.

"Hey, see for yourself."

Blue turned the page over and I saw that she'd been telling the truth. Those four words were the only ones printed there. *Nice Try, Miss Knight.*

Aside from the sarcastic, swirly penmanship, the only thing worth noting about the parchment was the seal it had been closed with—a red, sparkling spiral design that matched the shape of the skylights in the Scribes' library and the Capitol Building library.

"Getting off to an early start today aren't you, Knight?" Daniel said. "Doesn't it usually take you 'til at least midmorning to get on the bad side of someone new?"

"What can I say," I said, shooting him a glare. "I guess watching you at work has helped me sharpen the skill."

"It was a great try though, Crisa," SJ quickly interjected before he could respond. "Really. It is truly impressive that you found the Scribes at all. I am not sure anyone ever has. You should be proud."

"Thanks SJ, I . . ."

I paused as I registered something. "Hold on. Did you just say something *nice* to me?"

"Some would say *kind*," she replied slyly. "But, yes. I did."

Awareness struck me. The fourteen days were up! The witch's deal had expired!

"You're back! You're all back!" I exclaimed.

Filled with happiness and relief, I threw my arms around SJ, then Blue, then Jason, and then Daniel too (by accident). My eyes nearly popped out my head when I realized what I was doing.

"Sorry," I muttered as I tersely jumped away from him. "That was unintentional."

"I hope so," he said as he dusted off his jacket.

I shrugged, and looked at the rest of my group with a contented smile. "I'm so glad you guys are all, well, *you* again."

"Please, we were always us," Blue said. "You're the one who reminded us of that. Now come on, we'd better get back to our furry friends before they start to worry."

My group re-crossed the crater and journeyed back to the campsite. As we drew nearer, I started to hang back so that by the time we reached our destination I was at the rear of the pack with SJ. When Blue, Jason, and Daniel proceeded to rejoin the others I pulled her aside.

"So, um . . . Hi."

"Hi," she repeated. "Doing all right, Crisa?"

"Um, yeah, fine," I said.

There was an awkward beat.

"Oh, hey. I finally figured out that whole thing about what I contribute to our team's table," I said. "At least . . . I think I figured it out."

Before we'd gone to sleep the previous night, I'd had a conversation with Merilyn (a.k.a. the Therewolf formerly known as Not Blue). She'd told me how grateful she was that a leader like me had come along to organize the prisoners' revolt. If I hadn't, then her troupe might well have been under Pepperjack's control forever.

I'd responded by telling her that I wasn't a leader; I was just the one who'd thought of the plan. To mistake me for something else would be silly. How could I possibly be a leader when I didn't even have my own junk sorted out?

Merilyn actually laughed at this assertion. "Yeah, you're

right," she'd said. "What was I thinking? You're not a leader. You just keep an eye out for the big picture without losing sight of what's in front of you. You give direction that others listen to faithfully. And you consistently put everyone else's well-being ahead of your own. I mean, you must've passed on at least a half dozen chances to escape tonight because you kept coming back to save everyone else."

Her words had echoed in my head before I'd fallen asleep. And in the last few minutes during our silent walk back to camp they'd resurfaced, leading to the confession that spilled out of me now.

"I'm the leader, aren't I?" I said sort of sheepishly. "Or at least I tend to fill that role in our group a lot of the time?"

"Is that a question or a statement?" SJ replied, responding to the reluctance in my tone.

I took a breath. "It's a statement," I said more certainly. "As dumb or ridiculous as it may seem given my shortcomings, I am a leader."

At the very least I have the potential to be a leader. Maybe even a good one if I ever get my act together . . .

Iciness trembled my fingers. I held up my hand and watched it turn to liquid metal. Like it had earlier in the week, when the effect receded, the brand on my hand did not morph itself into a distinct word like I thought it would. Instead it merely flashed for a few seconds before returning to its former, blob-like state.

Hmm, according to that anticlimactic burst, being a leader clearly isn't the important characteristic that makes me, me *either.* Regardless, I still believed in the realization.

"Has that been happening a lot?" SJ asked, startled by the phenomenon.

"On and off," I responded. "It doesn't bother me much.

What does is this blob tattoo on my hand. If I never figure out my watering can quality, I'm not sure how I feel about it being branded there forever."

"I can understand that. I do not know how I would have explained a tattoo to my mother if my mark were still there. Thank goodness it has run its course." SJ lifted her own hand and looked it over. The "kindness" tattoo was no longer visible. It was gone just like the enchantment that had stripped her of the quality over the last couple weeks.

"That aside," SJ continued, "I am glad you finally figured something out. You are a natural leader, Crisa. I am surprised it took you this long to see it."

"Hey, I've been busy. Our Therewolf prison schedule didn't exactly allot time for daily meditation. And the only time I ever tried to formally lead anyone back at school was when I ran for captain of the archery club."

"To be fair I think you would have gotten the job if you had not tried to show off with those flaming arrows," SJ replied.

"Ugh, Lady Agnue was so mad."

"You burned down one of the detention towers, Crisa." SJ smiled. "She probably thought you did it on purpose."

I shrugged. "What can I say? Sometimes fate doesn't suck."

"Indeed." SJ laughed. "Anyways, I am very happy you came to terms with your role. Self-realization is a wonderful thing. It brings both peace of mind and strength." She patted me on the arm and began to walk away.

"SJ, hold up," I blurted out. "That's not all I wanted to tell you. I think we have some unfinished business that needs addressing. A lot's happened in the last two weeks and I'm well aware that I still owe you an explanation for certain things. But now that you're not magically unkind anymore, or a giant wolf, I wanted to see if you were, I mean, if *we* were good . . ."

Ugh, could that have been any less articulate? And I thought my attempts to make amends with her last night had been rough.

SJ inhaled deeply, letting me writhe before she coolly crossed her arms and responded.

"I am still upset with you, Crisa."

"Yeah, I kind of figured as much." I sighed.

"However, I want to assure you that this will not hinder our group's journey. For, despite the fact that you are currently unable to trust me completely, I do still trust you."

I took a step back out of surprise. "Really? Why? I mean, after everything I just . . . How can you?"

"Simple," she replied. "I know you, Crisa. Maybe I do not know all your secrets or motives or reasons behind every ridiculous decision you make. But those things do not matter. You do not need to know every single thing about a person in order to see who they truly are. I realize that might not sound logical, but it is true. And as I said, I know who you are, even if sometimes you seem to forget yourself or refuse to accept it."

I scratched my head. "Um, okay then. So you still trust me. That's good. But what about everything else? I know there's more you want to say to me than that."

"I think I have said everything that I can without causing further rift between us," she replied.

"Hey, SJ," Jason called out as he came jogging over. "Can you come here when you have a minute? One of the Therewolves has a question about those ice potions you made."

SJ nodded. "Yes, I shall be right there."

Jason trotted away and she started to follow.

"SJ," I said, stopping her again. "*So* . . . where does that leave us exactly?"

My friend released a steady exhale. "Let it lie, Crisa. As I was saying, I do not think it is wise for us to provoke the matter further given that we are to remain in such close quarters while we continue this mission."

She made to turn away once more, but I moved in front of her. "SJ, come on. You can't just pretend like you're fine with all of this. Look where that's gotten us up 'til now— two straight weeks of you slashing me with nasty comments and cruelty icier than those potions of yours. Both of which clouded your judgment and our ability to even be in the same room with one another for more than a few minutes."

"Crisa, I was under an enchantment."

"And now you're not. So please, in all honesty tell me what you're really feeling behind that naturally pleasant demeanor of yours. I need to hear it."

"You really want to know so badly?" SJ asked quietly.

Seriously, did I really want to know? I'd been acting like a jerk and an idiot, so whatever she had to say was probably going to make me feel awful.

"Yes," I replied in response to her question and my own. "I want to know."

"Fine." SJ sighed then swallowed hard. "I am myself again, Crisa, which means I can be kind. But that does not make up for the fact that I am hurt. We are supposed to be best friends. We have known each other for years and have been through everything together. There is absolutely nothing I would not do for you—no plan of yours I would not support, no trouble I would not help you get out of, no problem you could not come to me with. As I said, even despite your recent admissions of distrust, I trust you completely. Not just because you are our group's natural leader, but because of our personal friendship. So, yes, I am angry. But more than that, I am disappointed."

She took a breath. "Regardless, we have a job to do and a journey to take, neither of which can afford to be inhibited by such feelings. So I will not take them out on you. I will not tell the others about Natalie Poole being real or your ability to see the future in your dreams or your visions of Arian—"

"SJ," I interjected, surprised. "I didn't tell you about—"

"You were talking in your sleep again this morning. The others were not awake yet, but I was. That is beside the point though. What I am trying to say is that those are *your* secrets, Crisa. And you have to figure out why you are keeping them from us—your friends who know you better than anyone. Only when you figure that out will this bridge you have burned between us have a chance at being rebuilt, and will you and I truly be 'good'."

Huh. I'd been right. That did make me feel awful.

Much of what she'd said hadn't been news to me. Daniel and Chauncey had already nagged me about needing to accept myself in order to overcome all those issues SJ just listed off. Heck, even the residual blurry tattoo on my hand was a constant reminder of that.

Yet, in spite of my familiarity with this kind of lecturing, hearing it from SJ caused the issue to be driven home much deeper. She wasn't an enchanted object or a strange pig or my obnoxious boy tormentor; she was SJ. Listening to those words come out of her mouth made me feel as though I'd been blasted back by a bolt of magic stronger than the one that had shocked me last night.

I stood there like a statue as I absorbed the weight of her words, filled with a combination of humility and guilt.

I honestly thought she was finished with her lecture at that point. I mean, what else was there to say? Apparently I was a terrible friend and an enigmatic idiot with little to no self-awareness. However, evidently SJ was not done with me yet.

"One more thing," she said. "I realize that it probably did not come across all that well, what with the insults and bitterness I was filled with whilst I was attempting to say it, but did you understand what I was trying to tell you last night? What I said to you just after we escaped from the Therewolves' tunnel system?"

"You'll have to be more specific," I said wearily.

"Fine," she declared. "I shall."

My gaze dropped to the floor and I braced myself for whatever brutal words she had left to unload. But then, out of nowhere, something even more powerful happened. She gave me a hug. Not a half-hearted hug, or a patronizing hug; a real, everything-will-be-okay, best friend hug. The kind that I thought the wedge I'd created between us might've never allowed again.

"You may have a ways to go before you are able to do all that, Crisa," SJ said. "But until then I will still be what I always have been—your friend, and here whenever you need my help. All you have to do is take it."

She released me from her hug and began to head off to join the others, giving me a small smile as she glanced back over her shoulder.

"And I was too hard on you before," she added. "You *can* still feel free to thank me later."

CHAPTER 13

Enemy Mine

n hour later there was, in fact, a plethora of thanking going on.

This gratitude fest was not between SJ and me though, but between the Therewolves and our whole gang.

We were at the edge of the Forbidden Forest. The dark memories and ominous wildlife of its depths were behind us; the much less intimidating, downhill forest that led to town was ahead.

The Therewolves had spent the morning giving us humans rides out of the Forbidden Forest so that we wouldn't have to face its perils a second time around. Even with half our furry comrades staying behind to guard the campsite, every one of the former prisoners had been escorted out by noon.

My friends, Daniel, and I were the last group to be escorted to freedom. By the time we made it to the edge of the Forbidden Forest, the other humans had already gone, no doubt having returned to town as fast as possible.

I didn't blame them for not waiting. They'd already expressed their sincerest thanks to us earlier and were naturally itching to get back to their families.

Sydney—the Therewolves' new leader—had escorted

us out along with Merilyn. Having morphed back into human form, they wished us off with a myriad of hugs and handshakes.

"Thank you, my dear. Thank you all for everything," Sydney said as he shook my hand repeatedly. "We can at last live our lives again, and we owe it all to you."

He made the rounds to shake everyone else's hands while Merilyn gave me such a strong embrace she nearly broke my neck.

"Where will you go now?" SJ asked Sydney as he gave her a handshake of her own.

"Oh, we shall find a new part of the Forbidden Forest to inhabit. Perhaps something near a river or a tar pit."

"I'm sorry about your tunnel system, by the way," I said. "Now that I know you guys aren't bloodthirsty monsters I feel pretty bad about burying your home."

"No need to worry, my dear," Sydney replied. "That underground monstrosity was all Pepperjack's idea. We actually prefer to live out in the open. Being close to nature provides us with a greater, surrealist influence on our acting. It will fuel our training as we return to our true love—the purest, most valiant form of theater: comedic improv."

After a few more well wishes, Sydney and Merilyn returned to their beastly forms and ran back into the Forbidden Forest.

The five of us began to march forward. Town wasn't far. It was only a twenty-minute walk through this downhill, smaller forest to reach the stable where we'd left our Pegasi and carriage. From there it would be smooth sailing to our next destination. At least that's what I figured until another memory came rushing back.

I'd seen us walking through the very place that we were

walking through now in the dream I'd had last night. And then . . . then there had been something wrong.

I slowed my pace and looked around. Nothing seemed out of the ordinary. The tall trees, the intricately woven roots in the ground, the stones scattered here and there—everything appeared calm. And yet I knew what I saw in that vision, and what I felt now.

"Guys, something feels off here," I said.

"After everything that's happened, *now* you start feeling worried?" Blue asked half-jokingly.

"I'm just getting a bad vibe is all," I replied. "We should be careful."

"Yeah, we wouldn't want to upset any of these trees," Daniel mocked. "They might start taking swings at us."

"I'm not joking, Daniel" I said. "I don't really know how to explain it, but there is definitely—"

CRUNCH!

I suddenly heard the very clear, very memorable sound of a branch being crushed beneath an unknown weight. The noise sent a shiver of trepidation up my vertebrae. Instantly every hair on the back of my neck stood erect and the blood in my veins stopped cold. Without a doubt it was the same awful sound I'd heard in my dreams. And that meant—

Instinctively I spun around just in time to see a giant fireball headed straight for us.

"Get down!" I yelled.

I tackled the others to the ground and we hit the floor just as the flaming cannonball soared overhead. It barreled into the grass and left a trail of smoke in its wake.

My ears rang for real this time and it took me a second to get to my feet. I looked back in the direction the attack had come from. The trees blocked the view a bit, but soon enough

I saw him. There, not a hundred yards behind us, was Arian. To be precise it was Arian, eight armed henchmen, three additional dudes wielding crossbows, and six guys working together to operate a set of surprisingly portable, flaming cannonball catapults.

Jason cleared his throat. "Is that the same kid from the Capitol Building that tried to—"

"Yes." I nodded.

"And they're all here for—"

"Uh-huh."

"So we should probably—"

"Oh yeah."

And on that note of agreement, we all made a run for it.

It did not give any of us any pleasure to run from a fight. But if I'd learned anything from all the near death experiences lately, there was a very clear difference between running and running away. The latter being attributed to cowardice, while the former related to common sense.

The fact was, while it would have felt way more natural to fight, going against that kind of firepower would've been suicide. And seeing as how our ride out of here was not that far off, if we hurried we'd be able to escape without incident.

Bobbing and weaving through the trees, we retreated with purpose, dodging the constant stream of arrows and fireballs flying in our direction.

I stole a glance back at one point and saw Arian and his armed men gaining on us. The short look cost me, and I tripped over a tree root that sent me tumbling to the ground.

Eyes on the road! Eyes on the road!

I picked myself up and kept going. That is, until I flattened myself to the ground again to avoid being decapitated by another flaming cannonball.

Wait. The catapults are behind me, but this shot came from somewhere in front.

I got up and squinted through the smoke into the distance.

Oh no. There were more of them. And they were up ahead, intending to cut us off.

I'd underestimated Arian. I'd learned from my dreams last night that he had something in his possession now, some kind of tool that was helping him track me wherever I'd been. But I hadn't expected it to help him anticipate where I was going as well. Not only had he been able to use it to follow us out of the Forbidden Forest, he'd also obtained the foresight to instruct more of his forces to trap us on our way back to town.

"Now what?" Jason shouted as he and the others noted the additional threats.

"We split up," I responded. "As a group we're an easier target. All of you—do what you have to and get out of here. We'll meet back at the stables."

The others nodded in accord and our team broke apart. Arian's men were in close range now, so I drew my wand from my satchel.

Spear.

It was not a moment too soon. Just then one of our enemies appeared and took a swing at me with his sword. I blocked his blow then kicked his kneecap, elbowed his jaw, and slammed my staff onto his shoulder blade to drop him. When he hit the ground I leapt over his back and kept running, defending myself against more opponents as they passed by, morphing my weapon into its different forms.

Another fireball came at me as I approached the edge of a steep, tree-encircled slope. I'd been busy taking down another one of Arian's men and had barely seen the projectile coming. I sidestepped to narrowly avoid it.

Phew, that was close, I thought as I wiped the sweat from my brow. *I need to get out of range before—Eep!*

The attacker I'd just dropped had crawled up behind me and grabbed hold of my ankle. I fell to the root-laden earth, my wand flying out of my grip. It tumbled down the slope. I turned my head and saw the henchman smirking.

"You're not going anywhere, princess."

"Oh, I beg to differ."

With the very foot he was holding on to, I power-stomp-kicked him in his smug face. The punk was knocked out cold, and my ankle was freed from his greasy grip. With haste I stood and raced down the slope in search of my wand.

Where is it? Where is it?

"Looking for this?"

My breath caught in my chest at the sound of the familiar voice. Arian stepped out from behind a tree—his sword in one hand, my wand in the other.

"So tell me," he continued as he moved forward. "How does this work exactly? Only Fairy Godmothers can use wands because of their magic, so what makes you able to use this one? What makes you so special?"

He doesn't know about my magic yet. Unlike my visions of the dangers in this forest, my dream of him talking to that cloaked girl must be an exchange that's yet to pass.

I backed up the slope as he approached, but did so very carefully so I wouldn't trip over any more roots like I had before.

"Why don't you tell me what makes me so special, Arian," I responded. "You're the one hunting me, after all."

Arian shrugged. "It's not that complicated. As I said back

at the capital, your book and its prologue prophecy are of particular interest to our leader."

"Nadia, right?" I said as I quickly glanced behind me.

I'd noticed that the dude I'd face-kicked had dropped his sword. Without my wand it was my best bet for defending myself against Arian. First, though, I needed to get close to it. And to do that I needed to keep Arian talking.

"She wants me out of the way just like she wants to get rid of Paige Tomkins and Natalie Poole . . ." I continued.

Arian's eyes narrowed. "What do you know about them?"

"Enough, I assure you," I lied as I slowly eased my way backwards. "Anyways, don't change the subject. I must be pretty darn important for you to go after me first. I guess I'm flattered."

"Don't be. You were just the only one we could get to for the time being. What with Tomkins missing and Poole not yet existing."

We had just reached the summit of the slope. The sword I'd been after was only a few feet away, but I hesitated as Arian's words sunk in. "Wait . . . what?"

Arian suddenly lunged at me. I dove to the side and his sword stabbed into the tree I'd been up against. He threw my wand back down the slope then removed his blade from the tree as I rolled for the fallen soldier's sword.

Launching myself up, I raised the blade just in time to deflect another one of Arian's strikes. I moved it down to parry him again. Then I tersely blocked him on my right side, my left and up and down and right and . . .

Move, move, move!

Arian was coming at me with full slice-and-dice force, making it no easy trick to avoid being cut up like a fruit salad.

I hadn't fought anyone full force with a sword in a while, and truly had never been that confident with the weapon to begin with. Moreover, this guy was just as good as Daniel.

Who, in case you've forgotten, is really, really good.

I needed to get my wand in order to even the playing field with my own particular skill set. And I needed to do it without getting skewered like a fancy appetizer in the process. But I had no idea how to do that. Our fight had allowed Arian to move me pretty far away from where he'd tossed it.

Things went from bad to worse a second later when Arian's weapon knocked the sword from my hand completely.

Retreat with purpose! Retreat with purpose!

Zigzagging around the trees, I raced erratically through the forest. Eventually I ducked behind a particularly large trunk and sank to the floor to buy myself time to think of a plan.

"You can't hide forever!" I heard Arian call from somewhere not far off.

Ugh, he's right. I need to improvise here. I've done more with less . . .

I slowly peered my head out and saw Arian. He was some dozen feet behind the tree, but looking in the opposite direction. I hid behind the trunk again and clutched the nearest root tightly as I closed my eyes and summoned my confidence.

Just go and kick his butt—him and all his annoying friends. You can do it. Just get up from the ground and go.

I felt my hands grow hot, but I ignored the sensation. My eyes burst open with resolve and I grabbed a rock from the ground and threw it at a tree a few paces to my left.

The rock bounced off the trunk and the noise definitely

caught Arian's attention. As I listened to the sound of his approaching footsteps I grabbed another pebble and carefully slid up the tree trunk until I was standing.

When I sensed he was a couple yards away I gently tossed the second pebble out in front of me. It rolled innocently to the ground as if it'd been knocked loose on accident. Of course, it hadn't been.

The idea was to give away my location, but not let Arian know I'd done so on purpose. He had to think he was catching me off guard, when in reality I was waiting for him.

I knew making a direct dash for my wand was out of the question. Arian was faster than me, and he was blocking my path. I had no choice but to try and disarm him first. And since he had a weapon and I did not, the only chance I had of doing that was by fighting him from such close range he would be unable to fully extend his sword.

Between that and the element of surprise, it might just be enough to keep me from getting killed.

Arian held his sword in his right hand, which was why I'd drawn his attention to the left before redirecting it to the tree I was hiding behind. Placing myself on the same side as his blade put me in a much better position to block and disarm him. In theory.

I heard his footsteps crunching over the fallen foliage. He was close now.

Any second—

Arian's arm came into view as his sword swung around the tree, poised to separate my head from its shoulders.

I kept his strike at bay by simultaneously blocking his forearm with my left hand and his wrist with my right. He made to pull away, but I followed the momentum and harnessed it to my advantage. Instantly I tightened my grip around both parts of his arm, kicked his knee inward, and twisted his arm down.

I slammed my knee into his lowered chest and in the process cut his leg with his own sword. The blade fell from his hand as I'd hoped, but he recovered too quickly. Arian immediately followed up with a jab to my ribs that I was too slow to block. In that temporary stun, he wrapped the arm I was holding around my neck and pinned me against him in a tight chokehold that both my hands were trapped in.

"What's the matter?" he grunted as I struggled. "The damsel princess out of ideas?"

I gritted my teeth in anger and stomped down on his foot with the heel of my boot. With a thrust I turned our entangled bodies and slammed his back against the tree behind us.

I could've sworn I heard the bark crack when his head knocked against it. He released me from his chokehold, but before I could take more than a step, he grabbed my left wrist and twisted it sideways.

Something snapped. A bolt of pain shot through my arm, but I had no time to process the injury. As I lifted my leg to fire off a backwards kick, he kicked my knee outwards. My body fell to the ground. Arian kicked his sword back into his hand.

Adrenaline rushing through me, I automatically rolled to my right, barely avoiding the blade as Arian plunged his sword into the earth where I'd landed.

In a last ditch effort, I forcefully swung my leg around—sweeping Arian's out from under him. He dropped to the grass as I continued the momentum, using it to propel myself to my feet.

It was safe to say I'd never run faster. My heart throbbed loudly in chorus with the blood pulsating through my head. Combined with the white noise in my ears, it made for a beat like a violent symphony. If I added that to the blur of trees and smoke around me, it felt like I was trapped in one of my nightmares.

My eyes darted about as I searched for my wand. Finally, I spotted it resting on the forest floor twelve yards away. Checking behind me, I saw that Arian was on his feet and not far off. I bolted for my weapon with absolutely everything I had.

A burst of panicked yelling and shouting came from close behind me. It didn't sound like my friends, which led me to believe it was coming from Arian's men. I knew better than to waste my time by turning around to check, though. I didn't need to see the future to know that if I slowed down in the slightest, Arian would catch up with me.

Seconds later I reached my wand and picked it up without breaking stride. I spun around in anticipation of my inbound enemy. He was twenty feet away and closing. I braced myself to fight as he drew nearer. I was done running.

Alas, defeating Arian was not in the cards for me today. Without warning (and *definitely* without precedent) a giant arm swung out of the trees and flung Arian backwards. Only after a moment I realized that it wasn't an arm at all. It was a branch; a branch attached to a massive trunk with a set of golden eyes.

One of the trees had turned animate and was now stampeding about taking shots at Arian and his men. The thing must've wandered out of the Forbidden Forest.

Lucky for me, I guess.

However, it was pretty unlucky for Arian's forces. That had to be the source of the freaked out yelling I'd been hearing.

Taking advantage of the opportunity, I decided to save my battle angst for another day and seize my chance at escape. But then, of course, another obstacle dropped from the sky.

Literally.

Just as unexpectedly as the appearance of the rogue tree, the same dragon from Century City that we'd defeated ages ago suddenly swooped overhead and landed in the forest.

The earth shook when he impacted the ground—crushing several trees beneath his massive tail. I saw flashes of his silvery skin and gleaming, golden eyes through the foliage. When he let out a deafeningly mighty roar, I took that as my official cue to exit.

Let Arian and his jerky friends handle this one; I'm out.

My hunter and his forces now distracted by these new opponents, I made my way out of the forest with little more hindrance.

At the speed I was moving, I arrived at the town stables in minutes. Once inside, I saw my friends and Daniel arguing with the establishment's proprietor.

"What do you mean you sold our carriage and two of our Pegasi? You said we had thirty days!" Daniel yelled at the heavily bearded fellow.

"I'm sorry, I'm sorry," he said. "It's been over two weeks. No one goes into the Forbidden Forest that long and still comes back. I thought you were dead."

"Well, we're not. But *you* definitely are if you don't get us a ride out of here!" Blue retorted.

"Look, I don't have any more Pegasi, just the three others

that you left. But you can have that carriage over there." The bearded man gestured to a rundown vehicle in the corner. "Some of your stuff's even in the trunk."

The dragon's roars reached the stable.

"That will have to do," SJ said. "We must leave. Now."

Lacking other options, we hastily attached our three Pegasi to the rickety carriage and climbed in.

Without the other Pegasi and the levitation potion SJ had placed on our former carriage, there was no way we were getting into the air. We had to settle for escape by road. It wasn't as fast a means for getting away, but it was probably a safer option given that one of our enemies, or even the dragon, might've otherwise spotted us in the sky.

When Sadie and the other two remaining winged steeds were strapped in, we took off like lightning. With speed and fortitude, we rode out of the stables, leaving antagonists, monsters, and who knows what else behind in our dust.

CHAPTER 14

The Encounter

"J, are you sure you don't have any more portable potions up your sleeve?" Jason asked as he inspected the broken wheels of our carriage.

"I am sure," she responded. "I used the few extras I found on the Therewolf stage to escape those men in the forest. If we are to move forward, I am afraid we will have to think of something else."

All enchanted options having been exhausted, and no tools or supplies to help, the five of us surveyed our busted up carriage and tried to figure out how to proceed.

We'd been riding for a while and were in the clear in terms of attackers. That good fortune aside, two of the wheels on our rickety carriage had snapped under our weight a few minutes ago. Meanwhile, the gaping hole in the floor of the vehicle was growing wider—threatening to crack the whole thing in half.

We'd tried to fix it ourselves using wood from the trees, vines, and the different forms my wand could take. But none of our solutions proved reliable for very long. If we had some actual tools, maybe we could have salvaged the situation. Alas, we didn't have much to work with.

There had been no tools in the trunk of the carriage, just some bags of our stuff that the stable manager hadn't sold yet. Among these random items were a few empty canteens, extra throwing knives of Blue's, and some miscellaneous pieces of clothing we'd packed.

Although not helpful to our carriage problem, I was grateful for the latter. While SJ's SRBs kept us clean throughout the ordeal of the Therewolves and the Forbidden Forest, I was still feeling kind of gross. I'd been wearing the same thing for more than two weeks. My outfit was torn in multiple places, and its essence reeked of incarceration. So I was glad to find spare leggings and a dress that I could change into.

The others, too, opted for a costume change when we pulled over. They made use of the various spare clothing items as they tried to shed the memories of what we'd just lived through.

As I straightened out the hem of the long-sleeve, mustard yellow dress I'd put on, I wished fixing up the carriage could be this easy. If we were going to get to the shores of Adelaide any time soon, we would have to find another way of crossing the realm.

That's where we were beginning our search for Ashlyn— Adelaide. More specifically—the ocean off the coast of Adelaide near the underwater kingdom of Mer.

With the enchanted saltwater taffy from the Valley of Edible Enchantments, we now had what we needed to search the waters outside the lost princess's home kingdom. We also had something else to guide our search—a theory.

Before the carriage had broken down I'd told the others about my meeting with Harry the White Rabbit, sharing his revelation about the wormhole-esque holes in the In and Out Spell and showing them my new Hole Tracker.

In the process, I'd hit a few buttons on the rim of the

wristwatch. When I did, different holographic maps of Book started appearing, displaying upcoming holes in the In and Out Spell across the kingdoms. I'd noticed that some of these holes showed coordinates off the coast of Adelaide, leading to my theory . . .

No one had ever found a trace of Princess Ashlyn when she'd disappeared at sea a year and a half ago. But if holes (wormholes, as it were) regularly appeared in the ocean close to Adelaide, that alluded to the possibility that maybe the reason Ashlyn was never found in our realm was because she wasn't in our realm at all.

That night we met in Adelaide, Lonna the mermaid had expressed awareness that there were holes appearing in the In and Out Spell. So what if Ashlyn had actually been sucked through one of these holes in the ocean and was sent to another land altogether? That would totally explain why no one ever found her.

Brilliant, right?

The others thought so too. And they felt (as I did) that this theory was our best lead once we arrived in Adelaide. Now all we had to do was get there.

We couldn't count on our remaining steeds to transport us across the many kingdoms to the beaches of Adelaide. It was different when they'd had SJ's levitation potion and two other Pegasi to balance out the distribution of our weight. We would never make it like this.

As we searched for ideas, I kicked the dirt at my feet. It clouded in the air for a second and then danced upwards in the breeze—getting in my face.

I swatted and the stuff blew away from me, swept up by the wind into the sky. I watched it go. As it floated out of view and my eyes fell upon Daniel, I remembered the day we first met at Lady Agnue's. Just before our introduction I'd made the mistake of touching our school's In and Out Spell. Recalling the magic dust drizzling off it caused an idea to abruptly pop into my head. The legitimate kind, not the crazy kind. Which was sort of unusual for me.

"Hey guys," I said. "What about the magic train?"

An hour after ditching the faulty carriage, the five of us (plus our Pegasi) arrived by foot at the magic train station in the kingdom of Middlebrook.

The magic train was the only form of realm-wide, government-regulated transportation in Book. Stations could be found in each of our twenty-six recognized kingdoms.

It was not a free form of transport, so we were thankful for the small sack of gold the Therewolves had given us that morning as a thank you gift. The reward was enough to buy the five of us passage on the locomotive and board our Pegasi in the rear compartment with the other traveling pets.

I'd always thought of the magic train as a brilliant innovation. It provided speedy, smooth travel to citizens across the realm, and it served as a means to safely dispose of and regulate the use of magic dust.

The In and Out Spell that encompassed our realm dropped magic dust particles periodically. The majority of magic dust, however, was collected in the northern mountains. There was something about the cold climate and various classifications of rock there that caused the magic to be absorbed from the air in huge quantities—collecting in giant, crystallized chunks within the mountains

When gathered in large quantities, the concentrated dust acted like a strong and clean fuel. For this reason (and in order to keep the enchanted powder out of the hands of magic hunters who would've tried to abuse its power), the government passed a law making it illegal for citizens to collect it.

Furthermore, they'd set up a special department in charge of gathering the dust for the specific, mutually beneficial purpose of powering the magic train. The substance was now solely used to fuel this communal locomotive, making it faster and more energy efficient than any other form of transportation in the realm.

The five of us stood on the platform of Middlebrook's train station amongst a sea of other passengers. It was fascinating to see everyone from this side of the tracks. My family utilized the magic train from time to time. My mom and I, for example, took a combination of several train lines and carriage rides to get to and from Lady Agnue's each year.

However, as royals, the two of us had always boarded the train privately before it was open to the commons, so we'd missed out on all the hubbub the others and I were experiencing now.

Seeing it like this was definitely much cooler. The sounds, the smells, the luggage, the vibrantly dressed people of every sort—it was all so busy and bright in the best possible way. I would have gladly gotten lost exploring it for hours if we'd had the time.

Unfortunately, we didn't. And also unfortunately, the colorful bedlam was terribly confusing to navigate through, causing us to have to hustle even more.

None of us knew the way exactly. I had never been to this particular station. Neither had SJ or any of the others. The five of us wandered about like lost chickens for some time before finding the proper booth to buy tickets. Then we had to venture on an entirely different trek to locate the area of the platform where we presented them.

When we finally made it there, no one paid us any mind as we waited to speak with the man at the window. When it was our turn and we handed him our papers, the fellow behind the counter gave us five clunky necklaces in exchange. They were long, dark purple lanyard chains with miniature snow globes dangling from the ends of each one. I realized, of course, that it was not artificial snow inside these petite orbs. It was a small sample of magic dust.

Again, because of the way royals traveled, neither SJ nor myself had ever personally paid for tickets. Consequently, we were unfamiliar with these necklaces. Blue had to explain that they served as proof of having paid for passage, as well as being fun souvenirs.

I placed the rather lengthy cord round my neck like everyone else and proceeded to make my way to the train's entrance.

The platform was so crowded you couldn't help but bump into people. I had to fight to actively push my way forward and avoid being carried away like a leaf in the current of a river.

"Excuse me. Excuse me," I repeated as I brushed shoulders and rammed into one person after another.

Hmm, and I thought move-in day at Lady Agnue's was a chaotic affair.

This was just—

I rammed into someone with a very forceful thud.

"Oh, sorry," I said, composing myself. "I didn't mean to—"

I looked up to meet the gaze of the stranger I'd collided with. The instant I did I couldn't help but instinctively jump back.

The fellow I'd hit was super creepy. He had dark, shoulder-length hair pulled into a ponytail, a golden tooth like a prospector, and foggy eyes. The sheath on his belt appeared to be holding a dagger (a well-used one based on its worn leather grip). And the scars on his hands and chin were serious—definitely not the kind of thing a guy got from shaving.

The man wore a wrinkled camel-colored jacket that matched the tattered fedora on his head. He eyed me up and down for a second—squinting at me as he did so, his nose twitching. He seemed to be both interested in and perplexed by me. I didn't stick around to find out why. I hurriedly merged back into the crowd before any further exchange could pass between us.

As I boarded the train behind Blue and Jason, I glanced back and saw the man still standing in the middle of the platform amongst a sea of people. Only now he was joined by three other equally sketchy men wearing hats and earth-toned clothing. He whispered something to them as he pointed in my direction.

I ducked inside the train and followed my friends through the cars with haste.

Eventually our group found an empty passenger box and filed in. I looked behind me to make sure no one was following then quickly shut the door and released an exhale of relief. Regrettably, the others noticed the worried look on my face.

"Hey, you okay?" Jason asked as I sat down.

I thought about the question and realized I wasn't sure. I had a bad vibe about those guys on the platform and felt it was worth mentioning. But did I really *want* to mention it? That was another issue entirely.

I still felt weird about opening up to them. But lately I'd been keeping a lot of things from my friends and that was making me feel lousy. So I decided to test the waters and give trusting them with this particular insecurity a shot.

Awkwardly, I told the others about the guy I'd rammed into, the weird way he'd stared at me, and how he'd pointed me out to his friends.

I didn't know how I thought they would react to this information. I hoped they would reassure me that I was being paranoid, conclude that it was probably nothing, then drop the matter without further issue. Much to my despair, I got none of the above.

"I saw those guys," Daniel said pensively. "I'm pretty sure they were magic hunters."

"Oh, come on." I grimaced. "Just because they were creepy, dressed in earth tones, and looked like they'd been out in the wilderness does not mean they are magic hunters."

"Knight, unlike you, I grew up in the real world, not a palace. I know a magic hunter when I see one, and those guys definitely fit the bill."

"So, what?" Blue butted in, concern in her voice. "You think maybe the reason they gave Crisa those iffy looks was because they sensed her magic?"

"It's possible," Daniel shrugged. "Emma said they can sense it pretty well when they're within close range. It would explain why the one Knight rammed into was staring at her so intently. For all we know she's giving off a pretty powerful smell."

"Hey!" I interjected.

"Calm down, not an insult," Daniel said as he cut me off. "The point is, these guys are really good at picking up magical scents. So you'll want to keep a low profile until we're sure none of them got on the train. Just coming within fifty feet of them might be enough for you to catch their attention."

I wanted to disagree and assure the others that Daniel was wrong and I was in absolutely no danger. But then I remembered something.

On our school field trip to Adelaide earlier in the semester, our carriage had stopped in the middle of the road and a prison transport had passed in front of us. The magic hunter inside had stared at me in the same ominous way that the one on the train platform just had.

The secret spark of Fairy Godmother magic that Emma had given me did not pose much of a threat to me now because I didn't know what specific ability the magic had manifested in. Emma said that as long as I was unaware of this power and how to use it, I was safe from sending off a figurative flare of alert to magic hunters on a grand scale. But she also warned (as Daniel had just reminded us) that in close proximity a magic hunter might still be able to detect the slight magical scent I was giving off.

"Crisa," Jason said, recapturing my focus. "Did you notice if those guys got on the train with us?"

"No. I didn't see."

"Then I think it would best if you did not leave this compartment," SJ said. "It is too risky for you to go wandering about the train if those magic hunters are on board."

"Are you serious?" I exclaimed, now regretting that I'd said anything to them. "I'm not going to sit in here for the next ten hours hiding like a coward."

"SJ's right, Crisa," Blue seconded. "Those guys are dangerous."

"Thanks for the concern, but I can take care of myself."

Insulted and infuriated by their attempts to protect me, I made to get up and leave, but Jason grabbed me by the arm before I could go.

"Crisa, we are just trying to do what's in your best interest. Unless you can think of a way to turn off your magic scent or whatever, for your own good you've gotta stay here until we're sure the magic hunters aren't on the train."

I whirled back around to face Jason and the rest of them. When I did, however, my lanyard necklace swung a little too hard and hit the wall of the compartment. As it clanked against the wooden frame surrounding the door, a thought occurred to me.

"All right, fine then," I huffed. "I *do* have a way to 'turn off my magic scent or whatever'."

I shook Jason's hand from my arm and removed the lanyard hanging around my neck. Then I reached into my satchel and took out my wand, which I proceeded to morph into a knife.

Carefully I poked a hole in the snow globe at the end of the necklace. I made my way to the window at the back of the compartment, slid the glass aside, and emptied out all the magic dust that had been inside the orb.

"There," I said as I closed the window again. "Everyone on this train is carrying a bit of magic with them because of these necklaces. But I've already got a little magic in me. So without the extra that was in this orb, mine should be able to blend into the general magical scent of the other passengers. I won't send up any red flags even if the magic hunters are on board."

My friends looked at one another for a second.

"That's actually a pretty smart idea, Knight," Daniel said.

"Thank you, Daniel," I answered, in disbelief that he'd actually said something non-insulting to me.

"I can't believe it came out of you."

Aw, there it is.

CHAPTER 15

Public Transportation
& Personal Reflection

fter the train left the station we spent some time discussing the crazy that had occurred earlier in the day when we were exiting the Forbidden Forest.

I still felt weird talking about Arian. Despite the fact that I now accepted I could see the future, I think there was a part of me that had trouble accepting him. I was used to people rooting for my destruction—what with Mauvrey and Lady Agnue and all—but having an actual nemesis felt kind of unreal. With so many elements of my story still engulfed in mystery, it was like I didn't feel fully connected to the idea yet.

Regardless, the fact remained that Arian was becoming a far too consistent player in our present situation for me to ignore his existence. We needed to talk about him. So while I didn't want my friends to flip out with overprotectiveness again like they had with the magic hunters, as the train charged down the track I told SJ, Blue, Jason, and Daniel most of what I knew about him. Mainly Arian's name, that he and his team had been ordered by someone called Nadia to hunt down protagonists the antagonists deemed as threats, and that the reason they wanted me dead was because of what my book's prologue prophecy said.

The others had the same reaction that I'd initially had to this information—a touch of shock and a lot of confusion. They couldn't believe that antagonists were roaming the realm preying on protagonists. Could it be that no one of authority, like the Fairy Godmothers, knew about it? Or worse, did they know and just decide not to tell us?

The thought of the latter certainly made my teeth grind with anger. Lena Lenore was our Godmother Supreme. Much as I hated the woman, I thought we could at least count on her to do her job and watch out for us. What, was she so busy forging protagonist books with the ambassadors and the Scribes that she didn't have time to let us know antagonists were trying to kill us?

At least for the meantime I seemed to be the only person the villains were focused on. Jason, Daniel, Blue, and many other protagonists were marked as "possible threats" in their files. But only my name had been on their priority elimination list. As verified by recent events, the antagonists' current focus was solely on me.

It may have been strange to admit this, but that made me happy. Not because I had a death wish, but because being hunted was exhausting. I wouldn't have wished it on my worst enemy, let alone other innocents. If keeping the antagonists focused on me prevented them from being able to move on to anyone else, like my friends, then I would hold their attention for as long as physically possible, no matter the consequences.

Moving on, the whole "why me" aspect of the situation continued to be a hot point of confusion for me, just as it was for the others when I told them what Arian had said about my prologue prophecy.

"Do you think if the ambassadors and the Godmothers can manipulate the Scribes, the antagonists have a way of doing it too?" Blue asked, making a good point.

"I don't know," I said. "But of the groups of people who'd know for sure, one shot me with a magic bolt last night and the other shot cannon balls at us this morning. So outright asking them doesn't seem like a likely option."

I released an exhale, and with it some of my tension. In spite of my initial reluctance, it felt good to be on the same page with the others about this, and most things. The only information I chose to withhold was the bit about Natalie Poole and Paige Tomkins being Arian's and Nadia's next targets.

I couldn't tell the others about Natalie and Paige without explaining how I knew about them. And I wasn't ready to reveal the whole future-seeing, other-realm-seeping-into-my-head thing. Maybe that seemed stupid given that sharing the truth about Arian had eased some of my stress. But there was already so much happening that my brain and body felt like they could not take adding another plot point to the mix, especially one that was this ambiguous and personally unsettling.

It wasn't wrong to want to retain some privacy in regards to my vulnerabilities and maintain a bit of self-preservation. Didn't everybody deserve that?

Furthermore, although Arian's identity and his relationship to me were clear (making them easier to talk about), I was still missing some major pieces of the Natalie puzzle.

Until I understood more about her, I felt strongly about

keeping the matter a secret. I had a right to try and figure things out for myself first.

As the train chugged along, and we each fell into our own thoughts, I tried to do just that, picking away at what I'd already learned about Natalie from my dreams and the files I'd found in Fairy Godmother Headquarters and Arian's bunker.

Natalie existed on Earth, another realm. She was supposed to eventually fall for some guy named Ryan Jackson, who was her one true love—her O.T.L., as it were. However, Tara—one of Arian's lackeys—had been trying to keep them apart and making Natalie's life miserable because the antagonists (under Nadia's direction) needed to destroy her spirit. And this was due to the fact that on Natalie's twenty-first birthday (her Key Destiny Interval) she was going to be able to open something called the Eternity Gate.

Oh, and if that weren't enough, Tara (who seemed to know me) was responsible for Natalie's parents' demise. Natalie had a protagonist book in our realm. And according to Arian, she didn't even *exist* yet.

I spent the next hour or so trying to make sense of these different pieces of information, but ultimately exhaustion got the better of me and I drifted into nap mode.

I supposed it was a combination of the anxiety, the jolting train cars, and the smell of polyester seats, but my dreamscape was a turbulent flood of dizzying flashes and disconcerting circumstances.

I saw waves crashing against stone. A white boat with the name "The Seabeagle" written on its bow rose and fell on the light swell of a turquoise ocean. Seagulls flew across the horizon.

Next came a vision of an intense-looking guy in a grossly

dirty, sleeveless shirt. His shoulders had traces of blood on them, and he had no shoes. He was rappelling down some sort of metallic shaft with equal parts desperation and tenacity.

When that scene shifted, I saw a sandstorm violently whipping toward Daniel and me. We were in a desert—a greenish river on our left—and we were sliding down dunes as lightning snapped aggressively across the red and onyx sky.

These flashes soon faded to an image of an immense crystal formation, vaguely in the shape of a starfish and surrounded by a weird, aqua-colored glow. It stood on the platform of a grand cavern like a beacon.

The glow of this stone flickered for a beat until it went out like a dead nightlight. Things were dark for an interval. Then I found myself in the ballroom of Lady Agnue's.

I was dressed in a gorgeous gown. The body was blush-colored lace. Over it were whimsical, flowing pieces of ivory chiffon. The bodice was strapless and had crystals decorating it elegantly in a pattern that accentuated my shape in a surprisingly flattering way.

I glanced up at the familiar scene of a ball—protagonists in shimmering dresses and tailored suits; the sounds of laughter, clinking glasses, and orchestra music; radiant lights burning in the chandeliers overhead. Then I felt something unfamiliar that made me flinch. A warm hand was pressed against mine, causing my vertebrae to tingle. I looked up and saw Chance Darling, looking as handsome as ever in a beautiful suit. He was smiling at me.

I hadn't seen Chance since I'd gotten the prologue prophecy dictating I was to be his meek wife. And although I was beginning to believe that there was more to my prophecy than I had been told, seeing him still agitated me.

Yet, the dream version of me that my subconscious was currently trapped in did not protest to his touch. He led me out onto the dance floor and the two of us stepped into the flow of music. We danced and moved, but it felt like the world stood still. He raised his arm to turn me. I followed his lead, but when I came out the other side I found that I had twirled back into the void. I was still in my gown, but the ball and the prince I despised were both gone.

More images started to play around me. They came slowly at first. Natalie (a teenager again) was in a large white room. Her hair was in a messy bun. In one hand she held a paintbrush and in the other a palette. I saw her for only a moment before the image changed and I saw Mauvrey.

The seventeen-year-old princess was wearing a purple leather jacket fitted to her body that matched the color of her spiky heeled ankle boots. Her golden-blonde hair bounced around her with each confident step. There was a certainty and strength in her eyes that would've made powerful grown men stand down.

Behind Mauvrey was a dark green forest swirled with nighttime. The image was tinged with the gray smoke and orange hues of a nearby fire. The shades of all three blurred together like a pastel rendering that had been smudged over. I heard the sounds of yelling and fighting in the background. But they, too, were distorted and muffled, so they seemed surreal and far off.

When this scene was wiped from view I was back at Lady Agnue's. There was a brief flash of the waiting area outside of the headmistress's office and the tidy, currently unattended desk of our headmistress's assistant, Miss Mammers.

I was sitting on the couch facing the desk, alone in the room. Then I heard a door open. I cringed when I saw our headmistress, Lady Agnue, in the doorway of her den. Standing beside her was Lena Lenore.

The Fairy Godmother Supreme was dressed in a pastel pink pantsuit with light pink pumps that had glittering silver straps. They looked just like the ones I'd seen before blacking out in the Scribes' library . . .

Lena Lenore smiled in my direction, melding both congeniality and malice together as flawlessly as peanut butter and jelly. Then from her lips she spoke six words coated with an undeniable wickedness.

"Lovely to see you again, Crisanta."

The pictures in my head began to pick up speed, playing across my dreamscape quick and bright. I recognized the next few images as ones that I'd already seen before. Plastic patio furniture, a gray boat with a scarlet sail, lava everywhere.

The last in this stream was a visual of the heart-shaped locket with lime green crystals that had been around SJ's neck in my previous nightmare about Adelaide. My vision expanded around it and I saw the necklace bouncing against SJ's chest as she ran. She was with Blue, Jason, and Daniel. The four of them were bolting through an orchard that looked familiar.

Adelaide Castle, I realized.

"Maybe we should've gone back to look for her," Jason commented as they zigzagged through the trees and foliage.

"We never would've found her in that maze," Daniel replied. "She must've known that when she came up with this plan. We just have to hope she meets us at the rendezvous point."

"And if she doesn't?" Blue called back.

My dream shifted. More flashes spilled through—a

massive log cabin in the snow; a creature that looked like a giant black lobster; then lastly, that powerful purple vortex.

A dream version of me stared into the manifestation of swirling energy. It overtook every angle of our shared view, pulling her and me inwards and closer to its heart. She and I merged together and I felt the force of the vortex tear me off my feet. Energy surged around me—crackling like a funnel made of lightning strikes. Then, just as I was being absorbed into it, I heard a voice.

"Crisa, can you hear me?"

It was the same calm whisper I'd heard in my dreams of that bathroom last night. Even in my unconscious state I could recognize the fragile familiarity. It was haunting, but also strangely gentle, almost caring.

"Crisa, if you can hear me, when the time comes you have to remember . . ."

I focused hard, but couldn't see where the voice was coming from. Everything was now lost in the purple vortex, the likes of which I was disappearing into with each passing second.

"Remember what?" I shouted into the field of sparkling energy that sucked me deeper inside. "Tell me!"

All I heard was an indiscernible muffle.

I started to shout into the void again, but a second later my attention was captured by the feeling of someone grabbing my arm. Like my previous dream of the vortex, before I could see who it was everything went dark and I was expunged from the scene like an unwanted thought.

Having been jolted awake, I sat up in my seat and rubbed my eyes. The others paid me no mind as I righted myself and squinted at the dimming sunlight streaking across our passenger box. SJ was also napping, and Blue and Jason were attempting to pass the time by reading through the withered pages of some book.

Daniel wasn't in the room with us. I assumed he'd gone off exploring.

Not a bad idea considering the alternative—staying in this cramped box staring out the window and thinking about my dreams.

I swung my satchel over my shoulder, told Blue and Jason I'd be back, then proceeded to slide out of the room to do some exploring of my own.

The train's interior design theme appeared to be red. As I moved through the locomotive, I discovered that the seats, carpet, and curtains varied in shade and texture, but all inevitably rooted back to this primary color.

Travelers crowded every compartment. Many chatted away in general seating areas. Some filed in and out of their own passenger boxes lining the walkways. Others lollygagged in the aisles, mingling with anybody whose path they crossed.

A handful of the compartments didn't connect with one another directly. Each time I reached one of these severed ends, I had to push aside a sliding door with a single window then walk across a covered bridge linking the cars together. Each bridge had barred, vertical railings on either side. They stretched from floor to ceiling, but the gaps between them gave way to a perfectly clear view of the landscape surrounding the train.

The bridges were only a few feet in width and about ten feet in length. At the end of some there were ladders that extended to the roof of the train through small, open hatches.

As I moseyed through the various train cars (all of which

were lit up by elegantly-shaped electric lanterns) I found myself periodically ducking to avoid pieces of luggage poking out from the overhead racks. I also had to be careful not to trip over any protruding suitcases and trunks that stuck into the aisle. That was dangerous work when you were on a moving locomotive and waiters carrying silver trays of cappuccinos and other hot beverages kept passing you by. The train employees must've been very agile, otherwise the dry cleaning bill for their crimson and gold uniforms would've been tremendous.

For a while I wandered aimlessly through the hulla-balloo—general curiosity being my only guide. But when I was about seven compartments into my exploration, my stomach growled like a wolverine and I realized just how hungry I was. I hadn't had a solid meal in a while, and there was the intoxicating smell of melted cheese in the air, calling to me.

My nose followed the scent through four more general seating compartments. When I opened the door to the fifth, my heart stopped.

The magic hunter I'd run into on the platform was there. He was settled in a chair near the back of the compartment next to six of his friends and was gesturing to some kind of map.

They hadn't noticed my entrance into the car, and I considered backtracking before they could. Before I got the chance, several other people came in behind me and began herding me down the aisle.

With nowhere to go, I started walking forward as casually as possible, trying not to draw attention to myself.

As I made my way down the aisle I vehemently reassured myself that my original idea was sound. Everyone around me was wearing a magic necklace. With the contents of my own commemorative bobble drained, my natural magical scent would be well hidden in the crowd. I should've been fine.

Still, that theory hadn't exactly been tested yet, had it?

I held my head high and moved through the car without hesitation. As I walked past the magic hunters I slowed my breathing and kept my eyes forward, glued to the exit.

For a moment I thought one of them was going to raise his head as I passed by. Fortunately, the magic hunter simply scratched his dry, worn neck and yawned before going back to his work.

I ducked swiftly into the next compartment. Once I'd securely slid the metal door shut, I leaned against it and let out a huge sigh of relief.

Whoo!

Crisa's Resourcefulness and Ingenuity: 1

Magic Hunters and Their Super Sniffers: 0

I was filled with gladness. Because (a) my plan to disguise my magic scent had worked beautifully, and (b) I now found myself in the very dining car I'd been pursuing.

The place was pretty full. Spotting an open booth by the back window, I made my way over to it and triumphantly settled myself in the crimson seat that faced away from the main door.

Finally, I was going to get three of my favorite things: food, peace, and being left to my own devices.

I needed a menu, but all the waiters were busy. As I waited, I cracked my neck a bit and gazed out the window. The sun had set and the countryside was sinking into shadow.

My image flickered in the reflection. As the electric light of the compartment contrasted the darkening world outside, my image became clearer. I found this to be cruelly funny for I so desperately wished I felt the same way inside.

With each passing chapter of this story I felt like I was disappearing. When I was at school I'd always walked with strength and confidence in my step, but I guess that was because I'd never been tested, so a majority of the time I was able to keep my doubts tightly sealed.

Now, being forced to face them, my whole essence felt shaky.

That worried me. For the weaker I was, the more chance I had of blending in with my prologue prophecy and succumbing to the damsel stereotype I was so ardently trying to escape.

With an exasperated sigh I rested my head in my hands and continued to stare out the window. The girl staring back at me seemed more tired than any girl her age should be, making her appear older, but definitely not wiser.

It was getting hard to see much outside. The night was falling so fast that the farmlands and villages we zipped by all kind of blended together. I wondered what kingdom we were in, and I wondered what normal people—commons who weren't fighting supernatural, prophetic forces or worrying about being killed—were doing right now. The sad truth soon dawned on me: I couldn't even imagine.

And yet . . . While I may not have been able to imagine what it was like to be a common character in Book, in thinking about the multitude of fates entangling me, at that moment I felt they were luckier than I was.

Many commons probably would've disagreed and called me a whiny, unappreciative princess for even thinking the thought. But the fact remained that they were more fortunate than they realized. And not just because of the whole "antagonists trying to destroy them" thing.

They were not held up to these impossibly high, impossibly regimented standards, the likes of which constrained every movement and tried to cull anyone different or unorthodox into silence. They didn't have the weight of the world resting on their shoulders because some outside force decided to put it there. And they did not have to worry about being someone else's idea of great, just their own.

It was true that everyone—regardless of archetype—had expectations to live up to. Expectations were like shadows. It was easy to forget they were there, but they trailed you wherever you went. All you needed to do was look back and see them elongating in your wake.

But with common characters, the expectations were their own. That was the difference. When you were a main character, you were born with the expectations of older generations and genre tradition—an entire realm's way of thinking saddled onto your path. Then when you grew up to be my age you had the expectations of the Author's prologue prophecies to deflate the rest of you.

I thought that was a lot to handle when I believed my prologue prophecy was solely about being a good little ordinary princess and marrying Chance Darling. If there was more to it than that, I wasn't sure how to proceed. What if Arian had been telling the truth and my fate was actually much grander—formidable enough to cause an entire kingdom of antagonists to come after me?

The truth was, I didn't know what to do with that.

My fingers grazed the window in front of me. It was cold. In locking eyes with my own reflection, I realized the look I saw reflected there was just as frigid. Much as my personality was filled with fire, my expression deepened into distilled ice the more I thought about my prophecy's two possible outcomes.

If I were trapped in my old prophecy, I'd be forced to be a normal damsel princess forever—perfect in a million stereotypical ways, but none of the ways I cared about. However, if my prophecy correlated with the hints I'd been getting from Arian, my life was going to be a never-ending montage of bad guys trying to waste me because they believed I was some kind of threat.

It was conflicting to want to stand out and separate myself from the conventions of the norm while feeling wary about a destiny that might very well grant me that wish. What got to me the most, though, was that no matter which of these two paths ended up being my reality, I was still chained to expectations. They were just different kinds.

That brought me back to the burden that separated my kind from common characters. Unless I found the Author and took my prophecy into my own hands, the shadow of expectation would not only be on my heels forever, it would wholly consume me. For I was first and foremost a protagonist. And a protagonist's life was about living up to expectations, whereas a common's life was just about living.

Ugh. Protagonist. I dwelled on the word. With everything that had happened in previous weeks, it seemed to be getting a lot heavier to hold.

I'd always considered it a loaded, vexing term. To some it meant hero, prince charming, warrior, champion. To others it meant leader, influencer, princess, damsel. To me, all I'd ever known it as was a title laden with bitter responsibility—a role for someone who was supposed to go out into the world and make their lives mean something.

But mean what exactly? I thought as I tried to reflect on what I'd accomplished in my time as a protagonist.

What does my life mean?

And what do I stand for?

These were questions I could not yet address. I had to earn the answers by overcoming the challenge of accepting myself. Unfortunately, I still didn't know how to do that.

The more I thought about the various running opinions of me—sources ranging from classmates, to headmistresses, to enemies—the more confused I became.

But, then again, why should I even care?

Maybe I couldn't change how any of those people saw me, and that was fine. I'd long suspected that was impossible anyway. But none of them sincerely knew my character, so their opinions didn't really matter. The only opinions that did were those of my closest friends. As SJ had pointed out, *they* were the people who truly knew me.

Alas, even after everything we'd been through, I still wasn't entirely sure what they thought of me.

I'd always hoped they saw what I wanted them to see—someone strong, smart, kind, sassy, the opposite of a damsel in distress, and a potential great hero and great princess. But with my track record, especially lately, I knew my odds of being seen that way were decreasing.

Still, I held out hope. I may have been running out of chances to do so, but I had to redeem myself in their eyes. For if my friends (the people who knew me best) could come to think of me as something other than a weak damsel princess and a delusional hero-wannabe, then maybe the world was wrong and there was more to me than that.

Hm. Perhaps in hindsight that was the key to accepting myself. My friends held the answer. They were the deciding parties. If they sided with my views of who I was deep down, then, in spite of everything and everyone else, I would accept that I really was this strong, admirable hero-princess I'd always aspired to be.

Conversely, if they didn't think that—if they agreed with the greater world about what I was—then I garnered it meant that really was my true nature and I would have to accept that too.

My innermost thoughts were suddenly disrupted by a waiter. Without saying anything, he refilled the bowl of creamers on my table then strode away. I blinked—coming out of my deep introspection—and stared at the petitely packaged dairy products.

Each table held an assortment of creamers, as well as other freebies including matchbooks, bread rolls, and fancy chocolates. I assumed these were all complimentary, so I grabbed two of the rolls, a handful of the individually wrapped chocolate truffles, and a couple of souvenir matchbooks and shoved them into my satchel.

My mother surely would've scolded me if she had seen such a blatant display of gluttony and hoarding. But then, my mother hadn't just been starved and imprisoned by half-wolf actors for two weeks.

Another waiter came by and gave me the menu I'd been hoping for. I began to peruse it with enthusiasm. My contentment, though, was short-lived. Just as I was about to settle on a pasta dish, someone's hand was on my shoulder. Out of instinct I grabbed the hand (as well as the arm attached to it) and twisted them both onto the table with a slam.

"Knight, let go."

"Oh, uh, sorry." I released Daniel and awkwardly smiled at the other passengers that had turned to stare at us.

I burrowed further into the booth to avoid their gazes while Daniel rubbed his arm and sat down in the seat across from me. I passed him the menu wordlessly and began to rub my own aching left wrist.

Amazingly I'd been able to ignore the pain of my injury until now, the consistent adrenaline and million other things I had to worry about overshadowing it. But my abrupt movement had aggravated it.

Arian had definitely sprained my wrist in the forest. And while I'd been trying to keep the injury from the others, it was becoming increasingly difficult to conceal. The more time that passed without proper care, the more swollen it became. Of course, Daniel immediately noticed what I was trying to hide.

"What happened to you?" he asked.

"Nothing," I said. "I fell."

"Yeah, sure you did. You know, Knight, it's not the end of the world to admit you got hurt out there. We've all got some cuts and bruises to show for the last few days. You don't have to lie about it."

"Leave it alone, Daniel," I warned as I snatched back the menu.

No sooner did I bury my face behind it, did he pull the plastic-coated shield away again.

"You make no sense, you know that?"

"*I* make no sense?" I repeated. "Daniel, you're the one who's literally said that everything about me irritates you. If that's true, then why are you even here?"

"I'm hungry and there were no other tables open. Believe me, I checked."

"No, not *here*," I gestured to the booth, "I mean on this journey with the rest of us; going back and forth across the kingdom from school to Century City to the Forbidden Forest to Adelaide."

"I already told you. Just like you, I want the Author to change my fate."

"Yeah, I remember," I said flatly. "But I also recall you saying that the only reason you were here was because of *me*. Care to explain that?"

Daniel diverted his gaze. "I don't know what you're talking about."

"Don't give me that," I said, not backing down. "I may not have gotten anything else out of you while you were under that watering can's spell, but I heard what you said to Jason backstage on opening night of the Therewolf production. And I want an answer. What did you mean when you said that I ruined your life and that you were only here because of me?"

Our staring match might as well have been the only thing of importance happening on the entire train. It blurred every other sound, movement, and person like a large cloud encircling the eye of a storm. I wondered just how long two people could actually glare at one another. We were both pretty stubborn, proud, and unrelenting, so I figured if anyone could have set the record it was us. The nail-on-chalkboard intensity dissipated, however, when Blue and Jason abruptly popped up next to our table.

"Hey, guys. Can we join you?" Jason asked.

"Yeah, I was just leaving," Daniel said as he got up from the booth.

He left the dining car and didn't look back.

Blue raised her eyebrows as she sat down. "What was all that about?"

"Nothing," I grunted. "Just Daniel being Daniel. I don't know how either of you can stand him. Especially you, Jason. I can't even sit with the kid for five minutes. How did you share a room with him back at school and not want to break his arm?"

Jason shrugged. "He's a good guy, Crisa."

"Yeah, yeah."

"No, really. Look, I know he gives you a hard time. But he doesn't mean anything by it."

I rolled my eyes. "Right. His constant mission to take blows at my self-esteem and his belief that I, quote, 'ruined his life' are completely unrelated."

Jason blinked in surprise. "You heard that, huh?"

"I was behind the curtain."

"Hold on," Blue interjected. "I think I missed something."

"Before the Therewolves' show started, Daniel and I got to talking and he said that Crisa ruined his life. Oh, and that he was only on this mission with us because of her," Jason explained.

"Exaggeration much?" Blue snorted. "I mean he only just met her a couple months ago."

Jason grinned. "That's what I said!"

"Really? Okay, jinx then!"

"Blue, jinx only works when we say something—"

"—at the same time," Blue chimed in just as Jason finished his sentence. "There. Now jinx." She crossed her arms in playful satisfaction.

Jason shrugged again, seeming to accept his defeat. I coughed to draw their focus back to our conversation. "Yeah, so anyway . . . Jason, any chance Daniel ever finished telling you what he meant when he said that?"

Jason blinked at me wordlessly.

"Jason?" I repeated.

He still didn't open his mouth. What he did instead was gesture at Blue.

Oh, got it.

I sighed. "Blue, un-jinx him please."

"Ugh. Fine," she said. "Jason, I release thee."

Jason exhaled overdramatically, which earned him an amicable punch in the shoulder from Blue.

"Sorry, Crisa," he continued. "To be honest, when I was under the influence of that watering can I really couldn't have cared less about Daniel or his problems. But even if I had it wouldn't have mattered. That night was one of the only times during our stay at Camp Therewolf that I got the chance to talk to him."

"Great," I huffed. "So it's hopeless then. I'm never going to know anything about what makes the guy tick."

"If it helps," Jason continued, "I think the way he acts and keeps to himself comes down to the simple fact that he misses his life before Lord Channing's."

"Fine, he misses his old life. Whatever," I retorted. "That doesn't give Mr. Cryptic a free pass to pose as a friend without earning our trust. And really, guys, how can he possibly do that when he is concealing so much about himself? How are we supposed to even feel comfortable with him around if we don't know what's going on inside that thick skull?"

"Come on, Crisa," Jason responded. "Maybe you're being too hard on him. It's not exactly uncommon for people to keep things to themselves. And doing so doesn't make someone bad or untrustworthy.

"Maybe you don't understand why Daniel gives you a hard time or blames you for things or even the specific reasons why he's on this quest with us. But whether you admit it or not, you know you can count on him because you know who he is despite that. When you got your prologue prophecy and fell off your Pegasus in Adelaide's Twenty-Three Skidd tournament, he's the guy who tried to help you instead of stopping Blue from taking the winning shot. He's the guy who went back for you when we were trapped at Fairy Godmother HQ—diving into that watery deathtrap without thinking twice about it because he wanted to make sure you were okay. He drove the carriage to Emma's, had your back at the Capitol Building, kept you from getting barbequed by the lightning daffodils in the Forbidden Forest, and even turned himself into a Therewolf because your plans told him it was necessary for the good of the group."

Jason looked at me earnestly and I saw the same intense blue eyes of the ten-year-old boy who'd hidden under that tablecloth with me back at Lady Agnue's all those years ago. The eyes of someone who—from the very beginning—had been an ally in my way of thinking.

Until now.

For the first time in as far back as I could remember, Jason and I were seeing things differently. And for the life of me I wished it wasn't so. He was technically my oldest friend. Having him on such an opposite stance from my own made me feel a cutting combination of foolish and ostracized. Was I the only one who felt there was something off about Daniel?

"In the last few months the guy's conspired with us, worked with us, and fought with us at every turn," Jason went on, trying to appeal to my reason. "So yeah, maybe he keeps things to himself, and maybe that's annoying. But he's been there for us *and* for you since this whole thing started."

"Jason's right, Crisa," Blue chimed in. "I get how much he bugs you, and that whole 'ruined his life' statement obviously doesn't help. But you've gotta look past that and see the big picture. Daniel's been a good friend to all of us and we *can* trust him. You need to believe that. Otherwise things going forward are just going to get harder."

I twiddled my thumbs on the table between us. My gaze drifted back to the window and I uttered the only response I could think of.

"I don't know."

Not the most eloquent reaction, but what else could I have said? Blue and Jason made some really good points. Daniel had been there for all of us since our fates had been intertwined. He'd certainly proven himself to be a friend . . . hadn't he?

Ugh, but he was *Daniel*.

He was the aggravator of my patience and provoker of my worst qualities. Even after all we'd been through together, I still couldn't see him as a friend or trust him. I didn't know whether this conclusion attested more to his character or to mine, but it was how I felt. And I could no more change that than I could change him.

After a minute Jason broke the silence—redirecting my gaze away from the creamers on the table back to him.

"Crisa," he began carefully. "I get that this is kind of rough for you, and I can still see you backtracking. So let me give you another example that might resonate a bit better."

I raised my eyebrows. "Okay."

"All right, now don't take offense," he said. "But from what I've seen over the years, I think it's pretty safe to say that you don't like to rely on other people and prefer to handle things for yourself. Right?"

"Well I wouldn't say—"

"Oh, he totally hit the hammer on the nail, Crisa," Blue interrupted.

Jason nodded. "Blue, you know where I'm going with this. You wanna take it instead?"

"Yeah, sure," she said, sitting up straighter. "The point is, Crisa, even if you have a tendency to push us away when we try to help you, and keep stuff to yourself a lot, we trust you. Not just to lead the group when the situation calls for it, but as a friend. If we didn't, we probably wouldn't be here."

The words of magically unkind SJ from our time in the Therewolf theater echoed in the back of my mind: "*We are here because of you and your big ideas.*"

I hung my head as guilt burned inside of me like a spicy taco.

"Yeah. I know," I responded with a sigh. "It's my fault for dragging you guys into this. What's happened to you so far is on me. Almost getting killed, eaten, magically altered—it's all because you trusted me even though I didn't deserve it. And . . . I'm sorry."

"Crisa, I don't think you get it," Jason said. "What Blue's saying—she means it in a good way."

I glanced up. "How's that?"

"If we hadn't trusted you, we wouldn't be so close to breaking the In and Out Spell around the Indexlands or finding the Author. We wouldn't have discovered that the realm's ambassadors are messing with protagonist selection. And we wouldn't have found out that Mark might be in trouble."

Blue nodded. "Plus, think about all those people we freed

in the Forbidden Forest. And the Therewolves we helped. And, well, your quick thinking's saved us a bunch of other times too. If we hadn't trusted you, do you really think any of that stuff would've happened?"

"I, I don't know . . ."

"Well I *do* know," Blue replied bluntly. "It wouldn't have. You were wrong before, Crisa. You do deserve our trust. Like Daniel, maybe you don't always share as much as you should. Maybe your inexplicable behavior can be frustrating every now and then. But despite that, we know we can count on you to do what's right. You've proven that time and again. And that's enough." She held my gaze tightly in her penetrating blue eyes. "Crisa, you have to let that be enough."

"Blue's right," Jason said in agreement. "If we hadn't trusted you, I guarantee a lot of stuff wouldn't have worked out the way it did. We might not even be sitting here now. And the same goes for Daniel. So believe me when I say that if you don't start realizing you can count on him—like we count on you—then it's only a matter of time before that distrust causes something to go wrong or someone to get hurt."

But what if . . . I mean, how can I . . .

I started to retreat inwards, pulling away like I always did. But then Blue leaned forward and touched my hand.

"Crisa," she said sternly yet softly. "If we want this to work then we have to trust each other. It's that simple."

All I could do was sit and stare as her words hung in the air. Blue and Jason had just given me a mouth full of humble pie followed by a self-reflection sandwich, both of which made my stomach hurt.

I needed time to process, but the looks the dynamic

duo were giving me told me that they wanted some sort of immediate affirmation that their words had gotten through.

The thing was, I couldn't really provide one. Their logic was sound, but that didn't mean it contained more truth than my instinct. Both mattered here. And with so much at stake and so many unanswered questions concerning Daniel and our fates, I had to be careful with every step I took.

"So then . . ."

I looked up to find our waiter had returned with a notepad and a pencil. His gaze fell upon me with unintended weight as he asked me the very question that Blue and Jason's eyes were also silently posing.

"What'll it be?"

CHAPTER 16

Traingoer's Remorse

 roast beef sandwich, three glasses of peach iced tea, and a side of steaming hot guilt later, I was continuing my solo exploration of the train.

I'd parted ways with Blue and Jason after dinner. They'd gone on to explore other areas of the train while I continued ahead. We were currently at our fifth stop for the day, and Adelaide was only two stops away. I decided to use what was left of my time to go and check out the rest of the locomotive—namely, the non-commercial parts.

Those areas were clearly not intended for passenger access, but I didn't care. I had a curious instinct about the world, and was drawn toward places I was not supposed to be. It was one of the riskier aspects of my personality, sure. But it was also the part that brought the most color to my day-to-day.

At present, I was skulking through the different refrigeration compartments, having just slipped through the kitchen behind the dining car. The half dozen train employees I passed paid me no mind. Either they didn't care what I was doing or were too distracted by their upcoming end-of-dinner-service-break to notice.

It wasn't long before I found my way into the last

refrigeration car: the meat locker. The steel door slid closed behind me with a sucking noise that caused me to jump.

Everything in the metallic compartment was characterized by frost. My breath fogged up the sole window as I looked out at the night sky. The only lights illuminating the inside of the car were a pair of electric lanterns—one on the left wall and one on the right. Not much light considering the size of this place.

The meat storage unit was shockingly large, causing me to presume that the train didn't transport many vegetarians. When I first entered I couldn't even see the other side. There were dozens upon dozens of giant slabs of meat hanging from the ceiling, impairing my view.

It was like walking through a protein labyrinth. In addition to the slabs, I had to watch my step to avoid being entangled by the pounds of sausage links scattered across the floor like slumbering snakes.

Hmm. Is that even sanitary?

As I wandered through the maze of meat I tried to suppress the voices in my head that nagged me to heed what Blue and Jason had said before dinner. Alas, a good lecturing like that was hard to shake.

They hadn't been wrong. Logically speaking, Daniel had earned my trust and my friendship over the last couple of months. Plus—as my friends so blatantly pointed out—I had my secrets too. So to an objective observer my behavior could be seen as just as annoyingly cryptic.

Maybe I was no better than he was. Worse, maybe he was right on the carriage ride to Emma's when he told me we weren't so different.

I shuddered at the thought. Blue and Jason may not

have been wrong, but they also didn't fully understand. Daniel didn't treat them the way he treated me. Our whole relationship felt like a magic trick—a construct of misdirection, deception, and uncertain outcomes.

On the ride over to Emma's he'd reassured me that he didn't dislike me as a person. Nevertheless, one look into his eyes and I knew he was holding something back. He definitely bore some kind of deeper ill will toward me that extended beyond natural irritation. His claim that I had "ruined his life" confirmed it.

Knowing this, how could I possibly put my faith in him? If I was that positive that someone had ruined my life, then I darn sure wouldn't be looking out for their best interest. And I certainly wouldn't want to be so close to them all the time either, unless I had some sort of "keep your friends close, keep your enemies closer" motive going.

I paused for a second as the thought sunk in.

What if Daniel was just biding time keeping an eye on me until he had the right opportunity to get me out of his way?

It was a radical notion, but one that held weight the more I considered it, especially when my thoughts fell on Arian. Was it all just coincidence that the boy whose life I'd supposedly ruined had wormed his way into my world at basically the same time that Arian and his antagonists had set their sights on me?

Arian's first attack was at the Capitol Building in Century City, where Daniel used to work before coming to Lord Channing's. Daniel had only appeared at school this past semester, years after common protagonists typically started. And he'd only become Jason's roommate because Mark (who had a file in Arian's bunker) was out of the picture. Wasn't it fair to hold a little doubt about Daniel's true intentions? I mean, for all I knew, he very well could've been working with Arian.

Maybe lumping them together was a step too far, but the idea flitted across my mind nonetheless. Arian did mention to Tara in my recent dream that he had an ally in my inner circle . . .

I exhaled in frustration, which Daniel so often made me do. Of all the people out there who'd tried to bring me down, could this hero be the one I most had to worry about?

My internal monologue came to a halt as I reached the other side of the meat locker. Wanting to get past the foul smells and the equally rotten feelings about myself, I exited the chilly place as fast as possible.

Instead of emerging into another compartment, I now found myself standing on a small platform. This ledge was connected to the next carriage by the same kind of thin, railed bridge I'd come across earlier. The only difference was that here the floor-to-roof railings were much farther apart—about a foot and a half between each one.

It was a windy night, so despite our train being at a standstill the cold air whipped around me with rapid palpitations.

We'd arrived in the kingdom of Dobb a few minutes ago, and I could see people boarding the train from the station we were currently parked at. I carefully made my way across the bridge before any of them could spot me. It was fairly easy. Had we been in motion that would have been a different story.

This bridge did not feel as stable as the others. The metal flooring seemed way less walked on, making it more slippery under my boots. And it seemed less even as well, as if since passengers didn't typically come this way the train builders had skipped over the final smoothing.

Eventually I reached the other side of the bridge. Beside the door was a ladder that led up to the roof just like I'd seen on the outside of other cars.

I entered the large compartment ahead. It appeared to serve as some kind of employee locker room. Instead of passenger seats, a couple of ruby red couches sat beneath a big window that faced the train station. There were lockers against both walls with name labels framed in silver. A few coat closets lined the wide aisle space. Above them were some high-up bed nooks built into the walls. They were modest, like the holes a gopher might sleep in, but they looked comfortable. Between their seclusion and coverage, I imagined any one of them would be a good place to take a nap or hide in, depending on how your day was going.

I walked across the thin peach carpet until I reached the door on the other side. I pressed my face against its glass porthole like a child looking into a candy shop window. The adjacent car was something magnificent.

The engine room.

It was huge and constructed from a mix of bronze and iron. From the station platform, workers were hoisting sacks of magic dust inside. They were emptied onto the floor surrounding the firebox at the head of the train. The resulting piles looked like sparkling sand dunes.

Most of the workers wore pressed crimson uniforms. A couple of them monitored the dying blaze up front, which produced a strange orangey-purple smoke as a result of its magical fuel source.

Neat.

I pulled out a roll from my satchel and began to munch on it while I watched them work.

After a few minutes I decided to make my way back to our passenger box. I'd been gone a while and garnered that it was time I returned to my friends. I rotated away from the engine room and began the reverse journey.

As I strode back through the locker room car, my eyes drifted toward the window that faced the station platform. I'd been to Dobb a couple of times since meeting SJ (this was her home kingdom), and I'd always found their people's style of dress to be beautiful. They wore outfits comprised of a lot of silver silk and shimmering gold undertones, making the crowds look unceasingly elegant and enchanting, like walking embodiments of starlight.

People were still bustling in and out and gathering around the locomotive. I watched them hustle along. There were adults, children, nobility, commons, seniors, and . . .

A half-chewed bite of roll dropped from my mouth.

Arian and a group of about ten men were on the platform. I scurried to the window just in time to see them board one of the passenger cars somewhere down the line.

It seemed Arian hadn't been kidding when he said he'd found a way to track me. In spite of this, I still couldn't believe how fast he'd managed to do it.

I had to get back to the others quickly. We needed to get off this train.

With haste I hustled across the train's various bridges and compartments. Every so often I ducked inside an empty passenger box if I saw the compartment door ahead start to open. I didn't want to risk the chance that the passengers about to enter were Arian and his men.

Finally, I reached the car I'd seen my enemy enter into

from the platform. Before proceeding inside, I surveyed it through the door's porthole.

He didn't appear to be there anymore, but the magic hunters still were, so I moved as speedily as I could without drawing attention to myself.

A couple minutes later I burst into our passenger box.

"We're leaving," I said.

SJ looked up from the *Maidens' Home Journal* magazine she was reading. "Sorry?"

"Arian's here, and he brought friends," I explained to her, Daniel, and Jason. Then I glanced around. "Where's Blue?"

"She went to explore the rest of the train. She said one of the conductors was going to show her the engine room."

"We must've just missed each other," I thought aloud, figuring she'd passed me when I was hiding out in one of the passenger boxes. "But we need to find her before—"

I staggered forward as the train jolted into motion and we rolled away from the station. It was too late. We were on the move again.

"New plan," I announced. "We find our way to the luggage cars, grab the Pegasi, and escape on their backs. Adelaide's not that far now, and they should be rested enough to take us the remainder of the way."

"What about Blue?" Jason asked.

"I'll go find her while you guys get ahead."

"No way," Daniel said, grabbing my arm as I headed for the door. "They're after *you*. We can't have you wandering all over the train."

"He's right, Crisa," Jason agreed. "I'll go get Blue. You go with them."

"Fine," I said. I shook Daniel's hand off me in disgust. "But be careful."

I turned to the door again, but this time SJ grabbed hold of my elbow before I could exit the compartment. "Crisa, wait," she said.

I swear, if one more person grabs me today . . .

I spun around. "Now what?"

"The stop the train just made, it was in Dobb—*my kingdom.* My parents and I take the train from here to Lady Agnue's every year," SJ explained.

"And?" Daniel interjected.

"*And* I know the route that is coming like the back of my hand. In about fifteen minutes we will begin to pass through a series of mountain tunnels. When we go through them the conductor will turn off the lights throughout the train so we do not attract the vampire bats that dwell there. Between that and the fact that it is already night, all the train's cars will go black and no one will be able to see a thing."

"So since we don't know where Arian and his troops are," I said, finishing her train of thought (no pun intended), "we should make our move then. When the darkness can conceal us."

"Exactly," SJ affirmed.

Jason blinked in surprise. "That's brilliant."

SJ smirked. "Hey, not just a pretty face."

"All right, first things first," I said to Jason and Daniel. "I've been on this route a couple of times myself, and while we won't be able to see a thing when the lights are out, if we just keep going straight we'll be fine. If I remember correctly, pretty much everyone stays seated during the dark intervals. But for passenger safety the train conductors always make sure the aisles are completely clear before we approach the tunnels so no one will trip over anything. SJ," I turned to my friend, "you know the route best. You wanna walk us through it?"

SJ nodded and snatched a piece of parchment and a quill from one of the passenger box cubbies. She swiftly began to draw our trajectory as she spoke.

"Okay, there are a total of six mountain tunnels that the train will pass through, resulting in six episodes of darkness that vary in length. In between the tunnels the intervals of light will become longer. When the train enters the first tunnel, Jason will head for the engine room to find Blue while the three of us go toward the luggage cars."

I looked to Jason. "Once we reach the luggage cars we'll wait there for you and Blue to catch up. You guys should use the remaining tunnels to conceal your journey back to us. Got it?"

"Got it."

"Good," I said. "Now all we have to do is wait."

CHAPTER 17

I Make the Wrong Decision

J fiddled with her slingshot, Jason tapped his foot anxiously, and Daniel stood by the window.

In a moment of lapsed judgment, he reached inside his pocket and checked his mysterious golden pocket watch. I guess he thought we were all too distracted to notice the slight glance he stole at its contents. But he was wrong. As he took his hand from his pocket, he saw me looking at him.

A weird moment passed between us. He didn't avert his eyes quickly like someone ashamed. I didn't look away like someone embarrassed. We just held each other's gaze for a long, hard beat.

The train sped on. Eventually Daniel's attention moved away from me and back toward the window. I stayed focused on him, though.

I had a lot of enemies on this train—Arian, antagonist soldiers, a whole slew of magic hunters. But I knew what each of them wanted from me. All were direct in their intentions. Not knowing Daniel's made me wonder if the enemy I should really be worried about was standing right across from me.

I tore a piece of fabric from my dress and used it as a makeshift bandage to wrap my injured left hand. By wrapping the cloth tightly around my wrist and in between my thumb and pointer fingers, it soothed some of the pain and immobilized the joint to give it a bit of support. This wasn't a permanent fix, but I figured it would do for now.

The lights in our cabin began to dim. It was time.

We filed into the hallway as everything went black. Daniel was ahead of me and behind SJ. He was close enough that I was able to make out his shadow. But anything outside a one-foot radius was a total blob of ink. Swiftly but carefully, we moved from one car to the next, the train's wheels rumbling beneath us.

Soon enough the lights came back on and the three of us sat down in available seats before anyone could notice our presence. It was a general seating area. SJ ducked into a chair in the third row. Daniel and I slid into a pair of seats on the aisle of the fifth.

As we waited I wondered if Jason had found Blue yet. I wondered when SJ had developed such stealth. And I wondered how long my injured hand would tolerate being ignored. Then I stopped wondering and leaned out from my chair to take a look at the aisle ahead.

Just like ones we'd come down, this one was also clear. Unlike the first time I crossed the train, all the luggage was now either fully stashed beneath seats or strapped firmly in the above-head compartments.

My attention came back to Daniel. I eyed the pocket where he kept his watch, then the sheath strapped to his back.

If I could just get him to be honest with me about something . . .

"Daniel?" I asked, quietly so as not to call attention to our conversation.

He met my gaze. The lanterns of the train car defined his

bone structure in sharp shadows. Meanwhile his dark brown eyes had deepened to an almost beastly color.

"When we were about to break out of the Therewolf camp, why did you ask me to make sure I brought back your sheath?" I gestured to the plain, unremarkable thing that held his weapon. "You were adamant about it. Why was it so important?"

"Does it matter?"

"Would it make a difference if I said it did?"

Daniel adjusted the strap of his sheath, but I think it was more of a reflex than a conscious decision. I waited with bated breath, realizing only then how much his secrets deprived me of air.

"I appreciate you getting it for me, Knight," Daniel said slowly. "But just let it go, okay. I'd rather not talk about it."

"So the usual answer then." I sighed—not frustrated, just sad. The lights in the train began to dim and Daniel, SJ, and I rose as darkness settled.

We continued to advance from one car to the next until we entered the last passenger compartment before the luggage cars. I made my way forward, but after a few steps I suddenly tripped over something that protruded into the aisle. In an attempt to not draw attention to myself, I stifled my natural "Eep!" as I toppled over. The sound of me landing on the roughly carpeted floor was concealed by the train turbulence.

Ugh, what the heck? All this stuff is supposed to be stored.

And why had I been the only one to trip? SJ and Daniel were ahead of me. Shouldn't they have fallen over the suitcase too?

Obviously they hadn't. Nor had they noticed my fall since they appeared to be moving on without me. I perceived the sound of the door opening ahead, followed by the subsequent noise of their feet moving across the bridge that connected this compartment to the luggage cars.

Just as I got to my feet, someone's hand covered my mouth and yanked me back.

Immediately other hands began to grab my arms. I struggled and thrashed violently as I tried to get away or get out a sound.

It was far too dark for anyone to see I was in trouble. But in my peripheral vision, I noticed a light. It was like a tiny spark, and it was running down the aisle as if being conducted by a thin metal wire. As my eyes followed its route I realized this wasn't just a spark. It was a small flame. And it was making its way in the direction of SJ and Daniel like a . . . fuse.

Oh no.

I side-kicked, rear-elbowed, and backwards head-butted at my unseen assailants. Somehow I managed to break free. I raced forward in a feeble attempt to outrun the fuse rapidly burning its way down the line.

I didn't make it in time.

A couple of yards before I reached the door, an explosion went off. I was thrown back into the car—landing in a pile of other passengers who'd also been tossed to the ground. When my eyes finally blinked open, I discovered that the lights of the compartment had come back on, but a large haze of orange and purple smoke still hindered my vision.

I scrambled to my feet and bolted to the rear doorway. When I got there I found myself facing empty track.

Smoke rushed past me as we sped away from the tunnel. The explosion had detached the luggage cars from the rest of the train, severing the bridge that once connected us. I was barely able to see the disconnected cars roll to a stop as my own compartment raced on with the rest of the locomotive.

I looked down and saw that the steel, which had formerly linked to the bridge, had been completely burned through. On closer inspection, I discovered that the metallic edges were singed with the glittering magic dust that powered the train. There also appeared to be bits of torched purple lanyard crusted onto the area where the explosion had erupted.

I heard movement in the compartment behind me and turned to face what was coming.

The car was littered with luggage and frazzled people who were struggling to get to their feet. Directly behind them were Arian and several of his men. When he saw me looking at him he began to push even harder to get through the swarm of passengers.

I whirled back around and leaned out over the open space where the door had been. Unlike some of the others, this car did not have a ladder attached to it.

The lights started to dim again. I took the remaining few seconds to scan the layout from here to the other side of the compartment. Arian and I locked eyes just as the last lantern fluttered into blackness.

As the train plunged through the next tunnel I hurriedly maneuvered my way back across the chaotic car. I couldn't see a thing, but worked from memory as best I could to hurtle myself over the fallen people and luggage then crawl beneath the rows of chairs and seated passengers.

General commotion echoed everywhere, allowing me to elude Arian's capture. I eventually slipped out the other door into the next compartment. Once I had, I got to my feet and made a full on break for it.

With little to no regard for the luxury of keeping a low profile, I sped through the cars. The lights came back at some point. From then on I kept my eyes peeled for Blue and Jason. They had to be around here somewhere. And I needed to find them ASAP so we could figure out a way to get off this train and reconnect with the others.

As I continued I noticed that the rest of the passengers seemed oblivious to the explosion that had happened at the rear of the transport. It was pretty far back, and with all the lapses of darkness and mountain turbulence, they must've either not sensed it or chalked it up to a particularly bumpy ride.

I shoved my way past a haughty waiter as I burst through the dining car. Bobbing and weaving around one obstacle after the next, I proceeded through the kitchen and the various refrigeration compartments that followed.

With all my strength I soon heaved open the hefty door to the meat locker. The engine room wasn't too far ahead now. When I arrived there I would tell the conductors to stop the train, and hopefully I would find Blue and Jason too.

The door suction-slammed behind me. I crisscrossed through the various hunks of hanging protein until—

BAM!

I thought I'd run into a really thick cut of beef, but then I looked up and saw the fedora-wearing magic hunter.

I reached my left hand into my satchel for my wand, but all I had time to grasp was one of those matchbooks I'd taken from the dining car. Two seconds after I bounced off his chest the hunter grabbed me. Yanking me by the wrist, he pulled me in close with one hand while he drew his dagger from its sheath with the other. He moved so fast I didn't even have time to blink. The dagger was at my throat before I could finish a heartbeat. I would have been impressed had it not been for the sharp, cold blade I now had pressed against my neck.

Behind the hunter, two of his equally sketchy companions appeared. They entered through the other door, carrying several massive sacks of the magic dust that powered the train. When they saw our strange confrontation, they set their sacks down.

"Parker," a hunter wearing a black tweed jacket said. "Come on. The others have secured the engine room. We need to help them prep the bridge for the explosion."

"Hold on," Parker said as he studied me.

He pulled me in even closer. I resisted, but not enough to prevent him from taking a long, deep sniff of my left arm. His nose twitched and his eyes sparked with recognition.

"This is the girl from the platform," he said. "I was right. She's a carrier."

"Why didn't we sense her on the train then?" another magic hunter wearing a green scarf asked.

The one called Parker noticed the empty orb on my lanyard. He twisted my injured hand, causing me to wince. Then he lifted up the lanyard with the tip of his dagger and brought its dangling orb close to his face.

"Not if she was blending in," he said, comprehending what I'd done. He turned to look back at me. "Thought you were pretty clever, didn't you?"

My eyes narrowed. "I have my moments."

The other hunters came to join Parker in the overcrowding of my personal space. As they did, the train shook with an abrupt jolt of turbulence that caused one of the hunters to knock over his sack of magic dust.

My eyes widened as the sparkly powder fell to the ground a few feet from the back door. It spilled in a crescent shape around the exit, managing to coat several links of sausages.

"You idiot. Look what you did," the hunter in the black tweed jacket said.

He reached down and picked up a fistful of magic dust and chucked it at his clumsier, green scarf-wearing accomplice.

Green Scarf dodged, causing the splash of dust to stick to a large chunk of beef hanging between them. In retaliation, Green Scarf grasped two handfuls of magic dust and chucked it at Tweed Jacket.

Tweed Jacket rapidly moved out of the way. Most of the dust got on an adjacent dangling cut of pork, but some still managed to stick to his sleeves, and Parker's too.

Parker cleared his throat and clutched my injured wrist tighter, making me wince again. The other hunters refocused. Green Scarf ripped the lanyard from my neck. Then he and Tweed Jacket compared it to the ones around their own necks and took in my scent.

"I don't believe it. She smells like Fairy Godmother magic," Tweed Jacket said.

"Yeah, but stronger somehow," Green Scarf added. "More powerful than any Godmother scent I've ever been around. What do you think, Parker?"

Parker's dry, cracked lips formed into a small, malicious grin. "I think there's only one way to find out. Hold her down."

Oh, I don't think so, you—

The steel door I'd entered through abruptly slid open. Facing us now was Arian and a posse of five sword-wielding companions. They barged into the frosty place and rushed through the meat maze to the center of the compartment.

Parker hurled his dagger at Arian's head. The aim was perfect, but regrettably so were Arian's reflexes. He dodged the blade with ease. The same could not be said for the guy who'd been standing directly behind him.

Hmm. I guess that makes it four sword-wielding henchmen.

Arian didn't even blink as his fallen attendant collapsed to the ground. He simply continued to approach us.

Parker yanked me back a couple feet in response. I swallowed hard at the burst of pain in my hand, squeezing the matchbook I had concealed within my fist.

"Stand down," Arian said as he drew his sword. "I don't know what your business is here, hunters, but the girl is mine."

"I don't think so, Jack," Tweed Jacket countered as he whipped out a rather rusty looking knife in retaliation.

He and Green Scarf stepped forward, meeting the opposing forces in the middle of the compartment and blocking Arian from coming anywhere near me. This would've been great had it not been for Crusty the Magic Hunter (i.e., Parker) still latched onto my arm.

I glanced over Parker's shoulder. The exit was barely five feet away.

"We found the kid first," Tweed Jacket continued. "Her magic's ours."

"Her magic . . ." Arian raised his eyebrows, finally understanding why I could work my Fairy Godmother wand.

After a pause he shouldered the realization and readdressed the hunters. "Look, you can have her magic," he told them. "I just want her head when you're done. Deal?"

The boys on both sides of the standoff exchanged looks; silently deciding whether or not the terms were acceptable. Their macho staring match was so intense that they didn't notice the lanterns inside the compartment were beginning to flicker.

"Works for me," Parker finally replied.

The light dimmed more and more with each passing second.

"Actually," I interrupted, raising my free, non-injured hand as if to ask a question. "If I could interject . . ."

In the next instant everything went black. The moment it did I curled my raised hand into a fist and punched Parker directly in the throat. He released me and I reached out for where his lanyard had been, purposefully entangling my hand within it.

I tightened my grip around Parker's necklace and pulled back—strangling him with the lanyard while my other hand grabbed his arm. He was my human shield as I swiftly backed up through the darkness.

When I felt myself touching the steel of the door I kneed Parker in the back, released my grip, and shoved his body forward—knocking over the hunters who'd tried to come after us.

In sync with the thud of the impact I lit a match from the matchbook clenched in my fist and threw it on the ground. It immediately caught onto the littered magic dust.

An immense semicircle of brilliant, orange and purple flames blazed in a protective barrier around me. Just as quickly as it grew, it began to set off a series of subsequent smaller explosions as the sausage links that had been coated by the fallen powder ignited.

The sausage links spread the fire throughout the entire compartment. As the meat products erupted, I escaped through the door.

Rocky edges of tunnel whizzed by. I couldn't see them

terribly well, but I could feel their proximity in the same way a claustrophobic person could detect walls even if their eyes were shut.

The bridge connecting to the next car, on the other hand, was all but lost to me in the dark space. I could hear it rattling—metal jolting and bouncing around with the tracks' turbulence—but I might as well have been wearing a blindfold.

I'd already considered the bridge fairly unstable when we'd been parked at the station. Now it rocked back and forth so threateningly you would have thought it was trying to break free. Still, it wasn't like I could afford to be choosy about my means for escape.

As I crossed it, I knew the train was going uphill so I hung on to the railings as I pulled myself forward. I made it about halfway before the screeches started.

The vampire bats.

Beastly screams filled the tunnel, getting louder and louder until the creatures rushed into view. While everything else about the tunnel was a study in darkness, the vampire bats were a pop of unwelcome color. Each of their bodies was a bright, glowing shade of cobalt blue that filled me with dread. Hundreds of them were coming toward me, swirling in a condensed swarm.

I crouched down, keeping my eyes shut as I stayed as low and close to the railing as possible. The roof of the bridge created an overhead barrier, but I was still exposed from the sides. I felt the whoosh of the bats zooming in and out of the bridge's railings. Their screeches were deafening. Their leathery wings lapped against my face. I periodically felt the scraping of tiny claws against my back and arms as the bats chaotically thrashed about in the darkness.

I tried to remain calm. I tried not to freak out. All the while I fought the instinct to pull out my wand and hide behind its protective shield form.

If I so much as let it peek out of my bag, the situation would get far more dangerous. There was, after all, a reason that the train extinguished all unnatural light when we passed through these tunnels.

Thankfully, a loud boom from within the meat locker suddenly scared off the bats, freeing me from their assault.

When the creatures' high-pitched wails dissipated, I opened my eyes and saw that the meat compartment fire had grown. It was now noticeably visible through the window of the steel door. I guessed the explosion I'd just heard had been the result of one of the fires finally catching onto the slabs of meat that Tweed Jacket and Green Scarf had doused with magic dust.

Not wanting to risk another run-in with the vampire bats—I bolted across the rest of the bridge as fast as possible. When I'd traversed the clanging deathtrap, my hand grasped for the door. I slid it open, ducking inside the car's equally dark, but infinitely more promising innards.

Phew! Ok, maybe here I would be—

The lights flickered back on just in time for me to see some guy flying in my direction. I dove out of the way to avoid getting body-slammed.

"Crisa, hey!"

I whipped up my head to see Blue. She leapt forward and punched the aforementioned guy in the face. He was knocked out cold, but she didn't stop to admire her good work. Instead she spun back around to readdress the rest of the chaos in the room.

There were eight other men in the formerly quiet

compartment—all dressed in similarly grungy earth tones, which made me believe they were more magic hunters. Parker's other friends no doubt.

Presently, four of them were knocked out like the one Blue had just face-smashed. The others were still very much awake.

"What are you doing here?" Blue asked as she threw a rather impressive roundhouse kick at one of the attackers.

"What am *I* doing here?" I grabbed my wand from my satchel and hopped to my feet.

Spear.

"What are *you* doing here?"

"We're trying to save the train," Jason said as he ducked the swooping strike of a taller hunter. He rammed the blunt end of his axe into the hunter's lower back then turned to elbow another assailant in the jaw.

"Well . . ." I blocked with my spear then slammed the staff into one of the hunter's foreheads. "I'm trying not to die on it."

Blue sucker-punched the last of the standing magic hunters. He dropped to the floor. "How's that working out for you?" she asked.

I glanced back in the direction of the meat locker. It was far off, but I could still see the bright orange and purple blaze caressing the compartment window.

"Um, let's see. There was an explosion at the back of the train. The luggage cars with our Pegasi were separated from the rest of the transport along with SJ and Daniel. Arian and his lackeys found me and are hot on my tail. Oh, and the magic hunters are now actively trying to kill me. So overall, I definitely think it could be going better."

I made for one of the unconscious hunters, removed the

lanyard from around his neck, and began tying his hands behind his back with the rope-like necklace.

"What about you guys," I asked. "What happened here?"

Blue and Jason followed my lead and began to tie up the other incapacitated men.

"Well, I came in here to find Blue," Jason began. "But she was hiding in one of the overhead bed nooks. She'd heard the magic hunters coming and hid in order to get the drop on them when she had the chance. They were trying to steal all the magic dust and then cause an explosion to separate themselves from the rest of the train so they could get away."

"They sieged the engine room during the first blackout," Blue cut in as she finished tying up her third man. "And since there were too many of them for me to take on by myself directly, I waited to catch them off guard. Jason showed up during one of the intervals of light and hid with me. When they came out of the engine room and the train went through the next tunnel, we took them by surprise together."

"What about the train employees in the engine room?" I asked as I finished binding the last man. "We should go see if they're okay."

"Agreed," Blue nodded.

The three of us quickly made our way to the engine room. When we opened the door we discovered the conductor and several other workers tied up on the floor, presided over by two more hunters.

Blue and Jason stepped forward. In perfect sync they punched the hunters in their faces—knocking both out simultaneously.

Blue, Jason, and I freed the bound workers then tied up the magic hunters. The freed workers immediately went back to shoveling dunes of magic dust into the fire. The conductor, meanwhile, dusted off his pleated pants and composed himself.

The man had a very large, moist forehead with age lines across it like creases in a cliffside. His brown mustache was thin, but the goatee it curved into was bushy. And he had the most delicate, almost pixie-like eyes I'd ever seen on a grown man.

He enthusiastically slapped Jason on the back. "Thank you so much, children!" he bellowed. "That was quite the jigg-pokery we were in, wasn't it?"

"Um, yeah. You're welcome," Blue said. "But listen, you still have to stop the train. Like, now. There was an explosion by the luggage cars, these magic hunters need to be taken into custody, and, well, we *really* have to get off."

"An explosion you say! Good heavens! Was anyone injured?"

"I don't think so," I replied. "But you've got to stop the train before it's too late."

At that, the lights went off and we plunged into the fifth, and second-to-last tunnel in the series. This time, however, we could still see. The blaze of the train's firebox roared with life and filled the engine room with warm streaks of light. The conductor took out a damp handkerchief from his breast pocket and dabbed nervously at the sweat on his forehead.

"I wish I could," he said. "But we've already begun our ascent of the last mountain. If I should stop the transport now, it would only roll backwards and plummet down the tracks until we came to a stop. Or, more likely at this speed and incline, crash to a stop. We must keep going until we level out and reach a safe unloading zone, which will be just a few minutes after we've exited the final tunnel and crossed the bridge that connects Daulgrin Lake and Britner Canyon. Once we pass the canyon, we'll arrive at the next station. Before that, children, I'm afraid my hands are tied."

"Ugh, what are we supposed to do until then?" Blue huffed.

"For starters, this," I said.

I locked the door to the engine room. Then I grabbed a couple spare shovels used to scoop magic dust and shoved them in between the pipes around the doorframe—creating an extra barrier to reinforce the door.

The train lights came back on and I paused to glance out the porthole in the door. The adjacent compartment was still empty. Arian and the magic hunters had not made it out of the meat locker yet. As time passed, this made me more concerned than thankful. I may have made it difficult for them to follow me, but they definitely should've made it out by now.

"Something's not right," I declared to my friends. "I don't think we should just be waiting here. When the magic hunters and Arian's men do eventually come, this door isn't going to hold forever. When it gives way Arian and his lackeys will have me trapped and once the hunters have taken the magic from me, they'll have nothing stopping them from gaining control of the train. They'll overtake the engine room again, blow the bridge, and speed to victory while the rest of the transport plummets back into the mountain until it crashes."

"All right then. What would you suggest?" Blue asked.

I glanced around the room and spotted a ladder that led to a hatch in the ceiling. I walked over to the thing and inspected it. "We go up. Or rather, I go up."

"Lay that on me one more time?" Jason said.

"The magic hunters are after *me* now," I explained. "They'll probably want to finish that mission before they go back to stealing the magic dust. It's not exactly every day that someone with actual Fairy Godmother magic walks into the room. Fairy Godmothers never leave the safety of their floating headquarters unless it's for a Godkid. For a hunter, this is an opportunity of a lifetime. So I figure I can distract them—lead them away from the engine room and keep them occupied until we reach the next station—while you guys stay here."

Blue scoffed. "What? No way!"

"Guys, the only person that can make this distraction work is me. Both of you need to stay here and protect the engine room in case any of the hunters catch on to what I'm doing and turn back, or don't bite at all and go on with their original plan."

Plus, if this doesn't work there is no way I'm letting you get hurt because of me.

It's just not happening.

The bright glow of the zealous fuel fire—flickering in shades of tangerine and mauve—accentuated the expressions on my friends' faces. They looked at me like I was crazy.

"Crisa," Blue began, "I don't usually argue with your plans. But making yourself human bait? I mean it sounds kind of—"

"Stupid? Dangerous? Self-destructive? Yeah, I get that. But if it keeps those magic hunters out of here and the rest of the train safe, then it's our best option. It'll only be for a short time anyways. We only have one tunnel left before we reach that bridge and make it to the next station."

"What about Arian and his buddies?" Jason said. "They'll be right behind you too. You realize that?"

"Yeah, I know. But trust me, I can handle them on my own."

I noticed a collection of the train's special lanyard necklaces hanging from a hook in the corner—orbs plump full of magic dust. I snagged a handful and held them up to the conductor. "Can I have these?"

He blinked in surprise. "Of course, but whatever for?"

"I have an idea." I hung the six extra lanyards around my neck then turned to readdress my friends. "I'll wait for the hunters to get here before I go. They have to see me head for the roof otherwise they won't know to follow. And remember, no matter what happens, *do not* come after me. I can take care of myself and you're needed here."

I stashed my wand into my boot and clenched the dining car matchbook in my fist. Then I handed Blue my satchel. For what I had to do, I needed as little weighing me down as possible.

It was at that point that Jason waved for our attention. "Guys, they're here."

Blue and I rushed to the window. Sure enough, Parker and the two other magic hunters from the meat locker were storming the compartment. When they saw my face they began to race toward us in eager, angry pursuit. I made for the ladder.

"Crisa," Blue said suddenly.

"Yeah?"

"Just tell me you've thought this through and I'll believe you, okay? I just need to hear you say it—you know what you're doing, right?"

I met her gaze with confidence as I grasped the metallic handles. "Definitely."

And by "definitely" I mean "not really." But that's neither here nor there since I am doing this one way or the other.

The magic hunters' faces were at the window then. I winked at Parker and propelled myself up the ladder. Throwing open the hatch in the ceiling, I crawled out of the train.

Finding my balance was tricky once I got up there. The combination of high winds and the uphill trajectory did not make for the most stable footing. But I didn't wait to ease myself into being more comfortable. I had to make it over the bridge. I dashed in its direction, the train's souvenir necklaces bouncing against my chest.

When Arian and his friends caught up with me in the meat locker I'd realized that none of them were wearing their necklaces, despite the fact that I'd seen them wearing the bobbles on the platform earlier.

This led me to believe that *they* had been the ones that engineered the explosion at the back of the train; not the hunters. The metal clasps formerly connecting the cars had singes of magic dust and purple lanyard clinging to them. Arian and his boys must've figured out these little orbs could double as small explosives and decided to use them to cause the accident.

While entangling quite a few had caused a big bang, I reasoned that the explosive qualities of the lanyards could still be useful on their own. And it appeared the opportunity to test that theory had arrived. When I was ten feet from the bridge Parker's head came into view, poking out through the ladder hatch at the tail end of the car.

"There she is!"

He tried to finish scaling the ladder, but before he could

fully ascend I removed one of the necklaces, struck a match, lit the part of the lanyard just above the orb, and hurled it at his head.

He ducked out of instinct and the janky accessory fell into the hatch. A second later a moderate burst of orange and purple fire spurted out, the flame having worked its way down the remaining bit of lanyard and reached the orb.

Colorful smoke gushed from the area. I jumped across the opening and raced down the roof of the bridge. The unstable, metallic structure vibrated under the force of my footsteps.

A quick look back confirmed that Parker had cleared the combustion. He was on the roof and he wasn't alone. Not only were Green Scarf and Tweed Jacket with him, so were three of the magic hunters that Blue, Jason, and I had tied up in the locker room car.

Contrary to what you might think, this didn't concern me much. I'd managed to put a decent amount of distance between us, and I was ready for what came next.

I hit the deck—dropping flat on my stomach and grabbing hold of the creased edges of the roof for dear life.

Parker and his friends glanced at one another before realizing why I'd suddenly pancaked myself. At that moment the train was abruptly sucked into the sixth and final tunnel. My pursuers barely had time to take cover before we were consumed by the hole in the mountainside.

I heard a scream or two and the thump of a body against metal. I kept my head down and concentrated on the sounds of the wheels plowing over the tracks beneath us. Oh, and once again I tried not to freak the geek out when the vampire bats came.

I gritted my teeth and resisted the urge to scream as I felt the surge of their vicious wailing. Unfortunately, that's when a set of claws got caught in my hair and violently yanked me sideways. I rolled onto my back and accidentally opened my eyes.

All around me was a tidal wave of small, contorted blue bodies. The roof of the cavern was only about three and a half feet above me. As a result, the surging creatures were close enough that I could see their tiny eyes as they whizzed by. They were red and twinkling, like bloody, faraway stars.

I was grateful that they didn't seem interested in me, but soon the vampire bats' presence caused me greater difficulty nonetheless.

Up 'til that point the creatures' wails had been awful enough. But at that moment something changed. When the bat flipped me over, the movement caused the end of my wand to poke out of my boot. It started to emit the silvery glow it always gave off when in dark spaces.

This did not go well.

In response to my wand's unnatural silver illumination, the bats began to wail ten times louder. The sound didn't just pierce my eardrums; it shook the cavern. Pulses like sonar began to emit from their mouths, causing the tunnel to quiver and rocks to fall.

In tune with the violent change, the creatures' bodies turned from bright blue to bright red, matching their eyes.

I rolled back onto my stomach as chunk after chunk of mountain stone rained down. Sharp, jagged wings flapped everywhere as the high-pitched screams echoed at an unheard of frequency. It was all so visceral I wasn't sure what would break me first—the rocks, or the screeching wails that made my brain feel like it was about to implode.

After a minute that seemed like an eternity the train

emerged on the other side of the mountain—freeing me from the nightmare.

When the transport exited the tunnel the bats followed, ejecting into the night sky. As the echo of their cries filled the air, their wings spread out and turned blue again, calming down in the presence of the moon's natural glow.

I immediately jumped up. The three remaining hunters were already on their feet. Repeating my earlier trick, I lit and launched another lanyard fuse. The small fireball erupted in front of them, knocking one hunter off his feet. I fired a second lanyard, then a third.

By then all three magic hunters had been thrown back against the roof and I was free to hurry down the line.

The entire train had made it out of the mountain and was leveling out as it began to cross Daulgrin Lake. The metal bridge we zipped over was hundreds of feet in the air. The looming, nearly full moon cast its white light onto the navy waters below.

I continued to run—the heat in my cheeks making up for the bitter cold of the air. But then I started to get this weird pang in my gut. Something was wrong. I yanked my wand from my boot. Its silvery luminescence ignited like a reflex.

This is too easy, I thought as the train made it to the lake's halfway point. Things were never this easy. The lanyard thing was a good idea, and it was working to keep the magic hunters at bay. But they weren't the only ones after me.

Where was Arian? And where were his men?

As I hopped from car to car, putting more space between me and the hunters, my questions were soon answered. I was in mid jump when one of Arian's men took me down.

It occurred terribly fast, but somehow still felt like slow motion. I was leaping over the ladder hatch of another bridge when he reached up and grabbed hold of my ankle.

He didn't get enough of a grip to pull me down, but I still plowed into the roof of the bridge, crashing forearms-first. The impact knocked my wand out of my grip. I desperately reached out to grab it, but it was too late. My beloved weapon rolled over the side of the train.

I scrambled to my feet to look over the edge, but Arian and the man who'd just attacked me were suddenly on the roof, having risen from the hatch.

The lackey reached me first. I blocked his right punch and struck him in the chest. He staggered back a step— enough room for me to get in a roundhouse kick that sent him flying off the roof and to the waters below.

Arian came at me then. His fist drove straight toward me, but I slammed it down, blocking and parrying with a punch to his face. He took a swing at me. I ducked beneath it and spun around his side. I hit him in the ribs and blocked another one of his strikes. But a second later he managed to nail me in the stomach with a right hook then rapidly thrust his hand up to my neck.

He had me by the throat. Instead of lifting me off the ground, he swept my leg out from under me and slammed me down against the roof. I grunted as the stars in the sky blurred and dream déjà vu pulsed through my veins.

Arian continued to pin my larynx against the roof with one hand while he reached for a knife on his belt with the other. Before he could grab it, I jabbed my forefingers into the soft part of his throat just above the clavicle, kicked his knee outwards, and grabbed him by the side of the face— swinging him down and smashing his head into the roof beside me.

He released my throat and I grasped the very knife he'd

meant to use on me. I leapt to my feet. As I rose, three more of Arian's men came at my rear.

The first swung his sword and I was barely able to keep from getting chopped. Alas, when the second and third slashed at me I was forced to dive out of the way and roll so close to the edge of the train that I almost fell off.

"What does it take with you?"

I looked up to see a disgruntled Arian getting to his feet, clutching his head where I'd slammed it against the roof.

"I was about to ask you the same question," I replied.

He and his men were coming closer. They thought they had me. They thought I was without plan and without weapon. Unfortunately for them, neither was true. I dropped down, stabbed Arian's knife into the roof with one hand and grasped onto a railing on the side of the train with the other.

Having been on this route before, I knew that when we came to the edge of the lake the bridge abruptly plummeted into a steep slope before evening out over Britner Canyon. Arian and his men clearly had no idea. When the train dove into this very incline, while I was safe, they flew forward. Arian and one of his guards did manage to grab hold of the railings, but the other two were thrown off.

The moment the locomotive leveled out I jumped up and fired a lanyard at the last guard. He was only beginning to get back up, so he was off-balance enough for the eruption to blast him a solid ways back. He landed with a thud on the roof, hitting his head so hard he was knocked out. We zoomed into Britner Canyon and I set my sights on Arian— fully intent on knocking him out as well. But then something glinting in the moon's glow caught my eye and distracted me.

Holy bananas, is that . . .

It was. It was the magic mirror from the Treasure Archives.

Having fallen out of wherever Arian had been keeping it, it was sitting on the train roof two feet from where Arian was standing—its reflective glass glaring moonlight at me.

Suddenly I understood. That was the object Arian had been talking about in my dreams—the tool he'd been using to track me. The little witch in the Forbidden Forest had said she could get a hefty price for it and that she knew people in Alderon. She must've sold it to Arian at some point when we were imprisoned in the Therewolf camp. He, in turn, had been using it to find me in the same way I'd originally used it to locate Emma. All he had to do was utter my name into the looking glass and its magic would give him a real time view of me, sound and all. It was so easy it was sickening.

Arian saw the combination of shock and recognition on my face as he picked up the mirror and returned it to the leather holster he had beside his scabbard.

"That's how you've been doing it," I thought aloud. "That's how you've been one step ahead of us. You were cheating."

"My mission is to kill you. Did you think I was going to play fair?" Arian asked as he stood upright. "I should thank you, though. This stupid mirror isn't always the most helpful if the places in the background are too general. But you, Crisanta Knight, are always so admirably thorough with your plans. All we had to do was watch and listen as you explained every one of your next moves to your friends, then beat you to the punch when you tried to make them."

"So the explosion . . ."

"We figured it would be simpler to take you if you were on your own. So we readied the lanyards at the rear of the

train, planted the fuse during the first blackout, and waited
to trip you so that you'd fall behind and be separated from
your little group."

Arian drew his sword. Behind him the three magic
hunters I'd left in my dust earlier were about to catch up
with us. I fired my last necklace bomb at them. They were
not close enough for the blast to blow them off the train, but
it forced them to temporarily drop to the roof.

I spun on my heels and ran in the other direction. I made
it to the next car, but was cut off when another pair of Arian's
guards rose from the ladder hatch on the next bridge. The
first wielded a sword, the second a crossbow. Further down
the line two more men climbed up and started heading
toward me.

I skidded to a stop and whirled around to see Arian
moving in closer with a smug look on his face. The magic
hunters I'd just downed were getting up, fully intent on
joining him.

Arian sighed in an exasperated sort of way. "You made
our jobs easy, Knight. Once we'd gotten past your meat
fire, all we had to do was take out the mirror and listen.
When you were in the engine room you explained your
plans so nicely. We had the hunters here follow you with the
intention of chasing you far enough away from your friends
that you'd be unable to call for help. Then the rest of us
spaced ourselves throughout the train. That way no matter
how much ground you covered while you were up here,
you'd eventually get cut off and be trapped on both sides."

"Great exposition-packed diatribe, Arian," I said as I
backed up. "If your obsession with offing me and that lovely
scar on your face weren't enough, I'm now totally convinced
that you have all the makings of an excellent antagonist."

"And if your damsel in distress proclivities weren't enough, the weakness that got you into this situation has convinced me that you have all the makings of an excellent princess," Arian returned in snide.

And I thought I couldn't hate him any more than I already did.

With every step my pursuers (eight in total) backed me closer to the edge of the train. I didn't have my wand or any other kind of weapon to defend myself with as I'd forgotten to pull Arian's knife from the roof. The odds did not look good.

Arian saw the panic in my face. "It's over," he said as he closed in on me. "No one is coming to help you."

"You might wanna revise that statement!"

A small knife suddenly hurtled into the calf of the guard closest to me. Without hesitating I thrust my foot into his kneecap—dropping him like a sack of potatoes. Blue and Jason swiftly climbed onto the roof and were at my side.

Jason used his axe to deflect the guards' blades as they came swooshing down on me. Blue balanced out his efforts with her hunting knife.

"I thought I told you guys not to follow me!" I said as I sidestepped the sword of another guard then kicked him into an adjacent attacker.

Blue elbowed a magic hunter so hard in the jaw it knocked a tooth out. "Seriously? That's the first thing you say?" she asked.

"You said you would protect the engine room." I trapped one guard's arm and snapped it.

"You said you could handle this on your own—that you knew what you were doing," Jason countered, fully engaged in weapon-based combat with Arian.

I snatched the sword from my broken-armed opponent. "I still do. I still can."

"Not from where I'm standing!" Blue shouted as I barely blocked an incoming strike.

"Then stand—" I turned around to shoot Blue a glare, but my eyes widened with panic when I saw Arian behind her with his sword raised. I tackled her out of the way.

"—somewhere else," I finished as we both fell out of his range.

It looked like she was about to respond, but I didn't give her the chance. I saw the guard with the crossbow taking aim. I pushed Blue out of the way just before his arrow stabbed into the roof where we'd landed.

The ricochet caused my body to roll off toward the edge of the train. And of course who was waiting for me when I got there? Arian.

He vehemently kicked me in the ribs before I could defend myself with my sword. Then he kicked me again. And again. And again.

I was in no position to block his foot or make any kind of countermove. To be honest, his kicks were so hard and brutally persistent that I didn't have time to react in any way at all. Each one crippled me more and sent me closer to the edge. From the look in his eyes, I saw that he didn't want to just end me anymore. He wanted to savor doing so.

On his fourth kick the sword fell out of my hand and I came to the very rim of the rooftop. I caught a glance at the vast expanse several hundred feet below. We'd crossed into an area of the canyon that was abundant with tall, lean rock formations sticking out of the ground like spokes in a lawn. (If that lawn was a gigantic rocky hole and those spokes were 400-foot shafts, that is.)

I turned my head slightly. Blue and Jason were busy fending off other members of the attack team. They were too distracted to come to my aid. As Arian delivered his fifth and final kick to my diaphragm, Blue finally managed to see me out of the corner of her eye.

"Crisa!" she shouted.

It was too late. I tumbled off the edge.

I reached out and grasped hold of the railing that lined the roof. My body swung against the side of the train, bouncing off it in the same way those lanyard necklaces had bobbed against my chest when I'd been speeding down the line.

Both my hands clung from the railing, but my injured one was in no condition to support my weight for very long. Meanwhile, the way I was outstretched caused my injured ribcage to burn with agony.

Both my hands began to slip from the railing. The wind, the night sky, the feel of the metal against my fingertips—it was all too familiar to bear. My dreams had caught up with me just like Arian had caught up with me. And at that moment I wasn't sure which of the two was crueler.

Arian stood there for a moment, appreciating the precariousness of my fate. Then he crouched low so as to get a better visual of the anguish on my face. The way he looked down at me, I couldn't tell if he intended to strike my hands so I would fall immediately, or if he was content to watch me slip off on my own terms. He'd stored his sword in its scabbard, so I assumed it was the latter. This must have been just too good for him to pass up—watching me fall to my demise because of my own weakness.

"I'm not hearing any clever responses or comebacks," he said. "What's the matter—no jokes left, princess?"

Honestly, even in this situation I probably would've still tried to crack one or two had I not been in so much pain. I had to settle for gritting my teeth and glaring up at him.

Arian raised his sword.

My heart stopped.

Then, suddenly, he was knocked from view. Out of nowhere an arrow had pierced his shoulder. The combination of its force and suddenness caused him to tumble backwards out of sight. I turned my head in the direction the shot had come from.

Daniel.

It had taken me a second to realize it was him, but I recognized his Pegasus instantly. The creature's body was black, which would have ordinarily blended into the night. However, when in flight, Daniel's Pegasus had burning, silvery eyes and a pair of matching holographic wings that cut across the darkness.

As the steed rapidly approached, Daniel fired more arrows at targets on the rooftop.

When he drew closer I noticed SJ was a slight distance behind him. She was mounted on Sadie with our third Pegasus (attached to hers via a long rope) following her as they flew across the canyon. While the creature's brilliantly colored wings—purple and green for Sadie, blue and purple for the other Pegasus—were very eye-catching, SJ's discomfort was more noticeable. It was clear even from this vantage point that she was steering with great difficulty.

Like most princesses, the girl had learned how to ride horses when she was little. But even though every other kind of animal in the realm had a fondness for SJ, horses had always had a weird disinclination toward her. Between that and her aversion to being this high up, I knew flying a Pegasus was the last thing she ever wanted to do.

I guess desperate times call for desperate measures.

Daniel called back to SJ—pointing at me then the other side of the train. I couldn't discern what he'd said, but in response SJ and her Pegasi broke off and veered right. They disappeared over the train where I could no longer see them. Daniel, meanwhile, kicked his own ride into high gear and sped toward me.

"How's it goin'?" he shouted as he came closer.

"Uh, you know, hanging in there!"

He fired another arrow then stored the bow he'd been wielding across his shoulder.

"Jump off when I tell you!" he commanded. "I'll catch you!"

Uh . . . what?

I looked away from him and that's when I saw it. The bridge crossing the canyon was coming to an end. I could see the track entering the forest ahead and, just beyond that, the next train station poking out through the trees. We were almost there. Which meant that there was no need for me to jump or trust Daniel. I could definitely make it that far without losing my grip and falling. I hadn't exactly been practicing pull-ups and other forms of upper body strength all these years for nothing, now had I?

"Um, that's okay. I'm good!" I called back as my fingers grasped the railing tighter.

Daniel followed my line of sight then yelled at me in frustration. "Knight, don't risk it! Stop being an idiot and for once in your life just let me help you!"

"Daniel—"

"Come on. Just trust me!"

I stared at him for a second.

Trust him? Trust the boy whose motives I don't know, whose actions I don't understand, who claims I ruined his life, and who may be looking for a way to get rid of me?

I glanced down at the drop to the canyon below.

It would be so easy for him to miss me if I jumped; so easy for him to let me fall . . .

I shook my head. While Blue and Jason may have felt that they knew who Daniel was in spite of his enigmatic nature, and that he'd proven we could all count on him, I still had very real doubts. And in that moment I refused to take a chance on them or him.

"No!" I responded resolutely. "I can make it on my own!"

"Knight—" Daniel started to argue, but then he was abruptly forced to jolt his reins to the left.

A crossbow had been fired by one of the guards on the rooftop and Daniel barely maneuvered his steed out of the way to avoid being hit. The two of them fell back, and then bobbed and weaved again to evade a second shot. I'd been so distracted watching the scene unfold that I didn't see what was coming for me in the same instant.

"Argh!"

Something blunt and hard rammed into the fingers of my injured hand, causing me to release my grip on the railing.

My body swung from the one hand that still held on. I looked up and saw Arian. He was crouched above me holding his sword with the handle-side down. Without another word he rammed the base of his weapon into my other hand and my grip gave out completely.

I dropped into the wide-open mouth of the canyon. I didn't scream. I didn't shout. The feel of the fall was too consuming. Bitter darkness rushed around me like I was being swallowed.

That's when I spotted Daniel. His Pegasus flapped its silvery wings and he hovered in the sky for a moment, completely frozen. He didn't come after me. He didn't move at all. For a solid beat, he just watched me fall. And then . . .

"Knight!"

Daniel's voice shot through the darkness with almost as much speed and power as his Pegasus. They plunged into the abyss in rapid pursuit. With a heroic swoop, the pair caught up with me. Daniel grabbed me by the arm and pulled me out of my drop. He steered his Pegasus to the closest rock formation and dropped me on the flat surface before landing beside me.

I immediately crumpled to the ground.

While the idea of partaking in such damsel-like behavior in front of Daniel, or anyone, filled me with disgust, I couldn't help it. I felt broken in more ways than one. Arian had given me a serious beating. Worse still? The people closest to me had witnessed it. I could only imagine what they must think of me now . . .

Shuddering at the thought, I attempted to will my adrenaline to overcome the weakness, the pain, and the shame I felt over both.

As I knelt on the cold, hard stone, I gazed back at the locomotive. I saw SJ riding Sadie, and Jason and Blue riding the third Pegasus. They were circling underneath the bridge and coming to meet us. When Daniel had come after me, SJ had flown to the aid of Blue and Jason so they, too, could escape by means of our winged steeds.

They were approaching us quickly now, and would soon be within landing range. While I was very glad to see they were okay, I instinctively shifted my focus to what lay beyond them—the far away figures of the enemies I'd left behind on the train.

Despite my inability to see things clearly through the combined distance and darkness, I had no doubt that Arian was looking at me. I could feel his penetrating glare across the canyon in those last few seconds before the train sped into the forest.

A shiver passed through me. The physical pain in my body felt insignificant in comparison to the understanding that came with it.

We'd be seeing each other again soon, he and I. With or without my dreams, of that I was certain. Arian had his mission, and like me with mine, he seemed determined to see it through. What's more, he had the magic mirror. Which meant there was nowhere I could hide that he wouldn't soon find me.

CHAPTER 18

In Too Deep

onna! Lonna!"

My loud whispers rose over the sea breeze as we made our way along the wet rocks of the dark beach.

After a couple hours of flying, the five of us had finally crossed into the kingdom of Adelaide. Now we were searching its shores for the only acquaintance I thought might be able to guide us where we needed to go. The ever elusive but lovably frank Lonna Langard—one of the princesses of the undersea kingdom of Mer.

Searching a coastline for a single mermaid was a difficult task. But anything was easier than the uncomfortable journey we'd taken to get here.

The flight over had been rough in two senses. For one, I was currently in a substantial amount of pain. Two, I'd been traveling with four people who were super mad at me.

SJ and I were already in a weird place. Daniel was extremely ticked off that I had preferred to plunge to my doom rather than accept his help. And Blue and Jason were upset that I'd done this after they'd explicitly lectured me about how we needed to trust each other.

The two of them were also peeved about how I'd reacted

318   CRISANTA KNIGHT - THE SEVERANCE GAME

when they'd come to my aid—showing aggravation instead of gratitude.

I got why that would irritate them. But they'd misunderstood my reaction. I *was* grateful that they'd been there. If they hadn't, I could have been killed. But that understanding aside, they'd abandoned the train's engine room without being certain that the magic hunters wouldn't attack again. And worse, in coming to my aid they'd put themselves in danger. If anything had happened to them while trying to protect me, I'd never forgive myself.

The way I saw it, if my weakness caused me to get hurt, that was my problem. I didn't want my friends risking their lives for me. I cared too much about them to be okay with that. Furthermore, I was just as adamant about retaining my dignity in their eyes.

How was I supposed to prove to them that I could be strong if they never gave me the chance? No. This was not how it was supposed to happen. I needed to become a hero on my own.

I was either going to come out of this saga a stronger archetype by my own devices, or succumb to the damsel proclivities of my old princess archetype in the same way. They couldn't save me, and I didn't want them to.

As a result of my friends' frustrations, none of them had been in the mood to chitchat on our way over here. None of them had wanted to ride with me either. They'd paired up on the other two Pegasi, leaving me to fly Sadie solo.

This hurt, but not enough to make me regret my actions. They could be mad at me all they wanted. In spite of the close calls, if I had to do it all over again my choices would remain the same.

I would still instruct Blue and Jason to stay and guard the

engine room because it was for the good of the other people on the train. I would still be mad at my friends for coming to save me because it put them in the crosshairs of a fight that was mine to contend with. And above all else, I would still not trust Daniel to catch me. That was definitely one leap of faith I had not been ready to take and likely never would be.

It was true he'd caught me. He didn't let me fall, and that mattered. But there was that moment when I'd been falling that he'd paused. He didn't come after me right away. The hesitation only lasted a few seconds, but it was there. And that mattered too.

Our group had landed in the backyard of Adelaide Castle. It was dark and in the earliest hours of the morning, so no one saw us. From there I'd steered us toward the back of the palace where the dumpsters were. It was as secluded now as it had been when I'd jumped out that bathroom window on the night of Adelaide's ball almost six weeks ago.

The castle stable was nearby. Not knowing how long we'd be gone, we snuck our Pegasi inside where they'd have hay, water, and warmth until we returned.

We took the path I'd taken to the beach on the night of the ball, avoiding the beam of the lighthouse and the attention of the one guard half-consciously patrolling the area. Now we were on the sand searching for the mermaid princess I'd met here months ago.

I'd hoped it wouldn't be too hard to find her. I realized there was plenty of sea and plenty of fish in it. But at the time of our encounter, Lonna had pointed out a rock formation that she liked to frequent when it wasn't occupied by enamored Mer-people.

"Lonna," I called out again as we drew near the rock in question. The others and I carefully made our way across a span of slippery stones that stretched into the ocean. "Lonna!"

At last I saw her. She was facing the other direction and leaning against the wet rock taking in the moonlight like a sunbather absorbing the summer's warmth.

"Lonna," I repeated.

She still didn't hear me.

"Lonna!" I snapped louder.

"Awwg!"

Lonna spun around and half ducked beneath the water— only leaving her enormous purple eyes, blonde widow's peak, and the tops of her fingernails visible as she eyed us behind the safety of her rock.

"It's okay. It's me," I said softly as I stepped closer and moved into the moonlight.

Lonna propped herself up a little higher. She smiled with delight when she recognized my face. "Hey, Poofy Dress! I remember you. Uh . . . what was your name? Carly?"

"Crisa."

"Right, right. Long time no see." She tucked her wet blonde hair behind her ears then noticed the others. "Who're your friends?"

"Lonna, meet SJ, Blue, Jason, and Daniel. SJ, Blue, Jason, Daniel, meet Lonna."

Introductions out of the way, I crouched down low so Lonna and I were at eye level. "So, Lonna. I sort of need a favor. It's about the holes in the In and Out Spell."

Lonna raised her eyebrows. "Girl, did my dramatic hair toss and swim away the last time we hung out not get the message across? I may like breaking rules, but this is serious business. Mer-people are not supposed to talk to you, or *any* two-leggers, about the holes."

GEANNA CULBERTSON   321

"Yeah, I remember. But if memory serves, you also said that if I wanted answers I had to find them for myself. And I'm here to tell you that I did. I know that the holes in the In and Out Spell are wormholes that lead to other lands."

Lonna tilted her head in surprise. "How did you figure that out?"

I considered telling her about Harry the White Rabbit, but for the sake of time I decided there was a better, faster way to get the point across.

"With this." I held up Harry's Hole Tracker, which was strapped to my wrist. "It's a Hole Tracker. It locates holes that appear in the In and Out Spell. Earlier today it showed me one off this coast. It's gone now, but it looks like another one has opened underneath the ocean about fifty miles out. Do you think you could get us to these coordinates?"

I pushed a small button on the side of the watch where the third hand pointed to a tiny glowing circle that had turned black and started to pulse. In response (as I'd discovered from fiddling with it during our earlier carriage ride) a projection of light emanated from the watch, displaying a viridescent map. In the area off Adelaide's coast there were degrees of longitude and latitude beside a black, swirling dot.

Lonna took my right wrist in her hand and pulled me closer, studying the map. She furrowed her brow as she calculated something. Eventually she shrugged. "Yeah, I can get you there. Let's do it."

"Hang on," SJ said, seeming surprised. "You are a princess of Mer and humans are not supposed to have access to waters that extend into your territory. You are just going to take us to this location without so much as asking why we want to go there?"

Lonna blinked, also surprised. She glanced at me and tilted her chin toward SJ. "What's her deal?"

"She likes rules," I explained.

"Then we have fundamentally different values," Lonna huffed. She tucked another strand of hair behind her ear then took a couple of casual strokes backwards. "Crisa, is your mission important?"

"Yes."

"Will it bring any harm to or inconvenience my people?"

"No."

"Then we're good. Well, there might be one slight problem, actually. In order to get to that spot you'll need to hold your breath underwater for like two hours. I don't suppose any of you can do that, can you?"

I grinned. "Now that you mention it . . ."

The last time I'd been swimming was when we'd been trapped inside that watery deathtrap at Fairy Godmother Headquarters. Needless to say this was a marked improvement.

We'd been jettisoning through the ocean at a quick and easy pace for a while now thanks to Lonna. She'd been using her mermaid powers to control the currents to carry us the whole way. We didn't even have to kick; we just floated along as we were guided by the forceful but gently moving funnel Lonna had conjured around us.

Apparently mermaids were at their core another form of magical creature. Each had a little bit of magic inside that sustained a single power. Just like me, but without all the Fairy Godmother backstory and restriction, or the risk of being pursued by magic hunters on the surface.

Lonna's power was controlling currents, and I couldn't have been more grateful. The private, powerful rush of water was moving us at an extremely fast speed, but we barely felt a thing inside it. That was lucky for me. The injuries I'd accumulated within the last twenty-four hours would've by no means allowed me to swim on my own for two hours. Traveling like this I hardly had to exert any effort at all. The caressing waters almost felt therapeutic.

I clutched my tender ribcage—worried by the thought of the fully realized pain that would return the second we left Lonna's gentle waters.

Trying to take my mind off it, I reminded myself of the positives. The most prominent of which being that we were all still breathing.

The saltwater taffy we'd gotten from the Valley of Edible Enchantments was working perfectly. One solid bite was all it took for the magic to kick in. The moment we'd ingested the taffy, a set of gills had appeared on our necks. They were shimmering and turquoise—making it look like we were suffering from some sort of bejeweled rash. The skin between our fingers, too, had changed. It had turned sparkling turquoise and stretched—giving us webbed digits.

The final side effect of the taffy's magic was the flux in eye color. The whites of our eyes had been washed out with a shade of pale blue, and our pupils were now rimmed with glowing rings of rose gold.

It was a weird combination of side effects, but we couldn't argue with the results. We'd been breathing underwater for a long time. We even had plenty of taffy leftover in case we wanted to make journeying to oceanic holes in the In and Out Spell a regular venture.

For the majority of the swim I had been keeping my

distance from Daniel and my friends. The current allowed plenty of room for it. Still, I decided that being confined together in these waters presented the best opportunity for me to try and smooth things over with Jason and Blue.

Lonna was leading our group about twenty or thirty nautical feet ahead with the pair of them slightly behind her. The wormhole we were after—as represented by the black circle on my Hole Tracker—was pulsing more rapidly with each passing minute. I figured this meant we didn't have much farther to go before arriving at our destination. So I didn't have much time left to garner up the courage to talk to my friends.

Using my arms and legs, I slowly propelled my body forward within our contained current, my webbed fingers allowing me to cut through the water with ease. Soon enough I reached Blue and Jason. When neither of them acknowledged my presence I decided to just delve right into what I had to say.

"Guys," I began, "about the train—"

"Just because we can breathe underwater doesn't mean we have to talk, Crisa," Blue said, cutting me off.

Ouch.

"Look, I know you're mad, but I don't really think—"

"You mean you *didn't* really think," Blue interrupted a second time.

All right, not cool.

I felt my pride begin to overshadow my good intentions, and my mouth opened before my brain could stop it. "Hey, I'm not the one who left the engine room defenseless because of some baseless urge to come to my rescue," I retorted.

"We're not the ones who came up with a plan that put

ourselves in a risky position where we would inevitably *need* defending," Blue shot back.

She huffed indignantly—her wavy hair swishing around her like a clump of seaweed. "Crisa, keeping stuff to yourself and pushing us away on a personal level is one thing. But it's like I said before, we trust you when it matters. Mainly because we thought we could always count on you to do the smart thing—the right thing—instead of letting your pride interfere with your judgment. But tonight you proved us wrong. You took advantage of our faith in you. You picked your ego over common sense and ended up outnumbered and outmatched on a train roof because of it.

"It was stupid, Crisa; stupid and selfish and totally uncalled for. Oh, and while we're on the subject, I hate to break it to you, but that thought to come to your rescue was anything but baseless given how many times you've almost been killed in the last couple weeks."

The very pride she was accusing me of flared up inside even more and I narrowed my eyes at her. "I can take care of myself, Blue."

"Really? Cuz it sure didn't look that way when you were cornered without a weapon by, like, ten dudes. Or when you were dangling from the side of that train."

"Agree to disagree."

"Unbelievable."

"Hey, what do you want me to do—apologize for the actions of the psychos that put me in those positions?"

"Of course not, Crisa," Jason interceded. "That's not what matters here. Look, you needed help. It's no big deal. That's why we were there, and that's why Daniel was there too. But taking advantage of our trust to convince us you didn't need help, being mad at us when we gave it to you anyway, and then choosing to take your chances with a death drop rather than accept Daniel's help, that's just . . . I don't even know what to call it."

"Careless, rude, idiotic, ridiculous—"

"Blue, I think she gets it," Jason interjected.

"Does she?" Blue asked. "Because after she so thoroughly ignored our advice about counting on all of us and trusting Daniel, I'm not sure how much is actually seeping in."

Bitterness burned in my throat. "If that's how you feel then maybe you should stop preaching your words of wisdom and just let me make my own decisions when it comes to who I should and shouldn't trust."

"Fine," Blue said flatly. "Trust whoever you want. I don't care. Better watch out, though. Given that you don't want to count on any of us, it looks like that's gonna be a real short list."

The statement took me off guard, causing me to stop kicking as I had been doing to keep up with them. I was carried backwards by the current, away from Blue and Jason. My hair flowed around me with a mind of its own. I didn't fight the flow of water, and instead let it take me past Daniel to the very rear of our group where SJ floated.

I started lightly kicking again to keep pace with her. After a time, despite the fact that she and I were not on the greatest terms either, I could not help but vent my frustrations in a desperate attempt to get a bit of understanding from someone.

"Can you believe Blue?" I finally asked her.

SJ looked at me with a puzzled expression. "Given that she told me what you did and, more importantly, what you did not do, yes. I can."

I rolled my eyes. Why had I even bothered? She was equally disappointed in my behavior as of late and was in no position to offer the kind of consolation I sought.

"At least you got a whole new swell of members to the Crisanta Knight Hate Club," I said in response.

"Oh, settle down," SJ replied with an almost amused huff. "We are not exactly having T-shirts made. And anyways, Blue does not hate you. None of us do. She and the others are simply upset by your lack of faith in them. Right now it only seems worse because she is all worked up the way I was initially. Give her a little time and I am sure she will cool off. Plus, look on the bright side—we are underwater, so I imagine doing so will not take very long."

I blinked as I processed her words. "SJ, did you just make a joke?"

She gave me a small smile. "You looked like you needed it."

I nodded. "I did. You're a good friend, you know that?"

"I know." She shrugged. "And so are Blue, Jason, and Daniel. I only wish you would trust us the way good friends are supposed to."

"I know, I know," I replied with a sigh. "I'm working on it."

"For your sake I certainly hope so. Blue and Jason filled me in on what they told you when you were having dinner earlier. After everything that happened tonight, I hope you see now that they were right. If you do not start really trusting us, then it is only a matter of time before something goes wrong and someone gets more than just their feelings hurt."

"Don't be so dramatic, SJ. Everything turned out okay, didn't it?"

"Through luck, not design," she said earnestly. "You fell off a *train*, Crisa. And before that you came close to being killed in many more colorful ways. You are okay; it is true. However, you definitely would not be if it were not for the good fortune of having friends who ignore your foolish wish to handle everything on your own and consistently show up just in time to save you."

"You don't know that for sure," I argued. "I mean is it really so absurd a notion that I didn't need saving, that I could've gotten by without any help?"

"I do not know, Crisa. Why not ask that gigantic rock monster who would have crushed you to dust had I not come to your aid in the Therewolves' tunnel system?"

I glanced at her. "All right, fine, point taken. Maybe I did need your help then. But don't try to generalize it into some sort of lifelong pattern. That was *one* rock monster, *one* time."

"And what about tonight?" she asked.

"Okay, yeah, maybe I needed help tonight too."

"And in Century City, and at Fairy Godmother Headquarters, the Twenty-Three Skidd tournament," SJ listed. "The Forbidden Forest. Oh, and let us not forget the matter of your wand. If it were not for the previously unknown fact that it floats, and that I spotted its glow on the lake when Daniel and I were trying to catch up with the train, it would be lost forever right now."

I glanced down at my soaked-through satchel bobbing along at its regular place across my shoulder—my wand securely tucked inside.

I had to admit SJ had been quite the savior for me tonight in regards to my precious weapon. Like she'd said, if it hadn't been for her, the thing would be lost somewhere in the realm's largest lake versus safe within my bag. I had been flat-out overjoyed when she'd returned it to me post our train escape—overjoyed and relieved and beyond grateful.

"I appreciate you finding my wand, SJ. You know that I do," I responded. "I don't know what I would've done if I'd lost it. But all those other times—"

"All those other times were no different," SJ interrupted. "You needed us then just like you needed us tonight. I am only glad we know better now than to believe you when you insist otherwise."

My cheeks flushed with a combination of anger and embarrassment. "See, this is exactly why I don't just ask you guys for help in the first place."

"Because you are too stubborn to admit that you need it?" SJ countered.

"No, because then you'll all start thinking that I can't get by without it, and I can't have that!"

I realized that my heart was pounding faster and I'd inadvertently been clenching my fists so tightly that my knuckles had turned white. I quickly looked away from SJ. My mouth had just admitted something that neither my brain nor my heart had meant for it to.

"What are you talking about, Crisa?" SJ asked carefully, noticing my withdrawn reaction.

"Never mind. Just forget it."

"Crisa—" she started to probe.

Thankfully she was kept from finishing the inquisition. Just then our *current* current was evaporated by a distant Lonna as we came upon our entrancing destination. The wormhole floated in the waters ahead. The thing was as large as a Therewolf's face, the deepest black possible, and swirled in a clockwise motion, small sparks coming off it like tiny warnings.

"Whoa," I heard myself say as I swam up to join the others.

"I know, right?" Lonna said, grinning. "Okay, boys and girls, here's the scoop. I've got zero idea where this thing leads. The few Mer-people that have gone through holes in the In and Out Spell don't exactly come back to tell the tale."

Lonna pointed at her tailfin and smiled in a self-satisfied sort of way. "And yes, that pun was intended."

I couldn't help but smile a bit. This was my kind of mermaid.

"All I do know for certain is that you'll end up somewhere in the water," she continued.

"If no one that's gone through a wormhole has ever come back, how can you know for sure?" asked Blue.

"The holes that appear in Mer are two-way streets," Lonna explained. "All Mer-people have met fish that accidentally crossed over here through holes in whatever ocean resides on the other side. Some holes appear at regular spots and times, you see. So you can literally just hang out and wait to meet whoever passes through and ask them what their journey was like. I've heard you experience a lot of barf-inducing disorientation. So my advice: brace yourselves and think *a lot* of happy thoughts."

I floated toward the hole and nodded. "Good tip. But seriously, Lonna, thank you for—"

"Breaking a million and one Mer-people rules by getting you here? Don't worry." She winked. "I'm happy to do it. Your fondness for living on the edge is the main reason I like you. In any case, good luck! I hope you guys find what you're looking for."

Me too, the voice in my head echoed as the others came beside me and we stared into the depths of the wormhole—

this tear in dimensions, worlds, and the consistency of what we'd been taught to believe our entire lives.

"If you don't die going through there, bring me back a souvenir!" Lonna shouted as she started to swim away.

"Will do!" I called back.

And with that, the five us swam through the hole and into the unknown.

CHAPTER 19

The Seabeagle

oing through an inter-dimensional wormhole feels a lot like being inside a spinning salad bowl.

The five of us tossed and turned uncontrollably—our bodies lost in turbulence and our perspective blurred by gushing waves of green, purple, and blue. The sparks that had been surrounding the hole's entrance zipped around like energetic piranhas. They bit at our skin; sometimes I even felt like they'd entered my bloodstream and were burning through my veins. Needless to say, thinking happy thoughts definitely did not help.

The wormhole eventually spat us out into an ocean. Unlike the body of water we'd entered from, this one was warm, turquoise, and tropical. Even from the depths we emerged in, I could see streaks of sunshine. Just as we noticed this, we also witnessed the black hole we'd come from suddenly seal itself off. It vanished into the wall of infinite blue surrounding us.

With nowhere to go but up, the others and I headed for the surface. As soon as oxygen hit our lungs, the gills on our necks vanished. Holding up our fingers, we saw that the webbed skin went with them, as did our weird eye colors. Air must've been the trigger that stopped the taffy's magic.

The enchantment having ended, we took in the sunny atmosphere of our new environment.

None of us had obviously ever been to another realm before. So none of us knew exactly what to expect. As such, we were simultaneously wide-eyed and on guard.

As far as first introductions to new worlds went, this one was about as welcoming as it could get. Everything in sight was picturesque. The sky was a lazy shade of cyan. The scarce clouds were white, poofy, and casually floating about. And the seagulls flew with dancer-like grace as they meandered from left to right without worry of destination.

I glanced around and saw that in almost every direction there was nothing but ocean and open space. That is, except for some hundred meters away where a modest boat was anchored. Its paneling was white, its sail was forest green, and painted on its side were two unmistakable words: *The Seabeagle*. Without a doubt it was the same boat that had passed through my dreams on the magic train.

"That's where we need to go," I said, nodding in the direction of the vessel.

"How do you know that?" Jason asked.

"Just trust me," I replied automatically.

They all gave me a unified look of disbelief. I guess I didn't blame them. After the magic train, it was a bit presumptuous (and idiotic) to think they'd put their faith in me again so soon.

Still, we had no other option but to go toward the boat. And since this was not the time to have the whole "by the way, I have psychic dreams" conversation, I had to leave it up to my go-to fallback: classic, simple sarcasm.

"Ugh, fine. Don't trust me." I shrugged as I continued to tread water. "You can stay here and doggy paddle to your hearts' content until another boat sails this way to pick you up. I'm sure one will be by soon, what with this being the middle of nowhere and all. Me? I'm gonna go hitch a ride on the one that's already here."

With that said, I started to slowly swim for the boat. The others begrudgingly followed like I knew they would. After all, what other choice did they have?

After a short time of paddling (in my case, painful paddling since I no longer had Lonna's magical, current-controlling buffer), we arrived at the humble vessel. The boat bobbed along in the water directly beneath the beating sun. I squinted to gaze up at it.

I was about to ask the others for suggestions on what to do next when a figure stepped in front of the glare—providing a shadow that allowed me to see both the boat and its passenger more clearly.

The man was dark skinned and muscular like a lumberjack. He had a pleasant face, from what I could tell, and thick locks that matched his charismatic facial hair—a mustache and trimmed beard combo that added to his rugged charm.

"How did you kids get all the way out here?" the man asked as he stepped toward the boat's railing to get a better look at us.

"It's a long story," Daniel responded. "Uh, where is here by the way?"

"Uh, that'd be Bermuda," the man said, confused by the question.

He studied us for a moment. Blue's hooded cloak, Daniel's sheath, and the axe on Jason's back must've seemed peculiar to him, especially when compared with the open flannel shirt, tank top, khaki shorts, and sandals he was wearing. Now that I thought about it, outfits and accessories aside, five kids treading water in the middle of the ocean probably seemed a bit odd to him too.

"You kids aren't from around here are you?" the man asked.

"Um, not quite," I said.

"Uh-huh," the man nodded. "So did you find your way to the hole by accident or on purpose?"

"I . . . I'm not sure what you mean."

"It's all right. I know a lot more about those crazy wormholes than you might think," the man said. "Look, just wait here. My wife can explain better than I can."

The man turned around and disappeared from view.

"Ash, doll! Will you come here for a sec?" I heard him shout. "I think you might want to see this!"

A minute later the man returned with a woman at his side. This woman wore floral shorts and a blue blouse that matched a brace strapped to her right knee. She was about the same age as the man (somewhere in her mid to late forties) and had big, curly, chestnut hair and matching eyes. I immediately recognized her face from the many pictures I'd seen of her in Adelaide Castle during our school field trip.

"What's with all the hullaballoo?" the woman asked as she approached the railing.

The man did not need to answer the question. She stopped tersely when she saw the five of us floating in the water.

The woman stared at us in a way that suggested as much happiness and surprise as it did sadness. I stared at her as well, thinking that this was both too good to be true and very confusing given her age.

"You're Ashlyn, aren't you," I said. "*Princess* Ashlyn of Adelaide?"

The woman repeated the name out loud as if she was remembering something long gone. "Princess Ashlyn of Adelaide . . ."

Then she snapped out of her haze and smiled down at us warmly. "Sounds like a good name for a girl in a book, doesn't it? Oh well, since none of us are in one anymore, how about you just call me Ashlyn. It's a little less formal, a little less fairytale, and a little more me these days."

CHAPTER 20

Love, Sacrifice, & TV

y dream of *The Seabeagle* was not the only vision to come to fruition within the next several days.

I currently found myself sitting on the plastic patio furniture I'd recently seen flashing through my head. Having ridden Ashlyn's boat to shore, we were now at her house and sitting on her front porch. The chairs and round table were white with yellowed edges. I sat in one facing the ocean. It was a beautiful backdrop of blueish green that deeply contrasted the cream color of sand just before it.

Upon the table rested a platter of sandwiches (also from my dreams). They were ham, cheese, and turkey. Like the fresh pitcher of strawberry lemonade beside them, they'd all been made by Ashlyn and her husband Donnie (the man from the boat).

If you haven't caught up yet, Ashlyn was the daughter of the Little Mermaid, and the woman we believed would fulfill the next item on Emma's In and Out Spell list—"The Heart of the Lost Princess," also known as our "Something Pure."

The specifics of *how* were not clear to us yet, but for the meantime another question occupied our thoughts, a question Blue no longer seemed able to leave unspoken.

"Why are you so *old*?" she asked Ashlyn.

"Blue!" SJ gasped.

"What, you know a better way to phrase the question? Come on, we're all thinkin' it."

She was right. It had been boggling my mind that Ashlyn looked so much older than she should've been. We'd been in search of an eighteen-year-old. And this woman was *definitely* not eighteen.

"I suppose I should've expected that question," our hostess replied. "I forget that in Book-time it really hasn't been that long since I left. What's it been, about a year?"

"Uh, like a year and half," Jason answered.

"Wow." Ashlyn shook her head. "It really is crazy the time difference between our two realms. For me, here on Earth, it has been almost thirty years."

"I thought we were in Bermuda?" Jason replied.

"Yes, dear," Ashlyn responded. "But Bermuda is not a realm, it is an island *on* Earth. And the time here moves about twenty times faster than it does in Book."

"Hang on." Blue held up her hand. "Correct me if I'm wrong, but did you just say you *left* Book? As in, you ditched your home world by choice not some freak accident or kidnapping or shark attack like everyone else there thinks?"

"It's a long story," Ashlyn responded forlornly.

"Well, if you're willing to tell it, we'd like to hear it," Blue said. "Can't feel like that long of a story to us since this place moves twenty times faster than we're used to, am I right?"

SJ shot Blue a disapproving look as Ashlyn sighed and took a sip of her lemonade. Then, with Donnie affectionately holding her hand, she told us her story. Unlike the kind we were used to in Book, however, this one was not so much the stuff of fairytales.

It started romantically enough. The story began after the

events of the Little Mermaid we all knew (Mer princess meets human prince; they fall in love; they break a ton of rules; she turns human; shenanigans and magical complications ensue; happily ever after).

Married, the former mermaid and her husband had a daughter named Ashlyn. The princess was born and raised by the sea, the likes of which she grew up longing for just as much as her mother had desired to be amongst humans. Alas, the Sea Silence Laws prevented Ashlyn from being a part of that world.

These strict regulations forbade contact between the Mer people and the majority of the realm. They limited ocean access to "government" approved (a.k.a., Fairy Godmother approved) personnel for fishing purposes and separated the ocean into Mer-only and human-only areas. So despite her aquatic heritage, Ashlyn was forbidden from the deep ocean and its mysteries.

Of course that didn't stop her from going after it. Her aquatically-altered genetics designed for underwater breathing and fast swimming abilities were not the only things she'd inherited from her parentage. Like her former Little Mermaid mother, Ashlyn was willing to break the rules to get what she wanted. So, whenever she was home from Lady Agnue's, Ashlyn would sneak out of Adelaide Castle at night and make her way to the ocean.

During her early childhood the princess had discovered a secret route in the cliffside that wormed its way through an assortment of underwater caves and rock formations. It was by this escape route that Ashlyn was able to live out her dream of aquatic independence.

However, like in most fairytales, there was a twist in her story.

The incident took place during her senior year at Lady Agnue's. Ashlyn was home from school for spring break. Initially she was content to return to the tranquil privacy of her typical late night swims. But that first night proved to be anything but tranquil or typical. While exploring the depths of the ocean miles from the shore, Ashlyn stumbled upon something new.

It was large and black and surrounded by sparks—and she had to know what it was. Curiosity getting the better of her as it so often does in protagonists, Ashlyn swam toward it and became the first human in Book to cross from one realm to another through a hole in the In and Out Spell.

This hole, like the one we'd just found, deposited Ashlyn in the waters of Bermuda. And that's when Ashlyn met Donnie. And everything changed.

She said that the moment they'd laid eyes on each other it was like a thunderbolt struck their hearts and made them realize that until that moment neither of them had ever really been alive.

Overdramatic much? I thought as I drank from my own glass of flavored lemon beverage. *Ugh, stuff like that makes my teeth hurt from the sweetness. I mean the romantic nonsense that is, not the lemonade. The lemonade, actually, could use a bit more sugar.*

With an hour in Book equivalent to nearly a day on Earth, Ashlyn was able to spend a great deal of time getting to know the handsome young man fate had introduced her to without anyone back home being the wiser. Each of her afterhours swims converted to almost a week of time with Donnie. And once she discovered a consistency with which certain wormholes appeared in that part of the ocean, she was able to flawlessly regulate her transitions and spend even more time with the boy she loved.

Unfortunately, soon everything changed again—this time with far less desirable results.

It seemed that Ashlyn and I had a common enemy: a certain Lena Lenore, a.k.a. Book's resident Fairy Godmother Supreme and all-powerful micromanager.

When the holes had started forming in our realm several decades ago, Ashlyn explained, Lenore had apparently been the first to notice. However, instead of sharing that information with the general public, the Godmother Supreme insisted on keeping the discovery quiet. She succeeded in doing so for a while, using her Godmother task force's magical intervention to conceal the inconvenient wormholes as they appeared.

Alas, as the years passed and the number of inter-dimensional tears increased in number and unpredictability, Lenore realized something else had to be done. Which, evidently, was why *she'd* been the core person to push the passing of the Sea Silence Laws.

Yup. That's right. You heard me.

Holes in the Forbidden Forest and northern mountains were easy to keep secret because, as Harry had pointed out, they were hard to get to. But Mer was not like that, at least not to Mer-people.

Lenore knew that her Godmother task force wasn't going to be able to keep Mer-people from finding out about the holes forever, and that once they knew there would be nothing stopping them from telling humans about the holes' existence. And so *she* had instituted the Sea Silence Laws to keep the truth from reaching the rest of the realm.

Regrettably, one thing she hadn't been prepared for was a half-human, half-mermaid teenager finding some of these holes, figuring out the pattern with which they appeared, and then using them to come and go between worlds as she pleased. *That* was most certainly not a part of the Godmother Supreme's plans. And once she learned of this disruption in her tightly regulated system of secrets, she had to put an end to it.

During the third week of Ashlyn's spring recess, Lenore appeared to our princess before she could slip through the wormhole for her usual rendezvous with Donnie.

At their confrontation, Lenore cast a spell on Ashlyn. The effects of the magic would take hold in five minutes, Lenore said. Once they did, Ashlyn would no longer be able to swim. The water of the ocean would paralyze her and cause her to sink like an anchor.

Thus, if she did not wish this to be her fate, she had to choose: Book or Earth. Choose Book and Lenore would wipe the princess's memory, remove the aquatic-death enchantment, and then poof her back to home. Once there, Ashlyn would wake up and never recall anything about the hole, her underwater ventures, or Donnie.

Or Ashlyn could choose Earth and swim through the hole a final time, with any luck making it to the Bermuda shoreline before the magic kicked in and completely immobilized her.

Blue, SJ, Jason, Daniel, and I sat in complete silence as Ashlyn told this part of the story. Her eyes turned glassy and bloodshot as painful memories surfaced from wherever they'd been hiding like a dormant virus. I saw her knuckles begin to whiten as she squeezed Donnie's hand for the strength that she needed to get through the retelling.

Ashlyn explained that she couldn't bear the thought of leaving her home, her friends, and her family. She knew that if she left right at that moment then no one was ever going to know what happened to her. Her mother, her father, her sister . . . no one.

On the other hand, if she agreed to stay she would never see Donnie again. She wouldn't even remember him. And that notion would've broken her on the spot in a much more visceral, instantaneous way than Lenore's magic ever could.

So she made a choice.

She picked Earth. She picked Donnie.

The instant she made her decision, Ashlyn dove through the hole and swam like mad before her clock ran out and the magic took hold. And, thankfully, she made it.

"We were married a year later and have been together ever since," Ashlyn said as she finally wrapped up her story. "We settled right here in Bermuda because of Donnie's tourism business, and so we could keep an eye on the holes in the In and Out Spell like his family always has. Holes open up regularly around this island, forming portals to a hockshaw of other lands, not just Book. We have the timetables down pretty thoroughly now, so we're able to steer most people away. But over the years, residents, tourists, even the occasional boat or plane have been susceptible to getting sucked through."

"So people on Earth know about In and Out Spell holes?" Daniel asked.

Ashlyn shook her head in amusement. "Nah. Earth people like fantastical stories almost as much as Book people do. For decades they've blamed the disappearances that used to happen around this region on a supernatural thing they made up called the Bermuda Triangle. Donnie and my efforts have severely minimized the number of boats and aircraft affected by the wormholes, but the legend of the triangle remains. It's silly, but it's good for business so we don't mind."

"Wow," Blue commented. "That's nuts."

"Yeah. But hey, that's life isn't it? Our version of happily ever after might have more tropical storm warnings and hurricane advisories than most, but it's ours and we love it."

"No." Blue shook her head. "I meant how you got here. You left everything behind just like that to be with him." She gestured toward Donnie. "No offense, but that's crazy."

"Love makes you do crazy things," Ashlyn said. "And I love Donnie more than anything. So while I miss Book and my family and the feel of the ocean against my skin every day, I've never regretted the decision. Lenore asked me to choose between worlds and at the end of the day I knew that the one that mattered most was the one that had him in it. He was my world, you see. Even after thirty years I still feel that way. He and our four children are where my heart is."

Ashlyn's hand went to her neck and her fingers grasped hold of a delicate, silver chain that had been tucked inside her blouse. She pulled it out and I saw a metallic, heart-shaped locket edged in lime green crystals. Ashlyn proceeded to open the locket and take out a small picture of her, Donnie, three young girls, and a small boy.

The Heart of the Lost Princess . . .

That had to be it! That was what we'd come here for— the second object that we needed to break the In and Out Spell around the Indexlands was the locket around Ashlyn's neck. Not just because it made sense, but because I'd seen that exact same locket in my dreams several times already.

The others and I exchanged a quick glance that our hosts didn't notice. Even without the knowledge of my visions, it seemed they knew this locket was what we needed to continue our mission.

"The kids are inside right now if you want to meet them," Ashlyn said—unaware of our epic realization as she closed her locket. "Donnie can introduce you once he's shown you the guest rooms."

"We appreciate the hospitality, Ms. Ashlyn," SJ interceded. "But we are just here to collect . . ."

Blue elbowed her.

"A few spell ingredients," SJ finished. "We cannot stay very long."

"Believe me, you won't be," Ashlyn said. "At least not in terms of Book-time. You will have to stay for a few days of Earth-time, though. I may not have used them for a few decades now, but I know perfectly well that the next hole in the In and Out Spell back to Book isn't due to open until three o'clock Monday. So the five of you will have to bunk here until then."

"We could not impose," SJ said.

"You are not imposing; I am insisting," Ashlyn stated happily. "Over dinner you can all tell me your own stories about what brought you here. For now, go and get settled. And say hi to the kids on your way. They'll be thrilled to meet you. I think they're in the family room watching TV."

Ashlyn and Donnie began to direct us inside. I grabbed my soggy satchel and an extra sandwich while Blue loaded a plate with several more. Then, as an afterthought, she looked up at Ashlyn with a hint of curiosity in her brow.

"What's *TV*?"

CHAPTER 21

Magic Build-Up

shlyn and Donnie had four kids—Arabeth (fifteen), Mary Roberts (ten), and twins Michael and Tina Louise (six). Together, they made up the clan of the Inero family.

All but Arabeth had expertly tussled dark curls. She had long black hair much like SJ's. The twins had eyes like their mother's—a warm hazel brown ringed in amber. Mary Roberts and Arabeth took after their father and had eyes bluer than the coastline, which was visible through almost every window in the family's enormous beachside property.

Arabeth was very athletic. She was always either swimming in the water, running barefoot down the beach, or climbing trees. An entire closet in the hallway was stuffed full of her action-adventure equipment for a myriad of activities from rock climbing to bungee jumping.

Mary Roberts, meanwhile, was more calm and focused. Unlike her older sister who was constantly dashing about, she preferred to sit in a windowsill reading a book. I didn't get to talk to her much throughout our stay, but when I did I perceived that she was fiercely intelligent, just extremely modest about it.

The twins, Michael and Tina Louise, reminded me a great deal of chipmunks (not the fire-breathing kind we'd run into in the Forbidden Forest, just the normal kind that hung around public parks). Inseparable, the pair popped up when you least expected them. And they had these naturally curious expressions on their faces that suggested everything and everyone was absolutely fascinating.

That first night we all had dinner together, my friends, Daniel, and I told the story of how we'd come to be there. Since we didn't want to bring up the whole "we want your locket" business yet, we'd agreed on a cover story for that part of the tale before dinner.

Rolling with SJ's earlier comment about our reason for being here, we explained that in order to break the In and Out Spell around the Indexlands we needed several Earth plants, and we'd travelled through one of the holes to find them. It was a lie that worked well since while we were stuck here, SJ—with Ashlyn and Donnie's permission—planned on brewing a fresh batch of portable potions with whatever ingredients she could find and the many recipes she knew from memory.

That dinner was the most time my group spent together during our stay. After the meal we dispersed to pursue more individual activities, which would occupy our time and give us the space we desperately needed from one another.

Having received our hosts' blessing, SJ headed for the kitchen to begin her potions work. Daniel went with an eager-to-learn Arabeth to the front yard to teach her the basics of sword fighting. And Jason and Blue joined our remaining hosts in the family room to watch the "TV."

It was an interesting and sufficiently awesome contraption, this TV. Ashlyn described it as pre-recorded theater in a box and explained its concept in more detail after Blue's inquiry.

Blue and Jason went on to discover the family's collection

of VHS tapes that went with the TV. These devices contained pre-performed storylines that could be re-watched again and again from any starting or stopping point.

They were definitely an innovation worth more of my time. Alas, my interest in them was exceeded by the awkwardness I felt around Blue and Jason. As such, I did not join them for the VHS viewings that evening. Instead, I found my way to the garden out back and sat in the metaphorical bed of isolation I had made for myself.

The house (which was more like a rustic mansion) had enough rooms for me to find a solitary place inside. But I preferred it out here.

I kicked at the dirt, my boot catching the sheen of one of the many multi-colored lanterns that lit up the area. The sun had set long ago, and despite the tropical climate I was starting to feel the night's chill.

Or on second thought maybe that was just my friends' cold shoulders . . .

At least I wasn't wet anymore. That was definitely a plus. After emerging from the ocean the others and I had dried crisp and clean thanks to SJ's SRB's.

If only I could've said the same for my satchel. My beloved bag had been far from unaffected by the ocean's composition. The thing was weirdly discolored now and the material had hardened drastically. I began poking around inside and discovered that nearly everything inside was ruined. The only things that didn't appear to be destroyed were my wand and . . .

Hello, what's this?

Inside my worn bag I found a perfectly crisp white envelope. Its color remained unchanged, and its seal unweathered. I pulled out the object and turned it over to find a name printed in sparkly red pen on the upper right hand corner.

"Debbie Nightengale," I read aloud.

I thought back to that night in Adelaide six weeks ago and the sparkly woman who'd come to my aid in the shimmering lightning storm gown. My eyes widened when I realized what the envelope was.

Dang, I forgot about this.

My Fairy Godmother trainee Debbie had given me this envelope when we'd first met the night the others and I broke into Fairy Godmother Headquarters. It was a survey of her performance, and Debbie had said that since it was printed on magic paper it was impossible to destroy or ruin. She'd also mentioned that I would be unable to lose it until I filled it out. I guess at that point the magical document would just poof itself back to headquarters or something.

It seemed I'd underestimated her claims on both regards. I mean, for this thing to still be with me after all this time and still be in one piece—that was just nuts.

Well, I guess if it's with me for the long haul then there's no need to end the procrastination by filling it out now, is there?

With a shrug, I shoved the envelope back into my satchel and removed the other untouched object inside—my wand.

Might as well practice. Not like there's anything else to do out here.

I stood up from the grassy knoll I'd been sitting on and stepped away from its perimeter of carroty orange flowers. With a steady exhale I harnessed my dwindling concentration and focused on the wand.

Spear, I commanded.

The silvery weapon that had never failed me began to extend and thicken in the manner I'd become accustomed. Suddenly, about halfway through the process it felt as though someone had jabbed a knife into the arm I was holding it up with.

Surprised by the pain, I dropped the wand into a bush by my feet, causing it to snap back to its original shape.

I lifted my arm to examine where the pain had come from. Rolling up my sleeve, I was shocked to discover a bruise had developed on the skin several inches above my wrist. Not only that, but around the injury was a small haze of golden sparks. They fizzled around the wound like a flurry of tiny, electrical snaps. After a few seconds the sparks disintegrated into the air as curtly as they'd appeared, but the bruise remained.

"What happened to your arm?"

I spun around, rolling down my sleeve as quickly as possible. Ashlyn had entered the garden and was eyeing me with concern.

"Nothing. I, um, fell," I replied.

"Ignoring that clear exaggeration of the truth for now, what I am more interested in is what happened to the rest of you," Ashlyn said as she gestured to my entire person.

"I don't know what you mean." I shrugged.

"You're hurt. I can tell."

Ashlyn walked purposefully toward me, but her leg with the knee brace wobbled a bit with each step, causing a slight limp. Nevertheless, she moved as if she didn't notice the impairment at all. Perhaps she was just used to it.

She took my arm into her hands and gingerly held it up like a doctor examining a patient.

"It's just a few bruises. I'm fine," I tried to reassure her.

But I couldn't fend her off. I winced as she gently applied pressure to the area of my diaphragm where Arian had laid into me on the train.

"Right. Of course you are," Ashlyn replied.

She pointed authoritatively to a hammock tied between a pair of trees a few feet away. "Lie down. I'm going to have a look at you."

"Ashlyn, really," I protested. "It's not necessary."

"Crisa, I'm older and wiser, darn it. So lie down before I call the twins out here and have them tickle tackle you again."

I shuddered at the thought. I'd experienced one of those tickle tackles before dinner and, because of my injuries, the pain had been excruciating. Reluctantly I gave in and climbed onto the hammock. Ashlyn leaned over me and pressed her hands onto my ribcage with delicate accuracy. I cringed at the touch.

"Hold still," she said.

I clenched my fists and did as she commanded, despite the discomfort of her prodding. After a minute Ashlyn shook her head in disbelief.

"Well, I think it's safe to say I haven't seen a specimen this bruised up since I visited that roadside fruit vendor selling two-week-old pears. Honestly, it's amazing that you were able to keep going on as long as you did in this condition, Crisa. You're pretty banged up. I assume that you and your friends drastically undersold the danger of some of the adventures you told us about over dinner?"

I looked away from her.

"It doesn't matter," Ashlyn said. "I'm not your mother. You can do whatever you want and don't have to tell me about it. Just try not to move while I fix you, all right."

"Fix me?" I glanced up her. "How are you going to—"

"Crisa, sweetie," Ashlyn held up a finger. "Talking counts as moving."

I wanted to protest again but decided against it. Ashlyn laid one of her palms on my forehead and the other on my stomach. She closed her eyes for a second. When she re-opened them they flashed bright blue. In the next instant, the same kind of aqua-colored radiance began protruding from her hands.

When Lonna had first activated her current-controlling magic, the same kind of glow had consumed her hands and eyes. The only difference was that while her glow had dissipated into the waters around us, Ashlyn's spread over my entire body with a flowing movement that emulated a rippling tide.

I suddenly found myself feeling lighter. It was as if every ache in my body was being lifted. The sensation was strange, but it brought immediate relief. It was like lying in a bathtub and then gently having all the water raised off of you in one fell swoop.

Eventually Ashlyn removed her hands and the radiant light vanished into the air. When every trace of it was gone, I sat up and swung my legs over the side of the hammock.

I felt great. Better than great, really; I felt renewed. I moved my left wrist and sensed no presence of the sprain that had once been there. My ribs felt fine. My body pulsed with pain-free invigoration. Even that bizarre bruise I'd developed a minute ago was gone.

"How did you do that?" I asked.

Ashlyn smiled proudly. "It's one of the benefits of having Mer-people blood pumping through your system. Not only did I inherit the ability to swim like a mermaid and breathe underwater, I was also born with a touch of magic. All Mer-people have some, you know. It allows them mastery of a single power."

I nodded. "Yeah, I've heard. A friend of mine, Lonna, she can control currents."

"Sounds like my little sister Onicka. She could control waves."

"Really?" I perked up. "That's pretty cool. So your power is . . ."

"Healing. It's a pretty useful one as far as powers go, especially when you have four children," Ashlyn joked. "What about you. What's your power?"

I gulped and considered denying that such a thing existed, but one look at Ashlyn and I knew I couldn't fool her. Her eyes were burrowing into my soul like some kind of all knowing, pure-intentioned Great Dane.

"How did you know?" I finally asked. "That I have magic, I mean."

"That wound on your arm a minute ago," Ashlyn said. "I know it well."

Ashlyn raised the sleeve of her baggy sweatshirt and revealed three large bruises on her arm. Each was freshly made and fizzling with blue sparks similar to the golden ones that had previously been emanating from mine.

I almost fell out of the hammock in surprise. "Oh my gosh, why are you . . . I mean, how did you . . . Are you okay?"

"I'm fine. I'm used to it," Ashlyn replied calmly. "Magic works differently here, Crisa. On Earth there are no spells, no witches, no fairies, no enchanted objects. At least there's not supposed to be because, unlike Book, Earth isn't a Wonderland. So when you try to use our type of magic in this world, the realm sort of rejects it. Hence the bruise you received on your wrist. Every time you use unearthly magic here, the realm reacts with negative consequences that cause harm to whatever, or *whoever* is the source. The bigger the magical output, the bigger the side effects. That's why I got these," she said gesturing to her own bruises. "Healing you took a decent amount of my power."

"If we aren't supposed to use magic here then why did just use yours to help me?"

"For starters, girl, you were falling apart," Ashlyn responded. "But I was also due to use a little magic anyways, so it was a win-win."

"Wait, I'm confused. How's that a win-win? You just said that using Book magic on Earth is bad and that it causes punitive harm."

"That's all true," Ashlyn admitted. "But it doesn't mean we can just turn off who we are. We're magical creatures, you and I, and when we go too long without using our powers they sort of *retaliate*. It's called Magic Build-Up, and . . . Oh, how do I explain this?"

Ashlyn tapped her finger to her chin and blew a curl out of her face. "Okay, so basically it's like this. The force of our magic accumulates the more time goes by without our using it. And if we go long enough, eventually it overflows like water from a dam—expelling itself from our bodies in one giant burst whether we want it to or not."

"Awesome."

"Yes. But more than anything it's painful. It causes this terrible feeling to develop in your hands that's so intense it feels like they're on fire, and it will persist until you release the magic."

I blinked as if I was adjusting to some sort of bright light. An internal one that is, like a bulb turning on in my brain as Ashlyn's words triggered a familiarity that was way, way too close to home.

"Holy bananas, is that what that is?" I couldn't help but exclaim in excitement. "I've totally had that happen to me. Like a lot." Then I hesitated.

"But wait, Ashlyn, until recently I didn't even know I had a magical power. So if I'd never been using it at all, why hasn't this Magic Build-Up thing happened to me more often? I only get it once in a while, and always at the weirdest times—move-in day at school, our ball at Adelaide Castle, Therewolf prison revolts . . ."

"Ignoring the whole 'Therewolf prison revolt' thing, which raises a whole different set of questions," Ashlyn responded, "there has to be some sort of connecting thread between all of those events that would explain it. What were you doing just before I got here that caused you to develop the bruise?"

I swallowed my inclination toward secrecy and stepped off the hammock. Ashlyn had been so forthcoming and helpful with her explanations. I felt like in the privacy of this garden I could be honest with her too.

"I was practicing with my wand," I said as I collected the fallen, but not forgotten weapon from the bushes where I'd dropped it. "It was my godmother's, and it's enchanted to take the shape of whatever weapon I will it into."

Ashlyn examined it. "So if you have a wand and you can make it work, am I correct in assuming that your magic is Fairy Godmother-based?"

"That's right."

"Well, don't wands only work for their respective Fairy Godmothers because their specific magic is tied to them and that's all the wands will recognize?"

"That's how I understand it," I said.

"Then there you go," Ashlyn declared. "Whether you

realized it or not, all these years you've been using a bit of magic every time you operated your wand—keeping yourself from getting Magic Build-Up so long as your usage of the wand remained regular."

Light bulb number two went on in my head. I thought back to the three most recent occurrences of the strange burning episodes on my hands.

Normally I used my wand every day, but prior to move-in day at Lady Agnue's I had gone a while without practicing with it because of my mother's constant supervision. This explained the incident on move-in day while I was unpacking.

An entire week had passed during our field trip to Adelaide when I hadn't used the wand. This explained the episode at the Adelaide Castle ball that had led to me plunging my hands into that seagull fountain.

And being in Therewolf captivity had prevented me from using my wand for two weeks, resulting in the massive burning episode that occurred midway through our escape.

As I thought back to other instances of the Magic Build-Up I'd experienced over the years, the more I became certain of the explanation. Whenever I went longer periods of time without using my wand, that's when the burning episodes took hold.

Understanding this, now the only anomaly that remained was the instance of Magic Build-Up I'd experienced in the Therewolves' lair. That occurrence had been noticeably different from the others, given the increased levels of pain and the whole glowing thing.

Reasoning that Ashlyn might've had an answer for that too—what with her having had an answer for everything else thus far—I decided to just plain ask her.

"Does the amount of time without using magic correlate to the intensity of the burst?"

"You got it," she said, reaffirming my suspicions. "The longer the span of time without using your powers, the more extreme and painful the Magic Build-Up will be when it reaches its boiling point. Once I almost went an entire month here on Earth without using my powers and my inevitable Build-Up was so strong it felt like my whole body was on fire. And when I finally released the magic I ended up inadvertently curing the hearing loss of every elderly person within a sixty-mile radius."

"I know exactly what you're talking about!" I responded. "That awful pain thing happened to me just recently after I went two weeks without using my wand. It was so bad my hands even started to glow."

"Really?"

"Yeah, hasn't that happened to you?"

"No. My glow only comes when I use my magic intentionally. Channeling it to the point of producing an aura like that takes a lot of focus. It's never been strong enough to just happen on its own. Magic usually is never that strong."

"Oh," I said.

My excitement paused and I rubbed my arm awkwardly. I'd thought for a moment that Ashlyn might've had the answers to everything; that she and I were the same. Now I wondered if maybe we weren't.

"Hey," I said, changing the subject, "at least in your case the consequences of your Build-Up were favorable. Curing hearing loss is great. Meanwhile, who knows what kind of havoc my magic has been wreaking when I was unknowingly expelling it."

"The results were helpful to a lot of other people, yes,"

Ashlyn responded. "But it was harmful to me. Like I said, the level of magical output on Earth corresponds to the level of punishment for releasing it. While healing your various injuries caused me to develop a few nasty bruises, a burst as powerful as the one I'm describing caused a lot more damage. How do you think I got this limp? That Build-Up disintegrated so much cartilage around my knee that even after years of physical therapy it still hasn't returned to normal."

"Oh, I'm sorry," I said carefully. "That sucks."

"A bit," Ashlyn agreed. "But if anything, it was a lesson learned about the dangers of going too long without using my magic—a lesson that I hope you'll take to heart."

"I will." I nodded fervently.

"Good." Ashlyn nodded in return. "So then, no more wand work while you're here, just to be on the safe side. You'll be going back to Book in few days, so Build-Up isn't really a risk you have to worry about."

"All right, I hear you."

"And no other magic either . . ." Ashlyn started to say. Then she paused and tilted her head. "What can you do anyways? You didn't answer me before—what exactly is your power?"

"I have zero idea," I admitted.

Ashlyn gave me a skeptical look.

"Really," I assured her. "You can ask the others. I wish I knew what my power was. Honestly, part of me feels guilty not knowing. Obviously once I figure it out I'll have way more magic hunters chasing me because my magic scent will get stronger, and I've had enough trouble with them already. But if I could use my abilities, then maybe I would have a better means to protect my friends from the antagonists that are after me. Lately I've been feeling so useless. Everyone keeps having to save me and I have no means to ensure their safety in return. At least if I could use my magic I could tilt the odds in our favor." I sighed. "I don't know. At this point I'm beginning to think I might be incapable of figuring it out—what my power is, and what I am too. Or rather, *who* I am . . ." I trailed off, a little embarrassed to have opened up so much.

Ashlyn seemed to think on this for a moment. Then she brushed another curl off her face. "Somehow, I don't think so," she said. She slapped her hands to her legs decidedly and got up to make her way back toward the house.

"Wait," I said, following her. "What do you mean by that?"

Ashlyn shrugged. "Just look at what happened in the last five minutes," she replied. "The explanation behind your Magic Build-Up was not that hard for you to find. The answer was in front of you the whole time. You only had to truly want to see it in order to make the connections. So I have a feeling that when it comes to discovering the truth about your powers, and the truth about who *you* are, the situation is no different. Which means you only really need to ask yourself one question."

"What's that?"

"Do you really *want* to see it?"

"Hey, Ashlyn!" Blue called out as she suddenly came stomping into the garden. "I was wondering if I could ask you something about this VHS thing, I—"

Blue stopped in her tracks when she saw me standing there. "Oh, uh . . . am I interrupting something?"

"No." I shook my head quickly. "We're all through here."

"All right. Well in that case, Ashlyn, I was wondering if

you could tell me a little bit more about this." Blue handed Ashlyn a small rectangular box.

"I thought Donnie explained to you about movies and VHS tapes," Ashlyn said.

"He did," Blue responded. "I meant what's *this* movie? It looks interesting."

"Oh this? This is a classic—*Die Hard* with Bruce Willis," Ashlyn explained. "It's actually a part of a series. We own all three if you want to watch them."

"Okay!" Blue said excitedly.

"Don!" Ashlyn called inside the house.

Donnie came out through the screen door. "What's up, babe?"

"Will you watch *Die Hard* with the kids, please? I have some things to do so I can't, and I have a feeling they're going to have a lot of questions."

"Really? It's an action movie. How much stuff actually needs explaining?"

"Well, off the top of my head: guns, cars, computers, curse words, helicopters . . . Need I go on?"

"Point taken," Donnie said. "Sorry, I forgot that Book's not completely caught up with the times here. I'll watch it with them. Come on, Blue. I've got a hunch you're going to like this."

Blue took the VHS tape back from Ashlyn and trotted eagerly after Donnie. Ashlyn began to follow but then glanced back in my direction. "Aren't you going to join them?"

"Not right now," I responded hesitantly. "But hopefully soon."

CHAPTER 22

The Pooles

t's a girl."

A white smocked nurse handed a small bundle over to a sweat-soaked woman lying on a bed. This woman looked tired, but was glowing the way new mothers always did. And her luminous aura perfectly matched the bright canary shade of the blanketed package she'd just been presented with.

Gingerly the woman took the parcel then smiled down at its contents—a pink, squealing baby.

"What's her name?" the nurse asked.

A man in a smock with dirty-blond hair and dimples came over to put his arm around the new mother—staring affectionately at her, then the child.

"Natalie," said the woman. "We'll call her Natalie after my godmother. Don't you think?"

"Natalie Poole," repeated the man. "I like it. Sounds like a character from one of those old comic books you love."

The woman smiled. "You're right. And with a name like that maybe she'll grow up to be a smart, strong hero just like one of them. And just like someone else I know . . ."

The woman elbowed the man playfully. He responded by brushing aside a strand of her maple-colored hair and kissing her on the forehead.

"Or maybe she'll be a brave, beautiful princess just like her mother," he added.

"Or maybe she'll be both," the woman countered happily. "And everything and anything else she wants to be too."

The man hugged her tighter. As he did, the whole scene was absorbed into a bright light that merged into sunshine.

I now found myself in the most amazing garden I'd ever seen. It seemed to be circular, with evergreen foliage making up the entire perimeter. There were flowers of every sort and a gorgeous view of the valley below.

In the center of the garden, in the middle of a large pond, was a huge topiary hedge carved into a spiral design. It was just like the mark from our prologue prophecies, just like the skylights in the Scribes' library and the Capitol library.

Many trees surrounded the pond. Some were normal; others were more fantastic. They were giant, and their tops were spilling with intense fuchsia flowers. At first I thought the trunks were made entirely of bronze, but then I realized they weren't true trees at all. They were hollowed out structures designed to help the flowers grow upwards.

Many people were enjoying the scenery—couples, sole adventurers, whole families. Then I saw the man and the woman I'd just witnessed in the hospital room, along with a small girl of about five years old. She had streaks of dark red in her wavy maple hair, and was dancing through the wildflowers as her parents took in the landscape.

The man and the woman called her over. The whimsical child raced over to them and tackled her father with a hug and a flurry of giggles.

Another flash of white light later and the mood changed drastically. The tall street lamp at the center of the image shone brightly against the dark night—a steady palpitation of rain beating against it and the encompassing world.

Water poured over the sidewalks and spilled into the gutters like the world was ending. On the steps of a building next to a lone tree stood the same woman. She was holding an umbrella, but her tears drenched her face just as thoroughly as the storm would have.

Beside her was an equally grief-stricken Natalie, who seemed to be about fifteen years old. The two of them were having some kind of conversation with an official-looking man. He wore a navy raincoat that had silver polished buttons and a fedora that concealed the majority of his face in shadow. His very presence seemed grim and unyielding.

While they were talking, the door to the building opened from the inside. Several men wearing jackets that read "paramedics" proceeded to exit. They carried a yellow stretcher holding a black body bag that repelled the rain.

It was the most morbid sight I'd ever seen. Although I didn't know the family, I couldn't help but feel the urge to cry out in sympathy. Unfortunately, this was an urge I could not realize since I was not actually there.

Still, my subconscious was beginning to feel much more in control of its surroundings. Like in several of my visions back in the Forbidden Forest, I suddenly found the power to move through my dreamscape. Only this time that control felt much stronger. I was able to will my spirit to get closer to the scene and make choices about what parts to explore next.

I moved past Natalie and her mother and went inside the building. It was the same apartment complex I'd visited in earlier dreams of Natalie's life, minus some wear and tear. The paint on the walls was less chipped, the decorative artwork not as faded, and there were fewer scratches on the floors. Yet, it still emanated that sense of a foreboding, ticking clock that was only amplified by the crackling storm just outside the main door.

I made my way into 3C—the apartment that I remembered belonged to Natalie. Once inside I saw that it was much like I remembered, but for a few extra trinkets and art books scattered here and there. And a broken glass in the corner of the kitchen . . .

I was tempted to go over to it, but then I heard something akin to a light whistle coming from the other direction. I migrated toward the noise and found my way into a bathroom.

The sole window in the lavatory did not appear to be open, but as I approached I heard a slight hiss and saw rain seeping in from beneath the frame, proving otherwise. The thing had been left ever so slightly ajar and the harsh wind and rain were making their way through.

I drew nearer.

The window was clouded pretty heavily with water, but the street lamps in the alleyway outside illuminated the shadows beneath me. There were a few tipped over trashcans, a stray cat scurrying for cover, and a girl—her hair blonde and her pace fast—splashing down the pavement.

Her face was familiar. Even through the weather's wrath and this distance I could tell that I'd seen her before. And then just as resolutely I remembered where from. It was Tara, Arian's right-hand leading the charge for Natalie's destruction.

She merged her way into the shadows of the otherwise abandoned alleyway and vanished from view. Then my dream, which had been dominantly silent until now, was vehemently filled with sound. In fact, it exploded with it. The downpour of the storm, the body-shaking cries of Natalie and her mother, the noise of glass breaking against tile, the thunder, and then—

Daniel.

Everything went silent as my focus narrowed on him. His back was to me, and he was standing on the great, flat plane of a cliff overlooking the ocean. The sun beat against him. A large black bag was slung over his shoulder as he stared toward the right edge of the cliff, watching something in the distance.

After a few moments he tore his gaze away and began to walk to the left. The plateau he stood on was very wide; the left edge must've been at least four hundred feet away. But time condensed like an accordion; it only took the blink of an eye for him to reach the other side. His eyebrows crinkled, then panic shot across his face. Abruptly he bolted away from the edge and sped past where my metaphysical form had been watching him. I turned to follow, but when I did he vanished, as did everything else.

I was standing in a white void now, alone except for one other person. She was about ten feet away and was watching me ardently.

"Crisa . . ." she said.

The woman was in her mid-thirties and had light brown skin and dark, curly hair that fluffed around her shoulders. She was wearing a soft-looking pair of gray sweatpants and a teal zip-up jacket. Most notably, she appeared to be banging on an invisible wall.

I couldn't see any kind of boundary separating us. But when I stood in front of her and held up my hand I felt something akin to glass, only more warped. Some kind of force field was between us, and the woman was banging her fist against it.

When I looked her directly in the eyes, however, she stopped.

"Crisa . . . can you see me?"

I nodded in disbelief. This was the woman whose voice I'd been hearing in my dreams since that vision of the lavatory with Arian and Tara. She was right here. But who was she?

"Crisa, can you mktjkjsopg fahkqrhlkodf me?"

Her voice was going in and out again, and as it flickered so did her image. She was fading by the second. She seemed to realize it too, because she started talking faster. Unfortunately, her hastening did not remedy the disintegration. It was all a bunch of whispery half-words and gargling static now. There was only one word I was able to catch in full just before she vanished:

"Dragon."

Those two syllables pierced the void with shocking loudness. As they shook my skull the void's perimeter began to break apart. Like the shattering shards of a mirror, chunks of white fell away to reveal inky blankness. I ran and dodged them as they came down. All but the last one. A giant, dagger-like fragment of the void abruptly plunged into my path, causing me to fly backwards. The next thing I knew I was rolling off the bed in Ashlyn's guest room.

I hit the ground with a thud and was subsequently buried by the sheets I dragged with me. When I broke free I saw sunlight streaming in from beneath the curtains.

Wild dreams and my rude awakening aside, for the first time in a while I felt refreshed. Being free from injuries and having an actual bed to sleep on versus an old mat on the floor of a Therewolf prison did wonders for the body and the mind. And what's more . . . I smelled bacon!

I grabbed the robe Ashlyn had lent me and sped for the kitchen.

The others (who had their own guest rooms) were already there with the rest of the Inero family—the table laden with breads, breakfast meats, jams, and pastries.

When my friends and Daniel saw me, I froze.

I'd avoided them last night and wasn't sure how they were feeling about me now that they'd had the night to sleep on it. Part of me half expected them to throw the basket of muffins at me. Much to my relief, they didn't. All I got was a nod of acknowledgment from Blue as her way of signaling that it was okay for me to approach.

Not exactly a warm welcome, but I'll take it.

I put my pride aside and accepted the invitation to sit down at the breakfast table. The tension between us still felt heavy. But with nowhere to go, I swallowed down the awkwardness and took a bite of rye toast. Neither of which tasted particularly sweet going down.

CHAPTER 23

My Responsibility

aving been restored to my prime, I spent the remainder of the week joining the various members of the Inero family in whatever endeavors they undertook.

These activities kept my mind and body busy for most of my days. However, when I was not occupied I could not stop thinking about my dreams.

Since we'd arrived at Ashlyn's I'd been having way fewer dreams than normal, which I was grateful for. Unfortunately, the intensity of the ones that lingered remained strong.

I spent a great deal of time thinking about these haunting visions, costing me more than my peace of mind. Although Ashlyn had warned me not to use magic while we were here, I always kept my wand on me. And about once or twice a day—staring off into space, lost in daydreams—as I twirled it through my fingers, I accidentally transformed it out of habit.

I would immediately halt the reaction as it brought me immediate pain. But the small burns or bruises this inflicted were nothing in comparison to the mental weight of my nocturnal foresight.

I'd more or less had the same dream theme running through my head every night we'd been at Ashlyn's. I kept seeing Natalie, her happy family, and then the end of this happiness beginning with her father's death that rainy night in the city.

Sometimes the specific scenes changed, but the story stayed the same. Natalie was born to two people very much in love. She was raised in a world filled with familial bliss. And then, like an apocalyptic thunderstorm, everything came crashing down.

Natalie's father died. Her life outside her home began to be characterized by a constant stream of torment. Her mother eventually fell ill. And Tara kept the boy Natalie had feelings for so far away they might as well have existed in different realms.

It was an awful thing to watch. Furthermore, I didn't understand why I was seeing Natalie at so many different ages. I was supposed to see the future, right? So why was I suddenly seeing her past too?

That irregularity aside, all my dreams about Natalie caused me to come to terms with one concrete pair of truths. To start with, everything that went wrong in Natalie's life had been the design of that blonde antagonist known as Tara. Under the orders of Arian and this Nadia character, she was responsible for all of it. Tara was the one who would destroy Natalie's future in the many ways I'd seen, and in whatever ways I'd yet to witness too.

And then there was that other truth. The one that involved me. It was simple really: I had to stop her.

I didn't really understand why Tara, Arian, and Nadia were trying so hard to break Natalie. But I did know that I couldn't stand by and let them wreak havoc on her life.

First and foremost, it was an unacceptable notion and I just wouldn't have it. And second, there seemed to be a lot more at stake than the life and livelihood of one innocent girl. Otherwise, why else would the antagonists be working so hard to destroy her?

Something big was meant to happen with Natalie, something about her Key Destiny Interval and the opening of the Eternity Gate.

I did not know what this gate was or where it could be found. Nor did I have any idea what a Key Destiny Interval was. But with each passing night I became more desperate to learn the truth. Since I'd first seen those words printed in the folder I'd taken from Fairy Godmother Headquarters they'd been popping up in my life like a recurring zit. I closed my eyes and remembered them clearly:

- *Magic Classification: Category 1, 2, & 3 priority*
- *O.T.L. Candidate: Ryan Jackson*
- *Key Destiny Interval: 21st birthday* *(cross-reference* Eternity Gate*)*

O.T.L. stood for One True Love. I knew that now. But I had no idea what the Magic Classification thing meant. Neither Tara nor Arian had ever mentioned it. And without any concrete knowledge of the Eternity Gate, the only other piece of information I had to work with was Natalie's Key Destiny Interval. If it and the Eternity Gate were both tied to her twenty-first birthday, I figured if I was going to do something to save Natalie and stop the antagonists, I had to do it by then. This was when their actions around the girl's destruction were meant to climax. Which meant it was my deadline too—the day she turned twenty-one and not a day after.

Unfortunately, doing it by then was an ambiguous goal given that my recent dreams had left me completely at a loss for just how old Natalie was. Between the wide variety of ages I kept envisioning her at, and the way time moved on Earth in comparison to Book, for all I knew her twenty-first birthday could've been tomorrow.

Oh, and there was another problem too. I had zero idea how to go about finding Natalie and stopping the antagonists from hurting her.

To say I had obstacles would've been an understatement. Still, I was convinced I would find a way. I had to.

Regardless of the implausibility and the missing information that stacked the odds against me, I was completely set in my decision. I was irrevocably and consciously committing myself to figuring out a way to help Natalie no matter what it would take. If for no other motivation than— as the only person who knew what was coming for her—it was my responsibility.

I could no more explain this instinctive protectiveness I felt toward Natalie than I could my ability to glimpse into her future. Nevertheless, I felt certain that the compulsion was a just one. She mattered. Putting aside everything with Arian and Tara and this Eternity Gate, even forgetting the strange fact that she had a protagonist book in our realm, Natalie had been in my head for far too long now for me to continue writing her off.

For whatever the reason, her fate was tied to mine. And as such, I gathered if I was going to go to such great lengths to alter my own destiny on this mission, I should start looking into ways to change hers too.

I owed her that much. Moreover, I had this nagging feeling that where she and I were concerned, our journey together was only just beginning.

CHAPTER 24

Collecting a Heart

 ike me, the others found their own ways to pass the time while at Ashlyn's. Throughout the course of our stay we only met up for meals and to discuss our mission—what came next and, more pressingly, what we were here for.

Since that first afternoon we'd arrived in Bermuda, our entire group had come to the conclusion that Ashlyn's locket was the "Heart of the Lost Princess" we were looking for. Putting aside my dreams of the necklace (which only SJ and I knew about), it just made sense.

To start with, it was literally a heart that belonged to our world's designated lost princess. More poignantly though—with the locket's contents being a picture of Ashlyn's family—it was also a symbol of Ashlyn's heart. It represented her unbridled, unsullied true love for Donnie and her children, which had caused her to sacrifice everything she once held dear. Thus, it qualified as the "Something Pure" we needed for Emma's list.

Having agreed on that, the only issue that remained was getting Ashlyn to give it to us. She wore it all the time, so we figured it was pretty important to her. And since we obviously weren't about to steal it, we had to garner up the courage to flat out ask her for it.

SJ, Blue, and I were elected to speak to Ashlyn about it together—deciding that since the three of us attended Ashlyn's alma mater, we had a more natural bond with her than the boys did. We also settled on waiting until the day before our departure to have this talk in an effort to put off the task for as long as possible and buy more time to put ourselves in her good graces.

Time, as always, moved too quickly. Before we knew it, the day in question had arrived. SJ was finishing her last batch of portable potions in the kitchen when I came to find her. With great delicacy, she laid the glass orbs on a rack to cool by the window.

"All set?" I asked as I glanced over the tiny, colorful fruits of her labor.

"Almost," she said, taking off her oven mitts.

The small orbs twinkled in the afternoon sunlight. There were nearly three dozen of them—red, jade, and silver. Evidently she'd found all the ingredients to construct most of the same potions as before. However, there was also a lone indigo potion that I didn't recognize.

"What's this one?" I asked as I reached for it.

SJ swatted my hand with an oven mitt. "Crisa, they are hot! Must you always get into mischief?"

"Is that a serious question?"

She shook her head. "Never mind; you are hopeless. In regards to the portable potion, I was experimenting with some ingredients I found to see if I could create a brew I memorized on our last night before leaving Lady Agnue's."

"What does it do?"

"It is supposed to induce a temporary earthquake on the spot of impact, but I have not yet tested it. In all honesty, I am not sure I ever want to. The recipe required a lot of tropical plants, the likes of which are all but impossible to acquire in Book but are readily available here. So I was too tempted not to give it a go." She hesitated. "This may have been an irresponsible choice. I do not know how powerful this potion will be when released. The images in my special potions book back at school seemed to suggest that it could be . . . cataclysmic."

"Oh, is that all?" I said.

"Maybe I should just destroy it now, before it finishes cooling and the seal hardens," SJ thought aloud. She grabbed a pair of tongs and reached for the orb, but I stopped her.

"SJ," I said. "Why did you make this potion?"

"I told you, it was too tempting to pass up putting all these ingredients to good use."

"I'm sure that's partially it," I replied. "But you have hundreds of potions memorized. I'm sure you could have thought of a different, less powerful brew to make. Heck, even I seem to recall a memory potion we learned in class a few months back that uses half the plants you have on this countertop."

"What is your point?"

"My point is that something inspired you to create *this* crazy powerful potion specifically. So what was it?"

SJ sighed. "I just thought that with everything that has been happening, and all those antagonists and magic hunters chasing us, it might be wise to have a little something extra up my sleeve—a Plan B, if you will. I realize now that brewing such a powerful thing was a reckless and impulsive decision, though. And carrying around a potential category nine earthquake in a sack for the rest of our journey is hardly logical."

"SJ, logic is important. But so is instinct," I said. "There

380 CRISANTA KNIGHT - THE SEVERANCE GAME

was a reason your gut told you to make this earth-shaking potion, and I think it would be a mistake not to listen to it."

My friend looked at me, then the potion. After a moment she put the tongs back on the counter. "Fine," she said. "But if that thing accidentally goes off and we all fall through crevices in the earth, it is on you."

"So the normal agreement then."

SJ gave me a look.

"Joking," I said. "Come on, where's your sense of humor?"

"I think I left it on the magic train."

I diverted my gaze and swallowed down the enduring guilt. "Um, if you're through here," I said, clearing my throat and changing the subject, "we should probably go meet up with Ashlyn."

"You go ahead. I will find you again in a few minutes," SJ said, beginning to clean up the counter.

I shrugged and made my way out of the kitchen. As I wandered down the hall I started to hear voices coming from Michael and Tina Louise's room.

"Help! Help!"

I recognized Tina Louise's voice and darted for the door. It was cracked ajar, and I pulled the silver knob to step inside.

I hadn't been in their room yet and was met by an explosion of color. Everything—from the rainbow patchwork comforters on their bunk beds to the color pencil drawings they had on their walls—was a playground of bright shading. Currently the twins were dressed in costume. Michael was wearing his blue pajamas with a red cape and matching red eye mask. Tina Louise had on a light pink leotard, a hot pink tutu, and a sparkly tiara. She was on the top bunk waving around a plastic magic wand, stuffed unicorn clutched under her arm.

In front of the bunk bed was an assortment of other stuffed animals—bears, dragons, rabbits, dogs. They were positioned outwards in front of the bottom bunk. Michael faced them, waving a plastic sword.

"Everything okay in here?" I asked, confused.

Michael raised his eye mask and grinned. "It will be once I defeat these monsters." He gestured at the battalion of stuffed animals. "I am defending my kingdom and fighting for my honor."

I glanced up at Tina Louise. "And what about you?" I asked.

"I am the princess," she responded (a sort of "duh" expression on her face) as she pointed to her tiara. "I am trapped in my tower and am waiting to be rescued."

It's hard to express the exact combination of feelings that struck me then. So I'll settle with saying that it felt like I got punched in the stomach.

I walked over to the bunk bed, looking down at Michael then up at Tina Louise. "Why do you have to wait to be rescued?" I asked steadily. There was a toy chest next to me filled with many more props. I grasped a plastic sword with a bejeweled hilt and held it up to her earnestly. "Why don't you just climb down and fight the monsters too?"

"Because that's not the game," Tina Louise responded. "We are playing princess and hero. Michael fights, and I stay up here until he saves me. That's what princesses do."

My cheeks boiled. I was about to open my mouth again when there came a knock at the door. SJ stood under the frame waiting for me.

"Come on, Crisa," she said. "It is time to find Ashlyn."

I still wanted to argue with Tina Louise and Michael, but I didn't think getting into a bickering match with a pair of six-year-olds would improve SJ's current view of me. So with reluctance I put the sword on the bed and followed SJ out of the room, closing the door behind me.

"Are you all right?" SJ asked. "You look upset."

That's because I was upset. But I hardly thought she'd understand why.

"I'm fine. Where's Blue?" I replied.

"I was hoping you knew."

"Beats me." I shrugged.

I hadn't been spending that much time with anyone in our group this week. But of all of them, Blue was definitely the person I'd seen the least. Today, for example, I saw her at breakfast for, like, five minutes before she scampered off to who knows where.

"Are you guys ready?" Ashlyn asked as she came down the hall. She was wearing her locket and a mid-calf, flowing dress that was flawlessly white. "You said you wanted to talk to me at three o'clock, right?"

"Right," I said. "Though we were hoping Blue was going to join us. Do you have any idea where she is? It feels like she's been vanishing all week."

"Actually, I think she is in the family room with your friend Jason. But I'm not sure you'll want to pull her way."

"Why?"

"She's in deep *Die Hard* mode. Come on, I'll show you."

Intrigued, SJ and I followed Ashlyn to the other side of the house. When we arrived we found the door to the family room closed and the sounds of loud explosions and screaming coming from inside.

Ashlyn opened the door. Blue and Jason were plopped on the floor in front of the TV—their eyes glued to the set so intently they looked like they'd been hypnotized.

"I think this is the twelfth time she's watched it this week," Ashlyn whispered to us. "And she's watched the second one a good half dozen times too."

"What about the third one?" I asked.

"She watched it once, but then put it away. I think she's trying to pretend it never happened. Most of us try to."

SJ walked straight over to our frozen friend. "Come along, Blue. You can finish watching later," she said as she reached for the remote control. "It is time for us to—"

"Touch that remote and you lose a finger," Blue said without removing her gaze from the television.

SJ quickly pulled her hand away and scurried back to the doorway where Ashlyn and I were standing. "Crisa, do something," she whispered. "I have not seen her this far gone since she realized she could get course credit for bear wrestling over the summer. She is obsessed."

"What do you want me to do? *You* she still likes. Forget a finger, if I tried to turn off that movie she'd probably take my whole hand."

"Ladies," Ashlyn said softly. "Why don't the three of us have our chat without her? I feel like it would be best to leave Blue alone for now. Trust me, you don't want to disturb a person when they're lost in Bruce Willis world."

Ashlyn glanced back at the TV and raised her eyebrows as she smiled. "Mmm, he sure is a whole lot of man. Am I right?"

SJ followed her gaze to the TV.

"I will have to take your word for it," she replied.

Ashlyn began herding us out of the room. Just before leaving I caught one more look at the TV screen. The ever-resilient Bruce Willis and his once white sleeveless shirt were covered in various degrees of soot, sweat, and traces of blood. Having lost his shoes at some point, he was presently rappelling down a large, metallic shaft barefoot as he tried to escape whatever bad guys were after him.

Hmm, so that's what that was . . . I remembered seeing this very image in one of my dream flashes on the magic train.

"Speaking of spells," SJ continued once we'd closed the door to the family room. "Ashlyn, there is something we have all been meaning to ask you. It is what we wanted to talk to you about today, and it is quite important."

"What is it?"

"I think you'd better sit down for this one, Ash," I said. "It's our turn to tell you a long story."

Sitting on the same plastic patio furniture as before, SJ and I told Ashlyn the truth about why we'd really come to Earth and the item we were after. We began with an apology for lying, which she thankfully accepted. When we finished, she gave us a single nod.

"That's what you truly want, what you need in order to be happy?" she asked slowly. "To reach the Author?"

SJ and I exchanged looks.

"Yes," I said simply. "It is."

"Then I want you to have it," Ashlyn stated, and without hesitation she took off the locket and passed it across the table.

SJ and I were both in shock. Could it be really that easy?

"Ashlyn, are you absolutely certain?" SJ asked. "You have already given us so much, it seems wrong to ask you for such a special, personal possession."

"Donnie gave this locket to me a few years back for a birthday," Ashlyn explained. "But I have had plenty of birthdays and have received plenty of lovely gifts over the years. Not to mention I have extra copies of the picture inside this one. So it is no grand loss, really. And even if it were, I would still insist that you take it. Everyone deserves a chance to find happiness; the costs of it are just different from person to person. So if *this* is yours, then I'd be honored to help you pay it. Goodness knows the price could be higher."

Ashlyn stopped and stared out at the open water—a thought no doubt skimming across her mind in the same way a seagull on the horizon was currently skimming against the shimmering surface.

"Just do me one favor?" she said after a beat.

"Name it," I said.

"Once you've found what you're looking for and have no more use for the locket, return to Adelaide and find my mother. Give her the necklace and tell her the story I told you. And tell her . . . tell her that I miss her. And that I hope she can forgive me."

I smiled softly and nodded. "We'll deliver the message."

"You have our word," SJ agreed.

My friend took the locket and placed it around her neck. My memory flashed to the various visions I'd had of her wearing the locket on Adelaide. Part of me felt secure and another part felt unsettled as I watched this slice of the future lock itself into place.

With a wistful smile, Ashlyn bid us adieu and went inside the house. She was on a quest to find a reluctant Mary Roberts who had a dreaded appointment with the hairdresser at the turn of the hour. SJ and I got up too and started walking along the beach.

After a while we began talking. It was nothing of importance—what Mary Roberts would look like without her bangs, memories of when Blue tried to convince our entire floor at Lady Agnue's to let her give them Tinker Bell haircuts, that time Mauvrey freaked out and tried to get me suspended for using her hair brush.

It had been a while since SJ and I had been on completely good terms. Even our potions conversation in the kitchen had felt riddled with tension. But right at this instant everything felt like it used to. It felt like my best friend and I just enjoying one another's company.

"The necklace looks good on you," I commented when our conversation had shifted to how relieved we were that things with Ashlyn had gone so well, and that she hadn't been mad at us for lying.

"Thank you," SJ responded. "I hope it is all right with you that I hold on to it. I figured that since your dream had me wearing it, that is what I should do."

"Sure." I shrugged. "But you could have just as easily chosen not to wear the necklace if you didn't want to. It's not like it's going to cause some sort of mega universal time ripple that would make everything go crazy if you don't. I mean, just because I dream it doesn't mean it has to be that way, right?"

"I am not so certain, Crisa," SJ responded. "Everything you have envisioned has come to pass. Has it not?"

"Yeah, but all I'm saying is that maybe the future can be changed. That's the main idea behind our whole quest, isn't it? That we can alter what fate holds for us?"

"I suppose," SJ said slowly. "But we are traveling to the ends of our realm to accomplish that goal. If rewriting the plans the Author has for us was really as easy as making a choice—for example choosing not to wear this necklace— then we would not be here, would we?"

I rubbed my arm sheepishly. "I guess not."

"But speaking of your dreams," SJ continued slowly. "Crisa, I have been thinking about something lately. That vision you had the night before we entered the Forbidden Forest in which we were on the beaches of Adelaide—that portion of our future is fast approaching, is it not?"

"I imagine so," I admitted. "If the wormhole going back to Book lets out in the same area, all signs seem to be pointing to us ending up there."

"Does that mean that strange purple vortex you described consuming you will also be coming soon?"

"It might be," I replied. "But then again, my dreams don't seem to go in order very often, so maybe not. I'm not sure to be honest."

"Have you had any more dreams that better indicate what it is?" she asked.

"Sadly, no," I responded. I had experienced more dreams about the vortex, but I hadn't seen anything past what I'd originally described to her.

There was a quick pause on SJ's part. When I looked at her, I realized it was because she was studying me—trying to peer into my answer and my soul to get a better sense of whether or not I was being completely forthcoming.

I met her eyes confidently, trying to reassure her. "SJ, I really haven't. There's nothing new to report on that front. I promise you."

She seemed to believe me at that and moved on to her next question. One that I did not appreciate and that she seemed far too interested in learning the answer to.

"Are you afraid?" she asked.

I felt my fists clench.

For a moment this made me wonder if maybe that was

because a small part of me truly was afraid. Then a split second later I mentally tackled this vulnerable part of my subconscious—angry and ashamed at even the near admission to such weakness of character and fragility of spirit.

Get it together, Crisa, I chided myself.

I'd worked too hard to have my friends see me as something more than this helpless damsel stereotype I'd been running from. I certainly wasn't going to throw in the towel on that fight now. Because if I did, then they wouldn't. And if they didn't, then I really wasn't. And if I wasn't, then I was just . . . just . . .

You know what, no. I'm not even going to go there.

I just can't.

I did not make eye contact with SJ as I responded to her question.

"No," I replied. "I'm not afraid. Not of Arian, and not of anything else either."

CHAPTER 25

The Art of Fighting the Inevitable

 didn't know if it was all that talk with SJ or if it was just my subconscious's way of warning me to be ready, but for the first time since arriving in Bermuda I did not dream of Natalie Poole.

Streaks of lightning and bursts of lava were intercut with flashes of my friends running through the Adelaide Castle orchard. Eventually all these tumultuous images faded to one—dream me in Adelaide's cliffside tunnel system.

Shadows followed her as she ran until she reached a dead end. Her path had taken her to a cavern that was half-submerged in water. She stood on the edge and looked down at the forty-foot drop to swelling waters. The ceilings were high and curved. The only light came from the tunnel dream me had just entered from.

"No place left to run, princess."

Arian and a cluster of his men approached from the tunnel. His expression was a perfect cross of smug and resolute, while dream me's was cold and focused. He had something in his hand. It was the magic mirror, its glass glaring at me like a verdict.

Dream me backed up toward the brink. The water below

rose and fell from the tides that must've been feeding into it from the outside. I could almost hear the sound of my doppelganger's heart beating—hard, fast, anxious.

More flashes came. I saw the gray dragon that had stalked us from Century City. His sharp scales and ferocious golden eyes stood out against the powder blue and white backdrop of the sky he was soaring through.

Then there was Mauvrey. She was in a black gown leaning against the wall of my school's ballroom—a monthly ball in full swing. Following her eye line, I saw she was watching Blue and SJ. My friends (like all the other girls in the vicinity) were in similar black attire. Mauvrey checked her watch impatiently, clearly waiting for something as she kept an eye on them.

When that scene faded, I entered the void—still, quiet, eerie. My consciousness stood in the empty chasm for a second. Then the purple vortex consumed my vision. It took my breath away and surged everywhere. I felt someone grab my arm as it tried to swallow me, but the scene vanished just as curtly.

I was left with the same dream I'd had earlier of Arian talking with the cloaked girl through the Mark Two compact mirror.

The words in their conversation were the same as before, only this time I found myself comprehending most of their meaning. For example, I understood that their "small, wicked friend" was the witch in the Forbidden Forest, and that the tool she'd given them to track me was the magic mirror.

In turn, this vision caused me to finally realize that the cloaked girl must've been the mysterious thief who'd broken into the Treasure Archives earlier in the semester. She had been the one to smash the cases and take those other items. It only made sense given that Arian was now berating her about the witch being able to provide the very prize that she'd "failed" to acquire (i.e., the mirror again).

But who was this cloaked figure? Who was this girl who'd attempted to steal the magic mirror from the Archives? Why had she taken the enchanted pea, cursed corset, and genie lamp? And what was this *new* object Arian was planning on using to capture me with?

"Now then," Arian said in the dark chasm of my nightmare. "The other item you have is just what we'll need to take the girl when we cut her off at the beaches of Adelaide tomorrow. I'll be coming by tonight to pick it up, so meet me in the usual spot at half past two."

"All right." Cloaked girl nodded. "But why exactly? I understand its purpose in regards to Paige Tomkins, but how can it possibly be useful in this situation?"

"Four words," Arian responded like he had before. "Crisanta. Knight. Has. Magic."

It was there that the dream ended, as it had previously. But after the scene faded I came upon a new vision. Arian was there, only this time he wasn't talking out of a Mark Two. He was talking in person to his men—whose numbers had increased significantly since the magic train.

"I don't want any screw ups this time," Arian barked. "Make no mistake, if any of you lets her get away, Nadia will have your heads. Assuming I don't take them first. Understand?"

"Yes, sir," the soldiers replied in unison.

"Good." Arian nodded. "Now, according to the mirror and the Earth timetable, she should be here within the hour. So be ready. And remember, we want her captured *alive*. We just have to be within fifteen feet of her for our tool to work, so do whatever it takes to get the job done. Meaning if *any* of her friends get in the way, what are you to do?"

"Kill them!" the soldiers bellowed.

"Exactly," Arian said.

That was the end of my dream, and the end of my night's sleep. I rolled awake but there was no sunlight streaming from under the curtains. It was too early for that.

I slid on my boots and wrapped myself in a blue blanket. From there I quietly slipped into the hallway and down the stairs. The orange sunrise was just beginning to peak out over the edge of the water, so I unlocked the screen door of the kitchen and made my way outside.

The sky was gray, gold, and empty. The gulls that usually flocked across it had yet to start their day. Not even the flowers seemed to be awake. They just drooped bashfully while waiting for a more sensible hour to arrive. Something I probably should have been doing. But I just had too much on my mind to allow it.

Of all the scene fragments that had flashed through my dreams, the only one I didn't understand was the purple vortex. Everything else revolved around Adelaide, but the vortex had appeared out of the void. The thing made me feel uneasy, but as I strode across the Inero's dock I decided to let the matter go.

My dreams often got flashes of random, out-of-order junk—bronze animals running about, Bruce Willis scaling a vent, a log cabin in the snow. So more than likely the vortex had nothing to do with my imminent Adelaide timeline. Given that, I convinced myself not to worry about it. Especially since I had much more concrete visions to worry about.

I sat down on the edge of the dock and let my boots dangle over the water as my mind swirled with possibilities.

Arian was somewhere on Adelaide waiting for me. He had the magic mirror, so regardless of what direction I took when we got there, eventually he would find me. Once he did, he'd utilize this new mystery object to capture me. And if anyone I was with tried to stop him from doing so, he and his men were fully intent on showing them no mercy.

My mind churned. I was beginning to get ideas of how to handle Arian and the mirror, but no matter how I spun the issue I realized I could not have my friends with me when I inevitably confronted him. What I wanted to do had a much higher chance of success if I was alone. Which meant I needed to figure out a way to shake the others loose once we got to the beach.

My dreams assured me that I would be able to do this; my visions of the situation had shown me alone in that cavern. However, the big question was how to go about achieving that.

Lying to others didn't seem like a good option given that (a) I had to stop doing that, and (b) none of them would believe me after all the ways I'd individually burned them.

But telling the truth—that in my dreams I'd foreseen Arian cornering me with a bunch of his men—hardly seemed like it would convince the others to let me go off alone. As proven time and again, they always came back to help me no matter what it meant for them.

Much as this had saved my skin on multiple occasions, I just could not have that here. Not this time, not with Arian coming for me the way that he was. Letting my friends get close to me would only draw them closer to a danger that was *meant for me*.

Moreover, asking them for help at this point would be like putting the final nail in the coffin of how they viewed me—sealing me within the identity of this weak girl who couldn't fight her own battles forever.

I grunted as I cracked my neck a bit—the tension there beginning to stifle me in more ways than one. The sun was getting higher, but my spirits were not rising with it. We were leaving this afternoon and I felt a great unease about what approached.

Soon a radiant sun began to fill the world with warmth. As the sounds of local Bermuda merchants opening their shops and kids coming out to play filled the atmosphere, I understood what I had to do.

My best course of action would be a half-truth. It was the only way to keep my friends out of harm's way, give my plan the best odds of success, and prevent the universal view of who I was from being permanently defined by weakness.

Settled on this, I looked up and saw the horizon had become dotted with the multicolored sails of passing ships. Amongst the collection I spotted the slender gray boat with the scarlet sail I'd seen in previous dreams.

I rose from my seat and stood there motionless. Closing my eyes, I inhaled deeply. The smell of the salt water and the caress of the ocean breeze were not nearly as calming as they'd felt in my dreams of this moment all those nights ago. They, like so many other things, were ruined for me now— tinged with the knowledge of what was to come.

A sensation I would have to get used to, I supposed.

"Hey, you sleepwalking or just taking in the sights?"

I spun around and found Blue trotting toward me. It was my final confirmation that there was no getting around how things were about to play out. SJ had been right; the futures that my dreams predicted could not be so easily altered.

"Just getting an early start to the day," I responded.

"You sure you're okay?" Blue asked. "You look pretty beat. And SJ's been looking out the kitchen window to check on you all morning with this worried expression on her face. But when I asked her what was up, she wouldn't tell me."

"Yeah, I'm fine." I nodded.

But wait, why does she care?

The confusion I'd seen on dream me's face in this vision suddenly made sense. Blue had been avoiding me all week due to her *Die Hard* obsession and her residual irritation with what I'd done on the magic train. So why on Earth would she be expressing any concern for me now?

"I'm surprised though," I said. "Between your Bruce obsession and what happened back in Book, I wouldn't have expected you to notice . . . or even care for that matter."

"Well, I'm not over either," Blue said slowly, "but I think Bruce would want us to move forward. Don't you?"

"I do," I agreed.

I bit my lip and glanced in the direction where my subconscious form had watched this scene unfold. I knew now what she hadn't known then—what I needed to do next. In preparation, I exhaled deeply as I gathered my courage to go forward with my plan.

Step one: tell the others about my ability to see the future.

"Which is why," I began hesitantly. "Which is why I need to tell you something, Blue. Something important." My eyes dropped to the floor.

"Blue, I can see the future," I stated simply. "All those dreams I have, well, lately they've been coming true. I knew about the magic watering can in the Forbidden Forest, the Therewolf cave and theatrical production, the room beneath the Capitol Building, Ashlyn's heart-shaped locket, and a whole lot of other stuff too. I even had a short *Die Hard* vision when we were on the magic train. Although I didn't really know what that was until a couple of days ago . . . Anyway, the point is that I can see the future. So, um, yeah. There it is."

I took a deep breath and wrung my hands as Blue stared at me.

To be honest, I thought she was going to punch me. It's what I deserved for not telling her the truth sooner. But, much to my surprise no punches were thrown. Instead her *arms* were thrown. And they were thrown around me. Blue hugged me for a solid few seconds and then stepped back and smiled.

"Crisa, I know," she said.

I blinked. "I'm sorry?"

"You and SJ think I'm such a sound sleeper because I'm always buried beneath, like, five pounds of comforter. But, girl, you don't just talk in your sleep. Sometimes you, like, *shout* in your sleep. I hear it all the time. At first I thought they were just dreams too. But when what you yammered on about in your sleep kept matching up with what was actually happening, I put two and two together. It wasn't that hard."

I was dumbstruck. "Blue, if you knew why didn't you say anything?"

"Hey, it's your secret. I figured you would tell me when you were ready."

"And you were okay with that?"

"For sure. I'm not all talk you know. Like Jason and I were telling you on the train—everyone has stuff they prefer to keep to themselves. And everyone has reasons for doing it, even from the people they are closest to. I knew it might take a while, but I was sure that you would tell us about your dreams when you were ready. Secrets are a lot like bandages—some people like to rip them off quickly, and some people need to do it slowly so they can prepare to deal with what's underneath. You and me, we tend to prefer the latter."

"What, you have some big secret too?" I teased.

"Yeah, actually," she said seriously. "I do." Blue sighed in a way that indicated more frustration than sadness. "It's about my prologue prophecy," she said slowly. "I may not have given you guys the most accurate description of what it actually, *technically* said."

"Ladies!" Ashlyn suddenly shouted from the screen door of the house. "Soup's on! Get in here before the waffles get cold!"

"We'll be right there!" I called back.

When Ashlyn had vanished inside the kitchen, I looked to Blue expectantly. Much to my dismay, she did not pick up the conversation where she'd left off. Rather, she linked my arm through hers and began to steer us back toward the house.

"Come on; let's join the others. We'll stuff our faces full of waffles, you can tell the boys the truth too, and then you can share with us whatever crazy plan I just know you've been cooking up out here."

"All right, let's go," I said. "But after I tell the others about my dreams, I need to talk to Ashlyn for a minute before I explain the whole of my plan. Oh, and remind me after breakfast that I have to ask Jason for a favor."

The two of us started across the dock, but a few seconds

later I stopped and raised my eyebrows at Blue. "Wait, what about your little confession? You didn't finish before. What did you mean when you said you didn't give us the most accurate description of what your prologue prophecy said?"

"Tell you what," Blue countered. "Don't do anything to tick me off from here on out and I'll tell you and SJ later, deal?"

I extended my hand dramatically.

"Deal," I said.

Blue and I shook on it. However, while the gesture had initially been extended in jest, at the last second it curtly transformed into something much more somber. Blue tightened her grip around my hand at the last shake— replacing the silliness of the gesture with an earnest solemnity as she looked me straight in the eyes.

"I'm serious, Crisa," she said. "No more lying. No more diverting. No more of this severance game you've been playing with us since the start. It's like I told you on the train, if we want this to work, we have to trust each other. But that's a two-way street. We've trusted you. Now you need to stop pushing us away and trust us too. And this, right here, is your second chance to do so. *So don't blow it.*"

Surprisingly, the boys took my revelation rather well. They were confused at first. And they required a bit more convincing from SJ and Blue. But eventually they believed me.

With that first step of my plan completed, I proceeded to move on to step two: telling them some of what I'd foreseen waiting for us on Adelaide.

I explained that Arian was in possession of the magic

mirror and that he would use it to track me down within the cliff's tunnel system. But I left out the number of men he had with him, the whole "trapping me at a dead end" bit, and that he apparently had some sort of special tool to capture me with. This was necessary if I had any hope of getting the others to go along with my plan, the most important aspect of which being that we needed to split up in the tunnel system.

When I came to this part of the plan they freaked out with objections. But I had expected their qualms. And I was ready with the right responses to calm them. That—combined with the trust points I'd earned for being honest about my dreams—eventually got them to agree to it.

Based on some of my other visions about Adelaide, I knew they would eventually catch on to my misdirection. But I also knew that by the time they did it would be too late for them to turn back and come after me. They would be forced into being safe while I handled Arian and his men on my own.

That's where step three of my plan came into play: mastering Ashlyn's secret route.

Our hostess had mentioned she'd used a hidden path to get from Adelaide Castle to the seashore. Her route went through several underwater caves, the likes of which I'd seen in my dreams. So I figured we could utilize them to escape the beach and elude my enemies as we made our way back to the castle.

This was a simple idea. What was not was passing on its details. Both Ashlyn's route and the other elements of my plan had to be whispered to one person at a time.

I'd learned all too well on the magic train that Arian was able to watch my every move through the magic mirror. And (by extension) he was able to listen in on our conversations too.

In order to combat this advantage, I decided to communicate the key aspects of our plan in a way that—even if Arian was keeping an eye on me—he would not be able to overhear. It wasn't like the magic mirror had a zoom in button or a control for volume like the remote to Ashlyn's TV did.

The idea received a gold star of approval from both SJ (our logic goddess) and Blue (our fairytale history whiz). Both my friends knew plenty more about the magic mirror than I did, and both assured me that the tactic was sound.

Once Ashlyn whispered to me how to find and navigate her route, I passed on these instructions, and my own, to each of my co-conspirators in the same way. It was a brilliant solution, and I felt confident it would allow me to debilitate Arian's hunt until I was ready for him.

With that, our plan was set. We were ready. I was ready.

I did feel bad about misleading my friends and capitalizing on their faith in me.

I'd allowed myself to appear vulnerable with my dreams so they'd have no reason to doubt me and think I was concealing something else. But in truth it was a trick. Like a magician, I'd had them concentrate on what I presented in my hands and not what I had up my sleeves.

This made me feel kind of gross. For although my intentions were good, I knew it was a deceptive means to an end. And I also knew from my visions that when they figured it out, they would not be happy.

Nevertheless, none of the grossness or guilt changed the fact that this was the way it had to be. It was the best course of action if I wanted to stop Arian from ever following me again, protect the others from his wrath, and keep "damsel" out of the universal perception of who I was.

Blue had been right. This was my second chance, my last chance in more ways than she knew. And I really had better not blow it.

CHAPTER 26

Warnings

aying goodbye to the Inero family proved to be more difficult than I'd expected.

I'd really grown to like Ashlyn, Donnie, and the kids over the last few days. We all had. Which made it sad to think we'd probably never see them again.

When a quarter past two o'clock came around we said our final farewells and boarded *The Seabeagle*. It was a magnificent boat—as majestic and graceful in appearance as it was in function. It skidded so smoothly across the water, I barely felt it moving.

My friends and Daniel were at the bow. I'd decided to migrate toward the back of the boat. Seagulls were hawking in my wake so relentlessly it was like they were just asking to get a shoe thrown at them.

As I passed one of the boat's windows, I overheard a heated conversation between Ashlyn and Mary Roberts. The young girl had insisted on coming with Donnie and Ashlyn to see us off while Arabeth stayed behind to watch Michael and Tina Louise. Now she and her mother were arguing about something.

"Mom, you don't understand," Mary Roberts pleaded. "I know it sounds crazy, but she's going to need me."

"Mary Roberts, that's enough," Ashlyn said. "I am not letting you travel to another realm because of one dream about an old man in a sparkly robe."

"Why not? Crisa can see the future in her dreams."

"Yes, but you can't. The night before last you dreamed you were an army general in the winning side of a Muppets war."

"But Mom—"

A small wave crashed against the boat, causing me to stagger away from the window. I took that as my cue to stop eavesdropping.

As I made my way starboard, the squawking gulls flew away, thank the skies. While *The Seabeagle* continued to sail to our designated drop point, I leaned against the railing and inhaled the rare quietude.

The ocean wind blew and beat against me as much as the sunshine did. I took a deep breath and gazed back at Ashlyn's house, which was now but a dot on the shoreline.

Wouldn't it be grand to never have to go back? To escape the responsibilities of being a protagonist? To not have to worry about challenging Arian or the Author or everything and everyone else back in my own, insatiable world?

As quickly as the notion came, I swallowed it—knowing full well that as tempting as it sounded, it was not for me. It was a nice idea, an easy path. But my life choices thus far had never been about taking the easy way out. If they had been, then I wouldn't be where I was in that exact moment, and I definitely wouldn't be me. While hiding away might've kept me safe and prevented me from getting hurt, it would've also kept me from being myself. And that was just not the way.

Even if I got shot down by the Author, or killed by Arian, or trapped in the cage of stereotypes my universe had built around me, I would rather go down swinging. So it didn't matter if this upcoming confrontation was to be my last or just another bullet point in the long list of battles I'd picked over the years—I was going to stand my ground. I was going to fight. Because that's what fighters did. And that's what I was. While so much about me was up in the air, I felt sure that this was a concrete bit of truth unaffected by my hero or princess status. I was a fighter—possibly by nature, but most certainly by choice.

My eyes drifted down to my tingling palm. I was becoming accustomed to the abrupt tinge of frost that emanated from my hand whenever the watering can's magic acted up. My skin turned to liquid metal. I flexed my metallic fingers in the sunlight, causing them to shine as the phenomenon ran its course.

When it concluded, I studied the smudgy image that remained on my palm. Just like I was growing used to the sensation, I'd developed an equal familiarization with the realization that nothing about the mark was going to be different afterwards. It merely flickered before leaving me alone—anticlimactically consistent every time.

I wondered for a second if maybe that was because I didn't have one of these "root strengths" the witch in the Forbidden Forest had proposed. What other explanation could there have been for the mark's irregular and random disruptions? The only options were that either it was malfunctioning or I was.

I shrugged, turning my attention back to the glistening ocean that swelled beneath us. I had bigger things to worry about. There would be no use knowing the elusive quality that made me special if I was dead. And in order to avoid that, I needed to focus.

"Crisa."

I pivoted around to find Ashlyn. She was wearing a sleeveless, button-down white shirt. It flowed in the wind and contrasted her neon pink shorts and matching sandals. Her curls blew in bunches around her face, but not as wildly as my own long hair, which flung about in the wind with a sort of majestic madness.

"We're almost there. Do you have everything you need?" she asked.

I patted my satchel, which was slightly lumpier than usual due to the slingshot I now carried inside it. After breakfast I'd enlisted Jason to carve me a quick makeshift one. It wasn't as sleek as SJ's, and definitely was a splinter risk, but it would get the job done.

"Yup, all set," I replied.

I sort of expected her to go back inside the boat then, but Ashlyn stayed beside me at the railing. Her face exuded a sympathetic but concerned look that seemed to indicate she wanted to give me a grown-up talking to.

I'd suspected it was only a matter of time. She may not have been my mother, but she was *a* mother. And letting a bunch of kids go off toward danger was hardly something she could stand by and watch. She was worried about us. One look at her and I could tell she was worried about me in particular.

"You all right?" she asked.

My grip tensed on the warm metal. I kept my stare on the ocean and nodded without hesitation. Still, I could feel Ashlyn's eyes on me.

She sighed. "Crisa, it may not be my place to lecture you, but . . . I just want you to know that it is perfectly normal to be afraid. You don't have to put on a brave face twenty-four hours a day. I firmly believe you would feel better if you just talked about it."

Ugh, why does everyone keep assuming that I'm scared?

"Ashlyn," I said flatly as I rotated to meet her gaze. "I appreciate the concern, but there's nothing to talk about. Honestly, I'm not scared of those guys waiting for us on the beach."

"Then what are you afraid of?"

"Nothing."

"Everyone's afraid of something, Crisa," Ashlyn refuted. "You may not want to admit it, but I have had enough life experience to be able to recognize fear in someone's eyes when it's there."

I crossed my arms—feeling a tad violated and a bit embarrassed.

Ashlyn patted me on the arm. "Hon, I'm not trying to upset you," she said more delicately. "But you have a long journey and a lot of challenges ahead, and I just want you to be as strong as you can be when it comes time to face them."

"Then why are you trying to make me acknowledge fear?" I countered, my voice accidentally cracking as the words came out.

"Because a person can't overcome fear without first facing it. If those people on the beach or Alderon or your dreams truly don't scare you, that's great; more power to you. But lying to yourself about not being afraid of anything isn't doing you any favors either. If anything, that kind of denial will only stifle you—hurt you in ways that maybe aren't so obvious on the surface but are formidably destructive nonetheless. Do you understand what I'm saying?"

My shoulders tensed. "Ashlyn," I started to reply. "I don't think—"

"Portal, ho!"

Ashlyn and I whipped our heads toward the bow. A small, black swirling hole had appeared just above the water ahead. *Thank goodness.*

I saw my four counterparts quickly make for the lifeboat Donnie had readied for us on the side of the boat. I started to head in their direction, but Ashlyn gently gripped my shoulders and turned me to face her again.

"Crisa, I know there are a lot of things you think you have to do. But you should consider what you're sacrificing in the process."

As if seeing past my carefully constructed walls of pretense, she nodded toward the others. "Would it really be the worst thing in the world to let someone in?"

I paused for a second.

"I—"

"Knight, let's go!" Daniel shouted.

My body pivoted to go after them, but instinct caused me to stop short and give Ashlyn a quick hug first. "Thank you again," I said. "For everything. And if I don't see you again—"

"Knight!"

"I'm coming!" I shouted back.

Ashlyn patted my head. "Go." She smiled softly. "Just remember what I said. The things I'm telling you may not make sense now, but they might very soon. And when they do, you'll have some choices to make."

"Choices about what?"

"Crisa, come on!" Blue yelled.

"Not *what*, Crisa," Ashlyn replied. "*Who.*"

I opened my mouth to push for further explanation, but my friends' incessant urging overpowered the curiosity. I abandoned this important conversation like I'd done with so many others in recent days and dashed away. I slid down the ladder on *The Seabeagle*'s side and landed in the lifeboat.

Daniel moved aside a rather large, dark shoulder bag he'd brought with him so I could sit. Then, with all of us on board, Jason and Blue used the lifeboat's paddles to guide us to the hole. As we waved and shouted our final goodbyes, we began to drift toward the otherworldly connector that pulsed in the afternoon sun.

Just before we were pulled through, I looked back one last time. Ashlyn gave me a reassuring smile. Donnie waved. Mary Roberts stood there a bit more solemnly. She leaned against the railing, staring after us pensively.

In the next instant we left them all behind. Our boat was absorbed into the wormhole's depths and we were sucked into the slice of limbo that existed between here and home.

CHAPTER 27

Fruition

ne inter-dimensional portal later, and the five of us had washed up on Adelaide's shore.

It was different being on the beach during the daytime. Every other occasion I'd been on these sands had been late into the night, causing the cliffs, water, and rocks to blend together in a giant, dark mass.

I'd believed that seeing Adelaide's beaches and cliffside in the bright sunshine would've been far more beautiful by comparison. Alas, they were not. The warmth that filled the atmosphere seemed almost ironic given the circumstances surrounding our return. The gulls flying around us might as well have been vultures.

The five of us started to make our way to the north end of the beach where Ashlyn said we'd find better cave access. There were plenty of other cave openings we could've taken—Ashlyn assured us that they all interconnected at some point. But because of the way they twisted and turned within, she'd advised that we keep from entering the tunnel system for as long as possible to shorten our journey.

Unfortunately, how long we could stay outside the caves was up to Arian. He and his men could've been coming from anywhere, at any time. We'd been trekking across the beach for some twenty minutes now without incident, but for how much longer? None of us knew just how much time we had before—

"Guys," Jason said suddenly. "We've got company."

My body shivered involuntary before I turned around to face the inevitable.

There they were. Arian and about twenty guards were five hundred feet away and headed straight for us. Time was most definitely up.

"Let's move," I ordered.

The nearest crack in the cliffside was fifty meters ahead. We bolted for it, our feet sinking in the sand as we raced uphill, but our speed remaining true.

When we reached the opening, we dived in without looking back. I didn't know whether Arian and his men had seen which cavern we'd entered into, but eventually the mirror would lead them to us.

The sun's reach ended within seconds of entering the cavern. However, just as Ashlyn had described, its lack of natural light didn't matter. The caves and tunnel system had their own form of luminescence.

Jutting out of the rocky surfaces were the most beautiful stalagmites and stalactites. They were smooth on the sides but had jagged points. And for some unexplainable reason they glowed either a soft mint green or a rich sapphire blue.

I would've loved to linger and marvel at their brilliance. But at the moment these crystals were not for admiring. Their main purpose wasn't even lighting our way through the tunnels. More than anything they were a way for us to navigate through them.

Ashlyn had explained that the number and size of crystals increased as we got closer to the center of the tunnel system—making it easy for us to gauge our way.

We maneuvered through the caverns rapidly—swerving, rotating, and changing direction whenever the measure of crystals indicated a necessity to do so. About five minutes in, we took a wrong turn.

I skidded to a halt as our latest pathway curved into a cavern that was half-submerged in water. The floor of this one dropped off more abruptly than the others and we barely had time to pump the brakes. Gravel from under my boots tumbled off the ledge, and I jerked myself back, just in time to avoid going with it.

There was only one other route leading out of the cavern, so we took to it at full speed. After a minute this path deposited us into a much larger cavern. It was the size of the banquet hall at Lady Agnue's, but the ground was not level. It staggered with elevations of different heights that encircled an enormous crystal at the center like a beacon.

Countless other crystals protruded from the ground and ceiling. They were so massive that they filled the cavern with a light that rivaled the luminosity of the outside.

We'd made it. This was most certainly the center of the tunnel system. Everywhere we looked there were other tunnels converging unto this spot like ours had. Which meant it was time for us to split up.

As if on cue, we began to hear the choppy sounds of footsteps and shouting. We couldn't tell from which tunnel they emanated, but the volume suggested that it would not be long before Arian and his men found their way here too.

My eyes darted about, searching for the marker we were after.

Nope, not up there.

Not there.

Or there.

Or . . . wait, there it is!

On the upper left side of the cave we saw the crystal formation we'd been searching for. It was shaped vaguely like a starfish and its glow cast a radiant light over the entire platform it was perched on.

I remembered the image well. I'd only ever seen it in a flash of my dreams, but knew it was the indicator we sought. Alas, it was terribly high up. This final elevation was a good thirty feet above us and the slope looked too steep and slippery to climb.

It was at that point that Daniel swung the black bag off his shoulder. Unzipping it, he removed a grappling hook attached to a big coil of rope. He took out an arrow and nodded toward me. "You remember Fairy Godmother HQ?"

I couldn't help but smile as I took out my wand and transformed it into a bow. "How did you—"

"I didn't," he responded. "But just because I can't see the future doesn't mean I can't come prepared. Arabeth had a bunch of climbing stuff in her equipment closet. I asked if I could borrow a few things."

"Glad you did," I said.

With that, I attached the rope to the arrow, fired, and sent the grappling hook sailing upwards. It firmly attached to the starfish stone.

I hadn't known about the relevance of the starfish until I'd spoken with Ashlyn this morning. I had so many dream flashes these days it was hard to worry about each and every one. But when our former hostess had described her secret route from Adelaide Castle to the ocean, I discovered that this particular vision was actually key to our escape.

"The starfish crystal is located next to a tunnel that'll eventually lead you to a crevice in the ceiling," she had said.

"Climb through and you'll find yourself in an area below a bridge near the orchard. After that you're home free."

"All right, guys," I said as Arian's voice echoed closer. "Time for you to go."

"Crisa," SJ replied anxiously. "I know this is the plan we agreed on, but are you certain this is the best way?"

"We talked about this, SJ. Unless you want to fire that earthquake potion of yours and just end this by burying us alive, this is the only way. You guys know it, and so do I."

"She's right," Jason agreed. "I hate that Crisa has to do this alone too. But it's for the good of the group, and the best option if we want a clean break out of here without Arian continuing to follow us."

"Exactly," I affirmed. "So go on, all of you. I'll meet up with you where we planned."

I worried for a moment that they were going to keep fighting me on the subject. Thankfully, SJ nodded in agreement and they all began to scale the rope.

Beneath the shadow of the grand starfish I watched them go up one by one. Daniel was the last to make the ascent. He grabbed the rope in his hand then hesitated, looking back at me.

"Knight," he said.

"Yeah?"

He eyed me for a heartbeat then waved off whatever thought had crossed his mind. "Just don't die, okay."

I didn't know what to say, and he didn't give me the chance to think of it. Without another word Daniel swiftly began climbing the rope and was soon hoisting himself onto the highest ledge in the cavern beside the others.

Daniel reeled in his rope and shoved it back in his bag along with the grappling hook. Then he and my friends disappeared from sight into the designated tunnel behind them.

I was on my own now. And I was glad. Not a minute went by before Arian and several of his men emerged from a tunnel on the upper right side of the cavern.

On seeing him, I started to make a run for a tunnel a few ledges away, but then I had the misfortune of discovering why it had sounded like Arian's men were coming from everywhere. It was because they really *were* coming from everywhere.

Three of Arian's followers suddenly appeared out of the tunnel I'd been aiming for. More came from four other openings across the cavern. They must've split up when they'd entered the tunnel system to locate me faster. Good for them. Bad for me.

Arian spotted me and I stood frozen like a fawn in the crosshairs of a hunter's crossbow.

"Get her!"

None of the henchmen had emerged on the levels below me, so I hastily descended in pursuit of the tunnel at the lowest level.

With a slight cracking sound in my knees and the crunching of loose rock beneath my boots, I landed on each new level with a thud, but also with success. That last jump, however, was simply far too wide for any person to cross in a single bound. I landed with the opposite of grace, my body crashing and rolling to the ground.

Ignoring my scraped palms and arms, I hopped to my feet and plunged into the new tunnel. Increased adrenaline pulsed through my veins. My mindset was clear, focused, and unyielding.

As I ran, more paths converged unto my own—the labyrinth expanding.

"Split up!" I heard someone yell from one of the routes behind. "She's in here somewhere. Find her!"

I pulled my wand from my satchel and changed directions. Regrettably, my new course led me to a dead end. I whirled around, planning to go back the way I'd come, but halted when I realized voices were coming from that direction.

Spear.

Going on the offensive, I moved to meet the first surge of Arian's men.

They came at me sloppily, like a pack of drunken boar. Perhaps the chase had worn them out. Perhaps they were taken by surprise that I was actually daring to face them. Or perhaps I was just *that* good. The first two possibilities seemed more likely. But no matter what forces of fortune were at work, I was grateful.

This group of guards was comprised of three men and no Arian. When the first man charged I ducked, jabbed the guard behind him, and spun around to sweep his leg. As I punched the second soldier, his armor showed the reflection of the third attacker coming at me from my blind spot.

I whirled around and smacked his jaw with the dull end of my spear. His head smashed against the wall. As he sunk to the ground I blocked two more incoming strikes before throwing a low roundhouse and a leg hock. This took down the second attacker—leaving only one man inhibiting my route for escape.

I raised my eyebrows at him. "Yeah, I'm gonna need you to move."

Jumping on the back of the guy I'd just taken down and

using him as a boost, I faked like I was going to attempt some wild high shot. Right as my challenger raised his sword to plunge it into me, I transformed my wand.

Shield.

The shield blocked his strike and pinned his weapon-wielding arm against the wall. I thrust my elbow into his chin then back-kicked him in the shin for good measure.

Spear.

Both my hands grasping the staff, I turned and spun around—simultaneously pressing on his arm with one end of my spear and on his lower spine with the other. Transferring his weight with the terse shift of force, I thrust him off his feet and onto the floor.

Wand.

I took off down the narrowing tunnel at maximum speed. The submerged cavern I was looking for was around here somewhere and I needed to find it before I had any more run-ins with Arian's men.

As if.

Rounding the corner, I didn't even have time to transform my wand before a large knife came at my side. Thankfully my reflexes were good. I blocked the strike. My left hand grabbed the attacker's arm. Then my right hand—still clutching my wand—hammered his bicep before whipping against his face.

I swung back to do another leg-hock combo, but the attacker grabbed me and twisted my hand before I could manage the maneuver. Interlocked, we struggled for a second before his weight outmatched mine and he rammed me against the wall. I grimaced, unable to wriggle free.

An idea came to my head. Not a good one, but it would do.

With aim and conviction, I head-butted him. He staggered

back, giving me a chance to get a better angle for a follow-up, less-headache-inducing move.

And stomp the foot, kick the knee; thanks for letting go of my arm.

Face punch.

Shield.

Face punch with the shield.

And . . . roundhouse!

The power of my kick jettisoning him against the opposite wall, I morphed my wand back to its original state and made another break for it.

Dang, why can't anyone ever see me do that?

When I screw up I usually have an amphitheater-sized audience. But I get in a good butt-kicking combo that literally brings a guy to his knees and there are no witnesses. So unfair.

I ducked into a few more tunnels as I tried to outrun Arian and his helpers. Despite the high stakes, I remained calm, for I was by no means trying to outrun fate. Rather than dreading Arian inevitably catching up with me, I was counting on it.

My dreams told me this confrontation had to happen, and I'd come to terms with that. But I hadn't seen what was going to come *after* Arian and I faced off on that ledge. Which meant this part of my future I could still design for myself. And what I'd chosen to design was a scenario where I would ditch Arian in a way he hadn't seen coming *and* get rid of the magic mirror in the process.

As long as Arian had that mirror he'd be on our tail. The words he'd spoken in my dreams had been true—there was nowhere I could hide that he wouldn't find me. Ergo, my only option was to destroy the mirror. And getting close to Arian the way my vision had foreseen was going to give me the chance to do it.

If I succeeded, I would eliminate his only tactical advantage over me and create an opening to escape without further interference.

The only thing I hadn't been initially sure about was how to escape Arian once he'd cornered me and I'd smashed the mirror. Luckily, Ashlyn had whispered some advice about that too.

She mentioned that while it was necessary to navigate a certain course through the caves on her way *back* to Adelaide Castle, in order to save time on her way to the ocean she'd found a short-cut: the underwater caves.

Throughout the tunnel system there were many caverns half-submerged in water. All these caverns had decently-sized crevices at their bases that allowed water from the sea to freely flow in and out. The crevices were direct paths to the ocean big enough for someone to swim through . . . someone like me, for instance.

I bobbed and weaved through the glowing stone passageways before I finally found another submerged cavern. The shadowy, bulging ceiling was high, the walls were curved, and there were no crystals. The only light came from the tunnel I'd just entered through. Looking around at its dimensions and the size of the drop to the swelling waters below, I became certain this was the cavern from my dreams.

For just a moment I leaned out over the ledge and watched the dark, distant waters. They breathed and moved with the currents outside—reassuring me that my next move was not insane. At least not totally anyways.

"This way!"

Arian and his forces were closing in.

With their footsteps drawing nearer, I readied myself for

the action I needed to take. First that meant backing away from this ledge a bit. Only when they came into view would I make a break for it—acting as if I'd only just gotten there. I couldn't let it seem like I was waiting for them; otherwise they might have suspected something was up.

I firmly shoved my wand into my boot. Then I drew the slingshot Jason had made for me from my satchel, as well as a sturdy, meatball-sized rock I'd picked up on the beach before leaving Ashlyn's. Finally, I zipped up the internal closure of my bag and secured its outside clasps tightly.

That's when I saw the shadows stretch across the floor like a conjoined silhouette. I dashed back toward the ledge of the cavern, halting just before I toppled over.

The timing was perfect. To Arian and his men it must've looked like they'd caught up with me right when I reached the supposed dead end, just as I'd planned.

"No place left to run, princess."

Keeping the slingshot concealed behind my back and the stone in my left fist, I turned to face the familiar voice.

Arian led the group of six men. The glow behind him darkened his frame and elongated his shadow on the ground that separated us. His expression was smug as he and the others approached me. When he was about ten feet away, he came to a stop and gave me a sadistic grin.

"Got you."

"You would think so, wouldn't you?" I said, eyeing the magic mirror he held in his hand. I clutched the stone tighter as I readied myself for an opening.

Arian gestured to one of his beefy followers. "Bring me the bag . . ."

There it was! Now or never—take the shot!

In the split second he looked away from me, I whipped

out the slingshot and released my meatball-sized ammo in the direction of the mirror.

My heart stopped as the rock made bullseye contact with the enchanted object, shattering the looking glass into a hundred tiny shards. In an instant that felt like eons I watched them fall to the floor.

Although they'd both reluctantly agreed to the plan, I knew SJ and Blue would've probably had an aneurism at the sight of the beloved treasure from *Beauty & the Beast* breaking to pieces. Meanwhile, I was indescribably relieved that my aim had been true.

I didn't wait to see Arian's response. When the first shard hit the ground, I dropped the slingshot, turned, and dove off the ledge.

My body plummeted in free fall for a few seconds. Then I plunged into the water.

The cold was a shock, but in a good way that recharged my senses and my strength. I swiftly pulled my wand out of my boot. It glowed instantaneously and I swam for the bottom of the pool, guided by its light.

The water had a strong current, but it was hard to see exactly where it was coming from. I made for the seaweed attached to the rocks on the bottom of the cavern, ripped off a piece, and set it loose. The seaweed was speedily sucked to the right and I pursued it until I was led to the crevice where the current was swelling in and out.

The strand of flimsy seaweed was sucked through and out of sight. I, however, was not small enough to do the same.

I peered inside the crevice.

Past the initial opening the underwater route seemed to widen. But at present, the opening was only a foot wide and too tight for me to fit through.

I wasn't disheartened by this. It was a problem that I had been ready for.

Axe.

Still retaining its luminescence, my wand morphed into the desired weapon and I hacked away at the area around the crevice. After a couple of swings, a large chunk of rock gave way.

Wand.

The new-and-improved opening sucked me out with a sudden rush of water that seemed just as desperate to escape as I was. My body rode the current and I kicked my feet to speed up the process.

After a short ride through the underwater tunnel I was deposited into the greater ocean. Everything in this new environment was quiet and still, which would have been pretty tranquil had my lungs not been about to explode from lack of air. I saw sunlight caressing the water above and I zoomed up with what may well have been my last second of breath.

My head burst through the surface and I filled my body with oxygen.

Mental note—should I live to see another semester at school, I should suggest we build a pool on campus so as not to be so unprepared for these types of underwater scenarios.

When I eventually caught my breath I swam for land. A minute later I washed onto the sand like a beached whale with messy hair.

My trusty SRB instantly sent a flurry of silver sparks up and down my limbs that cleaned and dried every part of my clothes and person. As the sparks danced around me I got up and took the first deep breath I'd taken all day.

I had done it. My Adelaide vision had successfully been

completed without my getting captured or killed. I had outsmarted the future. And now that the magic mirror was destroyed and Arian no longer had a way to follow my movements, I was free to find my friends and Daniel without bringing any kind of threat along with me.

I looked up and down the beach.

The last tip Ashlyn had shared was that the underwater tunnels always let out somewhere near a distinct part of Adelaide's cliffside. I saw that unique area now. I'd seen it the night I'd snuck away from Adelaide Castle and first met Lonna. It was a magnificent, intricate cluster of stone skyscrapers that converged at the top to form a plateau connected to the cliffside. Each one of the natural rock columns appeared thicker than an ancient redwood tree. And they seemed strong too, as if neither time nor circumstance could wither their magnitude.

I began heading toward the natural structure, admiring the crafty work of Mother Nature and the gods of terrain-shaping that had created it.

From a distance I thought the formation resembled an unimaginably large, stone spider with dozens of long, jagged legs sticking into the sand at odd angles. Or maybe it was more like a giant's hand with clenched fingers digging viciously into the sand. Either way, it was pretty impressive. More than anything, though, it was familiar and reassuring.

Having seen this marvelously menacing structure from the other side when I'd first come to shore the night of Adelaide's ball, I knew I was not far from the other route off this beach—the one I'd taken before.

Arriving at the grand cluster of rocks, I smiled at the thought. I was almost in the clear.

The rock entanglement stretched the entire width of the

beach, leading into the ocean. As I made my way through it, I discovered two things. The first was the humbling pressure created by the above plateau's shadows. The sun was at an odd angle, so its rays cut through the formation in uneven, elongated castings—making some areas bright and warm while others remained cold and dark.

Meanwhile, the second thing I realized was that the rock pillars were actually far taller, larger, and in much greater numbers than I'd originally perceived. The masts of natural stone surrounded me like a forest of rock. I couldn't even see through to the other side.

It was intimidating, but I was not deterred. I'd already made it through a labyrinth of cave tunnels and *actual* forests. I simply had to keep heading straight and would eventually find my way out. Or at least I would if I didn't keep tripping on rocks in the sand that were—

Whoa!

My face fell forward and my knees sunk into a damp patch of sand as my wand flew out of my hand.

Stupid rock, I thought to myself. I reached out my hand to collect the weapon, which had landed a foot away from me. But just as my fingers hovered over it a thin shadow blanketed the patch of sun where it rested.

"Hello, Knight."

Daniel?

I looked up and squinted into the glint of sunlight just before the shadow.

My heart shot into my throat.

Arian.

I didn't think. I didn't reply. I just grabbed my wand, sprung to my feet, and made a break in the other direction.

How did he find me? How am I going to—

I rounded one of the rock pillars only to run into one of Arian's henchmen. He tried to grab me, but I elbowed him in the head and knocked him back with a firm punch to the jaw.

Two more men were behind him. I turned on my heels to try and go around the other side of the rock, but was confronted by three additional attackers. I jumped back as a sword slashed at me then ducked a second blade that came at my head. I managed to kick one man against the rock, but then an attacker grabbed my left wrist from behind and pulled me back.

I spun around and slammed my fist into his face. He let go and I attempted to make another dash for it, but there was nowhere left to run.

More and more enemies emerged. They were appearing from behind every towering rock in the vicinity—encircling me at all angles.

Gripping my wand, I backed up slowly until I was pressed up against one of the stone pillars. The men continued to move forward and tighten their circle. I morphed my wand and pointed my spear at them defensively. To my surprise, a few of the aggressors backed up a step when I did. Maybe word of my handy work with their friends in the tunnel system had spread.

Other than the momentary ego boost, this gave me little comfort. I had been able to handle facing a few of them at a time, but now there were nine of them. And they had me surrounded on all sides. Maybe I could've taken five or six of them. But nine *plus* Arian? I was sassy, not stupid. More than anything though, I was nervous. I hadn't seen this coming and definitely didn't have a plan.

The only chance I had was to bide time until I had a window to jab the guy closest to me and make a run for it.

"Go ahead. Try and run," Arian said, reading my thoughts as he joined his men. "You won't get far."

He took a few steps confidently toward me. I wished I had the room to take a couple more steps back.

Arian's hair was tussled, and he had dark circles under his eyes and mud on his shoes. Yet he continued to emanate confidence. He was tired, but by no means tired out. His black eyes still shone; his stance remained strong and tall. Unlike me, he was just as comfortable now in his own skin as he'd ever been.

I didn't know whether to worry over or envy that.

He studied my raised weapon suspiciously. While he did so, my eyes darted back and forth between him and the men on either side of me as I attempted to calculate possible escape routes.

"You might as well give up," Arian said, interrupting my thoughts. "You're outnumbered."

I adjusted my stance confidently. "Yeah, but not as outmatched as you'd like," I countered. "I can see you've increased your number of lackeys since the last time I saw you. What, afraid I'll humiliate you with another implausible escape?"

"Take it down a notch, Knight," he scoffed. "You're lucky, not good."

I raised my eyebrows. "More like 'very lucky given that I've managed to elude you three times now' . . . wouldn't you say?"

The preciseness of this comment—a nearly exact quote from one of my earlier dreams about him—wiped the smirk off his face.

I could see the gears moving in his head as the familiarity of the statement rung in his ears. He momentarily paused, no doubt wondering about the coincidence of my specific wording. After all, he'd spoken the phrase in a private conversation that I shouldn't have known anything about. Unfortunately, Arian shrugged off the peculiarity a second later and refocused on me.

"You know what," he said, "it doesn't matter. You're done either way."

He snapped his fingers and one of the henchmen brought forward a dark-colored bag I'd seen them carrying back in the cavern. Arian reached inside and pulled out a chrome shining object that I hadn't seen in ages but was well acquainted with nonetheless.

My eyes widened. "Is that—?"

"The lamp from your school's precious shrine? It is."

Aladdin's formerly genie-holding lamp gleamed in Arian's hands. No one had seen it since it disappeared from the Treasure Archives and it looked smudged and dirty, but there was no mistaking it for what it was. Which meant my theory about cloaked girl being the person who'd broken into the Archives and stolen all that stuff was accurate. Whoever she was, she had done it. And she had done it for Arian.

I felt my jaw harden and my eyes narrow.

"So how did she do it?" I asked him. "How did your friend break into the school and steal all that stuff—Aladdin's genie lamp, Snow White's corset, the fake magic mirror, and the enchanted pea? And while we're on the subject, how did she even get *into* the school? Seriously, Arian, who is this chick? I know she's not the great Nadia I keep hearing so much about. So who is it then? Tara?"

Arian smiled like the question posed some sort of inside joke. "No. It is not Tara," he replied. "And it is definitely not

Nadia either. I hardly think stealing a few magic trinkets from a private school is a task worthy of the queen of Alderon."

Nadia was the *queen* of Alderon? I didn't even know that kingdom had a ruler. How organized were these antagonists?

"You'll meet her soon enough, but on her terms, not yours," Arian continued. "As to the stolen property, Knight, I'm afraid you're misinformed as usual. Our ally you're referring to retrieved the mirror, the corset, and the lamp for us. But she didn't take some stupid pea. What use could we possibly have for such an idiotic thing?"

"I don't know, Arian. You stole a mirror, a lamp, and a corset. How should I know where you draw the line on your antagonist shopping list?"

Arian gave me an irritated look. "You think you're pretty funny, don't you?"

"I've gotten mixed reviews."

Arian began to move toward me again. However, I had one more question to ask. It was partially to delay him, but also every inch of my being desperately wanted to know the answer.

"Wait!" I said, halting my enemy in his tracks. "Why me, Arian? Come on, you owe me that at least. You say you hunt and kill protagonists that pose a threat to you, but what makes me so special that you need to steal all that stuff from the Archives just to better your chances? You said it was my prologue prophecy, but even if that's true and my prophecy is not what I've been told, how important could it be that you need to go through all this trouble?"

Arian scoffed with disdain and amusement. I wasn't sure which bothered me more.

"Don't flatter yourself," he said. "You may be an interesting, unexpected wrench in our plans, Crisanta

Knight, but not everything we do revolves around you. When I found out that you had magic I simply figured we could use the lamp and the mirror to kill two birds with the same stones. Of course, now that you've gone and destroyed the mirror, the search for our more important target has to go on as normal. You, on the other hand, will not be able to do the same—thanks to this other stupid piece of magic junk from your school, which remains intact."

Arian gestured to the lamp.

Now it was my turn to scoff. The lamp was short and stout with an elongated spout. The entire thing was solid chrome except for a few old jewels decorating the lid—rubies so dirtied they looked like specks of crusted blood. While it may have been an important fairytale relic, nothing about it was formidable.

"In case you haven't noticed, Arian, I'm not a genie," I said. "And the only wish I'd ever grant you is a last wish."

Arian gave a long, sinister chuckle. "It's a real shame," he commented. "All that money the commons pay in taxes to support your little protagonist private schools and you still don't know a thing."

"Then enlighten me," I snapped. "What am I missing here besides a fair fight?"

"Just one basic truth, Crisanta Knight," Arian said. "Magic lamps aren't just for imprisoning genies. They're meant to absorb and contain the closet magical being in the area. As long as it's within fifteen feet, any kind of magical being will do. And that, my dear princess, is where you come in."

Wait. Hold up. The closest magical being in the area? That's . . . Oh snap, that's me!

Instinct told me to grip the staff of my spear and attack. Logic told me that I could attack as hard as I wanted, but I couldn't rely on my strength, skill, or gumption to save me this time.

Arian was not about to give me another opportunity to escape. He removed the lid from the lamp before I could move. In the next instant a vortex constructed of swirling shades of violet and lavender—the very image that had long been troubling my dreams—shot out of the lamp.

It was unimaginably bigger and brighter than it had looked in my head, bursting out horizontally and spinning toward me like a hurricane. I tried to resist its pull but to no avail. It sucked me forward with such power and speed I never had a chance. I was yanked off my feet and into its depths.

Just as the force was about to swallow me completely I felt someone grab hold of my arm. I looked up to see who it was, but my vision had gone blurry. All I could see were the purple swirls that encased me like a futuristic cocoon.

Nevertheless, wherever this mysterious aid was coming from, for the moment it seemed to be working. It was acting as a tether—anchoring me to the outer world and keeping me from being fully absorbed into the lamp.

Just as suddenly as this help appeared though, it stopped. With one final inhale, the lamp's vortex consumed me and my attempted rescuer in one fell swoop. The beach, the world, and everything in sight were ripped away from me. I blacked out to the sound of Arian's evil laughter somewhere on the outside of my new prison.

CHAPTER 28

Moving Forward

'd heard the term "bottled-up fury" before, but it wasn't until this particular moment that I learned where the phrase must have come from.

The interior of the genie lamp I was trapped in was shaped like a bottle of fancy, imported water. Despite the spout that extended from it on the outside, the only opening visible from within was the lid I'd been sucked through, which was now high above my head.

The interior décor had the feel of a nightclub lounge that hadn't decided whether it wanted to be retro or post-modern chic. Satin curtains hung throughout the space, draping across the ceiling. The carpet was royal purple shag and matched the throw pillows on the black leather sofas, which curved around the whole perimeter. Oddly shaped mirrors with silver and gold frames hung on the walls, which were covered with splashes of green, maroon, and purple paint. I assumed the blobs of color were the original decorator's attempts to make the place look artsy. But to me, they just looked like the aftermath of a horrible pie explosion.

Sigh.

At least they matched the multi-colored crystal balls that magically floated around the room providing light. These whimsical orbs were polar opposites to the sleek candelabras sitting on the chrome side tables. Those were dull gray and seemed too sharp and severe to match the otherwise quirky décor.

As if being in a candlelit room with no windows or doors and *a lot* of flammable drapery wasn't disconcerting enough, the flames crackled an eerie bright green, reminiscent of a witch's cauldron. It was creepy. If there were such a thing as a villains' primary color wheel, this shade definitely would've made the cut.

If this was the interior design that the lamp's former resident had been forced to put up with for ten thousand years, I felt really bad for him. However, if the décor reflected the genie's own personal taste, well, maybe the world had been better off with him stuck in here.

Since the moment I'd woken up inside of the lamp, I'd been trying to find a way out. Meanwhile, as I fervently toiled away with my wand on the lamp's lid, Daniel had just been sitting on one of the couches reading a book he'd found on the coffee table.

Oh yeah. Did I forget to mention Daniel was here?

Remember that person that grabbed my arm and tried to keep me from being sucked into the lamp? Well, that had been him.

As my dreams had foretold, my friends had eventually worked out the deception in my motives for our splitting up. At first this didn't matter. I knew from my visions that they'd come to the same conclusion I'd reached when concocting the plan. It would be impossible for them to find me in the caverns, so they had no choice but to go on and meet me at our agreed rendezvous point, which was where we'd left the Pegasi.

What I hadn't anticipated, though, was that Daniel would find another way to get to me.

When they were nearing the place where we'd left the Pegasi, Daniel noticed the giant plateau of that immense rock pillar formation. As it offered a clear view of the beach on either side, he'd told the others to go ahead and collect the Pegasi while he waited to spot me on the beach, assuming that by the time they returned I'd have come into view and they could make a straight shot for me.

While Blue, SJ, and Jason proceeded with this plan, Daniel had in fact spotted me washing ashore in the distance. But as he watched me trek across the beach, he'd spotted Arian's forces approaching from the other direction—a threat that I was clearly unaware of.

With no time to wait for our friends, Daniel took the grappling hook and rope out of his bag and propelled down. The cliffside was jagged and sloped out as it neared the bottom. So when he ran out of rope he descended the rocks without it like a rock climber.

When he hit solid ground he rushed to my aid, catching up with me during my dramatic confrontation with Arian. He'd snuck up behind the rocky pillar I was cornered against and tried to save me just as Arian had uncovered the lamp.

And that, regrettably, was all she wrote.

It was a good effort in theory. But apparently once the lamp's powers locked on to the nearest magical creature in the vicinity, they did not let it go no matter what. And, as it happened, the lamp would also suck in anything that was holding on to said magical creature. Hence the reason why I was currently sharing this tacky prison with the world's most mysterious teenage boy.

There was no way of telling how long we'd been trapped,

but it felt like a few hours. As time went on I was becoming increasingly anxious. I had no idea where we were going, what happened to my friends, or how to get out of here. And if I didn't at least find an answer to that last question, it wouldn't be long before I was delivered to Nadia, the queen of Alderon.

Needless to say it was enough to stress anybody out. Yet Daniel seemed to be taking the whole situation in stride. When I'd regained consciousness he had been pacing around tentatively and we'd exchanged a brief recap of how we'd ended up there. However, since then he'd been silent—calmly reading in the corner like he was waiting for the dentist or something.

Frankly, it was really starting to tick me off.

I tried not to let my frustration with him get the better of me—I needed all my focus to keep my balance. I was standing on a wobbly stack of three chairs, which allowed me to jab the weapon's blade into the crease of the lamp's lid in an attempt to get it open.

For a second I thought maybe this time I was actually getting somewhere. But then the highest chair in the stack toppled off, and it and I both went tumbling to the floor.

I landed with a muffled thud on the thick carpet. My spear, meanwhile, hung pathetically from the fissure in the roof for a beat before it, too, dropped to the ground beside me.

"You're never going to get the lid open that way," Daniel said without looking up from his book.

I ignored him, spat out some carpet fluff, and began re-stacking the chairs with unshaken resolve.

He sighed and put the book down. "Knight, seriously, you're gonna break your neck if you keep that up."

I continued ignoring him and picked up my spear. Daniel

got up and walked toward me. Just as I started to climb the first chair in my newly restored tower, he grabbed the other end of my spear to prevent me from making the ascent.

"Daniel, let go," I said, yanking the staff.

He yanked back. "I'm helping, not hurting, Knight. You have to stop."

"I'll say it one more time, Daniel. Let go. *Now*."

"Make me."

"Fine!"

I hinged my leg and kicked him in the shin.

"Argh!" he grunted, releasing my spear.

I snatched the staff away and approached the stack of chairs again. Before I could climb up, guilt set in like slow-acting poison and I lost my conviction.

I'd spent a lot of time resisting the urge to kick Daniel since we'd met and fantasizing about how good it would feel to actually do it. But I'd been wrong. It didn't feel good. Even though he was getting on my nerves, his being stuck in this lamp was my fault. And I had no right to take my frustrations out on him.

I returned my wand to normal and shoved it in my boot. Then with a humbled exhale I turned to face him.

"I'm sorry," I said. "That was . . . uncalled for."

"Really?" he replied in disbelief. "Because it seems like you've been dying to do that for a while now."

"That's true," I conceded. "But I shouldn't have actually done it. You're just driving me crazy, Daniel. I mean, we are trapped inside a lamp. A lamp in the possession of someone who's been trying to kill me and anybody that gets in their way for weeks. And here I am trying to find a way to get us out, and you're just lounging in the corner reading some book."

"I wasn't reading; I was researching," Daniel replied.

"Come again?"

Daniel marched over to the couch where he'd been sitting and retrieved the book I'd seen him flipping through.

"The genie that used to live in this lamp kept a journal," he explained. "I found it under one of the couch cushions. Among other things, he cataloged the ways he tried to escape over the years. There are some pretty interesting theories in here that he was planning on testing out while he was serving Aladdin but never got a chance to see through. I think maybe we could try a few for ourselves."

Daniel handed me the book and I began to page through it.

He was right. There were hundreds, maybe thousands of catalogued escape ideas that the genie had attempted, and just as many that he was planning on trying out in the future. The journal was stuffed from front to back with diagrams, spells, and notes.

I handed the book back to Daniel. "Why didn't you say something sooner?" I asked.

Daniel released a slight scoff. "Would you have listened?"

"Of course I would have."

"Really? Because last I checked, every time I or *anyone* tries to help you, you go completely mental."

"That's not true."

"Isn't it?" Daniel asked. "Of all the times we've tried to help you, how many times have you actually said thank you?"

"Well, I don't—"

"And how many times have you overreacted and gotten mad instead?"

"I wouldn't say—"

"And despite all the messed up junk we've been going

through together *as a group*," he continued, "how many times have you been completely honest with us about what's going on with you?"

"I was honest with you guys about my dreams just this morning," I protested.

Daniel raised his eyebrows. "Come on, Knight—*completely* honest?"

"Uh . . ."

"Yeah. That's what I figured."

"Hey, it's not like I lied to you guys. I just . . . left some stuff out."

"And what would possibly possess you to do that?"

I felt my face getting hotter. It was partly due to anger, partly due to guilt. But mostly it was due to not enjoying being cornered by Daniel and his unpleasant personal questions in an enclosed space where I could not escape from either.

"You wouldn't understand," I huffed as I stormed to the other side of the lamp.

He followed, refusing to let the matter die.

"Try me."

"Daniel, I just . . ." I turned my back on him and paced across the room again. When I reached the other side I saw he'd pursued me there too.

I had nowhere left to go. I was literally backed against a wall. He was so close to me—his face, his eyes, his everything burrowing into my soul in such a way that I felt like I was suffocating. My cheeks flushed, my fists clenched, my shoulders tensed.

Is this place getting smaller? Or is the air just dissipating at an alarmingly fast rate?

"Knight . . ." Daniel said, a bit more carefully. "Come on, just tell me."

My eyes met his for a beat then darted to the ground. My heart pounded twelve times faster than it had when I was being chased by Arian. Evidently I preferred a confrontation involving malevolent archenemies and the threat of elimination to one that involved an extraction of my innermost feelings.

Yet in the end I forced myself to acquiesce.

"Look, Daniel," I finally said, sighing. "The thing is, I knew Arian and those jerks were after me. And the more I dreamed about it, the more I realized they would stop at nothing to get to me no matter what or *who* they had to go through.

"Knowing that, how could I let the four of you in on everything that was going on? If I had, you wouldn't have agreed to let me go off alone and then you would've gotten the same targets painted on your backs that I've had on mine for weeks. I wasn't about to let that happen. I'd rather be handed over to Nadia on a silver platter or trapped in this dumb lamp for a million years than put you guys in harm's way on my behalf. So there, you wanted complete honesty—now you have it. Now you know. Stupid as it may sound, at the end of the day I'd rather throw myself to the wolves alone than drag others down with me."

Daniel didn't respond.

Having been honest with him made me feel bare. Silence had never seemed louder, and I writhed in its condemning tension until it became too much for me to handle. I glanced up.

Daniel was just standing there looking at me. Staring at me, really, in a way that made me feel like an animal at the Century City Zoo. But it was worse than that because at least those animals had cages or kennels or walls to separate them from the people who came to judge their behaviors. Me, I had nothing to create a sense of safe distance between Daniel and me.

I was fully exposed to him. And I hated it.

"So let me get this straight," Daniel finally said.

I balled my fists even tighter—bracing myself for his judgment.

"You would rather risk your neck going it alone than let one of us help you? You're that stubborn, that set on keeping us at a distance, despite what it means for you personally? I gotta say, Knight, it's definitely not your brightest idea. If anything it's surprising. I mean, most princesses would—"

"Most princesses would *what*?" I suddenly snapped, my eyes locking with his angrily.

This had been the longest day of the longest week of the longest month of my life. I had been through a lot, but antagonists and monsters and magic hunters aside, what I was most fed up with was people lecturing me on this subject. I'd had it, and I wasn't going to take it anymore.

"Most princesses would swoon? Sigh? Give you a handkerchief as a token of their gratitude? That's what you think I should do, isn't it, Daniel?" I said. "Be just another typical princess: fragile, docile, oh-so-grateful that a hero like you came my way so that I won't have to handle things for myself? You've certainly been trying to put me in my supposed place since the moment we met. Well, guess what? I'm tired of it, of *you*. I don't know what type of princess I am, I'll admit, or even if I'm a princess at all. But I'll tell you what I do know; I'm sick of you and everyone else trying to decide for me. I have been busting my butt trying to keep people, especially SJ, Blue, and Jason, from seeing me as this damsel in distress, but I can't catch a break from anyone."

I groaned and dropped to the leather couch behind me—the weight of the world depriving me of my will to stand.

"But then again, what should I expect?" I continued as I stared at the hideous carpet. "If the universe really wanted me to be something more, I don't think it would've engineered a life where everyone keeps pushing me in the same direction—putting me in the same damsel box no matter how much I struggle against it.

"As much as it kills me to say it, maybe you were right that night we broke into Fairy Godmother Headquarters. Maybe I'm not strong enough to fight what's coming. Maybe my fate will never be mine to decide and all I am is exactly what you and Lady Agnue and Arian and the rest of the world seem to think. Weak. And incapable of being any of the things I wish I was."

I hung my head as my angry words settled in the air between us.

I was out of breath and out of words. Most of all, it felt like I was out of soul. Like I'd expelled too much and was now an empty version of my former self—ripe for verbal attack and vulnerable for emotional destruction, both of which I was sure Daniel would not be able to resist taking advantage of.

"Are you done?" he asked.

I waved my hand acquiescingly. "Yes. Go ahead."

"Good," he said. "Because if you would stop overreacting for one second then I could finish what I was going to say. Which is that, yes, most princesses would gladly call for help at the first sign of danger and expect someone else to step in and secure a happy ending for them. But you're *not* like most princesses. You're stubborn, loud, *crazy*, short-tempered—"

"Daniel, if you're just going to keep listing insulting

adjectives, I'm going to go back to stabbing the ceiling with my spear," I said, getting ready to stand.

"Knight, you gonna let me complete a sentence?"

I rolled my eyes and sat back down. "Whatever. Say what you've gotta say."

"All right," he said flatly. "Here it is then. Yeah, you're all those things, Knight, I'm not going to sugarcoat it. But the fact is that it doesn't take a genius to see that beyond that surface stuff, you're a lot more too. For starters, you're brave. And you're resourceful. And unique and probably one of the toughest, strongest people I've ever met."

And I thought that after meeting carnivorous actor wolves there were no more great surprises left in life. But of all the things I'd been shocked by recently, this definitely topped them all. Had Daniel just given me a compliment?

"You think I'm strong?" I asked, utterly stunned.

"Well, not so much in the usual sense," Daniel responded. "I mean, come on, your sword skills suck. You still need a lot more practice with that spear. It wouldn't kill you to lift more weights with Blue. And you're not exactly—"

"Daniel."

"Right, sorry, old habits." He cleared his throat. "What I mean to say is that no matter what, or *who*, tries to stop you, you never give up. You keep going. You keep fighting. And you never back down. That's the very definition of strong. So despite what those other snob idiots at school think, I know that you of all people are not weak, and to say that you've got some hero in you would be an understatement."

I was flabbergasted. Like so truly, completely shocked that I almost slid off the leather couch. I held up my hand.

"Seriously? You, Daniel, think that I, Crisanta Knight—

this girl right here," I gestured overdramatically at myself, "has what it takes to be a hero?"

He shrugged like I was the one being ridiculous.

"If you took a detour from that pride parade of yours and let people in, let people help you from time to time then, yeah. I do think you could be a hero. You have all the makings of a good one. You just need to stop trying to do everything by yourself. Don't get me wrong; I respect the bravery and self-sacrifice thing you were going for. But what's the point of having friends if you can't count on them to have your back when you need them the most?"

I shook my head, my eyes glued to the floor as I wondered just how much more I would tell him. Emotional vulnerability (or any kind of vulnerability) was not my scene. Unfortunately, the defensive walls that kept me from ever being truly honest with anyone—including myself—were coming down. As consequence, I couldn't stop the pure, unfiltered admissions that followed.

"I understand what you're saying, Daniel," I replied steadily. "But you just don't get it. I've spent my whole life believing that I can show the world that I don't need saving. That I can overcome the stereotypes and become something more than what is expected—something better, or at the very least something that I can be proud of.

"Those beliefs are everything to me. They're what give me purpose and hope that there's a point to all this. If I don't have them, then what's left? A life that's worth nothing more than a piece in someone else's puzzle, a page in someone else's book?"

"I'm not following," Daniel said. "What does any of that have to do with you trusting us, letting us help you now and then so you don't have to carry the weight of the whole dang world on your shoulders?"

"I'll tell you what it is has to do with that . . ." I started to say.

The air tasted sour in my mouth and my heart hung in suspense. I bit my lip and tried to swallow the declaration burning in my throat. However, I knew it was time to relinquish the truth. And just like that it came out in a whisper; like wind escaping beneath the crack in a steel door that'd spent far too long pretending to be impenetrable.

"I can't trust you guys that way because . . . because I'm afraid."

"What?"

My vulnerability abruptly turned to bitterness, and my fragility to sullen fury.

"I said I'm afraid," I snapped.

I punched the couch resentfully, having finally uttered the words.

"Are you happy? I may not be afraid of things like magic hunters or Therewolves or even antagonists that are trying to kill me. But the lot of you were right. I am still afraid of something. And that something is all those beliefs of mine going up in smoke like one of SJ's red portable potions. I'm afraid of proving the world right about me, being proven wrong about myself, and, most of all, of having to accept that who I am is the very person I've spent my whole life praying that I wasn't."

The clenched fist I'd punched into the couch was starting to tingle from within, but I ignored the sensation and continued. My emotional purging was not yet done.

"That's why I've been acting like this, Daniel," I said

more wearily than before, "and keeping everyone I should be able to trust at a distance. If I trust you guys enough to ask for help, then it's like conceding that everything I believe in is wrong. It's like affirming that there is no such thing as a princess who can save herself. And that the world was right about me the entire time; I really am nothing more than another damsel."

"Knight—"

"No, Daniel. Don't you see?" I interrupted. "I'm a girl who wants to be strong in a world where everyone thinks I'm weak. No matter where I go, people are so sure of who I am—never leaving room for the slightest possibility that they might be mistaken. I've been able to fight against it all these years because those people don't know me well enough to make that kind of call. But there *are* people who can. My friends. They're the only people whose opinions do truly matter because they're the only people who do truly know me.

"So you have to understand why all those times I knew I was in trouble and needed help, I could never ask for it. Because if I ever completely lowered my guard—asked for help, or worse, admitted that I needed it—then your impressions of me would become the same as everyone else's.

"Why do you think I get so mad whenever you've tried to save me in front of the others? It's not because I'm stupid or stubborn. It's because I've been desperately trying to protect my image in the eyes of the last few people in the realm who might still think of me differently. And every time you swoop in and try to pull me out of danger, it only further drives home the opposite. It validates those awful things people think about me, those awful things people are so sure that I am. And if it keeps up—me needing to be helped and saved all the time—then sooner or later . . . there'll be nothing and no one left to prove them wrong."

I hung my head low under the weight of the truth. My body was shaking. I felt like I was going to cry, but I resisted the urge. This may have been the ideal time and place to do it, but my will to retain whatever composure I had left was strong.

Exhaling a long sigh instead, I looked down at my hand. It had been prickling icily throughout my rant, and only now was the sensation beginning to calm down. Traces of metal evaporated back into my skin. Temporarily drained in terms of speech, I took a moment to unclench my balled-up fist and take a peek at the marking inside.

If this is it—if this is the actual time the tattoo has chosen to reveal its true meaning—I swear . . .

I opened my hand fully.

Thank goodness. It's still blurry.

If the word "afraid" or something similar had appeared there—announcing itself as my defining quality—that would've totally driven me off the edge.

I was beginning to feel a bit less shell-shocked, and this caused me to notice that too much silence had passed since I'd finished talking. I looked up at Daniel. It felt pretty weird having exposed my soul to someone I really didn't know, or *like* for that matter. And the subsequent insecurity made my stomach knot.

I half expected him to burst out laughing. Much to my surprise, he didn't. He just held my gaze for a minute before coming to sit down next to me.

I scooched away from him slightly—taken aback by the proximity.

Is this a trap?

This feels like a trap.

"Knight," Daniel said firmly. "You need to get a grip."

"Gee, thanks, Daniel." I rolled my eyes. "Do they teach psychology at Lord Channing's? Because your approach to dealing with fragile mental health is just textbook."

"Oh, settle down. I don't mean it like that," he said. "Look, in my opinion you don't have anything to worry about when it comes to what the others think of you. I mean, I just told you how I see you and it was nothing like you were expecting, right?"

"Right," I replied hesitantly.

"But for the sake of argument," he continued, "let's say I'm wrong. Let's say Jason, Blue, every one of us agrees with the greater world's consensus about who you are—that you're just a weak princess and a terrible hero. Even if that were true, so what?"

"So what?" I repeated. "So everything. If not even my closest friends see me as being different, then who's to say or prove that I am?"

"Well, off the top of my head, how about you?"

I blinked. "What?"

"You heard me," Daniel said. "You keep going on about how worried you are about people defining who you are but, Knight, none of them really can. Despite what you might think, the only person who gets to decide that is you."

"But Daniel, I don't—"

"No buts," Daniel interrupted. "No excuses, no doubts, no second-guessing. I know you hate to listen to me, Knight. But even if you tune me out for the rest of your life, I want you to hear me now. You wanna choose who you are for yourself? Well, the bottom line is that it's that simple. All you have to do is choose. Everything and everyone else don't matter. They don't get a vote; they don't get a say. The only person who does is you because you and you alone can define who you are."

"That's easy for you to say," I responded. "You're a hero. Your archetype doesn't have half as many stereotypes working against it as mine does."

"Maybe not," he said. "But people still expect things from me. I'm not trying to compare my problems to yours, but they exist either way. I didn't ask to be a hero any more than you asked to be a princess. That's just the lot I was given. But that's my character archetype, not my character. I define my character, just like you define yours.

"And as to the whole 'saving you' thing," he went on. "I'm sorry if that's been getting on your nerves, but I wasn't doing it to show you up or because I thought you were weak. Neither were the others when they've tried to help you. We just didn't want you to die.

"With everything your archetype has going against it— the damsel stigma and all—I get why it would bother you. But I think you're overcorrecting. No one ever became a hero by going it completely alone. No one ever achieved anything of value completely alone. I may not have been a student at Lord Channing's for very long, but even I know that relying on others doesn't make you weak. If anything it makes you stronger because it forces your pride to take a back seat so you can achieve more than you would alone." He shook his head and let out a frustrated sigh. "At the end of the day sometimes people just need help, Knight. And letting a person help you doesn't mean you're helpless; it just means you trust someone else."

450 CRISANTA KNIGHT - THE SEVERANCE GAME

I leaned my head back against the wall. "I've been pushing people away for so long trying to protect myself. Trusting people like that . . . it's not so easy, Daniel."

"It can be if you let it. I'm not saying trust every person that waltzes up to you. But what about the people who've proven they can be counted on—the people who are always there for you even when you don't want them to be, like Jason, and SJ, and Blue, and . . ." he stopped, like something was caught in his throat. "Well, me too, I guess?"

I raised my eyebrows. "You've got to be kidding."

"I'm not. Give me one good reason why you can't trust us?"

"It's not the whole *us* I'm talking about; it's the faction that includes you. In terms of SJ, Blue, and Jason, you're right; I have no reason not to trust them. Driving them away was a reflection of my own faults and fears, not theirs. And that's going to stop from here on out. But you're a different story. You're not like the others, Daniel. You and I aren't even really friends. You're just sort of here. And as sure as I am now that I will learn to trust SJ, Blue, and Jason, I am just as positive that there is no way in the realm I could ever fully trust you."

"Why would you think you couldn't trust me?" he asked, seeming genuinely confused.

"Is that an actual question?"

"Yeah, it is. I know I give you a hard time and, granted, I could probably take it down a notch in terms of insults. But I've been on your side since day one."

"Like I believe that."

"I'm serious."

"So am I," I replied earnestly. "Daniel, we established our mutual dislike for each other from the get-go, which

I'm fine with. And yes, we've gone through a lot of stuff together since then. But none of that changes the fact that you're hiding something."

"What, I'm not allowed to have things I want to keep to myself?" Daniel countered. "Haven't you been doing the exact same thing this whole time? We literally just established that."

"Yes. But we also just established that my keeping stuff to myself was doing way more harm than good. You want to talk about pushing people away? Why don't you practice what you preach? You keep me and the others at such a distance it's like you're allergic to us. And what you do is arguably worse because there's a difference between keeping secrets that are about *you* and keeping secrets about *other people*— secrets that those people have a right to know."

"What are you talking about?"

"Don't play dumb; you know exactly what I'm talking about. I asked you about it when we were on the magic train and you dodged it then like you're dodging it now. That night we broke out of the Therewolves' lair, when we were backstage I distinctly heard you telling Jason that I ruined your life, that you were only on this quest with the rest of us because of *me*. That's a pretty massive thing to accuse me of, Daniel, and I think I have a right to know what you meant by it. How did I ruin your life? What the heck does that have to do with our quest to find the Author? And why . . . why are you really here?"

My questions seemed to strike a sour note with Daniel, because the rather human expression of sympathy he'd had on his face these last few minutes was replaced with a slight glare.

I didn't let it bother me though. This whole time we'd

been talking I'd been the one in the hot seat. Now it was his turn. He could glare a thousand daggers at me for all I cared; I was not backing down. Not this time.

"I can't tell you that," Daniel responded.

"Then I can't trust you," I replied bluntly. "How can you expect me to when you're keeping things like this from me? It's off-putting, Daniel—spending so much time with someone whose motives are so enigmatic. If you truly believe I ruined your life then maybe you're just waiting for the right time to get rid of me too. Take the magic train for instance. How could I have been sure that if I let go of that railing you wouldn't just let me fall to my doom?"

"Come on, Knight. Really?"

"Yes, *really*. What else am I supposed to think?"

"Well, not that I'm secretly plotting to destroy you, that's for sure."

"Then what?"

Daniel blinked and started to fidget the way I had just minutes before.

"I don't know. Think whatever you want," he said distantly. "But whether you buy it or not, I wouldn't do anything to hurt you."

His eyes did not meet mine anymore. We sat there awkwardly as I realized just how uncomfortably conflicted he seemed to be.

And I understood.

For a second I wondered if I should put my hand on his shoulder to show support or sympathy. But when I started to move my arm to do so, I thought better of it. We did not know each other like that. Our relationship could be characterized by a lot of colorful adjectives, but as it stood, there were still far too many walls between us to allow for such closeness. At least there were on his end. A great deal of mine had just been torn down.

Until that point, the tension in our relationship had been just as much my fault as it had been his. But that wasn't the case anymore. In the confinement of this cursed lamp, I'd let my soul slip to him. I'd allowed myself to be honest, vulnerable, and transparent in a way that made me feel equal parts embarrassed and relieved.

That was a strange thing to wrap my head around, as I'd never been that honest about what was going on inside of me with *anyone*, myself included. But it happened. Whether I liked it or not, Daniel now knew me—even the parts I preferred not to know myself. And I felt he owed me the same in return.

"Look, Daniel," I began anew—slowly, sensibly. "No one knows more about wanting to push people away and keep personal things private than I do. But how am I supposed to put my faith in you when you can't do the same with me?"

He didn't look up.

Ugh, this is hopeless, I thought. *He's just as stubborn as I am. Getting him to be completely honest is going to be like pulling Therewolf teeth. It might be possible, but only by extreme force. Which, in retrospect, maybe I don't want to use.*

I definitely wanted to know the truth about him. But if Daniel didn't want to tell me on his own, did I really want to be the person that pried it out against his will?

As satisfying as it would be to know what he meant by me ruining his life, it would mean nothing if I ripped it out of him. Forced trust is hardly better than no trust. And right now I needed a reason to put *real* trust in Daniel.

I sat forward and huffed a strand of hair out of my face, knowing what I had to do.

"All right," I finally conceded. "I'll tell you what, Daniel. If whatever you're hiding really is that bad, I'm not going to push you to tell me. But I am going to ask you to give me something else to go on instead. I don't care what it is, just give me a reason to believe in you. Be honest with me about *one* thing—your life before Lord Channing's, your prologue prophecy, what that magic watering can imprinted on your hand, whatever. Just give me something, *anything*, and I'll call us even. Okay?"

Moments ticked by without a response from him. I thought he wasn't going to bite, but then he reached into his pocket and pulled something out.

Before I could see what it was, he tossed it over to me. I caught it and discovered it was the golden pocket watch that I'd seen him looking at so many times before.

"I wanted you to save my sheath from the Therewolves because I hid the watch in a secret compartment at the base before they confiscated our stuff," he explained. "It was too important to me to lose."

I held the pocket watch carefully; its metal felt cold against the palm of my hand. Daniel signaled for me to open it, and with bated breath I did so.

Inside I found a picture of a girl. She was about our age with long, wavy black hair. Her eyes were a rich brown and her smile was mischievous. She was pretty, beautiful really. But I had no idea what her picture was doing inside of Daniel's watch.

"Her name is Kai," Daniel said.

"Sorry?"

"The girl, her name is Kai," Daniel explained. "We've been together for three years, but I've known her my whole life. She's everything to me—my entire world—and I didn't think anything would ever come between us until my stupid protagonist book appeared. When it showed up, not only was I forced to leave her and my life in Century City behind to attend Lord Channing's, my prologue prophecy said . . .Well, among other things it said we might not end up together. Worse, as a result of how my fate plays out, something might cause *her* to come to an end. And I do mean in the very permanent, mortal sense."

"That's why you came with us," I thought aloud, the truth sinking in. "That's why you want to find the Author. You want to change your fate so that you can save Kai and the two of you can end up together."

"Yup."

I took another look at the girl in the picture then closed the pocket watch to hand it back to Daniel. He refused to take it.

"There's more," he said.

"Daniel, it's fine, really," I assured him. "I meant what I said. You don't have to tell me everything. You were honest about this and that's enough."

"No," he shook his head. "You were right."

"I'm sorry, what was that?"

"I said you're right. As inconceivable as it is, in this particular case you are. I can't expect you to trust me if I'm not willing to do the same. So let me get this out before I wise up and change my mind."

He sat up straighter and turned to face me completely. "The thing that my prologue prophecy predicts might bring us to an end, bring *her* to an end . . . Knight, that thing is you."

"What?" I stammered.

For a second I thought he was joking. For a second after

that I *wished* he was joking. But he wasn't. It felt like a brick had hit me in the chest. A lot of questions ran through my head. But in an effort to not come off like a babbling idiot, I settled on just one.

"How's that even possible?"

"I don't know," he admitted. "The specifics aren't there, but the wording is clear. Within you lies the potential to seal both Kai's fate and mine."

"That's what you meant when you said I ruined your life, and that you're only on this quest because of me," I said softly. "I'm the potential foil to your happiness—your life with Kai—and you want the Author to change that."

He nodded.

I rubbed my arm awkwardly. "If that's true, how can you even stand to be around me?"

"My prophecy also says that you're going to be a key ally for us both. So despite what damage you could potentially cast on our lives, I get that I might need your help too." He sighed. "It's complicated."

"I'll say." I huffed and shook my head. "I . . . I'm sorry, I guess. I don't know Kai, and I don't really know you either, but I guess I owe you both some kind of apology."

"No. You don't," Daniel said. "It's not your fault. This prophecy is my responsibility and I accept that. Only I can change it, and I'm going to do everything in my power to do so because there's nothing I wouldn't do for her."

He reached for the pocket watch and I handed it back to him. However, I couldn't help but crinkle my eyebrows as I reflected on something in the process.

"What?" he asked.

"Nothing. It's just, after all this . . . who would've thought that what was motivating you the entire time was true love."

Daniel shrugged. "Hey, love makes you do crazy things."

"Yeah," I said, thinking back to Ashlyn. "So I've heard."

I paused for a second. "Thank you for telling me. It couldn't have been easy for you to admit that to anyone. And the fact that you were honest about Kai with me of all people . . . Well, it means a lot. So, um . . . thanks."

"You're welcome," he replied. "Tell anyone though, and I'll have to kill you."

"Get in line."

He smirked and the two of us sat quietly as we allowed our new understanding of one another to sink in.

I still couldn't believe what just happened. Not only had I just been completely, irrevocably honest with Daniel, but he had been honest with me in return.

All he wanted to do was change his fate, to make the future his own just like I did. For the first time I looked at him with total empathy. He really had been right all those nights ago when we'd talked on the carriage ride over to Emma's.

We were not so different.

"Changing the subject," I said eventually, clearing my throat and the air between us, "I am sorry you're stuck in here. That one is on me and I actually do feel pretty bad about it, especially now that I'm starting to hate you a lot less. I'm probably the last person you want to be trapped in a lamp with."

"You're up there," he said with another shrug. "But you're not the last. I would say you're more like . . . a solid third."

"Aw, I guess I'll have to step up my game then," I responded with a smile, remembering the night of our ball in Adelaide when I'd said the same thing to him. "Coming in third sucks."

Daniel returned my smile and stood up from the couch with a sense of renewed purpose.

"Where are you going?" I asked as he tucked the watch back inside his pocket.

He gestured to the genie journal we'd left across the room. "Like I said, there are some pretty good ideas in that book and I think we might be able to make one of them work. If we want to have a shot at getting out of here before Arian delivers us to Nadia, we should probably get started."

He was right. I was about to stand and follow him, but before I could Daniel offered me his hand to help me up. I hesitated to reach out, staring at his hand with both trepidation and uncertainty.

It was a harmless enough gesture. It was just a hand. And for the time being Daniel had proven that he was someone I could count on.

I knew that now. I knew so much now, in fact, that I was beginning to wonder if within the limitations of this lamp Daniel and I had just affected our fates in some small way neither of us had ever intended.

Our paths ahead were uncertain. Even with my own clairvoyance, I could not see what lay in store for him or me or us. But I felt like something had changed. Here, by our own design, not the Author's, something had shifted. *We* had shifted.

The quandary remained, though, as I considered taking his grip—had we shifted enough to influence anything with lasting outcome? The connection and clarity we'd forged in these last few minutes of valiant vulnerability were strong. But they were also full of torrid unpredictability.

He was the boy who drove me mad and pushed me to

my limits. I was the girl with the potential to bring down his true love. So while the decision to change our clashing relationship was a wise choice, it also bore one crucial, unforgiving question. A question that was as painful to consider as it was to ignore:

Would he and I really change?

I knew full well that change was possible. It had characterized my world since I'd gotten my prologue prophecy. Just as surely, I knew that I had changed throughout this journey. At this very moment I felt myself altering as my heart opened up and my head felt a real sense of clarity.

But that wasn't the question I was posing. I wasn't asking if we *could* change—like did we have the potential to. I was asking if we *would* change—as in, did we really want to.

There is a difference between change that just happens to you and change you actively fight for. The former is sudden and the result of something outside of yourself. The latter requires the constant, unwavering dedication to hold true in your selected course no matter what obstacles, temptations, or old habits try to tear you down.

I remembered how insecure Daniel made me feel whenever we talked. Would I really learn to be confident enough in myself to not let him get to me like that?

I recalled the hesitation Daniel had shown when I was falling from the magic train. Would he really get past the fact that I had the potential to bring an end to his true love?

It all seemed very unlikely.

Given what Daniel had always been to me—and what I apparently was to him—I was not completely certain that this newfound commitment to change our ways toward one another would hold.

And yet, as I glanced up at Daniel's open hand, I knew that I wanted to try. So I placed my hand in his. With one strong sweeping motion, Daniel helped me to my feet.

I held on for an extra moment—holding his gaze as I fought back the uncertainty—and finally, confidently, spoke my intentions into existence.

"Let's do this," I said.

End of Book Two

ABOUT THE AUTHOR

Geanna Culbertson adores chocolate chip cookies, watching Netflix in pajamas, and the rain. Of course, in her case, the latter is kind of hard to come by. As her dad notes, "In California, we don't have seasons, we have special effects."

On the flip side, she is deeply afraid of ice skating and singing in public. Although, she forces herself to do both on occasion because she believes facing your fears can be good for you.

During the week Geanna lives a disciplined, yet preciously ridiculous lifestyle. She gets up before dawn to train and write. Goes to work where she enjoys a double life as a kid undercover in a grown-up world. Then comes home, eats, writes, and watches one of her favorite TV shows.

On weekends, however, Geanna's heart, like her time, is completely off the leash. Usually she'll teach martial arts at her local karate studio, pursue yummy foods, and check out whatever's new at her fav stores. To summarize, she'll wander, play, disregard the clock, and get into as many shenanigans as possible.